On behalf of a grateful nation

"On behalf of a grateful nation ..." These words spoken over a folded flag closed the final chapter in a remarkable story. It was a story begun sixty years before in the skies over Germany. It took place over seven decades and two continents, and ended on an Oklahoma hillside on a warm early summer day.

The folded flag and the words were a part of United States military tradition. Each step, each movement and word the result of a thoughtful process crafted over years and intended to be dignified, precise, and predictable in its execution.

Indeed, it could have been indistinguishable in its outward appearances from any one of thousands of funerals carried out in the past fifty or more years for American soldiers, sailors, marines or airmen. But this was not an ordinary funeral. Among the one hundred fifty or more gathered at the cemetery, only a handful had ever met the young man they came to honor. They came because their hearts had been moved by a compelling story that at times seemed both strange and wonderful. The funeral was only one event in a chain of many occurrences. True, it would be the culminating event, the one that would bring closure and finality to the process begun so long ago, but the events preceding it were most unique and remarkable. Those events shaped this story, and made it all the more remarkable by their qualities. The courtesies of the hearts of many are at the heart of this story, and they began as the nation was engaged in war in Europe ...

Note for Librarians: A cataloguing record for this book is available from Library and Archives
Canada at www.collectionscanada.ca/amicus/index-e.html
ISBN 1-4120-1165-5

*Printed in Victoria, BC, Canada. Printed on paper with minimum 30% recycled fibre. Trafford's print shop
runs on "green energy" from solar, wind and other environmentally-friendly power sources.*

Offices in Canada, USA, Ireland and UK
This book was published *on-demand* in cooperation with Trafford Publishing. On-demand
publishing is a unique process and service of making a book available for retail sale to the
public taking advantage of on-demand manufacturing and Internet marketing. On-demand
publishing includes promotions, retail sales, manufacturing, order fulfilment, accounting and
collecting royalties on behalf of the author.

Book sales for North America and international:
Trafford Publishing, 6E–2333 Government St.,
Victoria, BC v8t 4p4 CANADA
phone 250 383 6864 (toll-free 1 888 232 4444)
fax 250 383 6804; email to orders@trafford.com
Book sales in Europe:
Trafford Publishing (uk) Limited, 9 Park End Street, 2nd Floor
Oxford, UK oxi 1hh UNITED KINGDOM
phone 44 (0)1865 722 113 (local rate 0845 230 9601)
facsimile 44 (0)1865 722 868; info.uk@trafford.com
Order online at:
trafford.com/03-1543

10 9 8 7 6 5 4 3 2

Kenneth Breaux

Courtesies of the Heart

Kenneth Breaux

Trafford Publishing
2005

Contents

With grateful thanks to
the men of the Eighth Air Force,
and to those who waited for them,
especially the children of the lost.

"They shall not grow old
As we who are left grow old
Age will not weary them,
Nor the years condemn
At the going down of the sun
And in the morning
We will remember them"

For The Fallen
Laurence Binyon

Introduction

In Nazi Germany in 1944, a solitary hiker seeks solace in a remote forest and instead discovers the bitter fruits of war. His resolve to perform a courtesy of the heart sets in motion a remarkable chain of events stretching into the next century, and places him in personal danger. In 1972, a retired US Air Force officer obtains permission to visit East Germany to write a book about German sporting weapons. Instead he finds a man with a remarkable story to tell and becomes his ally in a common effort to honor a fallen warrior. In Tulsa, Oklahoma, in 1974 a young mother discovers a dusty trunk full of memories and begins to learn of the father she never knew. In Kovarska, Czechoslovakia, in 1983, a group of young boys find a bundle of clothing belonging to an American airman, hidden since 1944, and resolve to learn more.

All these people set into motion the solution to a mystery that had spanned nearly sixty years. None knew of the other, yet all contributed to a remarkably rich and uplifting story.

I never intended to write a book, or to be a part of a team of most unlikely collaborators, all involved in the same goal. As I returned from Brussels, Belgium in April of 2001, I carried with me a remarkable story and a treasured object. The adventure was only just beginning, yet had it ended there it would have been no less remarkable. As I related the story of my trip to some fellow travelers, I was asked if I intended to write a story about it. Little did I know the story would expand as it has, much less achieve the results it has. *Courtesies of the Heart* is a tale of how people connect with each other, and the character revealed in those connections. It is about the relationships of events and people, which when taken together constitute both a mystery and a redemptive solution.

"There is a courtesy of the heart: it is allied with love. From it springs the purest courtesy in the outward behavior."

"Es gibt eine Höflichkeit des Herzens, sie ist der Liebe verwandt. Aus ihr entspringt die bequemste Höflichkeit des äußeren Betragens."

Johann Goethe

Prologue

It is mostly young men who go to war. It is logical then that the ranks of the dead in war are filled mostly by the young. Under the bone white stones in our military cemeteries we tally up their short years. It is difficult to define them by their histories, for men who died so young have little history. We define them all too often by the manner of their death.

William (Bill) Melbern Lewis, Jr., died nearly sixty years ago.
As I searched for his history, I became aware that there was precious little of his daily life to be found. Those who knew him did so for a brief time, either in high school in Tulsa, or in the few months he served with them in the military. After sixty years, memories are sometimes scarce.

The Lewis family in 1934. From left, Ted, Nola, William M. Lewis Sr., William M. Lewis, Jr.

As a boy, he had a paper route, and worshipped at the First Christian Church. He finished elementary school at Woodrow Wilson Junior High School and graduated from Central High School in Tulsa. He was in the school play, and was described by many as tall, blue eyed, likeable, and quick to smile. After high school, he studied at a local business school and went to work at the Dupont ammunition factory as an accounting clerk. He and his older brother Ted were a little over a year apart and the only children of their parents. They entered the Army only a few months apart in 1943. Together with David Jewell and his brother Clifford, the four young men spent time together in the outdoors around Tulsa and became close friends. All four enlisted in the military, and three became pilots.

By the time Bill Lewis reported to the draft board in Tulsa, his parents had divorced and lived far apart. Bill had already married by then. Eleanor Powless was a strikingly attractive woman who had gone to school with Bill and worshipped at the same church in Tulsa. They had fifteen months together before Bill left for active duty, and Eleanor went to California to meet him when she was able. By winter of 1943, she was pregnant with their daughter Sharon, and back home in Tulsa while Bill prepared to go to war as a fighter pilot with the Eighth Air Force in England.

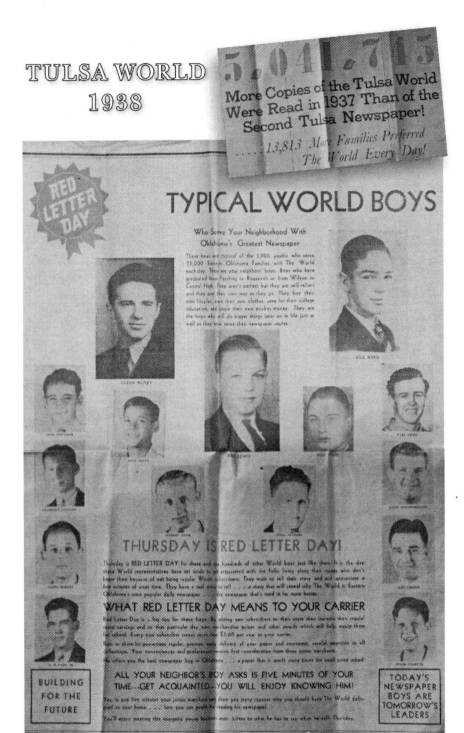

The Tulsa World paid tribute to their paper carriers. Bill Lewis is in the center.

Mission Day

On the morning of September 11, 1944, at four military airfields in Germany and England, young men intensely readied themselves and their machines for combat. World events had joined to place them in the cockpits and crew stations of military airplanes on this day. They might have been studying at a college, working in their home countries, or any one of a number of things, but on this day, time and circumstances dictated that they prepare for air warfare. Borne on wings of steel and driven by thundering engines, in just a few hours they would climb into the cold, brilliant blue heights above the continent of Europe and hurl their deadly machines toward each other. In the town of Ruhland, in far eastern Germany, the civilian workers at the oil refinery prepared themselves also. As a result of the new strategies of the allies, the petroleum processing facilities had come under new and concentrated attacks. Unlike the young men in their airplanes, they could only wait for the signals that an attack was imminent, and then scramble for safety.

Aerodynamics was not a new science, its principles having been investigated for decades before the Wright brothers flew. But the advances in such areas as higher speeds and altitudes and aerobatic maneuvers are typically driven by the military. By the 1930s, technology in aviation had made huge strides. In addition to the increased performance in the airplanes, weapons systems made great leaps in their deadly effectiveness. Bombs were larger, and dealt more destruction than ever before. Military airplanes flew higher, faster, and farther than anyone might have imagined just ten years before the outbreak of the war. Talented and brilliant engineers such as Willy Messerschmitt in Germany, and Edgar Schmued and Kelly Johnson in the United States gave their energies to the development of machines that had reached the state of the art.

The centerpiece of this combat would be the United States Army Forces B-17 Flying Fortress. The huge bomber had been in development since 1934, when the US Army began to apply new concepts of strategy to battle. The B-17 was designed to bring the fight to the enemy in a much different way, going far behind the lines of men and machines on the ground and attacking the enemy deep into his homeland. The world had never before seen machines such as these. Carrying thousands of pounds of bombs each and flying in massive formations, their efforts on this day would be directed at the refining capacity of the German industrial machine. With the roaring of their four massive engines, they darkened the skies as they gathered to form up for the flights across the channel. Their utility was such that by the end of the war in 1945,

Boeing Aircraft, Douglas, and Lockheed in shared production turned out 12,371 B-17s.

On this day, American fighters, primarily P-51 Mustangs, would accompany the bombers. For the early years of the war in Europe, fighters could accompany the bombers only on the very first and last segments of their missions. But this new plane, a sleek aerodynamic design that carried disposable fuel tanks, could travel the entire mission distance with the bombers, affording them protection that had not been available earlier in the conflict. Inspired by a British requirement, the plane had been improved with design changes and a new engine, and now acquitted itself well against the Luftwaffe in air-to-air combat.

In the German towns of Alteno and Welzow, Luftwaffe pilots readied themselves by performing checklists in the cockpits of the Focke-Wulf 190 and the Messerschmitt 109 as they listened for the alarm that would tell them that the enemy was near. The Focke-Wulf's in particular were designed and specially modified for attacking the bomber formations. The Messerschmitts were faster and more lightly armored, and would seek to engage the American fighters in direct combat before the bombers they accompanied reached their targets. The Messerschmitt design had been flying since 1939, and had seen action in the Spanish Civil War. German engineers had worked to perfect the machines of war, and now these young men would test their machines, and themselves, in earnest.

Since the summer of 1944, the German air force had been shepherding their now scarce resources of fuel and trained pilots. This day would mark a more aggressive approach by the Germans. September 11, 1944 would signify what the German defenders hoped to be a turning point. On this day, they would send aloft pilots armed with new tactics in what would become one of the largest aerial armadas since D-Day on June 6.

Each of these men had great trust in his fellow aviators, ground crews, and mechanics. Each had confidence in his country and the engineers and designers who gave him these machines to fly. But when they climbed into the cockpits and gun stations, radio compartments, and ball turrets, each would have to look into themselves to find the courage to endure one more mission. In Wormingford and Thorpe Abbotts in England, and Alteno and Welzow in far eastern Germany, the participants readied themselves for the great conflict that was about to erupt.

The Making of a Fighter Pilot – 1944

The Stearman PT-17 Primary Flight Trainer.

Among the young pilots who readied themselves for the mission on September 11, 1944 was a 22-year-old US Army Air Forces (USAAF) second lieutenant, William M. Lewis, Jr. Bill had enlisted in the Army on September 8, 1942 in his hometown of Tulsa, Oklahoma, just days after he was notified by his draft board that he was now classified 1A. He was called to active duty in March of 1943, having been appointed as an Aviation Cadet. On that day, Bill and 38 other recruits boarded a train from Oklahoma City to Los Angeles. His brother Ted soon followed Bill into the Army, also enlisting in 1942. By the spring of 1944, both young men had earned their commissions as US Army Air Force Officers. Both did well in their training. Ted was assigned to a B-24 Training Squadron in Washington State, while Bill went through most of his training in California and then in June of 1944, departed for England for an eventual assignment to an Eighth Air Force Fighter Squadron. On his departure, he would leave a young wife, Eleanor, and a new daughter, Sharon, born in April and whom he had seen only once. Married in January of 1942, their lives together had been interrupted by the war. They had shared a little more than a year with each other before Bill had joined the Army and began flight training.

Bill had his introduction to military flying in Oxnard, California. The selection processes for the Army Air Forces are outlined in the USAAF Handbook 1939-1945. Cadets accepted into the pilot training program were to be tested for 20/20 vision in each eye, uncorrected. They were required to have perfect color vision, 20/20 hearing, and be a minimum of 5'4" tall, and a maximum of 6'4." They would weigh no less than 114 pounds and no more than 200 pounds. Formal schooling was not required, but short exams were given to determine general intelligence, and tests to determine coordination. The stated goal of the selection process was to select the *"best and most quickly trained."* Having fulfilled these requirements, Bill reported to the Mira Loma Academy in June of 1943. The Mira Loma Flight Academy was a civilian school, like many during the war years, and it was contracted to provide primary flight training for the US Army Air Force. Quarters were built for the cadets, civilian instructors taught flying, and the United States Army Air Forces provided military instruction. Most primary flight training during World War II was conducted on similar premises. The demand for new pilots was great, and schools such as Mira Loma sprang up almost overnight, some being built literally within days. In the years prior to the attack on Pearl Harbor, the numbers of men in US Army Air Corps flight training declined dramatically. In 1937 for example, less than 200 Army personnel graduated from advanced pilot training. By some accounts, from 1941 through 1945 the USAAF is said to have qualified some 190,000 men as pilots from all schools, both civilian and military. Today, military flight training occurs over a period of about 18 months, but in the war years, the training would typically be completed in nine months. Cadets came from all over the US, and the schools were typically placed where the weather for flying and training new pilots was better than average. Repetition and confidence are keys to learning, and training young men to fly requires both in abundance. The trainees were subjected first to the language and vocabulary of flight. They would start with simple things. The definition of lift was one of the first, and then concepts such as roll, pitch, and yaw.[1] All of these concepts were taught in ground school, weeks before the fledgling aviators even approached an airplane. The basics of weather, simple flight instruments, and characteristics of engines would be among the subjects. Bill's flight log shows that on June 25, 1943, he and his instructor flew for exactly 20 minutes in a PT-13 trainer built by the Boeing Airplane Company. The PT-13, named the "*Kaydet*," was a biplane with fabric-covered wings, a 225 Horsepower

A BT-17 Vultee, the type of airplane Bill Lewis flew in Basic Flight Training.

engine, and an open two-seat cockpit. The airplane had been designed and built by the Stearman Company in 1925, which Boeing had acquired in 1938. For the young men who had scarcely earned their driver's licenses (some still had not), it was a hot machine. Weighing 2700 pounds and cruising at just over 100 miles an hour, it could be a challenge in the early phases. But it was a forgiving airplane in aviation terms; the quality most desired when training new pilots in the primary phase. You could make a mistake in the PT-13, and unless it was truly severe, you would live to fly again, if the instructors didn't wash you out of the program. Forty-four more flights in the PT-13 followed that first flight. At the completion of his Stearman flights, called the Primary Phase by the USAAF, Bill had accumulated 65 hours; 38 hours and 55 minutes of which were solo.

The completion rate for the candidates in the first phase was a little over sixty percent. Most of the washouts, as they were called, would be failed in the first ten hours of dual flying instruction. Reasons for washout included bad judgment, poor flying skills or a problem with coordination. Once the first phase was successfully completed, the drop out and washout rate would decrease significantly.

It was at Mira Loma that Bill Lewis would experience the first of two wartime reunions with David Jewell. Jewell, a close boyhood friend from Tulsa, spotted Bill. "*His head stuck up above the crowd, Bill was tall, and I recognized him right away.*" David Jewell, his brother Clifford, and Bill and Ted had lived on the edge of Tulsa, close to lakes and fields, and the four boys had spent their time fishing and exploring. Now, all of them were in the military. Bill, Ted, and David Jewell joined the Army Air Corps, and Clifford Jewell enlisted in the Navy. David (Buddy) Jewell had enlisted earlier, and had trained as a glider pilot prior to

An AT-6 Advanced Trainer.

16

entering the powered flight training program. In one of the coincidences of the war, they would become pilots and commissioned officers on the same day. In yet another coincidence, Bill would follow Buddy to their first combat assignment in England.

The P-38 Lightning. Bill flew these in his combat training and early combat missions.

The Vultee BT-13 Valiant was Bill's next airplane. The student pilots nicknamed it *"The Vibrator."* This phase of Bill's training began in Chico, California on September 2, 1943. The BT-13 was more like a combat aircraft. All metal in construction, it was a low wing produced in 1940, with a Pratt and Whitney power plant that was capable of generating 450 horsepower. At just a fraction less than 4,500 pounds loaded and with a top speed of 180 miles per hour, it was clearly a step up the performance scale. It also had an enclosed cockpit and a service ceiling of 21,650 feet, and had flaps and a variable pitch propeller. The variable pitch propeller was an example of how the USAAF introduced subtle changes in the training to bring student pilots into gradually more challenging situations. Now, the pilots could maintain constant RPM on their engines, but by changing the pitch or propeller blade angle, they could increase or decrease airspeed using the more sophisticated pitch control. The pilots were becoming accustomed to using oxygen and managing the systems of the airplane in a much more complex manner. The BT-13's range of 725 miles without refueling made it a practical machine for cross country flights and navigation training, and teaching fuel management to the students, and it was a transition to a bigger airplane with a different feel. Bill was aware that he was flying a machine of greater capability than the Stearman, but he had little love for the new airplane. In a letter to his brother, he complained that *"The Vultee flies like a tractor with wings."* The Vultee still had fixed landing gear, and no weapons, but it was closer to a fighter than anything the cadets had yet experienced. After five flights in the BT-13 with an instructor, Bill was signed off as safe to solo. The Basic Phase gave pilots more confidence, and with the majority of their time spent as solo, they were beginning to view themselves as well on the way to achieving their goals. Bill accumulated time rapidly now, and when he had finished the Basic Phase he had accumulated nearly 20 hours of instrument time and more than six hours of night flying.

Family separations in the war years of the 1940s were commonplace. Men were in training and overseas in combat. The life of a fighter pilot in training was Spartan and somewhat monastic. Eleanor had come out to be with Bill. She had received a letter from the Base Commander of the Santa Ana Army Air Base, admonishing her that it might be a mistake because she would *"find the living conditions expensive and you would be able to see him very little ... There have been many unfortunate and unhappy circumstances occurring in the past ... that have naturally reacted very adversely on their cadet husbands."* Undeterred, Eleanor left a few days later. She was successful in finding work, and the couple's tax return for 1943 was among the clippings and documents and other memorabilia the couple's daughter Sharon discovered in an old trunk. Eleanor had earned $617.12 working for Amerada Petroleum in Tulsa before leaving to join Bill, and another $189.80 while working for Contractors Pacific at the Port Hueneme Naval Base in California. Bill had earned $844.67 at the Dupont Ammunition plant in Tulsa, another $712.50 since he had joined the Army. In a letter to his mother, Nola, in September 1943, Bill gave her an idea of what his schedule was like:

6:30 Reveille
7:00 Eat
8:00 - Flight Line - 12:30
1:30 Eat
2:00 - Class - 4:00
5:00 Calisthenics / Drill

We are low on cash and waiting for payday. I have $1.50 and Eleanor about as much.

When Bill received his orders to Advanced Training in November, Eleanor and Betty Baggett, whose husband had trained with Bill and who was a fellow Oklahoman, left for Tulsa. They had trouble finding a decent place to stay, and when they finally did, it cost $10.00 a month and had no stove.

By the time Bill left Chico, he was well on his way to being a fighter pilot. His Class 44-A book, called the 44 BEAM, is autographed with the comments of his classmates. They were sentimental in a sense, because most of them would never come into contact with each other again.

"The best of luck and hunting, Baggy"
"Stay right up front and may the best be yours, Bob Austin"

"To one swell A.P. 'Okie,' sincerely, Kelly" [2]
"Good luck, see you in a 38, Bill"

There were a few days between training phases, and in early November of 1943, Bill reported to Williams Field in Chandler, Arizona for advanced flight training in the AT-6, a single-engine plane with a 650 horsepower engine. Seventeen thousand of these airplanes were built, and it is believed that nearly every single-engine pilot who trained in the U.S. Military during the war years flew this airplane as a student. Bomber pilots would transition to a small twin-engine trainer after Basic Flight training. Generally similar in power and service ceiling to the BT-13, it was only slightly heavier at 5300 pounds loaded, and cruised at a brisk 170 with a top speed of 205. Even though the AT-6 was comparable in performance to the BT-13, the pilots were using the airplane more aggressively. One thing students had to remember was that this airplane had retractable flaps. No more entering the pattern and on final approach without checking for gear down, these airplanes had retractable gear as well.[3] The details began to increase. In a letter to his brother Ted, Bill commented on the AT-6. *"It's a honey of an airplane. Will do everything you want it to do. It has a narrow landing gear, like a Stearman and it's a little tricky to land but if you stay on the ball it's OK. It lands at 90 per and that's going fast. If anything goes wrong you use brakes and throttle to save yourself, not rudder. If you kick in rudder the tail wheel goes out and you have yourself a nice little*

Class of 44-A, Squadron Two at Oxnard, CA.
Front row (L-R): *W.A. Prange, R.I. Potter, H.N. Varner, Jr., H.R. Weston.*
Second row: *J.R. Meyer, J. McMahen, J.L. Van Dam, W.M. Lewis, Jr., D.F. Jewell, Jr.*
Third row: *N.K. Williams, G. McAdory, T.C. Wilcox, R.D. Sanders, Jr., A.D. Scott, A.R. White.* Fourth row: *A.J. Hatfield, Jr., W.D. Montgomery, F.H. White, E.R. Johnson, S.A. Sampson, S.H. Reed.*

ground loop all your own. That's something I don't want to have." There were more things to remember, higher performance, less forgiving airplanes now. They were becoming fighter pilots.

There was still some dual instruction, but the rest of the syllabus was devoted to such things as solo flying in formation, air-to-air and air-to-ground gunnery, aerobatics, navigation and instrument flying, and transition. The skills developed in this phase were most closely related to the skills needed to fly high performance in a combat environment.

Despite the fact that training at Williams Field began with the single-engine AT-6, when Bill was stationed there, Williams Field was an Advanced Twin Engine Pilot School which prepared pilots for eventual assignment to the P-38. After completion of his single-engine training in the AT-6, he acquired several hours in the Army AT-9, a twin-engine trainer, followed by some time in the RP-322. The RP-322 was actually the export version of the Lockheed P-38, a twin-engine, twin-tailed fighter with two 1150 horsepower engines. It was identical to the model flown in combat, but did not have a supercharger as the operational models did. This was the first experience he would have flying an airplane with a tricycle landing gear. Most other fighters until this time, and the B-17 as well, were what pilots called tail draggers, and had two wheels mounted on the wings, and a small tail wheel. Flying airplanes with tail wheels required a cautious takeoff approach. The trick was to get enough speed to level the plane, making sure the tail wheel had lifted off the runway, then build more airspeed to generate lift across the wings, and to generate enough speed to allow the tail surface to provide directional control. If the pilot made the move too soon, he could rotate the pitch forward, and the propeller might strike the runway. All this had to occur while the pilot often had to estimate the lineup of the runway, since the forward fuselage obscured his vision until the nose rotated level. The US Army Air Forces had acquired the RP-322 as the final phase of training for pilots destined for P-38 squadrons. This would have made the transition somewhat smoother, as the receiving squadron would have a pilot with at least some experience in a combat aircraft. Bill's enlisted logbook closes out on January 5, 1944. The next day, he would finish advanced flight training and be commissioned as an officer. He accumulated an additional 24 hours in the Link simulator before his student logbook ends on February 3, 1944.

Bill's Honorable Discharge certificate is dated January 6, 1944. This is an administrative requirement still in effect today. Those who enter an officer's training program are first sworn in as enlisted personnel. When they complete the training, they are discharged from enlisted status

USAAF Second Lieutenant William Melbern Lewis, Jr.

to accept a commission as an officer. The reason given by personnel regulations is "*convenience of the government to accept a commission*," Section X, AR 615-360. Bill's enlisted summary states that he was 20 years, 7/12 months old at the time of his enlistment. He was 6' tall and had blue eyes, brown hair and a ruddy complexion, and was an accounting clerk prior to entering the Army. He had been vaccinated for smallpox, typhoid, diphtheria and tetanus. His enlisted pay was closed out with the amount of $125.50. His military specialty was AP, Airplane Pilot. He was now an officer, destined for a P-38 squadron either in Europe or in the Pacific. He had been in the USAAF for 1 year, 3 months and 29 days.

Bill remained in California, assigned to a stateside squadron, the 337th Fighter Squadron, where he accumulated more time in the P-38 on instruments and night flying, gunnery and formation and generally sharpening his skills as an aviator while waiting for orders to a combat squadron.

Bill Lewis came home in April, just in time to see his new daughter, Sharon, born on the 21st. The Tulsa Tribune carried this announcement:

STORK CLUB

Sharon Kay is the name chosen by Lieut. William M. Lewis, Jr., and Mrs. Lewis for their daughter born Friday afternoon at St. John's hospital. Lieut. Lewis, who is in the army air corps and stationed at Ontario, Calif., arrived Friday morning. He is the son of Mrs. Nola M. Lewis, Tulsa, and William M. Lewis, Portland, Ore. Maternal grandparents are Mr. and Mrs. R.A. Powless, 1415 S. Rockford Av., with whom Mrs. Lewis is making her home. She is the former Miss Eleanor Powless.

Bill was only home for a precious few days. His brother Ted was now stationed at an Army Air Base in Oklahoma, but the two brothers were unable to visit while Bill was on leave.

Ted had moved into the advanced phase of his training in twin-engine, and would receive his commission on June 27th at the Frederick Army Air Field in Frederick, Oklahoma, with class 44-F. On May 17th, Bill was nearly ready to leave for a port of embarkation. One of the final administrative functions was the requirement for a last will and testament. On that day, he wrote a simple will witnessed by David Jewell and two other USAAF officers, and he completed copies in triplicate of a Power of Attorney. All his preparation was behind him,

Eleanor Powless-Lewis with daughter Sharon Kay, 1944

and combat lay ahead. He was ready to go to war, or at least as ready as the US Army Air Corps could make him. David Jewell would leave before Bill, and would travel first to Scotland and then to the 55th Fighter Squadron. He would fly his first combat mission on June 4, 1944, just two days prior to D-Day.

In a letter to his brother Ted, written on May 9, 1944, Bill talks of his new daughter, and of his impending orders to San Francisco on May 17, where he would then report to a Port of Embarkation. *"I do think that I have a cute daughter but I might be prejudiced. The only thing that gripes me is that I won't get to see Eleanor before I go. Rough, isn't it?"*

The 55th Fighter Group

Wormingford, Essex County England
June 1944

Beginning in 1943, the Eighth Air Force descended on England in numbers. Its birth as a military organization came on January 28, 1942 in Savannah, Georgia. In just two short years, it had developed into a large force consisting of nearly 2,000 bombers and 1,000 fighters, and now it occupied sixty or so bases in England. At the time Bill Lewis arrived in England, the Commanding Officer of the Eighth was General James Doolittle. The first bomber mission of the Eighth was flown on the 4th of July 1942, flying in six borrowed British bombers.

The 31st Fighter Group flew the first fighter mission by Eighth Air Force pilots in six British Spitfires on July 26, 1942, but American pilots had been flying as volunteers with the Royal Air Force since 1940. By the time Bill arrived as a replacement pilot in the 55th Fighter Group, nearly 200,000 Americans were there. They were the pilots, ground crews, and administrative and support personnel of the Eighth and Ninth Air Forces, and by the end of hostilities, it was estimated that nearly 400,000 had served in the Eighth Air Force in England. Most of these were housed in the 60 or so bases in East Anglia, an area selected for its broad expanses of flat plains. They settled in on bases, some built out of farmland appropriated by the Ministry of Defence. Their bases had such names as Steeple Morden, Horsham St. Faith, Seething, Bury St. Edmunds and Bungay, and Chipping Ongar. My favorite is Great Snoring. Who could forget such a place? England had become the world's largest aircraft carrier. It must have been a strange sight. In the middle of what had once been farmland, between farms where wheat grew and in sight of thatched roof houses and quaint stone churches, there was now a great concentration of men and machines built for war. So dense was the concentration of force that many bases were no more than 10 miles apart. In the early morning, the stillness was broken by the roar of powerful engines as bombers and fighters taxied to the runways from their hardstands, or parking areas. As they returned, their crews fired flares from the bombers so those waiting would know that wounded were aboard. The ritual of counting began. Group and Squadron officers, mechanics, crew chiefs and fellow pilots scanned the returning flock with binoculars. Often they returned in distress, crash landing or worse in the English country-side. By the end of the conflict, more than 30,000 men of the Eighth Air Force would be dead or missing as a result of enemy action. Their combat casualty rate of 7.4 percent would be higher than the rate US Marines suffered in the Pacific campaign.

It was a strange way to fight a war, this coming into combat on wings, enduring furiously intense fights, and then returning to relative comfort and peace. While they were in peaceful surround-ings, the mental anguish of seeing their neighbors at peace in the pastoral settings must have been extreme at times, as they knew that tomorrow, or the next day, they would climb again into their planes and face death. The bomber crews of that era tell stories that will chill even the most hardened of veterans. Flying alongside another bomber to see it suddenly disintegrate, or watching chutes open partially or not at all; orange bursts of flame followed by a cloud of black smoke in the sky, and debris fluttering down; all these sights worked on the minds of the crews as they briefed and walked to the flights lines on the days that they were scheduled for a mission. All military aviation was then as it is now, voluntary. A man could withdraw for any reason, no ques-tions asked. How these men fought back their fear on those mission days is a study in courage.

Wormingford had a history of military aviation dating back to World War I, when it had been established as a fighter base to provide defense against German dirigibles or Zeppelins. As World War II loomed, it was investigated as a possible site for a heavy bomber base. Plans were completed, and soon the base possessed a 6,000' runway and two shorter intersecting runways. The USAAF specified that 52 hardstands or aircraft parking areas be built, and housing, dining, and maintenance facilities for nearly 3000 personnel were com-pleted. The work begun in 1942 was completed the following fall, and Wormingford was assigned to the Eighth Air Force as a bomber base. Shortly after this, the base was deemed unneeded by the bomber command, and the facilities became a fighter base occupied by the Ninth Air Force. Eighth Air Force again took possession in the early months of 1944. The 55th Fighter Group moved into facilities at Worm-ingford on April 16, 1944, and among their distinctions were the first Fighter Group to fly over Berlin.

A popular phrase of the time, attributed to the English, says that Americans were *"oversexed, overpaid, and over here."* But of all the accounts I have read, the tone does not seem to be hostile at all. In fact, there seems to be a genuine admiration expressed for the Ameri-cans. These were young men, far away from home, and, for the most

*Bill sitting in a P-38 Lightning. He flew these in combat before
the 55th acquired the P-51 Mustang.*

part, their conduct was good, if not perfect. Today, around many of the
old sites that have reverted to their agricultural lineage, there are small
memorials to the airmen who left England to engage the enemy and
never returned.

*"What one would remember most was the deep affection with which
our visitors regarded all things British. They showered friendship freely
upon us all which they viewed as so old fashioned and quaint. Duxford,
they considered, was quite an antique and clearly they were prepared
to fight to save it. Never mind your rank, you were treated as an equal.
If you were young, they had a special brand of affection for you. They
impressed upon all that whilst they had come to win the war they were
here to play as well as fight."* [4]

Upon his arrival in England in June of 1944, Bill was assigned to
the 38th Fighter Squadron, one of three squadrons in the 55th Fighter
Group. The tall young man with the strong Oklahoma accent soon fit in
with his fellow pilots of the 38th, one of who later described him as *"an
outstanding fighter pilot."* Bill had now reached the objective of all of
his training; to fly fighters in a war. He would now begin the process of
settling into the community of combat aviators.

The atmosphere was one of confident professionalism. There were diversions such as occasional parties and trips to the George Hotel and Pub in Colchester, trips to London on passes, but mostly life revolved around flying. One custom that did not survive the war was that of naming airplanes. Pilots of that era often applied names and nose art to their aircraft. In Dog Flight of the 38th, David Jewell flew "*Miss Boomerang Margie*," Eugene Holderman flew "*Betty Jane*," and Robert Rosenburgh named his airplane "*Picadilly Rose*." Arthur Thorsen had the opportunity to name two planes, "*Iki Aga*" and "*Six Gun Pete*."

The 55th had been formed at Hamilton Field, California as the 55th Pursuit Group, and included the 38th, 338th, and 343rd Fighter Squadrons. In May of 1942, they were re-designated as a Fighter Group, and departed for England in September of 1943. The Groups of that era were composed of three squadrons. Manning levels of the Fighter Groups typically consisted of about 250 enlisted men and about 50 officers. Squadrons did not operate independently but under Group control. Each Group had its own headquarters organization, with administrative, support, and engineering as maintenance was called at that time.

Despite the fact that Bill arrived at the 55th as an accomplished pilot with more than three hundred hours of flying time, the Eighth Air Force had its own indoctrination and training to accomplish. This was a theater of war, with its own rules, and its own requirements. By June of 1944, the Eighth Air Force had been in England more than a year, and its leaders had learned a great deal more than what was required to fly a high performance aircraft like the P-38. New pilots would have to learn aircraft recognition. Telling an enemy apart from a friend at 400 miles per hour or double that at closing speed is critical. The geography of the English countryside, the geographies of France, the Low Countries and Germany were taught. With sixty air bases in a small area, local flying regulations were enforced. The challenge of high altitude operations, and safety at altitudes was a topic for training. Pilots were photographed in clothes typical of Europeans. If a pilot was downed and evaded, resistance fighters would use these photos to create an identity card specific to that region. Training in Escape and Evasion followed this (German interrogators soon discovered that most squadrons used the same clothes to photograph pilots. One said that he could look at a picture and tell the pilot to which Fighter or Bomber Group he belonged. Another interrogator used the mess cards since the same mess sergeant usually signed the cards for the entire Group). Since all flights were over the Channel, new equipment such as life vests and dinghies were issued and training given. These were just a few of the issues facing new pilots arriving in theaters of operation for the first time.

There were other considerations. Any new pilot coming into a combat squadron would be examined closely; he needed to fit in with his new teammates. They needed to be able to trust him, and for the first several weeks they would assess his skills, temperament and compatibility and place him in the organizational structure where he would achieve the greatest good for both himself and the Group. He would become a member of a flight, six to eight pilots who flew usually in a four-ship formation of two elements of numbered positions one through four, with the flight leader occupying the number one position. At the time of the Ruhland mission in September of 1944, Bill was assigned to "Dog" flight, led by 1st Lt. Arthur Thorsen, a tall thin officer with a great sense of humor and a likable personality. In June of 1944 Dog Flight also included David Jewell, Robert Rosenburgh, Eugene Holderman, Robert Littlefield, and Robert Callahan. Pilots usually did not fly every day, but Dog Flight would be assigned to provide a four-ship element on each mission. Bill's logbook shows that he made only three flights for area familiarization and transition before his fourth flight, which was a combat mission. When Bill arrived, the Group had

The pilots of Dog flight of the 38th Fighter Squadron.
In plane – Robert Rosenburgh. Standing – left to right: Eugene Holderman,
Arthur Thorsen, Robert Littlefield, Robert Callaghan, David Jewell, Bill Lewis.

already made the move from Nuthampstead to Wormingford, six miles north of Colchester in East Anglia. He arrived in time to begin the transition from P-38s to the new P-51s. His log shows that he made his first flight in a P-38, followed by a second and a third in a P-51. He flew his first combat mission in a P-38 on July 12, 1944. In a letter to his mother Nola, on the 26th of July, Bill remarked that he had been on four combat missions and logged 14 hours and 20 minutes of combat time in the P-38. There were more flights, combat and training, and after July 19th, all of his missions were in P-51s. The Mustang had already gone through four lettered versions, and now most of the 55th pilots flew the latest, a P-51D. The 55th, which had been the first to fly P-38s from England, now became the first American Fighter Group to fly the new D models. Many of the D models had first arrived in England in early 1944, and now they came equipped with the new K-14 gun sight, which had been developed by the British. The K-14 was simple to use. It required the pilot to correctly identify the airplane with which he was engaged. Six diamond-shaped brackets were arranged in a circle on the sight, and turning a small dial on the throttle control column tightened or loosened this circle to set the wingspan. The same wingspan was used for the two most common opponents, the Me 109 and FW 190. Getting into position to fire and remaining there was everything. Not too many enemy pilots would cooperate by remaining a target for very long. Lieutenant Colonel (Lt. Col.) McGinn, leader of the 55th on the Ruhland mission, flew an airplane equipped with the K-14 that day, and his mission report is highly commendable when he talks of the success he had with the sight. In addition to the K-14 sight, some pilots were equipped with the test versions of the new anti-G suits, which allowed them to make tighter turns in maneuvering by preventing blood from pooling in their arms and legs. These suits are standard in modern jet combat aircraft.[5]

The Group's missions through the 24th of July were short relative to later missions. None exceeded two hours, five minutes. It is unlikely that the pilots thought they were short. There were learning, the new pilots and the more experienced. No one had flown this type of aircraft in combat before, though the British had experience with the earlier models at lower altitudes. No one had escorted bombers in large formations such as the bombers flew, no one had encountered high altitude anti-aircraft defenses or flak as the German acronym came to be known, or high altitude problems, or flown on oxygen for sustained periods.[6] The altitude alone brought on a host of new problems both in aviation physiology and in maintenance of aircraft under those conditions. For those unfamiliar with aviation, especially military flying, some understanding of the challenge is warranted. All flying is mentally intensive. There are few details in flying a high performance airplane that are unimportant. Add to that the challenge of flying in a very high performance, very fast airplane with several other high performance, very fast airplanes just a few feet from you, and you will get the concept. Radio call signs, navigation courses, rules of engagement, escape routes, flight characteristics and dangerous maneuvers of your specific aircraft create a highly challenging environment in which mistakes are often made only once. When a high performance aircraft enters a tight turn or otherwise deviates from a level course, the airplane "pulls Gs." The force of gravity in a four-G turn effectively increases the weight of the pilot by a factor of four. He is trying to fly the airplane with all the required subtle touches, and his head, hands and legs have become incredibly heavy. Even those relatively short missions of two or three hours were taxing.

One of the standard practices of World War II was that flight crews were issued "mission whiskey" after landing.[7] David "Buddy" Jewell, Bill's Tulsa friend, and later squadron mate in the 38th, says that a man's bicycle was a treasure. After a mission, the pilots often pedaled off to the George in Colchester for a little British lager. Neither David nor Bill were heavy drinkers, but both of them, David said, "liked to bend an elbow now and then." There was much to learn and much to overcome. There was much to fear, and much to live for, and the young pilots of the 55th experienced it all.

Bill wrote to his mother on 21 July:

You know from Eleanor's letters that I've been on three missions in my old airplane. I'm switching now as I've told her and I'm happy about the change ...

Haven't seen any enemy fighters yet and don't know whether I will. They seem to be quite scarce now as you can tell by papers, etc. I'm well and getting very good food and lots of rest. That's about all there is to tell.

Tell Ted congratulations for me. He can be glad he got to be an instructor cause that sweet old USA is wonderful. You really realize it after you get out of it.

All my love and take care of those two lovely girls of mine.

Your big bruvver, Bill [8]

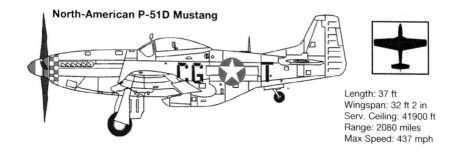

North-American P-51D Mustang

Length: 37 ft
Wingspan: 32 ft 2 in
Serv. Ceiling: 41900 ft
Range: 2080 miles
Max Speed: 437 mph

From the 19th of July to the 30th, the 38th flew mostly escort. From the relatively short mission times entered in Bill's log, the targets were probably close. Changes in strategy soon would dictate bringing the war closer to the German homeland. When the new external droppable fuel tanks were added, the P-51s acquired a combat range of just over 2,000 miles without refueling. Though their missions were still dangerous, the big bombers now had some protection from the German Luftwaffe by their Little Friends, as they called their fighter escorts. In the letter to his mother of July 26, he told her that he had "only" 300 hours of combat to finish his tour. He went on to add that from what he had seen so far, this war wasn't very dangerous.

> I haven't seen any enemy planes, and only a very little flak. So as far as I'm concerned, I don't know very much about war. And the way things are going there will be less and less of enemy opposition. I have very good quarters, concrete barracks with windows and a good bed with sheets, very comfortable. ... if you ever need anything I'll be ready to help you with all I have. You're my mom ... and I won't ever forget what I owe you. I wouldn't be where I am right now if it wasn't for one person — _you_.

David Jewell agrees with Bill's comment about the living quarters, but remembers taking showers and using the latrines when it was snowing outside, and the showers and latrines were not made with roofs. "_It wasn't much of a place,_" he recalls.

Bill flew ten combat missions after completing his familiarization training at Wormingford in July. On July 30th, Bill participated in a fighter sweep, a longer mission that lasted three hours and 55 minutes. Increasingly longer missions, five hours or more, followed this. On the 6th of August, the Group escorted bombers on a mission to Gdynia, Poland; a seven hour trip in Bill's log. August was an intense flying month. Bill flew twenty missions that month, and on two days, the 12th and 18th, flew two missions each day.

In an earlier mission on August 10, an unusual event occurred. The Squadron had another pilot named William Lewis. On this day, Bill flew as 1st Lt. Lewis's wingman on a strafing mission. William H. Lewis was shot down while the Group conducted strafing attacks on trains in France. Bill observed him as he bailed out, and returned to the squadron and reported the loss. 1st Lt. Lewis evaded for more than two weeks, and was returned to England in good condition on September 2 after having been discovered by members of the 7th Armored Division. William H. Lewis went on to a very successful wartime career with the 55th. He became an ace credited with eight victories. On September 5, 1944 William H. Lewis and his squadron tangled with a sixteen plane German formation and shot down every one. On that same day, another 55th pilot, William Allen, became an "ace in a day" when he personally accounted for five of the enemy fighters.

The August missions were varied; August 3rd was a fighter sweep, followed by five escort missions. The 13th and 18th were dive-bombing missions. All the escort missions were now lengthy. The new external tanks which made longer missions possible and enabled the strategy of bringing the war home to the Germans, and the need for the Eighth Air Force to show success in daylight bombing all exerted pressures on pilots and their leaders. The variety and intensity of the August missions reflected the movement of Allied forces on the ground. Since D-Day on the 6th of June, allied forces had made slow progress, but the breakthrough on August 1 at St. Lo had finally opened gaping holes in the German defenses. Now, they pursued the Germans with Infantry, Armor, and Artillery. Allied fighter aircraft

Bill Lewis's written mission notes from early August to early September 1944.

in August of 1944 often operated tactically, strafing German targets, dive-bombing tanks, trains, and columns of Infantry as they moved back to regroup and consolidate their strength.

By the end of August, 2nd Lt. William Lewis had added nearly ninety more hours of combat time to his flying logbook. He had accompanied bombers, dive bombed and strafed over Poland, Holland, France and Germany. He was a seasoned combat pilot, accepted by his fellow fliers, and by one account "an outstanding fighter pilot." With about 125 hours of combat time, he had nearly reached the halfway mark for fighter pilot tours. He had flown a total of 25 missions. There are no known logbook entries in Bill's logbook from September 6 until the 11th.

We know from Bill's log and from the Squadron and Group histories that Bill, along with many other pilots of the 55th, had never been in direct combat with German fighters. In various histories of the Eighth Air Force, mention is made of the lack of German fighter appearances in the summer months of 1944. While German aircraft had been aggressive in the previous winter and spring, August was a month of few opportunities for USAAF fighter pilots who sought out the Germans in air-to-air engagements. It is now widely known, and was speculated then, that the Germans were holding back resources for the time when the Allies moved into Germany. While pilots such as Bill Lewis had learned the new requirements of operating in the European Theater, many were still denied the experience of a one-on-one encounter with the enemy.

The Drive into Germany

Luxembourg – German Border
0530 hours, September 11, 1944

As dawn broke on the 11th of September, advance elements of the US Fifth Armored Division moved steadily toward the German border. Their objective was the ancient city of Aachen to the north, the early seat of Roman rule and later, the home of the Emperor Charlemagne. It was a city that held tremendous psychological and cultural importance for the citizens of Germany and their leaders. Though the Allies would not take the city for some two more months, the significance of this border crossing was evident to the German High Command. Not since the armies of Napoleon invaded more than 100 years before had an enemy army set foot on German soil. Since the 6th of June, in a little more than ninety days of fighting, the Allied forces had swept across France and the Low Countries, and now stood ready to invade the German homeland. It was not the "Blitzkrieg" or "lightning war" that Hitler had used against Europe in the early phases of the war, but an inexorable and relentless grinding away aimed at the German homeland. In the late evening of the 11th, a small American reconnaissance team moved quietly across the border. To their surprise, they saw no evidence of the German forces. The Germans had retreated prior to their advance, and as the 5th Armored crossed the Our River in force over the next few days, the Germans consolidated their strength in Aachen. The fighting would be brutal, but the outcome was never in doubt. The long, logistical tail supplied the tiger with teeth from across the Atlantic, and fresh soldiers and new equipment came in a steady stream to the shores of Europe. Within two months Aachen would fall and ultimately all of Germany. Now, the land campaign was paralleled by an equally bloody fight for control of the skies.

In the American Eighth Air Force, a huge aerial offensive had begun. In operations reminiscent of "Blitz Week" in June of 1943, huge formations of Allied bombers began to pound the German petroleum production systems. This was the outcome of discussions held at the Casablanca conference in January of 1943, resulting in the "Casablanca Directive." The strategy developed in the conference was a new emphasis on the destruction of German war production. In addition to the symmetric frontal opposition in which forces on the ground attempt to destroy each other, the fight would be brought to those industries that enabled the Germans to make war. This fight would target the enemy's cities, its automotive plants, aircraft manufacturing, transportation, and heavy equipment and precision machinery capabilities. For several days in September of 1944, the targets were to be Germany's petroleum producing facilities, most of which were located deep in the eastern part of Germany, close to the border of annexed Czechoslovakia. This attack on German war production was not a new phenomenon. Attacks such as the Schweinfurt-Regensburg raids in 1943, had been carried out earlier deep into Germany. But there were new tactical considerations now, and better airplanes, and the great leap-frogging over the German defensive lines on the ground was beginning in earnest.

The United States Army Air Forces (USAAF) planners had an enormous advantage over their German adversaries. Despite the fact that the US military was fighting essentially two separate wars over a huge amount of diverse geography circling nearly half of the globe, US manufacturing capacity had not been touched. Resources were finite, but their availability was a problem handed over to production engineers and factory managers. In Germany, the problem was different. At the beginning of hostilities the German military was fully prepared, and its adversaries were not. German production capacity was still not challenged to the fullest when the war began. As attacks on German industrial centers mounted, there was significant reserve capacity to fill production shortfalls. In fact, German war production generally tended to increase during the conflict, but it could never outstrip the production capacity of the United States and its allies. In another area, perhaps more important, the German population could not maintain a supply of young, combat ready troops and airmen to keep up with the Allied influx of men and materials.

There was also a significant shift in the conduct of tactical air operations. During the early years of bomber missions, a lack of range prevented fighters from accompanying bomber missions deep into Germany. At the onset of the war, neither Britain nor the United States had the capability of range in fighters to reach even the borders of Germany. So when the P-51 Mustangs acquired long-range capabilities, their first priority was bomber protection. Near the end of 1943, General Hap Arnold reorganized the European air assets. They were to be primarily strategic, with the Eighth in England and the 15th in the Mediterranean. Arnold gave new instructions to his leaders. They were to *"Destroy the enemy air force wherever you find them, in the air, on the ground and in the factories."* Within a short time, General Jimmy Doolittle assumed command of the Eighth, ready to carry out his orders. When Doolittle assumed command of the Eighth Air Force, he was already a charismatic figure. His success on the raids on Japan, only four months after the attack on Pearl Harbor, contributed to his leadership stature. Assuming command of the Eighth Air Force, he quickly echoed Arnold's declaration that the fighter role was now to destroy the German Air Force. His predecessors had carved out the fighter mission as one of primarily bomber defense. Doolittle would not abandon the bombers, but now his fighters would conduct independent sweeps on German airfields and generally seek out the enemy. Bombers would still have escorts, but the escorts would now act aggressively in the defense role. In the Ruhland mission on September 11, 1944, this role would be demonstrated visibly as fighter pilots sought out German defenders and carried the fight from purely defensive operations to aggressive defense.

Another factor in the air power story was Hitler's opposition to air defense. He was obsessed with the attack role. Because of this and other factors, he had often blocked attempts by Luftwaffe leadership to strengthen air defenses in favor of plans that favored strategic attack. Because of this stubborn resolve, Germany's citizens and her soldiers would pay a deadly price.

Mission 623

The official USAAF History and Chronology refers to all of the September 11, 1944 Eighth Air Force bombing missions collectively as Mission 623. Each of the Groups and their Squadrons though, would identify the mission by a separate mission or operation order number. Strategic Mission 623 was composed of 1,131 bombers and 440 fighters tasked with the attack of synthetic oil plants and refineries in Germany. The after-action reports indicate that the crews encountered an estimated 525 German fighters, and as many as 42 bombers and 28 fighters of the American Eighth USAAF were lost.

Thousands of young men were engaged in the fighting that day, in the air, on the ground or the oceans. Among the combatants, lives would be ended or dramatically changed. Families would be shattered, dreams broken, futures altered or denied. For Bill Lewis, this September Monday marked the halfway point of his combat tour in P-51 Mustang fighters. The twenty-two-year-old Lieutenant was approaching the downside of his required 300 hours of combat flying. He had already begun to think of going home to his wife Eleanor and new daughter, Sharon, now six months old. He was an experienced and competent combat pilot. He had flown nearly 150 hours in combat, including long-range bomber escort, dive bombing, and strafing. While we cannot be certain, Squadron records and Bill's own logbook give no indication that he had encountered any German fighters on his earlier missions.

The September missions planned at Eighth Air Force Headquarters at Wycombe Abbey reflected the strategy designed to focus on industries vital to the enemy war effort. On three consecutive days, from the 11th to the 13th of September, the refinery complexes in far eastern Germany were attacked in massive raids. Mission 623 refers to two distinct components. One segment of the mission was destined for refinery targets at Bohlen, Chemnitz, Brux and Ruhland. The Chemnitz force was a shuttle mission. This was an element of a larger operation whose code word was Frantic. Frantic operations had been instituted to establish cooperation with the Russians and to reduce the distance required for crippled bombers to reach safety. Shuttle missions would make the attack, then continue on to airfields in Russia where they were to rest, refuel, and return to home bases in England. The second stream of bombers was to attack the targets at Merseburg, Leuna, Lutzkendorff and Magdeburg. Magdeburg would receive two separate attacks within four minutes by two separate bomber forces. In addition to the above targets in the second group, targets at Misburg and

Hanover would be bombed. The targets were numbered, 1 through 10, in the following order: Merseburg/Leuna, Lutzkendorff, Magdeburg (2), Misburg, Hanover, Ruhland, Bohlen, Brux and Chemnitz.

For each of the ten primary targets, there was an alternate to be attacked if weather prevented bombing in those locations. There were also targets of last resort, which were planned so that the bombers would not depart Germany without dropping some ordinance over a target. With such a large mission, so many targets and so many airplanes, it was necessary for the coordination to be timed precisely. The first target was the Merseburg/Leuna refinery complex. It was scheduled for attack at 1150. In the next twenty-seven minutes, and ending at 1229, the remaining nine targets were to be struck. Mission timing and eastward progression was straightforward. Each element of the mission was to reach a longitude line at a precise time, then move on the next timeline in the plan. Thus at 1103, the supporting Fighter Group (55th) for target 7 (Ruhland) was to be at longitude 8 degrees East. The 55th's next checkpoint for navigation was at 1135 hours, at longitude 10 degrees, 30 minutes East. This places the Group along a line of bearing almost directly above the village of Oberhof at 1135. The actual mission summary and navigation Operations Plan (OPPLAN) obtained from the US Air Force Historical Research Agency under the Freedom of Information Act reveals a complex, highly coordinated mission that took place over extreme distances and involved more than 1000 aircraft. Originally classified as Secret, the Eighth Air Force Operation Summary shows the bombers and their escorts departing in three separate streams originating from East Anglia. One assembly point originated in Great Yarmouth, another over Southwold, and the third near the coastal town of Felixstowe. Here, the huge four-engine B-17 and B-24 bombers, each with a crew of nine or ten men, would gather until all of the birds were airborne, then assemble in huge formations to cross the channel. [9] All of this activity began early, well before dawn for the bombers. The crews would be awakened in their quarters to be told the mission was on. They would assemble and eat breakfast, followed by briefing, usually riding in groups in the back of trucks. There would be general briefings for all crewmembers. The briefing board was covered with sheets and uncovered once all the crews were assembled to reveal the route ribbons, which connected the takeoff points and final targets. Separate briefings might be held for various crewmembers such as navigators and radio operators. Crew readiness completed, they were off to the aircraft, most of which had been prepared the night before. There they would make radio checks and preflight the planes for a takeoff, which would begin at about 0730. Making their way to the continental coast in three massive streams, the bombers would be in relatively close proximity to each other until nearly 1120 hours or so, at which time they would begin to separate into 10 individual groups destined for their specific targets.

For the first half of the mission, the bomber Groups would be separated by about 20 kilometers, close enough on a cloudless day to see each other's formations. The bombers and escorts assigned to the Ruhland mission had the longest distance to the target. The distance "as briefed" was 1,310 miles. The total time would be 4 hours and 9 minutes for the fighters, much longer for the bombers. To think of it in other terms, it is just about one hundred miles less than the distance from Houston, Texas to JFK airport in New York, with all but the first and last 150 miles over hostile territory. The average speed over the plan geography, including combat, would be 320 miles per hour for the fighters.

As the swarm of noisy machines thundered into the air headed for the deep blue sky high over Germany, their young crews busied themselves with equipment checks, navigation plans, and all the other details of flying a combat mission. They would be alone with their thoughts for more than two hours on the cold fringes of outer space, and then the clash of men and their machines would begin.

(See mission map on pages 60 - 61)

The Defense of the Reich

Wormingford
September 10, 1944

The men of the engineering department of the 55th would work as long as required getting the 52 airplanes of the Group, including spares, ready for the takeoff the morning of the 11th. There was plenty to do. Military airplanes such as the P-51 are complicated machines. While it takes skill to fly them, it takes more work to maintain them. The support crews of the 55th probably worked through the night on some planes, because by the 0935 takeoff time called for in the operations order, those 52 planes had to be ready. The ground crews included armorers, radio specialists, sheet metal technicians and engine mechanics. These men had several months of technical training in their specialties, and often attended further training offered by the aircraft manufacturers at their facilities. While the Eighth Air Force pilots had the day missions and the British the night missions, this meant that the mechanics often had to work nights to get the planes ready for early morning takeoffs. In addition to addressing the usual problems caused by normal wear, mechanics were responsible for regular inspections and maintenance at 25, 50, and 100 hours of flying time. Armorers would load the linked machine gun ammunition, and if the question were asked, "Is the ammo loaded?" would reply with the comment "the whole nine yards." This referred to the fact that the ammunition for the three Browning M-2 .50 caliber machine guns on each wing, when fully loaded, would require 27 linear feet of space. The machine guns were formidable weapons. Air-cooled, they weighed 61 pounds each and fired 750-800 rounds per minute.[10] They were older weapons, developed fifteen to twenty years earlier.[11] When compared with the light machine guns on the German Me 109 and FW 190 though, the American weapons were much more effective. The Germans also employed the much more powerful 20 and 30 millimeter cannons that were frequently loaded with explosive shells, but not on each aircraft and not in large quantities. It is helpful to remember though, that even the P-51's "whole nine yards" of ammunition had a limited time in combat.

After the mechanics had done their work, the pilots would conduct a short preflight check and "walk around" of the aircraft. They had loaded the weapons, charged the oxygen tanks, checked the fuel, hydraulic fluid, radiator and supercharger coolants, battery fluids, oil, and a hundred other "little" things, any one of which found lacking could be disastrous. The mechanics, radio technicians, armorers, and sheet metal specialists in the maintenance units of the Eighth Air Force kept them flying under truly difficult circumstances and enormous pressures. These men were truly unheralded heroes. Without them the "Mighty Eighth" would not have gotten off the ground.

Ruhland, Germany
September 10, 1944

At the Brabag-Schwarzheide refinery in Ruhland, there was a tense quiet.[12] The oil producing facilities in the area had been taking a beating. There were massive attempts by German leadership to repair the damage done by these attacks. The US Strategic Bombing Survey, completed after World War II, states that as many as 300,000 workers were assigned to make repairs to these facilities. These repairs were often effective, but the attacks, especially by the Eighth AF, returned as soon as it became evident that a particular plant was back in production. There was a standard, wry comment often made by the German workers which said that the bombers knew just when to come, and it was always after the repairs had been made to the plant. Early in the war, the USAAF had disagreed with the British approach to heavy bombing. The British concentrated on night bombing, and often bombed German centers of population.[13] The USAAF approach was centered on targets of specific importance. These included, but were not limited to, such facili-

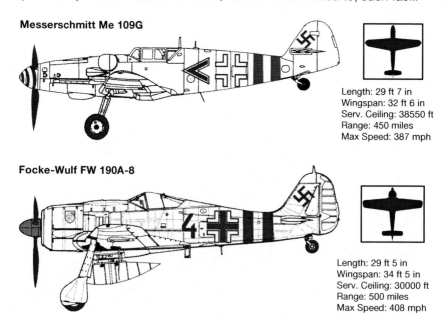

Messerschmitt Me 109G

Length: 29 ft 7 in
Wingspan: 32 ft 6 in
Serv. Ceiling: 38550 ft
Range: 450 miles
Max Speed: 387 mph

Focke-Wulf FW 190A-8

Length: 29 ft 5 in
Wingspan: 34 ft 5 in
Serv. Ceiling: 30000 ft
Range: 500 miles
Max Speed: 408 mph

The 38th Fighter Squadron Dog Flight pilots after briefing before one of the September missions. Back row – from left to right: Robert Maloney, Bill Lewis, Dudley Amos, Tunis Holleman, Norman Larson, sitting: Robert Callaghan, Dorman Castle.

ties as ball-bearing plants, oil production, railways and waterways, and electric power. Bombing at night was not a great deal safer than daylight bombing, and identification of such strategic targets was later abandoned for night missions. The Luftwaffe also had a highly developed night fighter defense, and British losses were often severe. One effect of the bombing campaign of both British and US forces was to severely curtail fuel availability. Not only was fuel in short supply for tanks and mobile artillery, but also for aircraft. In the early years of the war and generally until 1943, Luftwaffe pilots who were well trained and highly experienced made up the greatest percentage of the force. The fuel shortages and losses decreased the numbers of these pilots. Luftwaffe pilot training was diminished by this, and by the war's end, it had begun to create a huge problem.

Because the Luftwaffe had been under such pressure, the late spring and summer of 1944 had been relatively light for American fighter pilots as it related to air-to-air combat. But for this raid, the Luftwaffe would mount a vigorous defense. The German leaders knew that there was still a chance for them to prevail, and they had held back their air assets in order to train new pilots, gain confidence, and save resources for what was sure to be the greatest assault on their homeland since the beginning of the conflict.

The German Air Defense system had learned early in the war to monitor the radio frequencies of the British and American bombers as they prepared for takeoff from England. They were able to determine with great accuracy the numbers of bombers as they made radio checks prior to takeoff, and then they waited for the visual sightings as various early warning posts made their observations along the coast. On days in which the upper level weather conditions were satisfactory, contrails of the bombers were clearly visible, indicating the course and numbers of aircraft clearly. In the event of cloudy weather, they still had the use of radar, which had been developed early in the war. Reports would include the number of aircraft, location and direction. Much of this system owed its existence to the defense developed against British night bombing missions, but now it became valuable as the daylight missions by the Eighth Air Force increased. Large centers, often underground and placed deep in heavily protected bunkers, used direct telephone connections to the watching stations. Progress of the approaching bombers was plotted on large frosted glass panels. There were several such fighter control stations, the closest to England being Luftflotte 3 at Deelen near Arnhem in Holland. Historical evidence indicates that these stations controlled most encounters with allied aircraft. Though the Luftwaffe occasionally experimented with "free-hunting," it was not a common practice, and by 1944 the Germans had accumulated a great deal of experience with flight control procedures. Luftflotte 3 was responsible for defense in France, Belgium and Holland and as such encountered all the missions originating in England. The remainder of these stations stretched out in a line going generally south. Each of the stations in the system was responsible for alerting the various fighter Groups of impending action. It was from one of these that the pilots of Jagdgeschwader 4, based in Alteno and Welzow in the Cottbus region close to the border of Poland, would be alerted on September 11, 1944.

Clausewitz, the German General who served in the Napoleonic wars as a youth and later authored the classic *On War* in the early 1800s, would have been interested in the Luftwaffe approach. One of Clausewitz's dictums says that the defensive is the most perfect form of warfare. The Luftwaffe had surely read Clausewitz for their tactics in the defense of Germany offered them the security of mounting air-to-air defenses only when a clear tactical advantage could be applied. The air battle of September 11th would test their application of defensive theory. They would plan the timing of their defensive response against the bombers by calculating the takeoff times, estimated fuel states, ranges, and positions of the bombers and deploy their assets appropriately. This is the time in military operations when the successful union of intelligence and tactics becomes critical. The Luftwaffe intelligence officers painstakingly gathered details from crashed airplanes and interrogated their captured crews in detail. They knew call signs of the bomber squadrons, squadron designations from the markings on the fuselage. They recovered maps, briefing reports, and navigation charts and pored over these intensely. All these things, taken together, gave them a very complete picture of the capabilities of the aircraft and intentions of the forces as a whole. Another key factor in the relative German success against the missions in the summer and fall of 1944 involved understanding the American Fighter Groups strategy in bomber defense. The Luftwaffe studied the timing of the various Fighter Groups in the support role, and on the Ruhland mission there is evidence that the ability of the Luftwaffe defenders to predict the timing and coordination of the American attackers played a large part in their success against the bomber force. A very simple defensive goal of the Luftwaffe defenders was to find the bomber stream and attack just before they reached the target. This might disrupt the timing and therefore the accuracy of the bomb runs.

Wormingford, Briefing
0730 hours, September 11, 1944

It was a mild September day on the southeast coast of England, known as East Anglia, and as the pilots made their way to the briefing, there was a slight haze, with some typical clouds and a cool temperature. Across the channel near one of their first checkpoints, the wind was minimal and the day was cooler than normal with a low in the middle 40s and a high expected in the middle 60s. Even more importantly, the same cloud conditions seemed to dominate the entire continent, which might have been a problem for the bombers.

As the briefing began, the pilots of the 55th Fighter Group learned they would be escorting units of the 95th, 100th, 390th, and 486th Bomb Groups to a mission in the eastern part of Germany, near the Czech border. These first three Bomb Groups formed the 13th Combat Wing. The 486th Bomb Group was part of the 92nd Combat Wing. They would fly the lead, out ahead of the 13th Wing, and would be the very first over the target. The escorts would be assigned to a particular combat box of bombers, each box consisting of about 36 bombers.

Boyhood friends Bill Lewis and David Jewell during training.

The distances between boxes would be between 3-10 miles. Keeping the distance limited was important, because it hindered the German fighters' ability to penetrate the seam between boxes. Two other Fighter Groups would also be tasked with the escort mission for the targets at Böhlen and Brux. These were the 339th and 352nd, flying out of stations in Fowlmere and Bodney respectively.[14] Each of the Fighter Groups would operate to provide escort to the various parts of the mission, and at different times. Some would provide support for the initial part of the mission, or penetration, while others would support the bombers over the target or during withdrawal from the target. The 55th was to escort elements of the 13th Combat Wing to the Brabag synthetic oil plant at Schwarzheide near Ruhland, located about 55 kilometers north of the Czech border.

Heavy fighter opposition was not expected, and the mission planners had provided what they believed to be ample fighter escort, with 252 P-51 Mustangs and P-47 Thunderbolts for the 384 bombers. The weather was expected to be clear over the target, with a ground haze on takeoff and scattered low cumulus clouds from 3000' to 5000' all the way to the German border, expected to diminish as they neared the target. If the clouds held up over the target, it would make things difficult. The lead navigators and bombardiers depended on a visual sighting to begin the formation bombing run. Radar was available but was not always dependable for bombing. In the event of downed airmen and aircraft, their locations on the ground would be difficult to determine. Even if bombs were dropped on the primary target, the presence of clouds would obscure the results, and there would be little intelligence information at the completion of the mission. Sometimes, Pathfinder aircraft, equipped with special radar, would locate the target even if it were clouded over. Instead of dropping bombs to signal the Group that followed them, they would drop flares or smoke bombs of specific colors to indicate the target. Lack of a clear visual sighting of the drop points was difficult not only for the bombardiers and navigators. The Intelligence specialists depended on a series of photographs taken during the run to establish the effectiveness of the mission. Lack of these often made it necessary to send a special reconnaissance mission over the target to determine the results of the bombing. If the results were not satisfactory, another mission would be scheduled within hours.

The 38th and 338th were to remain with the 100th Bomb Group formation, while the 343rd went ahead to provide protection to the first combat box of the stream, composed of the 486th Bomb Group. It is believed that on this mission the 38th remained along the left side of the bomber formation until just before 1140. The 338th was probably a little behind the bombers and somewhat higher. This would place the 338th ahead of the 95th Bomb Group, which formed the last box in the stream. The actual placement of the squadrons was at the discretion of the flight leaders, but this formation was typical. There were to be four flights of four aircraft each. Spares would be assigned for the replacement of a pilot whose aircraft had early mechanical difficulties. These would fill in as the flight leaders requested.

Hellcat White flight of the 38th Fighter Squadron was to be led by 1st. Lt. Robert Tibor, who was the 55th's Group Operations Officer. He would also serve as the 38th's Squadron Leader for the mission. Captain McCauley Clark would lead Hellcat Red, Lt. Merle Coons Hellcat

Yellow, and Lt. Arthur Thorsen would lead the flight designated as Hellcat Blue. Bill's position was in the second element, flying the wing of Lt. Dorman Castle. Lieutenants Holleman, Lapham, and Courtney would fly as spares, and would fill in the assigned position of any of the aircraft experiencing mechanical problems. Leaders flew as the number one, with number two as their wingman, who was to protect their rear from attack. The number four man of each flight flew the wing of number three. Numbers one and three were to press the attack, while two and four protected them. The combination of one and two, or three and four, was called an element, and two elements composed a flight. Attacking from above was termed a "bounce." The pilots of the 55th were familiarized with the OPPLAN for the Ruhland mission. The OPPLAN was a document that spelled out the timing of the mission, the navigation checkpoints (bomber Groups used the term TP for turning points), and the takeoff and return times.

For the 55th, the Ruhland escort was numbered Squadron Mission #206, and Field Order #563, (Escort of 3rd Division B-17s). Engines were started at 0916. Takeoff time was scheduled for 0924 hours, landing at 1458. The Commanding Officer of the 338th, Lt. Col. John McGinn, was to act as Group Leader on the mission as well as flight leader for Acorn Squadron. As Group Leader, his responsibilities centered around three issues. The first of these was the takeoff time. He would have to ensure that the 52 Squadron aircraft required in the OPPLAN were ready along with their pilots at the time prescribed in the orders. Second, he was responsible for ensuring that the Group made the planned rendezvous with the bombers, on time and at altitude with those 52 airplanes. Third, the compass courses to the rendezvous and return were his responsibility. The actual return times would likely change for each element of the 55th. An early, intense engagement would deplete fuel and ammunition and affect an early return for the elements involved. Individual pilots might return alone if they encountered mechanical problems. The plan called for starting the compass headings at 0944. These gave the Group time to takeoff and assemble in formation before starting the first of several course changes. The first heading was to take them to the English coast, only twenty miles from their base at Wormingford. At 1011 hours they would turn nearly due east for the Belgian coast, an 80-mile flight over the channel. Twenty-two minutes later they were to be at the assigned altitude of 24,000 feet to prepare for the rendezvous with the bombers. Rendezvous was scheduled at 1106 in the vicinity of Verviers, Belgium. There were 10 more navigation checkpoints in the OPPLAN, including the time over target of 1224, and mission completion as briefed would occur at 1458 when they touched down at their home base of Wormingford.

After Bill and the rest of the 55th's pilots who were to fly the Ruhland mission had been briefed, they headed to the building that contained their individual lockers to don their flying gear and survival equipment. First came the flying suit or overalls, then a double layer of socks. They wore fleece-lined boots, leather helmet and goggles, a personal side arm such as a .45 caliber pistol, a leather flight jacket and gloves. Finally, they donned their life vests and parachutes, and checked the small CO_2 canister that they would activate to inflate their life vests in the event of ditching in the Channel. They may have carried a map, and often wrote the various routes and compass courses on the backs of their hands in ink. All this completed, they rode in one of the trucks to the flight line and headed for their airplanes.

We can't know what Bill Lewis might have thought as he gave his aircraft the pre-flight walk-around. But we do have a pretty good idea of what he had to do. Aviation is a jealous mistress. Many pilots leave the military with excellent training, great experience, and many hours in the air, and never pilot a plane again. Without the access to a government airplane, free fuel, and excellent mechanics, they cannot devote the time to flying that they know they need in order to fly safely. One aviation saying sums it up very well; *"there are old pilots, and there are bold pilots, but there are no old and bold pilots."* While this statement usually refers to obvious risk taking, it also refers to casual pre-flight inspections. Most careful pilots will characterize the pre-flight inspection as a search for reasons not to take off. Finding none, they fly. Bill would have checked the airplane he was to fly that day, walking around the plane with an eye toward finding problems; he would have first checked the tires for wear and proper inflation. The loss of a tire on takeoff could cause the loss of the airplane and maybe the pilot. The Mustang manual called for 3-$^7/_{16}$ inches of clearance and equal on both wheel struts. He'd check the Pitot tube; the small tube that told him of the plane's indicated airspeed, to make sure it was clear of obstructions. Inability to know airspeed could be fatal. The gun hatch covers would be securely fastened to keep "the whole nine yards" of ammunition from leaving the orderly arrangement of the armorers and jamming before firing. Before entering the cockpit, he would look at the caps on both gas tanks, making sure they were tight, and then check the Dzus fasteners, the little spring loaded devices that hold various service compartment covers securely in place, and the screws in the fairings to be certain that none were coming loose. All this done, he would have been ready to enter the cockpit and begin his preparations there at engine start time. He would have started the engine while his crew chief stood by, listening and looking at his instruments for signs that something was not quite right. Running the engine at 1300 rpm, he would check engine and coolant temperatures, magnetos and fuel mixtures.

The armorers, electricians, mechanics and sheet metal technicians had been awake long before their pilots. Many would not sleep at all the night before a mission, involved in preparing their assigned aircraft for the combat of this day. They took immense pride in the ships and were protective of them. They often waited out the tough missions with great concern for the fliers, and they were good at what they did. The crew chiefs were responsible for the total maintenance. They would coordinate and supervise the action of each of the various specialists who performed the work, and they would spend a little time before takeoff with each pilot discussing the details of what their preparation had discovered. But at takeoff, the plane was the responsibility of the pilot and no one else.

Once Bill accepted the airplane, which had been worked over by a team of dedicated specialists, his work as a pilot began. One of the first things he would do would be to check the seat height. It should have been high enough to see comfortably through the gun sight and over the cockpit. If a shorter pilot had flown the previous mission, it would have to be adjusted. Next, he would check the distance from his feet to the rudder pedals. The P-51 seat adjusted upward, but not forward, so that each of the rudder pedals had to be adjusted manually one at a time. It was a little detail, but an important one. Fighter pilots like to feel the airplane is an extension of themselves, and these items made them feel that extension. He would set the parking brake so that the airplane did not move forward during engine start and run up. The landing gear handle was supposed to be in the down position. The Mustang had no safety to prevent the landing gear from being raised while on the runway. He would reach forward and unlock the controls, which were secured by a mechanism at the base and forward of the control column, so that he could check the movements of the elevator and ailerons. He would fasten the safety belts and harnesses and set his altimeter to the correct barometric pressure, and open the oil and coolant shutter valves to the full open position while the battery cart was being connected for startup. The rudder trim was set to 5 degrees right trim so that the torque or force of the propeller would not rotate the airplane to the left and cause a stall and spin. Set elevator trim to 2-3 degrees, nose trim up if 25 gallons or less fuel in fuselage tanks, down if fuselage tanks full. Check hydraulic pressure and release by raising wing flaps to up position. Close the canopy. If the engine

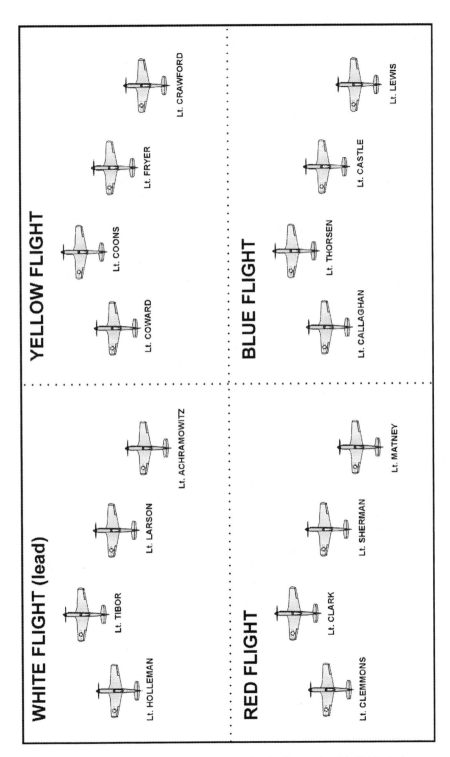

38th Fighter Squadron element assignments for the September 11, 1944 mission.

had been idle for more than two hours, the props were to be manually pulled to circulate oil. Open throttle and set mixture control to idle. Start engine. Check oil temperature between 70-80 degrees C., with a max of 90 degrees. Check coolant temperature between 100-110 degrees C., maximum of 121 degrees. Check fuel pressure at 12-16 pounds per square inch, maximum of 19. Check magnetos at 2300 revolutions per minute with a maximum drop of 100 revolutions per minute, set mixture at Auto Rich.

This and a few dozen other details completed, each pilot of the 55th reported ready for takeoff. Engine start was set for 0916, takeoff at 0924. At least one pilot that day returned right after takeoff. His wheels were stuck in the down position. This sometimes occurred when the drop tanks interfered with the flow of air past the wheel fairing, or cover, which encased the wheels once they were raised. Suction would be created, and the wheels stayed down. The solution was yawing, or moving the rudder pedals left and right to alter the airflow. Sometimes it didn't work, and on that day, Lt. Douglas E. Mayer of the 38th had to return at 0940 because of this. Lt. Mayer would miss the combat action over Ruhland. He volunteered to fly as a spare with another squadron the next day on an escort mission to Leipzig, flying a plane named "Mom's Pride." He was killed in action that day.

The Mustang presents an elegant architecture to the eye. It looks as though it belongs in the air. Some have even commented that if it were not an airplane, it would be an award winning sculpture. But the Mustang fully loaded presented a takeoff challenge. At 11,000 or more pounds, it was just half the weight of the loaded P-38 Lightning. But it had half the engines as well. Loss records of the 55th at Wormingford show more than a few takeoff accidents, when the aircraft carried a full load of fuel, several hundred pounds of ammunition, and struggled for altitude at takeoff. The Mustang performance charts indicated that taking off with a gross weight of 11,000 pounds, the airplane would stall at 107 miles per hour if power were lost. It was at the high altitudes and combat maneuvers that the P-51 would excel. At takeoff, it was as vulnerable as most airplanes.

Wormingford, Take-off
0924 hours, September 11, 1944

Take-off time arrived for the 55th. As the Mustangs prepared to line up for the taxi order, the bombers of the 13th Combat Wing had been aloft since 0735 and by now were formed up in the box formations and well over the continental coast and nearing Germany. The fighter pilots would catch up to them quickly after they climbed and opened the throttles. The pilots weaved their way to the runway, making "S" turns in the low cockpits so that they could see in front of them. Their engines ran at 1000 revolutions per minute as they taxied in order to prevent spark plugs from fouling. Another factor involved in the taxi process was speed. The Mustangs handled best when taxiing at about 35 miles per hour. Too much pumping the brakes could cause them to overheat, and when the airplane reached altitude, the metal would rapidly contract and, as a consequence, the wheels would lock on landing, causing an accident. All the care taken in the weaving taxi formation was for a good reason. Later, a pilot of the 55th would be killed in a collision between two aircraft while taxiing for takeoff. Usually takeoff

Lt.Col. McGinn was leader of the 55th FG for their escort mission on September 11, 1944.

was by pairs, lead and wingman. In some squadrons, if weather was bad and visibility was low, the leader took off and maintained the course called for in the flight plan. The wingman took off with him, but immediately turned right for several seconds before resuming the takeoff course. This way they could hope to avoid a collision in the clouds. Al Koenig says that the 38th did not follow this procedure. Instead, during low visibility they tucked in close to the element leader to have positive visual contact all the way through the clouds. This technique gave the pilots more confidence, and kept the number of pilots flying alone through a congested, low visibility air space at a minimum. Takeoff speed was done more by feel, but would generally be about 110 mph Indicated Air Speed. Best climb speed was at 170 mph, with 2600 rpm's on the engine. All these requirements were called out very specifically in the various checklists and manufacturers recommendations, but when it came time to take off, the pilots relied more on "feel" of the airplane than looking at gauges and dials. From an experienced pilot's point of view, takeoff was not a complicated affair, but it did require quick action if something went wrong.

Lt. Col. McGinn would be monitoring the 55th's assigned radio frequency, and as Group leader he would have been monitoring a separate radio channel that allowed him to communicate directly with the bombers at rendezvous. As the Group Leader, it was his responsibility to fly the fighter escort portion of the mission "as briefed." This meant arriving on time and at altitude for the rendezvous, with the requested number of fighters in the mission brief. He was authorized to make any tactical decisions and changes necessary to achieve this objective. By the time they reached altitude at the OPPLAN time of 1033, the temperature in the cockpits could be as low as -50 degrees, and the pilots would be easily fatigued. By the end of the mission and debrief, the pilots would be hungry and ready for their "mission whiskey."

The three squadron elements of the 55th were airborne at the precise time called for in the OPPLAN. At 0936 they completed their formation takeoff and joined before starting their first compass course of the mission at 0944. They would depart the English coast at 0949, crossing the Belgium coast at 1011. Rendezvous with the "Big Friends" was scheduled for 1106, after which the first of the four checkpoints leading to the target would be marked. It was getting cold as they climbed, but the heating system was reliable, and it was better in the P-51 than it had been in the P-38. The bombers labored on ahead of them, and in the unheated and unpressurized confines of the B-17s, the crews attempted to ward off the bitter cold by wearing electrically heated suits and gloves and covering exposed flesh. The 55th crossed the English Channel as the bombers prepared to depart France, and 22 minutes later they could look down on the low country islands and marshes of the Belgian coast. As they crossed the Belgian coast and neared Holland, the pilots heard the static in their radio headsets caused by the German air search radar as it recorded the contacts passing above. At 1040, twenty-six minutes ahead of the OPPLAN time, they made rendezvous with the bombers of the 13th Combat Wing. Had they known of the day's events, they might have looked down and to their left earlier as they passed over Verviers, as they were then scarcely 25 miles from Aachen and flying over the Allied armies as they flew east. The formation was due to reach Ranis, the first major land checkpoint, at 1149. After Ranis, they would begin a series of course changes which would bring the bombers and their escorts directly over the target at 1224. The bombers were to approach the target from the west-southwest, south of Eisenach, then take a more easterly course toward Gera and Jena, approaching the Czechoslovakian border, then begin their Initial Point preparations for the bomb run as they approached Ruhland from the southwest. Their accompanying Fighter Groups did not always follow the bomber track exactly. While their track would take them almost exactly over the Czech border, south and away from the other missions in the area before they began their run from the Initial Point (IP) into Ruhland, the 55th's planned track was somewhat to the north of the bombers. This is probably because the available intelligence reports indicated a more likely attack from the north.

From debriefing and crew reports we know that the bomber Groups took this long and indirect approach, possibly to avoid enemy fighters and flak which would be more prevalent on a direct approach, and to confuse the defenders regarding their objective. Even a few minutes of deliberation on the part of the German fighters would give the bombers an edge. Since Mission 623 involved other locations in the same general area, there was a great deal of activity in the air during the operation. The bombers were still about 55 minutes from the target when the combat began in earnest. They were about 200 kilometers from Ruhland as the fight began. Elements of the 55th Fighter Group were south of Erfurt, above the picturesque and wooded hills of the Thuringian Forest, the Thuringer Wald.

In a cold blue sky, with gentle September sun painting the rolling hills and forests below, the two groups of young men in the machines of war advanced inexorably toward each other. They prepared to meet in the ultimate contest in which many would die. Some would die alone in a shattered cockpit, hurtling toward the earth in a crippled aircraft. Others would die in the company of their fellow crewmembers, as the bombers were ripped apart by the murderous fire of the German Messerschmitts and Stürmjagers. All would die violently as the carnage began at 25,000 feet and descended to as low as 20 feet above the earth, and the wreckage of their brutal endeavor would be scattered in an area about 100 kilometers long and perhaps 50 or so kilometers wide. Nearly 60 years later, the wreckage of battle that was laid down on that day still litters the fields below.

Alteno and Welzow Airfields, Germany
Jagdgeschwader 4 area, 1000 hours, September 11, 1944

In the early years of the allied bombing efforts, Luftwaffe leaders wrestled with tactics and experimented with new weapons against the big four-engine bombers. In 1943, Hermann Goering ordered the establishment of a new group of fighters. These would be called "Sturmstaffel." Adolf Galland, the famous German fighter leader, had concluded that the main reason for failure against bombers was due to both formation and range. Fighters did not hold close formations and attacked at

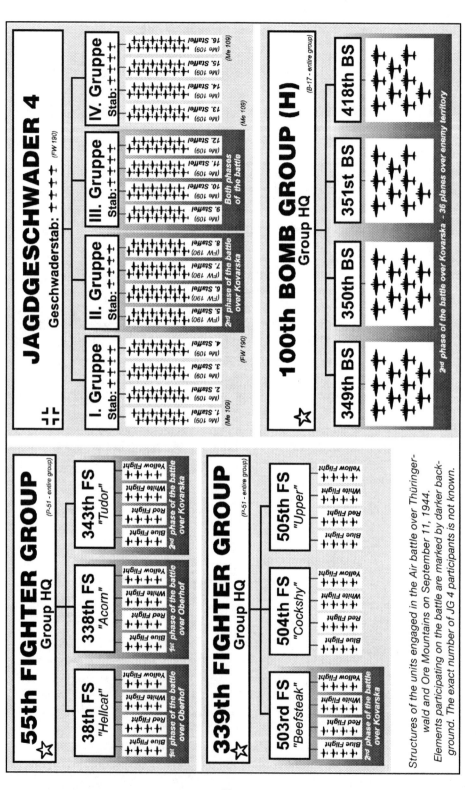

Structures of the units engaged in the Air battle over Thüringerwald and Ore Mountains on September 11, 1944. Elements participating on the battle are marked by darker background. The exact number of JG 4 participants is not known.

too long a range to be effective, Sturmstaffel tactics called for fighters to be much more heavily armed, keep close formations, and attack at very close ranges. The first of the Sturmstaffel squadrons was formed in 1943, and one of only three existing and specially equipped units would take to the air with Jagdgeschwader 4 (JG 4) on September 11, 1944.

The pilots of JG 4 were accustomed to quick starts and changes of the plan. As defenders, they adapted their fight to that of the attackers. While many Luftwaffe squadrons had begun the war in the west, in occupied France or the low countries of Belgium and Holland, the pilots of Gruppe I./JG 4 had begun the war during 1943, farther east, guarding the oil fields in Rumania. The squadron had moved dozens of times since their formation. But the Allied advances had surged, and now the pilots of JG 4 were assigned to the defense of Germany. In the summer of 1944, the Stab and II. Gruppe of the JG 4 were established and provided with the new and heavily armored FW 190A-8/R2 "Sturmböck." The airplane had been specially designed to penetrate and attack the heavy bomber formations of the USAAF. Major Günther von Kornatzski, a former leader of Sturmstaffel 1, was responsible for the new tactics to be used by the pilots. The III. Gruppe was established at this time. They stood ready in the eastern part of Germany, not too far from the border of occupied Poland, and the Geschwader which would fly against the Americans on September 11, 1944 would be a vastly improved and highly prepared group.

The fighters that rose up to meet the Americans were being produced in numbers, but the German approach to personnel staffing during the war was quite different. When readers first learn of the German aces and the number of planes they shot down, their first reaction is that they must have been exceptional pilots.[12] They were, as any military combat pilot must be, but the Germans had no rotation system. This was in direct contrast to the American system, where bomber pilots rotated out after a specific number of missions, or fighter pilots like Bill Lewis finished their tours with 300 hours of combat time. A German fighter pilot flew until he was shot down. If he landed on German controlled territory, he flew again even if he were injured. A Nazi official asked the German General Jeschonneck, during the time he served as Chief of Staff of the Luftwaffe, if increasing production of fighters to 350 per month would help. Jeschonneck is reported to have said, "*What would I do with 350 more planes?*"[16] As the Allied bombing campaign began to take its toll on fuel and the Allied fighters encountered and destroyed not only airplanes but also killed pilots, the problem of staffing the Luftwaffe grew severe. Young Luftwaffe pilots were now receiving minimal training compared to those pilots who flew at the outset of hostilities. This would be critical as JG 4 took off to meet the two squadrons of the 55th south of Erfurt.

As the alert came from the Luftflotte Headquarters, the pilots began their takeoff preparations. Quickly snuffing out cigarettes and laying books aside, they raced for the Messerschmitt's and Focke-Wulf's parked on the grass airstrips at Alteno and Welzow in response to the "Alarmstart" that told them that a mission was on. Throughout the German heartland, more than 500 pilots would be sent up to defend against the attacking bombers. On September 11th, the mission of JG 4 was to defend the area south of Chemnitz. It was into this area that the bombers of the 13th Combat Wing would make their turn northward toward the target a few minutes after noon. More than 50 Messerschmitts and Focke-Wulf's raced up from the fields at Alteno and Welzow. For many of the young German pilots, the 11th of September would be their first combat experience. For 21 of them, it would be their last.

A Duel of Eagles

In the air, south of Erfurt Germany
1130 hours, September 11, 1944

Lt. Col. McGinn, flying as group leader, organized the two squadrons in a defensive formation after the rendezvous west of Frankfurt. The 38th was abeam of the bombers to their left, while the 338th flew closer to the bombers and behind them. Early air defense tactics had always limited the fighters to "close" escort, meaning they were to remain in visual range of the bombers and were not allowed to sweep independently forward of the bomber track. Since General Jimmy Doolittle had assumed command, the tactics had changed, and now fighters swept the area ahead of their "Big Friends," miles ahead of them. The bombers were in the box pattern, with a high, middle, and low formation inside the box. In the early years of daylight bombing in Europe, bomber commanders were certain that the geometry of the box would render their formations impregnable to attack. The bombers had self-defense weapons at their nose, upper and lower turrets, and tail, and two waist gunners aft of the wings. By massing their firepower, which was formidable, they felt that the enemy fighters would be unable to penetrate the boxes. The bomber box was similar to the Infantry concept of interlocking fields of fire. The box was different though, due to the speed of air combat. It was necessary for the gunners to have incredibly quick reaction times. In the heat of combat, the P-51s and Me 109s often looked the same. P-51 pilots who pursued German pilots into the box sometimes found that they were being fired on by the B-17 gunners. The mobility and speed of aerial combat made the field of fire concept unworkable in the air, and severe losses soon changed the opinions of Eighth Air Force commanders. Once the P-51s with disposable fuel tanks were employed, the bomber boxes gained greatly improved and longer range protection, if not invulnerability.

The German Luftwaffe had also made modifications to their tactical formations. The attack on the Ruhland mission bombers made use of specially modified Focke-Wulf 190s. These airplanes were heavily armored in order to survive the firepower the box could deliver. Called "Sturmjäger" or "Sturmböck," they were to make a diving attack right through the firestorm of lead in the box and target individual bombers in the high, middle and low box as they flew through. The tactical purpose of the Sturmjäger was to cripple the bombers and especially to break the formation of the bombers' combat box, not to engage the American fighters. Heavily armored, they lacked the maneuverability of

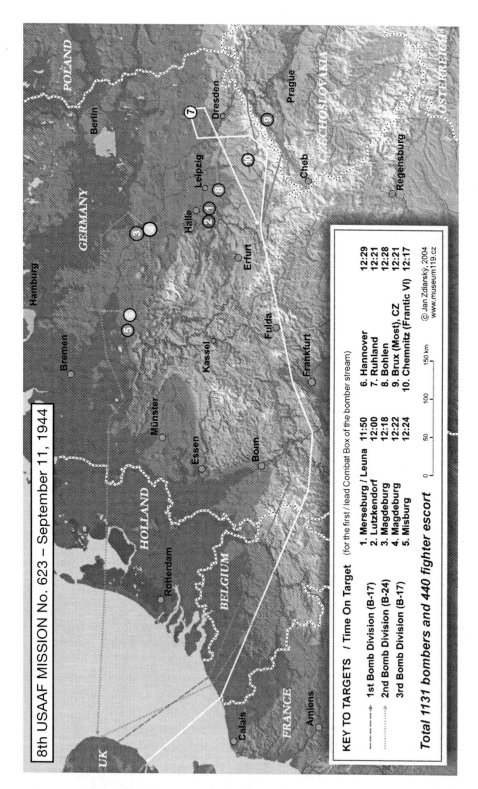

8th USAAF MISSION No. 623 – September 11, 1944

KEY TO TARGETS / Time On Target (for the first / lead Combat Box of the bomber stream)

	1. Merseburg / Leuna	11:50	6. Hannover	12:29
1st Bomb Division (B-17)	2. Lutzkendorf	12:00	7. Ruhland	12:21
2nd Bomb Division (B-24)	3. Magdeburg	12:18	8. Bohlen	12:28
3rd Bomb Division (B-17)	4. Magdeburg	12:22	9. Brux (Most), CZ	12:21
	5. Misburg	12:24	10. Chemnitz (Frantic VI)	12:17

© Jan Zdiarský, 2004
www.museum119.cz

Total 1131 bombers and 440 fighter escort

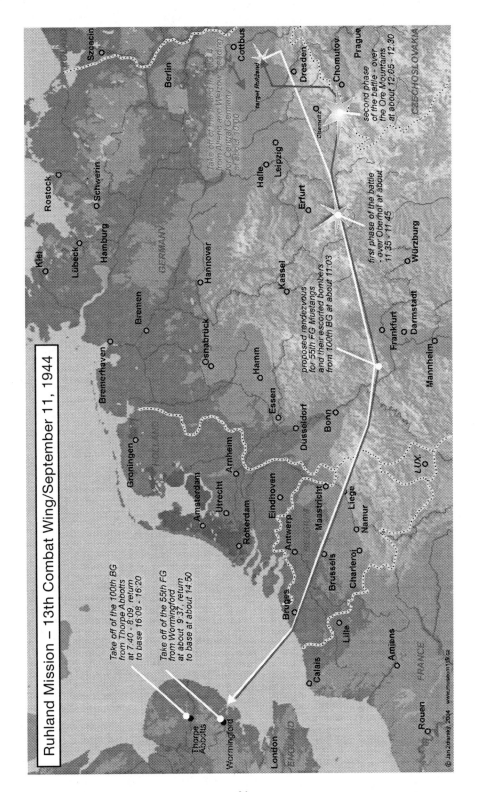

Ruhland Mission – 13th Combat Wing/September 11, 1944

Take off of the 100th BG
from Thorpe Abbotts
at 7:40 - 8:09, return
to base 16:08 - 16:20

Take off of the 55th FG
from Wormingford
at about 9:37, return
to base at about 14:50

proposed rendezvous
for 55th FG Mustangs
and their escorted bombers
from 100th BG at about 11:03

first phase of the battle
- over Oberhof at about
11:35 - 11:45

second phase
of the battle - over
the Ore Mountains
at about 12:05 - 12:30

Take off of the 100th and 390th BG
from Alnens and Wetzrow heading
for Central Germany
at about 10:00

Target Ruhland

© Jan Zdiarský 2004 www.museum119.cz

the Messerschmitt. Disabling a bomber could be achieved by a single hit on one of the four engines, causing the big airplane to lose altitude and speed, and fall out of the relative protection of the box, aborting the bombing run. Such disabled airplanes then became much easier targets for the German fighters.

At about 1130, the formation began to close in on the target. They were only about 19 minutes from the first of the major land navigation checkpoints, Ranis, when Lt. Col. McGinn noticed contrails to the left of the screening fighters and above them at about 30,000 feet. Several other 55th pilots saw this same formation, and estimated it to consist of as many as 150 enemy aircraft. As the formation passed to the south of Meiningen and headed due east on a course of 088 degrees, McGinn called for the 38th to move forward and join Acorn squadron in the forward screen. He then began a climbing turn to the right and radioed to the Group to follow. This was intended to place Acorn and Hellcat Squadrons in the sun, where they could begin their attack, and to place the two squadrons in an altitude advantage. Shortly afterward and while still in the turn, the Group was bounced by two Me 109s. McGinn called out for the Hellcat and Acorn pilots to drop their tanks.

The fight was on. Turning back toward the left and the original course, he saw two Me 109s who had appeared from somewhere other than the large formation seen earlier as they flew through the formation of P-51s. He pursued one that quickly reversed direction, and then saw the opportunity to chase the other. Firing just two ½ second bursts, he watched the aircraft roll over on its back as the canopy was jettisoned and the pilot bailed out. The second element of Hellcat Yellow flight, led by 1st Lt. Earl R. Fryer, had remained above with the rest of Hellcat Yellow to provide top cover from the second large group of German fighters. From the top cover group there suddenly emerged another pair of Me 109s. These two fighters commenced an attack on Hellcat Yellow, and Fryer turned into them. They broke off their attack and turned, giving Fryer an opportunity for a no-deflection shot from 550 yards astern of one of the two Germans. Fryer fired at that distance, then closed to within 200 yards and fired again. He had the speed advantage, and found himself quickly overshooting the enemy. As he pulled back for a third pass, the pilot bailed out of his crippled aircraft. By this time, the enemy top cover had been committed, possibly by the two Me 109s who had left the high cover group prematurely. Fryer's wingman, 1st Lt. Kenneth I. Crawford, had engaged the other Me 109, and quickly secured hits on the second German fighter, who also bailed out of his aircraft. Fryer and Crawford then engaged another pair of Messerschmitts and attacked them. In the pursuit of these two, Fryer and Crawford separated. Fryer went looking for more victims, and in the next few minutes of the fight that remained, scored two more kills.

1st Lt. Clifford Sherman was leading the second element of Hellcat Red when the fight began. Observing an Me 109 at his flight level and 9 o'clock to him, Sherman began a left turn to engage. He was seen by the enemy pilot, who then began to "jink" his ship violently as he tried to destroy his pursuer's aim.[17] Closing to within 150 yards, then to near zero, Sherman fired repeatedly with no visible results, and considered ramming the enemy fighter. He pulled out to the right and flew formation for several seconds, looking for evidence of his marksmanship. Pulling back again, he followed the German in a left turn, and opening to 100 yards, fired again. This time he was rewarded by seeing the cockpit and wing roots of his opponent disintegrate under the withering fire at close range. There was no bailout as the Messerschmitt caught fire and began to trail smoke and unburned fuel in a steady stream as it plunged to earth. Sherman did not follow the falling fighter, but set out to find another victim.

Arthur Thorsen led Hellcat Blue, consisting of Thorsen, Lt. Robert Callahan flying his wing, Lt. Dorman Castle as number three, and Bill Lewis flying Castle's wing as number four. Responding to Lt. Col. McGinn's call for Hellcat to come forward, Thorsen moved up with the rest of the 38th to meet the enemy with Acorn already engaged. As the flight moved forward, Thorsen was concerned about the movements of the top cover for the first group of attacking Me 109s. When he realized that they would not commit immediately, he joined the fight, which had now progressed down to the lower altitudes. He picked out a blue-nosed 109 and attempted to follow him, but the German executed a split-S and dove. Thorsen lost contact with Callahan, and the second element with Castle and Bill Lewis was forced to split as a result of a head on attack by more enemy aircraft. Closing to within 500 yards on another German, Thorsen fired from directly behind and watched as smoke poured from the enemy plane, which then went wildly out of control. Thorsen stayed with the stricken fighter, and then realized that he was in a vertical dive and exceeding 500 miles per hour. He had reached the cloud tops when he began a recovery, and pulled out of the dive at 300 feet above the trees in the Thuringer Wald. Groggy from the pullout, he regained his vision in time to see a tremendous explosion on the ground. The enemy pilot had jettisoned his canopy while they were still in the clouds, but never escaped the damaged aircraft.

Tunis Holleman, who had originally begun the mission flying as a spare, had assumed the number four position in Hellcat White. Waiting with the rest of the Hellcats as guard against top cover, he was quickly split up from his element and soon found an Me 109 with him in a tight diving turn. A second P-51 drove off the Me 109, and Holleman pulled out of the dive at 3,000 feet only to discover that another German was on his tail. He started another diving turn, and at 200 feet above the deck had apparently run out of ideas and altitude. The German was attempting to "square the corner and get deflection" when Holleman performed a reverse snap roll and recovered just 20 feet off the deck. The German who was pursuing him was unable to recover and struck the ground and exploded underneath and only slightly behind him. He would not be the only 55th pilot to claim a kill without a shot that day.

Walter Konantz, whose brother Harold was also a pilot in the 338th, claimed another enemy fighter in similar conditions. As the fight broke out, a single Me 109 dove across his flight path at a 45-degree angle. Konantz chased the enemy fighter as the dive increased to 90 degrees. At 600 yards distance, he could not set up a firing solution. As they passed through 15,000 feet, his airplane began to buffet violently, and he observed an indicated air speed of 600 mph. Though his own ship was shaking and nearly uncontrollable, he could see the same in the enemy aircraft as it bucked and skidded across the sky, barely in control. Still trying to set up a shot, he passed through 10,000 feet only to see the right wing of the Messerschmitt separate from the aircraft about four feet from the fuselage. He was the second pilot to score a kill without firing on the 11th of September.

Another three kills were attributed to a 1st Lt. of the 338th, William J. Ingram. Ingram quickly finished off two Me 109s in the opening minutes of the encounter. Looking for a third to complete his day, Ingram found a P-51 pursuing a Messerschmitt in a Lufbery.[18] The Mustang pilot apparently ran out of ammunition, as he told Ingram to take over from him and finish the German. Ingram zoomed up in a power climb and nosed over to get deflection, and fired, centering his strikes on the wing roots and canopy. The plane rolled over, and burning furiously, began a dive from 9,000 feet. His Individual Pilot Encounter Report filed after the mission and verified by the Squadron Intelligence Officer, Capt. Walker Gabbert, indicates that the unknown P-51 pilot is believed to have been either Bill Lewis or Kenneth Crawford. In the documentation involving Bill's loss, Ingram also filed a report saying that sometime during the fight, he saw a P-51 on its back and smoking. He believed this plane to be a 38th aircraft. No other pilots claimed to have encountered a similar situation during the melee.

For the next ten minutes, the Hellcat and Acorn Squadron pilots were engaged in a free-for-all while Tudor pilots continued on with their escort duties. The fight took place over an area ranging from south of Meiningen to Gotha in a generally northeast direction, a distance of about 75 kilometers. It lasted only ten minutes, or enough time for both Hellcat and Acorn squadrons to have depleted all of their ammunition and a significant amount of fuel in the high-energy maneuvers. At the end of this brief, furiously intense encounter, the pilots of the two squadrons would claim 25 kills and seven damaged enemy aircraft. At 1200 hours, the pilots of Hellcat and Acorn squadrons had done all they could. They set course for home. During the engagement, pilots had reported the presence of a single Messerschmitt-410, circling above the battle at 35,000 feet. Although the Luftwaffe frequently used "contact keeper" aircraft to fly above the Allied formations and identify their positions, this aircraft was later determined to be a British built Mosquito flown by Americans.

The author of the chronicles of the Peloponnesian wars, Thucydides, wrote, "*War is a violent teacher.*" For the fighter pilots of both sides, the lessons came quickly above the forests of Germany. The ten minutes of intense combat focused the minds of the survivors, gave them invaluable lessons on how they might fight next time. There were no second lessons for the dead.

The 343rd had been tasked with escorting the first bomber combat box to the target, while the 38th and 338th remained with the second combat box. The 343rd would find the enemy shortly after noon as their Big Friends came closer to the target. The greatest activity of the day was over for most of the 55th, and they had acquitted themselves well. But to the east, along the Czech border, the activity for the bombers was approaching its greatest intensity.

The weather briefing for the bomber Groups had been promising. At the bombers takeoff time, 0735, there was a 1/10 (10%) cirrus at 25,000 feet and visibility on the ground was 3,000 yards in haze. Cloud cover on the Continental coast was expected to be 2-4/10 (20%-40%) at 09 degrees East longitude, and increasing to 4-6/10 (40%-60%) as they approached 11 degrees East longitude, with no middle or high cloud layer. Visibility was somewhat restricted over Belgium but would improve considerably over Germany. The forecast for the time over target, 1224, was to be 4-6/10 small cumuli with tops at 6-7000 feet. The downward visibility over the target at Ruhland was expected to be 25 miles. This was important. Downward visibility with a 40 to 60 percent cloud cover should have given the bombers a window in which to allow the lead navigator to begin the drop. The rest of the bombers would simply follow as they observed his bombs falling. The lead navigator did not need to have perfect visibility, only a

Boeing B-17G Flying Fortress

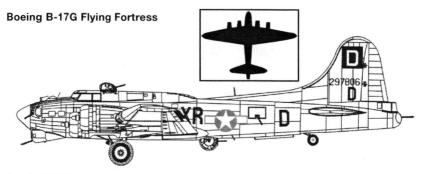

Length: 74 ft 9 in
Wingspan: 103 ft 9 in   Serv. Ceiling: 35600 ft   Range: 2000 miles   Max Speed: 263 mph

quick look would be necessary. The IP, or Initial Point, for the mission was the final navigation check before the bomb run. The bombers would be committed at that checkpoint. From this point until their bomb loads were dropped, they were committed to the discipline of a fixed course, speed, and altitude. Aboard the lead aircraft of each of the groups, the bombardiers assigned as leads made their final calculations and set these values into the bombsights, entering speed, altitude, and winds aloft. In the last few minutes before the run, the aircraft was placed on autopilot. The bombardiers of the following aircraft would wait for the visual sighting of bombs dropped from the lead aircraft. At this signal, they would release their bombs. It was here that discipline of the formation and the precise calculations became important. Flying at just above 200 miles per hour, each aircraft had a speed over the ground of about 3.4 miles per minute. Releasing the bomb loads ten seconds too early or late would mean an error of 1000 yards, and each second meant 100 yards of error. The tight formation was not just meant for the discipline of formation flying and defense, but to ensure that the greatest concentration of bombs fell on or very near the target.

As the bombers neared the target at Ruhland, the German defenders prepared to meet the Americans in even greater numbers than they had in the initial engagement below Erfurt and Meiningen. The initial engagement between 1135-1145 below Erfurt may have been a tactical move by the defenders. If a contact keeper was aloft, he may have been told to verify that the two initial squadrons engaged, and to follow their progress after the fight. Knowing that the bombers pressed on with only the single squadron elements of the 343rd may have been exactly what the Luftwaffe planned. Planned or not, the Germans took advantage of the situation. The 343rd would be at the last leg of an already long flight, not yet low on fuel but certainly not capable of a long engagement either. At this time, too, the 343rd had already turned back toward the west and had begun the trip back to England. It is also no coincidence that the bulk of the aircraft that came up to meet the bombers above Kovarska were the heavily armored FW 190s, and also some Me 109s.

The 100th Bomb Group provided four squadron elements for the combat mission of September 11. These were composed of aircraft from the 349th, the 350th, 351st and 418th Bomb Squadrons. The squadrons of the 100th were no strangers to combat in the air. The 100th had participated in the Schweinfurt-Regensburg mission on August 17, 1943. Flying from their base at Thorpe Abbotts on that mission, they had lost nine of 21 bombers flown. Earlier losses had earned them the title of "*The Bloody Hundredth*."

Just before the bombers changed to the course specified for the IP, problems began to develop. The wing leading the division had turned to go to the secondary target, avoiding Ruhland because of degradation in the weather, which prevented them from picking up key navigation points. As they made the decision to abort both the primary and the secondary targets, they sent out a radio message that they were proceeding to the last resort target, Fulda. This message went out on a channel that was to have been monitored by the Group. Inexplicably, this message was never received by the 100th. They had been separated by a distance of sixteen miles from the leader of the first combat box and had never been able to make up the distance to rejoin the formation. Now, the lead Group had aborted and made a turn to the left to pick up the last resort target, and the 100th Bomb Group continued on toward the target at Ruhland. This situation pointed out the necessity of maintaining a close formation. Once the bombers had spread out beyond the planned limits of the formation, the fighters could not adequately cover the wide distances and provide protection to the entire force.

In the air, Czech - German border
1205 hours, September 11, 1944

The 343rd had completed the remainder of the mission assigned. They had begun the course out of the target area when in the distance they saw the separated Ruhland mission formation at 1220. They observed two of the wings under heavy attack. Pursuing at full throttle, they attempted to engage the enemy aircraft, but reached the area too late to prevent the attack. The enemy aircraft had already headed out after their run against the bombers. They were able to make contact with some of the retreating German fighters, and claimed three kills. The 503rd Fighter Squadron of the 339th Fighter Group also took part in this phase of the battle. Their claim was 20 kills.

Helmut Detjens of JG 4, then an 18-year old Messerschmitt pilot, recalls that the German fighters had headed on an intercept course hoping to catch the American bombers. There were Me 109s and FW 190s in the group, and they were not aware of the earlier combat above Oberhof. After the 190s turned to the East, their 109 escorts separated into two groups. Although one began combat above Oberhof, the other continued with Fockewulfs. Many of the fighters had no radios installed, and pilots kept a sharp lookout on their flight leaders for the hand signal to attack. The group was almost out of fuel, and about to turn back to the east when they saw the bombers of the 100th approaching. The FW 190s of the group attacked first. Detjens patiently followed his flight leader intending to attack the bombers from behind. He quickly found a B-17, but was too close to the craft, bouncing in the turbulent wake and unable to get a shot. Finally, he waited until the big bomber slipped momentarily into his gun sight and

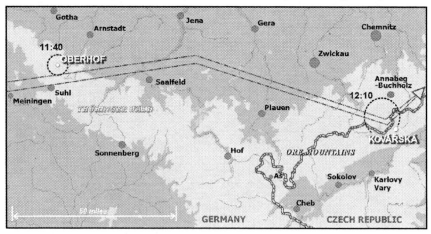

The eastern Thuringer Wald and western Ore Mountains at the Czech border, showing the bombers' formation and areas of both phases of the battle.

The tail section of the plane piloted by Lt. Albert E. Trommer rests on the roof of the elementary school in Kovarska. Items from this wreckage would be discovered in March 1982, and contribute to the remarkable thread of events leading to the recovery of Bill Lewis's remains.

fired a short burst. He did this several times and finally the big plane fell out of formation and started downward. As Detjens was completing his destruction of the B-17, he saw bright streams of tracers winking around his fighter and realized that he was being pursued by a P-51. Out of fuel and ammunition and without a radio, he looked around for a friendly airplane and joined another Me 109 that seemed to be headed in the right direction. When they landed he had no idea that he was in fact at his home field and had been following his squadron leader.

Wilhelm Wohlgemuth of JG 4 had much the same recollection. He does not recall there being two groups of German fighters that day, and thinks that what Thorsen and the other Americans must have seen was in fact another Geschwader headed east, because he is certain these airplanes did not come from JG 4. However, it was in fact Thorsen's group which engaged the pilots of JG 4 above Oberhof. He did remember that the FW 190s were lower and slightly ahead of the Messerschmitts. This could account for the perceptions of the 55th Fighter Group that there was a top cover group flying for the 190's on the 11th. He, too, says that the group was not aware of the combat to the west around Oberhof. Flying out of the northeast, his group flew under the bombers and then initiated a climbing turn to attack from behind and out of the sun. Although Detjens was unaware of combat above Oberhof, the separation of the Messerschmitt group into two

The Lawrence W. Riegel crew, 100th BG, one of the crews lost during the second phase of the battle over Kovarska.

formations seems to prove Thorsen's observation was accurate.

Over the Ore Mountains on the Czech-German border, the skies were virtually on fire. The sound of the bombers and the chattering of guns high above had alerted the village to the battle. Aboard the B-17s, it was clear that the bomber force was under an extremely heavy attack. In aircraft number 42-102657, the "*Boss Lady*," the crew watched as a swarm of about 40 each of Me 109s and FW 190s came from the six o'clock position firing 20 and 30-millimeter explosive shells at a range of 400 yards. On the first pass, a fire was started in the bomb bay and right wing, and 1st Lt. Albert Trommer, the pilot, gave the order to bail out. The copilot, Lt. Timothy Bradshaw, sent Sergeant Alvin Severson down from the cockpit to check on the Bombardier, Lt. Levi Groce, and the Navigator, Lt. James Wright. Confident that the crew now knew the condition of the aircraft and were making preparations for bailout, Bradshaw made his way to the escape hatch where he found Severson pulling at the hatch handle. Together they attempted to release the stuck hatch while the plane burned. In the first pass, Bradshaw had sustained a wound, and now Severson asked for Bradshaw to jump first. Bradshaw left the crippled plane, and was captured three hours later. Trommer, Severson, Groce, and three other crewmembers were never seen to exit the plane, and they were thought to have gone down with the ship. The selfless action of Sergeant Severson probably saved Bradshaw's life. The aircraft exploded directly over Kovarska, and the tail fell into the roof of the elementary school.

Mrs. Gerinda Krivankova was an eyewitness to the crash of two B-17s. *"We saw one bomber hit. It fell in two pieces on the village. One section was burning and fell on the upper part of the village. The second part, the tail, fell on the school.[19] I did not see anyone bail out ... we saw another burning aircraft, very low, fly over the village heading north west. Before it disappeared beyond the houses, we saw an airman bail out but he hit the tail section. As he came down in his parachute, we noticed that his head was at an unnatural angle. He landed about 150 meters away from us, in a meadow behind No. 97. We ran there but he was already dead. His head was missing ..."*

Lt. Riegel's ship had crashed on Kamenny Vrch, a wooded hillside to the northwest of Kovarska. The wood caught fire, and the remains of the bomber burned through the night, punctuated by the sounds of exploding ammunition. The people arriving at the site found several empty parachutes, along with the burned bodies of four crewmembers.

The fighters returned once more, making a similar pass from 6 o'clock low. Within only a few seconds, all of the airplanes in the low squadron of the 100th Bomb Group disappeared into the undercast, some out of control. None of the airplanes in the low squadron survived the encounter.

Aboard A/C # 42-97806, *"Now an' Then"* piloted by 1st Lt. Charles Baker, the crew communication system was shot out on the first pass. 2nd Lt. Donald Lienemann recalled after his release from a German Stalag that the fighters had approached them that day in a "Company Front." This formation was composed of six planes abreast and an interval of 15 seconds or less between Groups. This tactic, the "Company Front," had a great deal to do with the weapons employed by the Sturmgruppe the bombers faced over Kovarska. They would use their 30 mm cannons in close, but they had to use them in this way. At longer standoff ranges, the 30 mm cannons lost velocity and thus accuracy. They also had a very limited number of rounds for these cannons.

Lienemann believes that they were still about 25 miles west of the target when the attack took place. The instrument panel was heavily damaged, and a fire started in the bomb bay. Lts. Baker and Charles Chiles attempted to speak with the crew on the interphone system. Having no success, Baker rang the bailout bell, warning the crew that they should leave the ship. No one seemed to have heard the bell, and smoke entered the oxygen system, which had probably been compromised on the first pass of the fighter attack. Chiles went to the aid of Technical Sergeant Eugene Damrel, wounded in the encounter. He placed a tourniquet on him and then helped him into his parachute and returned to the cockpit. Baker indicated by pointing to Chiles that he should put on his parachute. Chiles donned the chute, and then placed a chute on Baker while he flew the damaged airplane. Baker was having trouble keeping the nose of the bomber up to maintain control. The automatic pilot assembly had been hit and damaged, and now lay in pieces on the flight deck in the cockpit. Baker, unable to place the plane on autopilot, signaled for Chiles to leave the craft. It was likely that the plane exploded then, because Chiles had no recollection of leaving the plane on his own. He found himself in his parachute, floating downward among the debris. Baker remained with the plane and died when it crashed into a young forest between Kovarska and Oberhals.

Only Chiles, Lt. Donald Lienemann, and Technical Sgt. Damrel survived. Damrel had his right hand shot off during the attack, but remained conscious and alert enough to release his ripcord. Lienemann believes that all six of the crew who perished had been unable to hear the interphone or the bailout bell. Just before he bailed, he saw the left wing shot off, followed by the aircraft surging madly to the left and up, and the right wing separated from the craft. Finally, he watched and felt the concussion of the fuel tanks exploding. Regaining consciousness at about 4,000 feet, Lienemann pulled his ripcord and had only about fifteen seconds of fall before he landed in a forest. In that brief time, he saw three men falling nearby, and he concluded that they must have been three of his fellow crewmembers, none of whom had opened their parachutes. He believed that they had never regained consciousness after their bailout, or had been killed in the initial attack. Lienemann was now hanging in his parachute 10-15 feet above the ground in a heavily forested area. Slipping out of the parachute, he left it hanging and buried all of his identification under the tree in which he landed. He set out for Switzerland, or its general direction, and stopping at a remote farmhouse at dusk, he satisfied his thirst by milking a cow. His luck ran out the next morning at the edge of a cornfield. Lienemann's next experience was repeated many times in the German held territories as the American sons of German immigrants brought the war to their cousins. The German soldiers that had captured him asked him his name, and immediately he was suspected of being a German deserter who also had the name of Lienemann, a sergeant, for whom they had been searching.

As he was being transported to the interrogation center, Lienemann sat next to another flier who had lost his shoes on the jump. He had been provided a pair that his German guard claimed to have taken from a dead flier, and this pair of shoes had been tied together with wire. Lienemann was sure that this pair of shoes had been taken from Lt. McGuiness. McGuiness wore flight boots, but kept his shoes wired together and tied in a distinctive manner to his parachute pack, so that he would have shoes in the event of a jump.

Fate had played a cruel game with Baker. He had been found medically disqualified for flying, and his orders would arrive a day later, on September 12, grounding him permanently. Baker's commitment to flying the disabled plane and keeping it stable long enough for anyone who was able to bail out saved the lives of the three men.

Horst Schmiedel of the town of Medenec recalls his experience. *"I was a small boy when it happened; I was with my granddad in the woods. Overhead we heard the battle; I don't remember how long it continued, but afterwards my granddad told me a plane had crashed. We found the site where there was a lot of metal plate. A dead airman hung from a tree by his parachute. My granddad told me to look away, there was nothing here for me to see."*

Helmut Hoffman of Kovarska relates … *"We were going to school in Vejprty when at about 11 o'clock there was an air raid warning. We should have run for shelter, but we ran back to Kovarska. Halfway there we heard the bombers coming from the west, many were burning and smoking. Then we saw another group of planes, this time German fighters coming from Chemnitz and watched them attack the bombers from above and below. Just before the attack, we saw two crew bail out from a bomber with a burning wing. One of the parachutes failed to open. The aircraft exploded and parts fell on Kovarska. Later, we saw another plane break formation and blow up over Muhthütte and Horni Halze (Oberhals). Before it exploded, we saw three airmen bail out, but again their chutes did not open, perhaps because they were too low. I found out later that they all were killed …"*

This aircraft was the plane piloted by Lt. Charles E. Baker, who died along with the bombardier, Lt. Raymond McGuiness, the radio operator, Sgt. David Gurman, and gunners, Sgts. Roy Johannesen, Fred Fischer, and David Rattin. Years later, on a visit to Kovarska, Donald Lienemann recalled more of how the crash happened, *"… the left wing and bomb bay were on fire. We left the formation still under attack. Everybody was firing. Then I saw a break in the left wing and shortly after our plane blew up. The wings and tail section blew away, and the cockpit began to somersault. I bailed out and lost consciousness. When I came to, I was very low. I managed to open my chute and landed on a wooded hill."*

Some planes of the 349th Bomb Squadron flew in the low squadron position on September 11. 2nd Lt. Warren Soden flew as Navigator in aircraft #42-97834 named *"Mud in Yer Eye."* Soden recalls being jumped by FW 190s as the force neared the IP southwest of Ruhland. From his position in the nose, he witnessed one B-17 as it started down after the fighter attack, and followed a damaged Focke-Wulf as it slashed through the squadron on the way down. *"Mud in Yer Eye"* had been hit on the first pass, and the controls had been damaged. *"Mud in Yer Eye"* was missing the usual fabric panel, which separated the nose from the pilot's compartment, and Soden could see the feet of his pilot, 1st Lt. Orville Everitt as he attempted to regain control, working the rudder pedals. The alarm was given, and Soden bailed out through the forward compartment hatch. He watched the airplane in a slow descent as it approached the 5000-foot undercast. Looking down, he saw it explode before reaching the clouds and watched as pieces of aluminum floated down. As he pulled his ripcord, the chute straps on his chest took the brunt of the opening shock, and he suffered a severe back injury. Captured immediately as he landed in a forest, Soden made the long train trip from Chomutov to Frankfurt and then to Oberursel for interrogation. As he was being transported to Frankfurt on September 13, he saw the nose gunner, Sergeant Edward G. Minton, on a stretcher. Minton, too, had suffered a severe injury when his chute opened. His spine was separated, and he died in a German hospital in 1945, only months before the end of the war. The tail gunner, Staff Sergeant William E. Kenney, was wounded in the attack. He had been shot in the lungs, and lost consciousness. He had no recollection of how he escaped the damaged B-17. Copilot 2nd Lt. John B. Manniello suffered severe head injuries in the bailout. He spoke with Minton in the German hospital where they were both patients. Minton told him before dying that all the crew except Everitt bailed out, and they were strafed by German fighters as they descended, then attacked again by German civilians at the Chomutov railroad station in the Sudeten as they awaited transport to Frankfurt. In addition to Minton, five other crewmembers were lost as a result of the fighter attack and subsequent explosion.

Lt. Trommer's ship exploded and came apart in the air over the town of Kovarska. All four engines crashed on the fields and meadows around Kovarska. The cockpit crashed on a road between houses. With a single bomb remaining, the bomb bay crashed on a house in town without exploding. A pupil in the elementary school has this memory.

"When the planes, came we were having a P.T. (Physical Training) class outside and were not in the school building. We had only a few seconds to run for our lives. My friends and I ran upstairs to No. 83 and saw the battle. The sky was full of American bombers, many of them burning. We also saw the German fighters and heard the guns firing."

Helmut Hoffman also witnessed the crash of a German Me 109 from JG4, one of four to crash in the Kovarska area that day. *"Some bombers flew very low, some of them were burning. German fighters flew overhead. A bomb fell so we had to "keep our noses to the ground" and therefore we did not see everything. But we clearly saw a German fighter that flew very close to us and climbed to a higher altitude. It was climbing very steeply and was still firing its guns to empty skies. Then it stopped, flipped over on its back to crash into the ground. We did not see it fall as this was over the horizon. Later we noticed that it was the plane that crashed in woods behind the chapel on the lower part of Kovarska. The wreckage was later found in the wood. I don't know if the pilot was killed, or if he survived."*

Kurt Frank of Kovarska was also a student in the elementary school on September 11. *"When the teacher took us from the class-room and into the cellar, me and my friend escaped. On the way up the hill, we saw bombers coming from Klinovec. We were worried and ran home. Then we heard shooting, and saw German fighters, one bomber cut in halves in the air on the course to Medenec. American heavy bombers were flying over Kovarska, sometimes even very low, some were burning. Many parachutes were in the sky. Then, really very low, one burning American (bomber) flew. I think it was the one who fell on Kamenny Vrch. I remember it seemed to me (to be) one of the low-flying German fighters shot at an American airman hanging in the parachute and surely hit him. My uncle, who saw it too, was later very angry...Then I saw about six American fighters coming from the course of Vejprty. Germans disappeared soon ..."*

At least one German fighter pilot survived the battle. He was reported to have walked into the town with his parachute in his arms, giving pieces of chocolate to the children.

The largest part of Lt. Orville Everitt's airplane fell with its bombs on Spitzberg Hill in a stand of trees. As townspeople approached the crater gouged out by the bomb load, they saw the shattered bodies of crewmembers pinned against the trees, torn by the blast. The bodies of the dead airmen could only be retrieved by cutting the trees. The tail section of the plane fell about a mile away.

Harry D. Everhart, a Staff Sergeant flying as a waist gunner aboard aircraft # 43-38076, named *"Aces and Eights,"* was the only survivor of the attack on his aircraft. The crew endured about ten minutes of fighting before their plane was struck and disabled. Hearing no alarm or other crew communication to bail out, he was busy shooting at the Germans when he finally realized that they had descended and were about to crash. The pilot was attempting to crash land near Kretscham, Germany. Thinking the rest of the crew was still in the plane, Everhart stayed at his gun and waited for the impact. He lost consciousness in the crash, and awoke to find himself several hundred yards from the crashed plane, which had fallen in a wooded area. Everhart was taken to a POW hospital in the town of Hohenstein-Ernsthal. During his 12-week hospital stay, an interrogator told him that all aboard the plane had been killed.

In the low squadron, the hardest hit of the entire Group, aircraft # 42-97154 was on fire. The fighter attack had wounded the pilot and flight engineer. A second attack destroyed the interphone system. Without a means of communication between the forward part of the ship, and with the fire raging in the bomb bay, the pilot and copilot, navigator and flight engineer were separated from the remainder of the crew. Before the interphone was shot out, the pilot, Lt. Wesley Carlton, had ordered a bailout. The copilot, 2nd Lt. Edward Neu, observing the engineer, Staff Sergeant Hike Bagdasian, to be seriously wounded, attempted to push the unconscious man out of the forward escape hatch. While he was trying to move Bagdasian to the hatch, the aircraft exploded, and his only recollection of the event was that he regained consciousness on the ground. The only survivors of this crew were Neu, and the navigator, Hugh Davidson. It is likely that the fire in the bomb bay may have prevented the crewmembers in the aft section from jumping, or that it ignited the oxygen system or the bombs and the aircraft was destroyed before they were able to jump. This plane fell in a wooded area near the town of Neudorf, Germany.

Missing Air Crew Report #8814, describes the experiences of the crew of 2nd Lt. Howard Schulte. Crewmembers reported that as the fighters swept past, the number four engine was shot out, and number three set afire. Several of the control cables were shot away, and a fire started in the pilot's compartment. Rapidly losing altitude and fighting for control of the aircraft, Schulte realized that his parachute had begun to burn. The copilot, Flight Officer Richard Keirn, was told by Schulte that he did not intend to bail out. Keirn left via the escape hatch, and observed the plane as it went into a steep dive and exploded some thirty seconds later. The navigator, 2nd Lt. Jerome Hutcherson, recalled that Schulte had lost consciousness due to the destruction of the oxygen system. Keirn, who was now flying the plane, had decided that the damage was too great, and unable to extinguish the fire, had ordered a bailout. It was then that Schulte regained consciousness, and told Keirn that he had not been wounded, as Keirn had believed. He concurred with the bailout order. No one saw

Schulte exit the damaged ship. As the bombardier, 2nd Lt. Kenneth R. Summers, left the stricken B-17, he watched for anyone else. He could see the left wing in a mass of flames, and believed that the plane had passed through 7,500 feet with Schulte still attempting to fly the ship. His opinion is that Schulte, because of his burning chute, had elected to stay and try to crash land the bomber, giving the crew time to escape. The aircraft finally crashed close to the German town of Machern, near Leipzig. Keirn survived and was released from a German prison camp in May of 1945, only to become a prisoner of war again in Vietnam, this time for seven years. All of this action occurred some fifteen minutes later, after the initial attack prior to the bomb run. This aircraft survived the initial attack and had made the turn back to the base when they were struck. Although Lt. Schulte's body was never found and he was long regarded as the second MIA of the Ruhland mission, the circumstances of his MIA status are somewhat different. Since the site of his bomber's crash is known, it is presumed that his body was consumed by the fire that occurred when the plane struck the ground.

Aboard 42-102695, piloted by Lt. Hugh Holladay, the action came at 1156 British time, only minutes before setting up the IP for the bomb run. Holladay believed the majority of the German fighters were FW 190s. The bomb bay and two engines were immediately set on fire. A great deal of this enemy fire penetrated the radio room. Sgt. Nick Marrale was in his gun position in the upper turret. He watched as the exploding 20-millimeter shells concentrated in the radio compartment below him, riddling the compartment and disabling the interphone system. Lt. Joseph Michaud parachuted safely, landing very near the heavily damaged section of the ship, which blew up shortly afterward. The shattered Fortress fell into the German village of Crottendorf, destroying two buildings.

The attack on the lower B-17 box of the 100th Bomb Group destroyed the entire low squadron of the 350th in a matter of seconds, and three Fortresses of the 349th composing the remainder of the lower box. Three of the aircraft were lost on the first pass, the remainder in the few minutes after. The total losses for the Group were ten airplanes of the 350th, three ships of the 349th and one from the 418th. Three other aircraft damaged in the attack nevertheless managed to survive.

"*Oombre Ago*" stalled and spun down quickly. The radio operator on this airplane, piloted by Lt. Raymond Hieronimus, bailed out during the spin. Hieronimus regained control of the plane and turned westward, crash landing in France. French farmers, who scavenged it for parts and aluminum, salvaged the aircraft.

Captain Ferdinand Herres was leading the high (right) element of the 349th Bomb Squadron aboard A/C # 43-37823. His aircraft was badly damaged by flak before the fighter attack. Herres and his crew left the box before the fighter attack, which probably saved their lives. They made it as far as the British coast, where they bailed out. Herres had turned the burning airplane out toward the sea, attempting to avoid the island and harming civilians. After he left the crippled airplane, it began a slow turn back toward the Isle of Sheppey where it crashed despite his attempts to steer it to sea.

"*Heaven Can Wait*" with pilot Lt. Harry Hempy and copilot Jack Janssen was damaged in the fighter attack, losing two engines. One crewmember, the tail gunner, Sgt. Charles Emerson, was severely wounded, and died later. The crew made a successful landing, and the aircraft underwent major repairs before returning to service.

Aboard the B-17 named "*Lady Geraldine*," copilot 2nd Lt. Grant Fuller and the crew were flying their third mission. They had been hit by flak before, but had never encountered German fighters. Flying in the starboard position of the high squadron, they could not really see the

Don Jones crew, 100th BG, left to right: back row - D. A. Jones, Art H. Juhlin, Ralph P. Farrel, Curtis L. Hooker, Kratsas. Kneeling - Don Stewart, Pat J. Gillen, Alfred F. Marcello, Grant A. Fuller (sitting), Sam L. Foushee.

low squadron under attack easily, but knew the fighters were looking for targets. To Fuller's surprise, as he watched the controls while his pilot flew the airplane toward the bomb run, he suddenly saw a German fighter just off the right wing and very close. He recalls that he and the German stared at each other through flight goggles for a long time as he wondered why neither the German nor the B-17 shot at each other. More than likely, the German was already out of ammunition, and the right element of the high squadron was a safe place for the fighter, especially when he got so close that the turret gunner could not fire for fear of hitting his own wing. The reason the Fortress gunners did not fire was probably due to the fact that the Fortress guns had protective "cutouts." These cutouts were firing limits, both mechanical and electrical, which prevented the gunners from complete freedom of movement as they fired, thus preventing them from accidentally hitting the surfaces of their own plane. This German pilot must have been very experienced. He knew how to approach the B-17 in its blind spots, and he must also have known of the cutouts, which protected him.

Of the 100th Bomb Group aircraft lost over Germany on September 11, only two crews survived the engagement and bailout without the loss of any members. These were the crews of 2nd Lt. Paul Corley, and Captain John Giles, the leader of the low squadron, all of whom parachuted safely and were ultimately released from the German POW camps at war's end.

The lead planes of the 95th Bomb Group, scheduled on the target just minutes after the 100th, observed the action from their position several miles away. They were to be the fortunate ones this day. The 95th would lose only one plane, A/C # 42-97334, the "Haard Luck,"[20] flown by pilot Vance Mooring. After the entire crew bailed out, the burning plane crashed near the German village of Schmalzgrube.

The Mustang escorts of the 343rd Tudor squadron had begun the turn toward home, their escort duties completed. Attacking what was actually a USAAF Mosquito reconnaissance aircraft and then realizing their mistake, they had dropped tanks and set course for Wormingford when someone called out that there were bombers in trouble to the south. 1st Lt. Wayne Rosenoff, flying number three in Captain Robert Brown's flight, engaged in a line abreast with Brown as number one, Lt. Phillip Gangemi as number two, and Lt. Floyd Blair in number four. As they engaged the enemy, they looked to the left and saw a P-51 with its right wing sheared off and burning. This was Rosenoff's airplane. He had collided with a German Me 109. Tudor squadron of the 55th added three more enemy airplanes to the Group total, bringing their tally for the mission to twenty-seven. The fight had begun at 25,000 feet, and had gone down to 10,000 feet before the enemy dispersed. As they climbed back up to altitude, they counted some 100 or more parachutes in the area, and on the ground they saw the thirty fires started by the burning wrecks of airplanes dotting the gentle rolling slopes of the Erzegebirge (Ore) Mountains. The 18 Mustangs of Tudor squadron began the 650-mile trip back to Wormingford.

After the initial combat above Oberhof, the 38th and 338th pilots headed home earlier than the flight plan called for, and the last of them touched down at Wormingford at 1345. As they debriefed, they waited for the missing pilots. Often a pilot would have engine trouble and make a forced landing on Allied territory in Belgium or France. Lts. Kenneth Crawford and Bill Lewis of the 38th were listed as "NYR" — (not yet returned). Debriefing of the pilots who fought the first encounter below Erfurt revealed that no one had heard from Crawford or Lewis during the encounter. As was often the case, pilots simply went missing, with no communication with their squadron mates.

Lt. Dorman Castle of the 38th had also been listed as NYR, but there was speculation, later proven, that he had landed at a friendly field in Belgium. In the original roster, Castle had been assigned as number three and Bill as number four of their flight. This may explain why Thorsen later indicated that Bill was flying the wing of Callaghan at the time of the encounter near Erfurt. From the 343rd, Wayne Rosenoff and Kenneth Williams were missing. Rosenoff's airplane was believed to have exploded in the mid-day encounter west of Kovarska, and those who witnessed the event were sure he had been killed. The fourth of the NYRs was 1st Lt. Kenneth Williams of the 343rd. Williams was leading the ships of Tudor Red flight. Red flight was nearest to the enemy fighters, which now numbered as many as 50 Me 109s and Focke-Wulf 190s. Red flight had intended to make a bounce on the fighters, now several thousand feet below them and to their right. Just as they prepared for the bounce, they were called back by the squadron leader to cover the bombers, and then the enemy fighters turned away from Tudor Red flight. Williams's aircraft began to stream black smoke and his wingman believed that he had run one of his drop tanks dry, causing his engine to stall. Williams called him on the radio and indicated that if he was unable to restart the engine, he would bailout when he reached 10,000 feet. At 12,000 feet, the flight followed Williams into a cloud base and lost sight of his airplane. Williams radioed then that he was leaving the airplane. Although Williams's flight leader reported seeing a parachute descending near Saalfeld, later evidence would prove that this could not have been Williams.

The procedure for declaring a flier officially missing could not begin sooner than 48 hours after the event. The Interrogation, as debriefing was called, would be detailed and would involve all persons who might have seen the actual crash or who might have had radio contact with the lost aviator. Radio communication was sometimes difficult, and pilots who had mechanical problems would often find a friendly field in France or Belgium, and set down for repairs for a few days until they could make their way back to England. Others would be shot down, rescued by the French or Belgians, and evade or hide, sometimes for weeks before returning to Allied control. There was no reason to think the worst. The intelligence officers would examine the individual pilot encounter reports, placing the pieces of the mosaic together carefully until they had a clear picture of what had occurred. Only then, when they were certain that a pilot was lost, would they begin the process of notifying the next of kin.

David Jewell had heard the news of the Not Yet Returned just after the mission. David recalls that he was upset when he heard the news, but not convinced that Bill had not simply made a forced landing somewhere. In early August, David Jewell had gone missing with Lt. Clifford Sherman. The two had been forced to land when Sherman's airplane developed engine trouble and were marooned at a Polish-Russian base where no one spoke English. It was ten days before a mechanic arrived and repaired Sherman's aircraft, and they were declared missing all that time. Maybe something like that had happened to Bill. He had gone to the barracks to look after Bill's personal effects, but another officer, Captain Boggess, had already secured the items and packed them for shipment. This was purported to be prevention against theft. It may have had that intent, but the Air Corps leadership was also keenly aware of the effect that an empty bunk and personal belongings had on the survivors, and they acted quickly to prevent morale from sinking.

Once the 48 hours had elapsed, a Missing Air Crew Report (MACR) would be created, making the loss official. The MACR itself is a succinct one-page document that does not reveal much more than the very basic facts. Other accounts would be appended to that document, and if the loss were to be confirmed as a Killed In Action, these accounts would become a part of the IDPF, or Individual Deceased Personnel File. We will have the opportunity to visit this document later, as it plays a strange part in the disappearance of Bill Lewis.

The 339th Fighter Group from Fowlmere had a second encounter with the German defenders. The 339th had been assigned to escort the bombers attacking target #8, Bohlen, scheduled for a time over target of 1228. The navigational track of target #8 placed them in a close proximity to the Ruhland mission, and this group witnessed the late stages of the battle along with Tudor squadron. They engaged in time to shoot down more fighters, with the top score claimed by a young lieutenant, Francis Gerard, who claimed four victories on September 11, 1944.[21]

For the 100th Bomb Group, the day had been deadly. As the survivors made their way back to England, the Interrogation teams waited for the sound of the big bombers over the horizon, and counted the specks in the sky. When the 100th mission elements departed Station 139, Thorpe Abbotts in Norfolk, they numbered thirty-six B-17s. Twenty-two would return. Those lost would include all of the low "C" squadron and two from the lead "A" squadron. For the overall mission that day, #623, the losses would total forty-two B-17s and B-24s, and nearly 100% of their crews, approximately 400 men.

Aftermath

The German fighters of JG 4 had risen in numbers, and they had been defeated in numbers. Intelligence accounts of the days combat indicated that JG 4 had suffered as much as 50 percent casualties. As many as 28 young and irreplaceable combat aviators were missing, and many of these were dead. Even among the survivors, many of the pilots had not been able to return to their home fields, and the next day, as the raids began again, they would be scattered throughout the area trying to return to their respective units. At the end of the day's fighting, the German pilots performed the same process that the American pilots did. The agony of waiting for the returning aircraft was doubtless repeated at Alteno much as it was at Wormingford. The German mechanics and pilots, eyes to the sky, looked in vain for the remaining pilots of their squadron, most of them dead in a trail of smoking wreckage between Erfurt and Chemnitz. Debriefing with the Group Intelligence Officers, they were asked questions about the number of American bombers and their escorts. How did they fight? Were any new tactics observed? What were the Quick Identification Markings (QIM) on the sides of the American fighters and bombers? How many kills, probable kills, or damaged were claimed? What were their losses? In which areas and at what times did they occur? Where possible, crash sites would be investigated and items recovered from the planes. At the sites where American aircraft had crashed, special teams of the German military would go to the field and determine the information required for the field intelligence reports. These reports had a specific format that required information regarding details of the crashed airplane and its equipment. Each crash was assigned a number and a type denoting whether it was a bomber or fighter. The field reports would be sent on to German intelligence, and accompanied the file of each POW associated with the crash so that interrogators might be able to use this information in the sessions with the prisoners.

There are no known reports of claims by German pilots of JG 4 that correlate to the downing of Bill Lewis on September 11, 1944. Many of the JG 4 pilots were flying their first combat mission when they met the more experienced pilots of the 55th. It is conceivable that the JG 4 pilot who shot Bill down died in the action only minutes later, or even in the same engagement. The 55th claims that day were numerous.

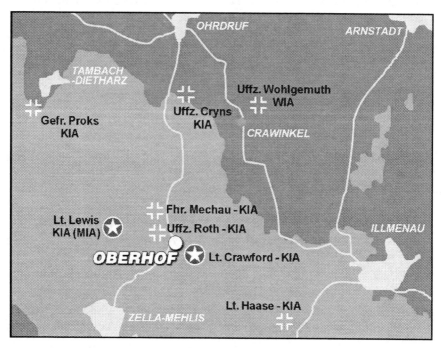

55th FG and JG 4 losses in the Oberhof combat area, September 11, 1944.

The 38th claimed 11 Me 109s, the 338th 14, and the 343rd claimed three kills. Totals for the Group were 28 German aircraft destroyed, none probably destroyed, and eight claimed as damaged.

Kenneth Crawford and Bill Lewis both flew the number four position that day, the most dangerous for a fighter pilot. He is charged with protecting the number three position as his wingman. Who protects the number four is up largely to chance, if at all. It could also be that Bill experienced mechanical problems as did Kenneth Williams, but there are no pilot reports of such an occurrence, nor any radio communications to that effect. There are no reliable visual reports either, except the one Mustang pilot who thought that he saw a P-51 smoking and inverted, but there is no certainty that this was Bill's plane.

The replacement crews of the 100th Bomb Group arrived some time after the "C" squadron of the 350th in the Ruhland mission were lost. "Chan" Finfrock was such a replacement. He arrived at the 350th's barracks on September 23, 1944. The barracks were nearly completely empty, all their crews lost on the mission. "... *going into those empty barracks that day ... I didn't think I'd ever make it home alive*," he recalled to his nephew Randy Finfrock of Tulsa.

Oberhof and Saalfeld, Germany
– Kovarska and Wranowitz, Czechoslovakia
1130 hours, September 11 - 0730 hours, September 22, 1944

On the ground, a long trail of aircraft aluminum, fires, and bodies and parts of bodies littered the course of the bombers and their escorts from Oberhof in Germany to Kovarska and Chemnitz in Czechoslovakia. The greatest concentration of wreckage and surviving American airmen was inside an area bordered by the towns of Chemnitz and Johan-georgenstadt in Germany and Chomutov and Cheb in Czechoslovakia. The airplanes had fallen across the mountain range known as the Erzegebirge in Germany and Krusne Hory (Ore Mountains) in Czechoslovakia. On the mountain slopes above Oberhof, where the first encounter had occurred, and in the Keltahlsloch, south of town, two American P-51s had crashed. In the first encounter beginning around 1135-1140, the two Mustangs fell near the town of Oberhof. In the towns of Hellingen, Tambach-Dietharz, and Ilmenau, the airplanes piloted by Hans Ammon, Josef Proks, and Alfred Haase fell. The Me 109s of Johann Roth, Günter Mechau, Jakob Cryns, and Wilhelm Wohlgemuth fell to earth in this area too. The German reports of those incidents are very precise.

The local police and Volkssturm teams dispatched to the crash sites of American airplanes followed a protocol, filling out the form known as the "KU" report or "J" report. Some researchers have said that KU typically referred to crashed bombers, while J was used for fighters. These reports were written in the field and sent by telegraph to the German Luftwaffe Intelligence section at Oberursel, a suburb north of Frankfurt where the information was analyzed and to other places such as regional airfield commands. Later salvage groups (Sonderkommando) came to the sites to provide further investigation, recover bodies for burial, and claim industrially usable wreckage.

The report first examined pertains to the crash of an American P-51 at 1135 near Oberhof.[22] This crash, according to the KU report, was found on the Oberhof-Tambach road, 3.5 kilometers northwest of Oberhof, in the Greifenberg forest. The aircraft was 99 percent destroyed through fire and explosion. The body of the pilot was "*in innumerable small pieces*" as a result of the crash.[23] The team investigating the site was not able to determine any identifying marks or other registration numbers of the aircraft in question. The identity of the pilot was undetermined at the time of the crash. The assumption was made that it was a P-51 Mustang, probably because the air defense stations and the "contact keeper" aircraft seen during the encounter knew that

**Some of the casualties of the fighter engagement
above Oberhof, September 11, 1944.**

*Lt Kenneth I. Crawford (55th FG).
His plane crashed only a few kilometers
southeast of Bill's.*

*Uffz. Johann Roth (JG 4).
KIA September 11, 1944. He is buried
in the Oberhof cemetery with other
German soldiers and airmen.*

*Uffz. Jakob Cryns (JG 4). He died in the
air battle of September 11, 1944 and is
buried in the Oberhof cemetery.*

*Gefr. Josef Proks (JG 4). He died in the
September 11, 1944 battle and was buried
in the Tambach-Dietharz cemetery.*

P-51 Mustangs were seen to engage in that area, and from reports from the survivors of JG 4. The teams were also directed to recover any radio equipment and the aircraft gun cameras from the crash. Often they also recovered the Browning Machine Guns, as these had unique serial numbers that could be traced to each aircraft.

In Oberhof, the pastor of the local church, the forester, the mayor and cemetery caretaker had heard the planes as they crashed. They went up the hill on the Tambach-Dietharz road and found Bill's crash site, but returned to the town unable to find much to bury or even to identify as human remains. They left with the same conclusion reached by the German Army crash team — there was nothing there to bury.

South of the town, about 1 kilometer from the center, a second Mustang crashed. This plane fell in the Kehltalsloch, a shallow depression between two peaks. This pilot parachuted from his plane, but according to the KU report, he died due to *"Bei missglucktem Fallschirmabsprung"* (bad parachute jump). He was found in the forest, suffering from head injuries. He died after midnight on the 12th of September, and was buried in the churchyard in Oberhof. He was identified by the German military as 1st Lt. Kenneth Crawford.

Lt. Kenneth Williams's body was found near a crater formed when his Mustang crashed near the town of Grünhainichen, near Chemnitz. The crater was described as filled with metal parts, and the pilot's death was also attributed to a failed parachute jump. The villagers of Grünhainichen found his identification tags and other personal effects, and they were sent to the Luftwaffe Intelligence Section at Oberursel for evaluation and recording.

Aside from an incomplete record of JG 4 losses compiled some days after the missions of September 11 there is no known record of the recovery of the remains of the German pilots fallen in the area of Oberhof on September 11, 1944, but today the cemetery surrounding the little chapel contains the graves of three young German pilots who died that day. Their names were Jakob Cryns, Gunther Mechau, and Johann Roth.

For the 55th Fighter Group, September 1944 was a month full of achievements. Early that month they began a series of missions deep into Germany that continued through the 13th, eight in all. Most of these missions were much like the Ruhland mission. Flying long distances and involving air-to-air combat, followed by strafing at low level after the escort duty was done, the 55th was awarded a Distinguished Unit Citation for the dates of September 3-13, 1944.

Today the town of Kovarska is populated mostly by Czech speaking citizens of the Republic. In September of 1944, Germans had repopulated Kovarska, formerly known as Schmiedeberg, after Hitler's annexation of the Sudetenland and the Munich Agreement in October 1938. As a result, the German citizens that met the downed fliers were of mixed political opinions. Accounts of the downed fliers and eyewitness accounts of the town indicate that while some were set upon and beaten by angry townspeople, others had an almost welcoming reception. Over

The German KU report No. J2081 for Lt. Kenneth I. Crawford.

the next several days, surviving airmen trickled slowly out of the rolling hills of the Ore Mountains to surrender.

The falling airplanes or their bombs killed no one in the town of Kovarska or its surrounding area on September 11, 1944.

Few pilots who landed among the German population would be able to evade for any length of time. In occupied France, though, there are numerous accounts of pilots who not only evaded but, with help from their French friends, managed to stay free from the Germans for long periods of time and many who ultimately returned to Allied control. For Wayne Rosenoff, shot down in the encounter over the Ore Mountains, the experience would last 11 days, until he was captured in Wranowitz, a suburb of Pilsen in Czechoslovakia. Rosenoff survived not only the collision with the German opponent, but walked some 100 miles from the point of his crash, crossed the border of the Sudetenland / Protectorate undetected, and was finally apprehended when he asked for food. A more detailed account of his lengthy evasion and his subsequent POW experiences can be found in Robert Littlefield's book "Double Nickel-Double Trouble."[24] Robert Littlefield was himself an evader in France after having been shot down. He eventually returned to the 55th and completed his combat tour.

What were the results of the bombing mission? In a report originally classified as Secret, the Lead Bombardier of the 390th described that Group's assessment. Of the twelve aircraft in the group assigned to the Ruhland mission, each aircraft carried ten 500-pound bombs. Nine of those aircraft returned to their home base with eighty-two bombs. Only one aircraft of the 390th dropped over the target, but that aircraft was also successful and struck the target. Nearly all of the remaining aircraft were either lost before the target was reached, or were unable to bomb due to the cloud cover obscuring the target. Other groups on the mission had much the same experience. The mission planning was jeopardized because of weather, communications problems, and the massive German attack just before the Initial Point was reached. The surviving bombers of the 100th continued on and dropped on the target. On September 11, 1944, the crews of the 100th Bomb Group were the only bombers who reached the primary target and dropped their bombs.

Although the refineries were being struck heavily in the early weeks of September, this was not a first effort. Records indicate that the same refinery group in the general area of the Ruhland mission had been attacked often over the last several months. The Ruhland missions of September 11, 1944 were more concentrated, however. The predictable nature of the course in to Ruhland, the distance required, and general experience of the German defenders who pressed the attack just before the IP made the effort on the bombers at the Initial Point successful.

From the Fighter Group's perspective, the mission was more productive. The German fighter losses were severe. Perfect hindsight begs the question; did the Germans plan the brief intense engagement below Erfurt? The participants who were interviewed do not think so. At the time of the engagement, the German pilots had been flying for about two hours, and were nearing the end of the fuel. The engagement was in fact accidental, as they had been searching for bombers all this time, and were almost ready to begin their return to the home field.

Tulsa, Oklahoma
September 11, 1944

Nola, Bill and Ted's mother, had been divorced for some time when her two sons went off to join the Army Air Corps. Alone and fearful, missing her sons, Nola worried about the two young men. That she was needy was revealed in a response from Bill to an earlier request. A letter from Bill had admonished her not to attempt to follow her sons around from camp to camp, as she had desired. It was bad enough, Bill said, that their wives followed them, but he would draw the line at having his mother come to stay. Now, with Bill in England, Nola did not heed his advice, and set off for Washington State to visit her son Ted, flying as an instructor pilot in B-24's in Walla Walla. She left sometime in early September and planned to return to Tulsa toward the end of the month.

Eleanor had returned home to Tulsa some months before to be with her family and Bill's mother. She had wanted to stay in Phoenix while Bill finished his advanced training at Williams Field, but could not find decent accommodations. She had joined the First Christian Church, and was living with her parents. Five of the wives of pilots in

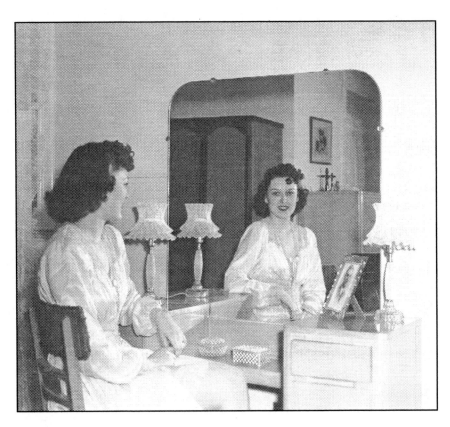

Bill's graduation class were from Tulsa, and she spent some time with them, but for the most part, she was occupied taking care of Sharon. Bill wrote to all the members of the family, and the news from those letters was shared by all of them. It was during the fall that Eleanor became more focused on the news regarding the Eighth Air Force's European missions, and began to save the newspaper clippings. The 1940s were very different for news distribution. There was no television, and if you missed the radio news, you had to rely on the next edition of the newspaper for information. Letters were extremely important, but the length of time it took for letters to arrive was often extreme. In a letter to his mother, Bill complained that her correspondence of June 28th had just arrived on the 20th of July. Air Mail was only slightly better, about a four-day advantage. Despite these difficulties, mail was really the only way to keep in touch, with an occasional telegram, but those were reserved for special events, and sometimes-tragic ones. The reception of something written in your next of kin's own hand was a treasure, something of a connection. The collection of letters and newspaper clippings grew almost daily, as Eleanor had begun to look forward to Bill's eventual return. It was possible that he would come home by Christmas.

Tulsa, Oklahoma
September 12, 1944

On September 12th, Tulsa newspapers carried the story of the Ruhland raid. The newspaper account tracks remarkably well with the official version found in the USAAF Combat Chronology.

The Tulsa Tribune:

Nazis Take New Bomb Blasting
LONDON, Sept 12 (AP)

In clear weather, the bombers struck visually at these objectives:

Synthetic oil plants at Ruhland,[25] northeast of Dresden, Bohlen near Leipzig; Magdeburg and at Brux on the Czech border ... The enemy, in desperation, lighted smudge pots around some of the refineries to conceal them in smoke palls. Some of the targets were even deeper in eastern and central Germany than those attacked Monday. ...

Eleanor was terribly restless and fearful. The newspapers carried the unrelenting news of battles. There were frequent death notices or notices of those missing in action, many from the Tulsa area. Her clippings of newspaper accounts were chillingly prescient. She had cut away an article from the 11th of September that detailed the Ruhland mission. The clipping was one of many in Eleanor's trunk full of memories. The word Ruhland is underlined in the original, as was Dresden, Bohlen, and Brux, and several other cities. It would appear that she had noted these at the time she read them, since several other locations were marked. She had saved two more clippings from the 13th, underlining the targets and the fighter losses. In a letter to Nola Lewis, visiting her son Ted, now an instructor pilot in a bomber group in Washington, she confided her fears:

13 September

Dearest Mom,
The Christmas overseas mailing starts the 15th of this month and I must get a box off. You don't need a request letter and I know you all will want to send Bill a box.
He is fine and has 111.30 hours. This big raid the 11th and 12th with around 49 fighters lost has worried me so much and I'm living for his letters of those dates.
I sure do love that man and miss him terribly. He'll be back soon and I'll be so happy. I can hardly wait. This is the longest we've been apart since we had our first date ...

Zella-Mehlis, Germany
September 13, 1944

In Zella-Mehlis, the townspeople had seen the action just to the north of them, and many watched as two parachutes descended into Oberhof, only eight kilometers or so away. Planes were falling all around the area, mostly German. On the 13th of September, a man from Zella-Mehlis set out for the hills north of Oberhof. A passionate nature lover, he often took solitary walks in the thick forest. He had seen the parachutes, but this day he wanted nothing more than a walk in the deep woods. He went to the same place along the Tambach-Dietharz road that the mayor and pastor of Oberhof had traveled on the 11th, the day of the battle. It would be his practiced eye, his critical sense, which would see the things in his forest that they did not see.

Uncertainties

Tulsa, Oklahoma
September 24, 1944

The system of delivering news to the relatives of the missing
or dead in World War II was not sophisticated. Those familiar with
current casualty notification, which requires two service members,
usually including a chaplain, and personnel who have been trained to
understand the reaction of those whom they notify, would not have
recognized the 1940s era methods. The War Department used telegrams, sometimes delivered by taxicab drivers who had no stomach
for this kind of trip. Some fortified themselves with alcohol before
making the delivery. It would be many years and a couple of wars
later before the system would be refined. The message was simple
and short; just two sentences. Even if there had been more information, it may not have been forthcoming. Censorship and security would
be observed, the details trickling out over time, only if and when the
military was sure of its reliability. Eleanor received the official notification that Bill was missing on September 24th, 13 days after the
Ruhland mission.

The brief, shocking telegram was followed in only two days by a
letter. On September 26, Eleanor received a letter from Major General

Ulio. His letter confirms the lack of certainty about Bill's MIA status, and defines the problems associated with Missing in Action personnel. His letter read in part:

... Experience has shown that many persons reported missing in action are subsequently reported as prisoners of war, but as this information is furnished by countries with which we are at war, the War Department is helpless to expedite such reports. However, in order to relieve financial worry, Congress has enacted legislation which continues in force the pay, allowances and allotments to dependents of personnel being carried in a missing status.

Permit me to extend to you my heartfelt sympathy during this period of uncertainty.

J A Ulio
Major General
The Adjutant General

With the reading of that concise telegram, Eleanor and her mother-in-law, Nola, would enter what was probably the most agonizing time in their lives.

They knew nothing more than Bill was missing. For the immediate future and well into the next year, they would be locked in battle between hope and grief, their spirits rising and falling with every scrap of news from the war. There is a special anxiety associated with the unknown, and they would have to bear this until for better or for worse, final closure would come. They chose to hope for the best but could not dismiss the grimmest of possibilities as they waited, reading the newspaper reports of those lost and those found alive.

Eleanor's worst fears had been realized when the telegram arrived on the 24th. She was uncannily accurate about the raids, even having underlined the target cities, among them Ruhland, in the newspaper accounts.

The morning after Eleanor received the telegram, she sat down to write a letter to Nola and Ted, and wired them as well. One can only imagine her feelings as she sat through the long night, composing her thoughts for the letter that she must now write.

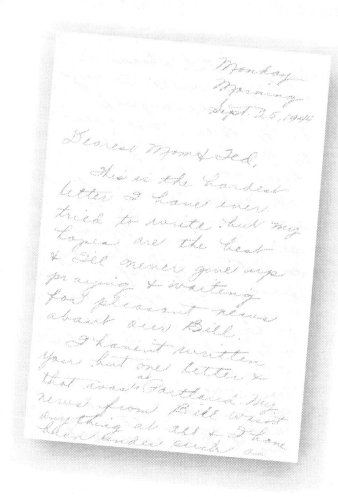

Monday
Morning
Sept. 25, 1944

Dearest Mom
and Ted,

This is the
hardest letter I
have ever had
to write but my
hopes are the
best and I'll never
give up praying
and waiting for
pleasant news
about our Bill.

(...) The
cable came last
night around
7:30 and said
he was "Missing
in Action" over
Germany since
Sep. 11th. I
received a letter written on the 11th at 7:00 am and he had had breakfast and (was) ready to go out and (it) was a very short note. He said he
would write again that evening but he never got back to write and my
heart and all of me feel he is allright, and I know Bill knows how to use
himself and will take care if he is able. I'll know if he is a prisoner of war
or in Allied country before too long and I hope you are here by then.

I am mentally sick but I must go on and keep that chin up and Mom
you do it too. 9 of 10 chances he is all right. Please tell Ted I wish you
were all here.

I knew you'd want the truth and Bill and I always had that understanding.

I cabled Bud (David Jewell) for any news and he had written the 12th
so he must know if he can tell me now. I will let you know immediately if
any word. I love him and need him so much.

Love Eleanor

Ted responded with a letter of his own on the 27th, in which he told Eleanor that she should hope for the best, that on his base there had been an officer shot down over Berlin who evaded all the way back to Allied lines. His letter was hopeful and supportive.

 "Listen Sis, I am going to think of this as just a forced landing or something like it ... I know that if there is any way to get back he will find it because he has one of the sweetest wives and baby in the world and he knows you will be waiting. Out of all the fellows that have gone down in Germany about seventy percent get back. There is an officer here on the field right now that walked back from Berlin Germany and he says the chances are good that he will get back. ... If he is a P.O.W. he will be free soon because this war is going to be over soon ... things are really happening." Ted closed by asking her to be brave and to keep on praying, adding; "Things like this are happening to many families."

Nola, who was enroute home on the train, had departed at 7:30 the morning of the 25th. The telegram had come to Ted at 11:30 that morning. Nola would not learn of Bill's loss until she arrived in Tulsa days later.

Eleanor's mother also wrote to Nola on the day after Bill was declared missing.

Seems the days are so full, but that's the way I like things. We are just waiting now to hear more about Bill. I feel everything is OK and that time will erase every thing. God is still the same Father, and he has never failed us yet.
Whatever the outcome we shall be comforted.
Keep your faith and tell Ted we are counting big on him....
With Love,
Mr. & Mrs. Powless

Buddy Jewell had no knowledge of what had happened that day over the Thuringer Wald. In a letter to Eleanor he told her what little he could. He was also unable to communicate Bill's status until the USAAF had officially declared him Missing In Action.

Sept. 27, 1944
"England"

Dear Eleanor,

I received your telegram today, and I was waiting till I heard from you before I wrote!

With all my heart I wish I had good news for you, but all I have is no news!

I was not flying that day Eleanor, so all I know is what I'm told.
There was a big scrap that day, and after the fight Bill was not around.
Nobody saw him or knows what happened! That's all we know Eleanor, so maybe he bailed out!

Promise me Eleanor, that if there is anything I can do, please don't hesitate to write me!

Your Old Friend,
Bud

Arthur Thorsen, the flight leader of Hellcat Blue on September 11, also wrote a letter to Eleanor in the month after Bill's disappearance.

Oct. 6, 1944

My Dear Mrs. Lewis,

I feel it is my duty to write you in regards to the fate of your husband Bill. You see, I was leading the flight and Bill was my number four man. There is nothing definite as to what happened to him, things like that happen so fast. I'll try and give you the details and take my chances with the censor. On the 11th of September we escorted bombers into Germany. As we neared the target we spotted about 50 Messerschmitt 109s bunching up to attack the bombers. Our group prepared for combat and pressed in for the attack. But I held my flight back, for above this first bunch of enemy aircraft there were about 75 more waiting to pounce on us if we made a move. I called my flight on the radio, told them about these Huns above us and started in toward the air battle, which had already started. They all acknowledged my call, including Bill.

Two 109s had pounced on one of our buddies, a Lt. Matney and so we drove into them and broke it up.[26] At this time the Jerries above us came screaming down and attacked my flight. They came head on. I rolled over on my back and went straight down. My number three man, Lt. Callaghan, rolled on his back too, but was forced to pop the stick and go straight up, as he and Bill bore the brunt of the attack. That's the last I saw of Bill. I radioed my flight a few seconds later, but by

that time everyone was engaged with the Huns. A P-51 was seen flying upside down with smoke pouring out of its engine and a chute was seen a few seconds later. That might have been Bill, we don't know, as he wasn't the only one missing that day.[27] *That's about all I can tell you, Mrs. Lewis. I hope it has helped in some way. All we can do is hope and pray — and I'm doing that. I feel, in some way, responsible for him. I feel responsible for all the boys in my flight. I can't say "don't worry, he's alright," for I don't know — but I can say, "don't give up hope until you hear from the Red Cross or the War Dept."*

This is the kind of letter I always wanted someone to write my wife if I should go down. Bill always talked about you and the child — he was very proud and happy to have both of you — but I suppose he's told you that many times. Bill was one of the best men in my flight and a credit to our country. You should be very proud of him. That's all I have to say for now. I would appreciate any news you might receive from the War Dept. about him.

Very Sincerely Yours,

Arthur L. Thorsen
1st Lt A. C.

This account is somewhat confusing. In the original flight operations plan, the Hellcat Blue formation is scheduled as Thorsen-Blue Leader (1) Callaghan is flying Thorsen's wing as (2), Castle is flying (3), and Bill Lewis is flying as Castle's wingman as (4). Castle is known to have landed at Brussels. Yet in Thorsen's report he indicates that Callaghan is flying as number 3, and in his letter to Eleanor he states, "he and Bill bore the brunt of the attack." Without an encounter report from Lt. Castle, we cannot know when he left the formation, or if Bill was flying his wing when the attack began.

What might have happened to Bill Lewis? The most obvious conclusion is that he was struck and killed immediately after the first group of Me 109s broke through the 38th's formation. A shell striking and penetrating the cockpit could have killed him. This would explain the absence of radio communication.

There was another more remote possibility, a structural malfunction caused by a rapid evasive maneuver. In most situations, this would not have been a problem. The P-51 though, did have a unique quirk, as with most airplanes. If the center fuel tank was partially full, the movement of fuel caused by rapid and violent combat maneuvers could cause the airplane to become unstable. Al Koenig, a squadron mate of Bill's while in the 55th, relates two stories of such events.[28] In the first, a General touring the 55th asked to fly in one of the Group's Mustangs. He returned from his flight badly shaken. The center tank had been partially full or partially depleted during the flight. The General was flying aggressively and engaging in dog fighting tactics when the airplane became unstable and began to tumble end over end. He recovered, only barely. In another episode, a 55th pilot was testing the new G-suits and trying to determine how well they worked in tight turns. He entered unstable flight, and the aircraft lost a wing. The pilot spent some time attempting to get out, having released his seat belt and harness when the airplane came apart. He was badly injured by being thrown around the spinning cockpit but managed to parachute. He was unable to talk much, but could say *"five-five"* when he was recovered at a British base. He went on to fly again. Al Koenig says that this condition of stability and fuel tank filling was never passed on to pilots officially, at least during his time in the 55th. Could this have happened to Bill? We know that Lt. Callaghan first started down at the beginning of the encounter with the German fighters, then reversed suddenly. If Bill were flying his wing, he might have followed him. This might have caused a problem with stability in the center fuel tank. At the time of his crash, Bill had nearly completed half of his combat tour. He was experienced in P-51 operations and might have known of the tank-filling problem. The only readily apparent answer to what happened to Bill was that he was killed in the first pass of the Me 109s. Later, we would learn of other possibilities that might account for his loss.

Walla Walla, Washington
2227 hours, September 29, 1944

By September of 1944, Ted was now flying in a B-24 Training Squadron as an instructor. He had been commissioned on the 27th of June, and was fully instrument qualified, with 324 hours of flight time, of which 117 hours were in the B-24. He had flown a reasonable amount of that time at night, but had not qualified as an instrument rated pilot in the B-24. On the evening of September 29, at 2227 hours, he took off with a more experienced B-24 pilot and a crew of four others for the purpose of local cross-country navigation training. The weather was "soupy," with a light wind out of the north and scattered clouds at 7,500 feet, and a layer of clouds over the Cascades range up to 11,000 feet. The flight plan indicated that the route of flight was to be from Walla Walla to Spokane, then to Ellensburg, The Dalles, Pendleton, and return to Walla Walla. At 2355, the crew reported in to Walla Walla airfield that they were over Ephrata at an altitude of 9,000 feet.

Ted R. Lewis. He died in a B-24 crash just 19 days after Bill was lost.

Shortly after midnight, a forest ranger station and an airport worker at Wenatchee reported seeing a fire in the mountains south of the town.

At 0700 hours, the rangers started out for the site of the fire. It took them several hours to reach the scene, and when they arrived at 1600, they found the completely destroyed remains of the B-24. All of the crew had been killed instantly. The condition of the wreckage made it impossible for the Army team of investigators to determine the cause of the crash. The B-24 impacted into the side of the mountain at 6,300 feet, four minutes after midnight. They were on course, but about 500 feet too low to clear the mountain. The official report states that the cause of the crash was "*collision with objects other than aircraft.*"

The US Army Counterintelligence units were concerned with possible sabotage, and they requested a weather analysis from the various stations on the route of flight that night. Most stations reported light winds, but one station reported winds of 31 miles per hour during the last few minutes before midnight. This report was submitted to the Counterintelligence groups with the notation "*highly doubtful,*" next to the station location. The Army did not seem to believe their own data. Forest rangers reported that there was a rain shower in the area of the crash that evening. Showers are usually characterized by relatively weak updrafts and downdrafts. Microbursts, however, are characterized by weak updrafts and very strong downdrafts. Pilots flying under IFR or Instrument Flight Rules, apply a concept known as MEA, or minimum enroute altitude. If you are flying from point A to point B under IFR and there is a 9,000-foot peak between the two points, you should maintain an altitude greater than 9,000 feet between the two points. Since this flight was for the purpose of navigation training, it is unlikely that any of the crew would have diverted from their flight plan through carelessness. The possibility is that a strong microburst forced them down along their planned course, and they were unable to recover the altitude in time. It was not until the middle of the 1970s that meteorologists and aviation weather researchers fully understood the concepts of the microbursts. There is another, more simple explanation as well. When transiting from an area of higher barometric pressure to a lower, aviators must reset their altimeters. Failure to do so might give a false reading of altitude, indicating a higher altitude than the aircraft is actually flying. If the aircraft entered an area of squalls, it is possible that this is what might have happened.

Nola had seen Ted for the last time. She would learn of his death on her arrival in Tulsa, at the same time she learned that Bill was missing. Though she still held out the possibility that Bill might return, she had lost one of her sons for certain. Nola and Eleanor would live out the remaining months of the war in a cloud of uncertainty, and with the hope that at least one of their men would return safely.

Nola was now a Gold Star Mother, and she placed the little flag out in front of the Tulsa home where her sons had grown to manhood, with a gold star signifying her loss.[29] She would remain active in the organization for many years.

Eleanor had saved a newspaper article from November 24, 1944 titled "Prisoners of War." It discussed the *new and exclusive clubs* that were springing up all over the United States. These were the Next of Kin Clubs, started under the auspices of the American Red Cross and the Army's Prisoner of War Information Bureau. These two groups, working in partnership with the National Catholic Welfare Conference and the War Prisoners Aid of the Y.M.C.A. had emerged to assist the relatives of the POWs and the MIAs. By October 1st of 1944 there were 55,000 service members known to be prisoners of the Germans or Japanese. Another 58,000 of that period were simply missing in action. The meetings could be emotional, with returned soldiers sharing their experiences with grieving relatives, hopeful for news of any kind. The article went on to say that relatives practically would not let such a speaker leave the meeting, so desperate was their need to know more. Eleanor and Nola would attend one of these in March of 1945.

Eleanor must have been heartbroken after she received the first letter from Bud Jewell; surely she and Bill's friend Bud would have known something. With Ted away in training, she would rely heavily on Bud for support and information. Having someone who knew Bill that well was a stroke of luck, but now it was all for naught, even Bud could not tell her anything more. Bud wrote at least one more letter to Eleanor, apparently in response to a question she had posed about the disposition of his belongings:

Jan 2, 1945
England

David Jewell with Sergeant Charles Senn,
standing in front of "Miss Boomerang Margie."

Dear Eleanor,

Hello again, I'm back again! I wrote you a couple days ago, but I didn't get all your questions answered, so I'll finish them this time!

You were asking me about Bill's clothes-well, here is the deal on that! Our squadron adjutant (Captain Boggess) has that responsibility! Soon as we land from a mission, if any pilots are missing, he comes to the barracks and packs all the clothes — he makes darn sure that nobody steals anything. After Bill went down I came to the barracks about an hour after the mission had landed and Captain Boggess already had Bill's clothes packed. .... Bill's bicycle is still here, and I will sell it for you. I assure you Eleanor that Capt. Boggess was a good friend of Bill's and he took good care of all of Bill's belongings!! ...

Well, Eleanor, I've got 2 victories in the air and 1 on the ground! I got one of my victories (a Me 109) in the Merseburg area (where Bill went down), so I got that one for Bill!! I got an FW 190 at a Berlin show in December!! I got that one destroyed on the ground way last Sept.!! That's my score till now, but I'm going to get some more before I come home (I hope ... I'm a flight leader now — I've had my own flight for about 8 weeks! ...

Well Eleanor, I'm about talked out for this time-Thanks again for the pictures and I'll not wait so long before I write as I did before the last letter.

Love,
Bud

Bud Jewell's reference to Merseburg gives an indication of how little the Army Air Force knew about the conditions under which Bill was lost. The combat over the area south of Erfurt took place at extremely high speeds and was over quickly. Most accounts of the mission encounter describe it as lasting ten minutes or less. In the tensions of the moment, no one would fault pilots for inaccuracies under pressure. Various early references to the crash placed the location at Gera, some 65 miles distance to the east of Oberhof, and also at the Merseburg location. It would not be until 1946 that a more accurate description of where Bill's plane fell was to be revealed, even longer than that for his next of kin to know anything more.

Eleanor Lewis waited, but she was hardly inactive. The written responses from the Adjutant General of the US Army, Major General Ulio, are witness to the fact that Eleanor was persistent and aggressive in her search. She wrote and sent telegrams to the Army requesting information. The letters from Arthur Thorsen and the War Department were not conclusive. With so many MIA and so much activity in the air, few pilots could be sure of what they saw, or who might have escaped from their aircraft. A fighter pilot's vision and perspective during a dogfight are limited; the pilot sees a tightly focused world of pursued and pursuer and knows little of the larger picture which occurs during the action. Eleanor's newspaper clippings reflect the terrible balance between hope and fear she must have felt when in 1945, men began to return from the POW camps in Germany. She had maintained a steady hope. After all, no one knew for sure that Bill was dead. Someone as highly regarded as an Army General had written to tell her this, and even Bill's flight leader that day, Arthur Thorsen, had told her to keep her hopes alive.

Her clippings from area newspapers reflect what she must have endured. *"Tulsa flier liberated"* or *"Area aviator returns home."* These may have been families she knew, or just a mirror of her hope that some day, she'd find that Bill had been a POW and was finally coming home. She kept up the pressure on the authorities, and the Army responded graciously and with seemingly genuine sentiment for her predicament.

Tulsa, Oklahoma
March 12, 1945

The American Red Cross organized a meeting in Tulsa in March of 1945. The invited guests were the next of kin of American prisoners of war and those MIA. Among those present were twelve repatriated former prisoners of war, accompanied by a Lieutenant Colonel. Most were Army Air Corps crewmembers that had been captured in Europe. These men had been traveling all across the United States since their return, meeting families throughout the country. One, an Army corporal, had received the Bronze Star for memorizing the names of 667 American prisoners of war missing after the Japanese ship carrying them sank. The Lt. Col. could not have been comfortable in his assigned role. He was to preside at a private meeting after the former prisoners had told their stories. At this second meeting would be the next of kin of those missing in action. He was reported to have up-to-the minute percentages figures on the number of men who were discovered alive and in the German system, and the *Tulsa Tribune* said that he urged relatives not to give up hope. Eleanor and her mother-in-law, Nola, had clipped the article from the paper and were doubtless at that meeting. A map of known German Prisoner of War Camps with their names was distributed at the gathering. For many, it was the most significant document they could have, short of a letter from their loved one. The caption above the pictures of the repatriated men said, "Army offering Information, Hope, to Soldiers Families."

In the few months remaining before the war officially ended, events accelerated in Germany. Prisoners began to return in great numbers, so many that the Army could not keep up with their own procedures for notifying family members of the men. In April of 1945, the Army authorized press and radio journalists to release information without the permission of the military. Many families would discover that their men were coming home from newspapers or radio correspondents present in Europe.

Eleanor was busy in her anguish. The activity helped her resolve the terrible weight of not knowing. On April 23rd, she sent a telegram to her Congressman, George Schwabe of the 1st District of Oklahoma. Schwabe responded on the 19th of September with a letter. He had contacted the Adjutant General immediately upon receiving her telegram, he said. The Adjutant General's office had responded to her inquiries on the 24th, and had told her that there was no further information forthcoming. His last paragraph contained the following statement — *"This is perhaps the last information we will receive on the case."*

The war was now moving rapidly to a close. German radio in Hamburg announced on May 1st that Hitler was dead. *"At the Fuehrer headquarters it is reported that our Fuehrer Adolf Hitler has fallen this afternoon in his command post at the Reichs chancellery, fighting up to his last breath against bolshevism."*

Eleanor's last hope was that Bill was alive and simply unable to communicate. She must have dreaded the end of the conflict and the imminent release of the POWs. It would mean that the end of her hope was near.

Tulsa, Oklahoma
V-E Day, May 8, 1945

The *Stars and Stripes* daily newspaper of the US Armed Forces had a half page high headline; GERMANY QUITS. All leaves and passes of the military personnel in the U.K. were extended by 48 hours. Huge mobs crowded into Piccadilly, where GIs gathered to celebrate along with Londoners. In New York City, impromptu ticker tape showers began only a few minutes after the news had been received that Germany had surrendered without conditions. Even in neutral Switzerland, church bells rang throughout the country for fifteen minutes. In Tulsa, Eleanor and Nola Lewis still held out hope.

Eleanor's trunk full of hopeful clippings had grown larger through the winter of 1944 and the early spring of 1945. She collected the newspaper clippings as men from the Tulsa area were liberated from the German Stalags. There was one about Bud Jewell, home on leave as a Captain with a Distinguished Flying Cross; while in another article Bud described how he shot down a German Me 109 for his third victory; another of a neighbor who was coming home; another about a friend. Cities celebrated with dancing in the streets, and a newspaper columnist in Washington, D.C. named Kenneth Dixon wrote a story titled *"It's too bad the dead can't dance,"* telling of the young men mourned and how someone else would dance for them. *"... crosses always bloom ... and they always cover the guys who can't be here today. But they are the dead, and they should be dancing tonight ..."* The Tulsa Jaycee organization joined with radio station KTUL and sponsored a prize contest for returning veterans who had been prisoners of war. Lieutenant Bill Eastman, who arrived home to see his youngest daughter for the first time, won the prize. Eastman won a five-room home, a car, and other gifts. *"It's like the second episode of a very swell dream,"* he said. *"First, I get home from a war prisoner camp, and now I find I've been given a house and a car and everything. It's all a little difficult to realize."* An earlier newspaper headline read "Both Sons of Tulsa Family Are Released," and talked of Bill Eastman and his brother John, both Air Corps Lieutenants. As the tired nation drew in a heady dose of euphoria, those families of the missing were guarded in their celebration. Perhaps they would still return, many must have thought, and then the birthdays and missed holidays, the relationships and suspended lives could resume.

Many if not all of the MIAs were known to be alive and coming out of the German Stalag system. The USAAF had hastily converted C-47s and B-17s in the field, and while they did not provide much space, it was still the quickest way back for the former POW's. Another news-

WHERE ALLIES NARROW GERMAN REACHES—The U. S.
Ninth army crossing of the Elbe river at an undisclosed point near
Madgeburg paced main Allied drives (arrows) on three fronts (heavy
neck. Operating under a security news Blackout, Ninth army forces
pounded toward Leipzig and a possible meeting with the Russian
Russian drive toward Dresden and Leipzig. In Italy Yanks captured
errors as British forces pushed toward Bologne. Canadians in Holland continued advancing toward the North sea and Russians extended gains beyond Vienna. Shaded territory is German-held.

Nazis Reported Shifting Panzers From East Front; First Army Nears Leipzig

BULLETIN

WEIMAR, Germany, April 12.—(AP)—Lt. Gen. Ge
S. Patton's 11th Armored division was less than 40 r
from the border of Czechoslovakia tonight. Patt
forces swept across the Saale river south of Jena.
Saale river crossings were made at points along a 30-
stretch by the Fourth and Sixth armored divisions.
day's gains brought Patton's men to a point south of H
burg, which is 128 miles from Russian lines.

U. S. Ninth: Advances four
miles beyond Elbe; crossing near
Madgeburg forced back.
U. S. First: Closes on Chemnitz and Leipzig, and chews up
dwindling Ruhr pocket with Ninth
army units.
U. S. Third: Captures Hof,
eight miles from Czechoslovak
border.

87th Infantry: Cleared S
25 southwest of Gera.

90th Infantry: Captured
near Czechoslovak border.

American, Soviet Planes Meet Over Reich Battle Zone

ADVANCED HEADQUARTERS,
U. S. NINTH AIR FORCE, April 16
(AP)—American and Russian planes
met and exchanged greetings over
the central German battle zone today.

Four Lightnings of the 474th
fighter group were the American
representatives in the first tactical
joining of the east and west air
battle fronts.

Leading pilots, led by Lieut.
Freeman of Chattanooga,
to recognize the Russian
first, but when identity
had there was a friend-
of wives and maneuvers
Allied planes departed
respective fields.

American and the Rus-
were speeding along at
level when the meeting
place. The Russians were apparently first to recognize their
allied pilots, and, for they suddenly started aerial acrobatics. The
Americans said they were impressed
by the daring of the Russians in
gazing in short flying at such a
altitude.

When the American pilots first
saw these acrobatics they were sus-
picious and climbed for altitude to
watch out on spotting.

Apparently sensing the American
uncertainty, the Russians tilted
their planes so that the Allied pilots
could see the small red star in the
black circle on the wings.

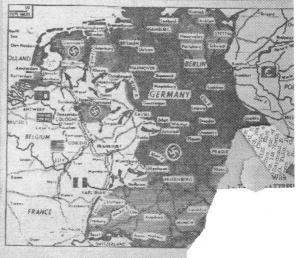

WHERE TWO FRONTS ADVANCE AGAINST
Allied advances (arrows) into the remaining Nazi-held terr
and deepening thrusts are the

*Some of the many articles gathered by Eleanor in the months and years following
Bill's crash. She sought out any information which might have given
her hope that Bill had survived.*

paper headline said "Many Tulsans May Have Been Freed From Nazi Prison Camp," and went on to describe the scene as the liberated soldiers mobbed the 14th Armored Division Troops as *one of the wildest liberations ever witnessed in Germany.*" This camp, known as Stalag 7A at Moosburg, contained about 110,000 Allied prisoners, and was the largest in the German system. The hope was dying hard with such bright, constant images in front of those who waited. For those families who had not heard, they waited in hope for their men to return, and many waited in vain. Eleanor and Nola Lewis were gradually, inexorably, coming to a fitful and uneasy closure. It was not until September 12 of 1945, exactly one year and one day after Bill had been reported as missing, that the Army Air Force finally issued a letter declaring him dead. Bill was finally gone, but there was still precious little information as to where and how he had met his end. Congressman Schwabe's letter proved prophetic.

Half a world away, in Schmiedeberg, not yet renamed as Kovarska, the end of hostilities was celebrated and the chaotic postwar resettlement began in the Sudetenland. The fifteen graves of unknown airmen lay unclaimed in the local cemetery from 1945 to 1947, when US Army Graves Registration personnel reclaimed them in two phases. The shattered condition of most of these bodies and the subsequent fires in the crashes made identification difficult. Many of these dead were simply identified as groups of casualties and buried temporarily in the European cemeteries of the American Battle Monuments Commission. Some were buried at Jefferson Barracks National Military Cemetery in St. Louis, Missouri. Only a few were identified individually, and most of these were buried in their home areas. With that exhumation and reclamation, the collective memory of the events of that tragic Monday in September 1944 began to slip away.

The 55th flew their last combat mission on April 21, 1945. This was Sharon's first birthday. They served very briefly after the war's end with the Army of Occupation, and in 1946 the Group was inactivated.[30]

Robert Littlefield of Dog Flight stayed on for a career, retiring as a Lt. Colonel and flying fighters. Eugene Holderman left the military to work for the Federal Aviation Administration, and he says, "*I flew a little,*" as a Reserve Officer. The others, Arthur Thorsen and Bud Jewell among them, came home to start their lives again. Bud had studied geophysics before the war. As an experienced combat flier and Captain with the Distinguished Flying Cross, he was sought after by the National Guard. He joined the Tulsa Air National Guard when they acquired P-51's and served as the unit operations officer. He loved flying, he said, but loved geophysics more. He made the decision to resign from the Guard just two months before they were activated for the Korean War. Al Koenig recalls that at breakfast on mustering out day, seven out of eight pilots at his table had decided to stay on, but by dinner only one remained, and Al made his decision to go to work at the Philadelphia Naval Shipyard. It was time to resume the lives they knew before the war. Dorman Castle was killed in the postwar crash of a P-80 jet. Lts. Thorsen, Castle, and Callaghan were the only members of Hellcat Blue who could have provided details of the combat action of the 11th, and by January of 2001, all three men had passed away. The mystery of the disappearance of 2nd Lt. William M. Lewis was lost in time.

By the early summer of 1945, all of the men who had been in prisoner of war camps were liberated. The official confirmation of Bill's death came in the form of a letter from the War Department in Washington on September 12, 1945, one year and one day after Bill was declared "Not Yet Returned" from the Ruhland mission.

Dear Mrs. Lewis,

Since your husband, First Lieutenant William M. Lewis, Jr., 0763247 Air Corps, was reported missing in action 11 September 1944, the War Department has entertained the hope that he survived and that information would be revealed dispelling the uncertainty surrounding his absence. However, as in many cases, the conditions of warfare deny us such information. The record concerning your husband shows that he was the pilot and sole occupant of a P-51 "Mustang" fighter aircraft, which participated in a bomber escort mission to Ruhland, Germany. During this mission enemy aircraft were encountered and at approximately 11:50 a.m., in the vicinity of Gera, Germany, a plane, believed to be your husband's, was observed to be damaged and smoking.[31] The records of this office further indicate that your husband was promoted to the grade of First Lieutenant, effective 15 September 1944 ... in view of the fact that twelve months have now expired without the receipt of evidence to support a continued presumption of survival, the War Department must terminate such absence by a presumptive finding of death. Accordingly, an official finding of death has been recorded under the provisions of Public Law 490, 77th Congress, approved March 7, 1942, as amended ....

I regret the necessity for this message but trust that the ending of a long period of uncertainty may give at least some small measure of consolation. I hope you may find sustaining comfort in the thought that

GEORGE B. SCHWABE
1st DISTRICT, OKLAHOMA

HOME ADDRESS,
TULSA, OKLAHOMA

COMMITTEES:
INDIAN AFFAIRS
MINES AND MINING
PATENTS
IRRIGATION & RECLAMATION

Congress of the United States
House of Representatives
Washington, D. C.

September 19, 1945

Mrs. Eleanor P. Lewis
c/o Mr. R. A. Powless
1415 South Rockford
Tulsa, Oklahoma

Dear Mrs. Lewis:

Further with reference to your husband, 2nd Lieut. William M. Lewis, Jr., concerning whom you wired me April 23 and on which case I reported to you in my letter of April 26, beg to say that I have a more recent report which I think I should pass on to you.

At the time we interviewed the Casualty Department of the War Department here on this case, we asked them to flag the case and give any further information they might receive in reference to your husband on their former report that he was missing in action September 11, 1944. They have told us this morning that his case was reviewed under Public Law 490 and that a presumptive finding of death was made as of September 12, 1945.

This is perhaps the last information we will receive on the case. However, if there is anything further that we can do for you from this office, I want you to feel at all times perfectly free to call upon me.

In the meantime, I want to express my continued sympathy and best wishes.

Sincerely yours,

George B. Schwabe, M. C.

GBS:CMG

The letter from Congressman Schwabe indicated to Eleanor that further,
positive answers about Bill might not be forthcoming.

the uncertainty with which war has surrounded the absence of your husband has enhanced the honor of his service to his country and of his sacrifice.

Sincerely yours,

EDWARD F. WITSELL
Major General
Acting
The Adjutant General of the Army

Back home in Tulsa and making plans to attend college again, David Jewell paid his respects to Nola and Eleanor Lewis. Eleanor, he remembers, was extremely nervous about her future, alone and with a small daughter. She had come to accept the fact that Bill would not return, and now her thoughts were of how she would provide for herself and Sharon. David could not find the words for Nola. He felt he should say something, but how could he console a woman who had lost her two sons? *"I just did not know what I could say to her, but I visited."* For David, the realization that his two close friends were both dead did not settle in until he was released from the Army and came home. It was then, he remembers, that it really hit him hard.

During the next 18 months, Eleanor coped with the sometimes-inane bureaucratic and administrative documents required by the military and civil authorities. There was a letter rescinding the promotion to 1st Lieutenant, remarking that since Bill had been killed two days before his promotion was scheduled to take effect, he would be listed on the casualty lists as a 2nd Lieutenant. Another letter came to instruct her to return the Purple Heart citation that listed him as a 1st Lieutenant, so that the Army could reissue the certificate with his proper rank. In turn, this change was reversed once more, and Eleanor would be paid the survivor benefits of the wife of a 1st Lieutenant, but Bill would be carried on the permanent rolls as a 2nd Lieutenant. Bill's will had to be legally certified, and there was an Army insurance policy to be paid out. Sharon, as his dependent, would be entitled to a monthly allowance until the age of 18. There was a rather curt missive from the Army detailing the proper manner of dispensing the cash found in Bill's personal effects at the time of his death. Thirty-one dollars and some change had been forwarded to Eleanor, and she was reminded that if Bill were in fact alive, she must account for the money when he returned. The box containing his belongings made its way from the various Quartermaster Depots to Tulsa. It was stored away and seldom opened. In it were the pilot's wings of both Bill and his brother Ted, newspaper clippings, squadron pictures, letters, flight logs and other memorabilia.

Eleanor was alone and dispirited. She was living with her parents when a young man in uniform came to the door. Sharon's only knowledge of her father was from the pictures of him in uniform. As Sharon called out *"my daddy, my daddy,"* Eleanor saw Nelson Williamson standing on their porch. Nelson had been at a party at his mother's home celebrating his safe return. When he heard about Bill's death, he left his own party and went to look for her. Nelson was one of a circle of friends, many from the First Christian Church in Tulsa, where Eleanor and Bill had been married. In December 1946, two years after Bill's death, Eleanor and Nelson Williamson were married. Sharon's grandmother had told her the story many times; how Eleanor had been surprised at seeing Nelson, and how Sharon crying out *"my daddy"* had unnerved Eleanor. Nelson Williamson had been in the Battle of the Bulge and had experienced the war on the ground. He finished

The Wall of Missing at the Luxembourg American Cemetery.
For years this was the only memorial to Bill Lewis.

LERMUSIAUX ARTHUR M	SGT	315 ENGR CMBT BN 90 DIV	COLO
LEWIS JACK H	SGT	40 TK BN 7 ARMD DIV	NEW YORK
LEWIS JOHNNIE E	CPL	4150 QM SV CO	NEW JERSEY
LEWIS WILLIAM M JR	1 LT	58 FTR SQ 55 FTR GP	OKLAHOMA
LOERA LADISLAO	S SGT	8 INF 4 DIV	TEXAS
LOSCHIAVO BARTHOLOMEW C	PFC	329 INF 83 DIV	NEW YORK

his college studies and began a career in the oil industry. The couple had two children, and Nelson later adopted Sharon Lewis.

Years passed. Sharon married, divorced and later remarried. Anyone who had wanted to trace her would have faced an impossible obstacle.

Sharon was conscious of her biological father's absence, from the earliest years when she saw someone in uniform and shouted "*my daddy*," well into her time as a teenager. In 1960, Eleanor wrote a lengthy letter to Sharon. In it she talked of falling in love at a young age, and giving up her goal of college to marry. Bill and Eleanor had married on January 31, 1942, when she was nineteen and Bill was twenty. She had done this even though she was uncertain that it was the right thing to do. After Bill's loss, she felt she could not go on. Her heartbreak was a constant, something that never left her, but she had to continue for Sharon. Nelson, she said, was the answer to her prayers for her and Sharon. He had given them a home, she had given birth to two more children, and they were financially secure. This, she told Sharon, was God's plan, and they should understand it.

For Sharon though, the feeling was different. She, as most of the other World War II children who suffered the loss of their fathers, simply had no frame of reference. She had no conscious memory of her father, no recollections however vague, nothing to hold on to. There seems to be a common dream among these children, that of seeing their fathers returning, walking toward them with arms outstretched to claim them. Those things that they never knew and could never know were the very things they sought.

Years later, when she was a young mother, she would discover an old trunk, stuffed with artifacts and memories to fuel her search. This would become the portal to the things she sought to know.

Sharon's search for knowledge of the father she never knew seems to be a common phenomenon among the children of World War II veterans, and perhaps of all wars. The stepfathers of the children of that generation were mostly veterans themselves. Eager to resume their lives, they pressed on with the widows they married, having children and forgetting their own often-dark memories. As I learned more about these children, they all seemed to have similar stories. Most seemed to feel that their adoptive or stepfathers genuinely loved them. Despite feeling loved, they seemed to also have the feeling that they were alone and disconnected in some way.

Tulsa, Oklahoma, June 1948

There would be another formal recognition of Bill's service and sacrifice. On Tuesday, June 1, 1948, Tulsans congregated at the Boulder Park War Memorial. Veterans and Gold Star Parents and others, 1,500 strong, met to place wreaths on white crosses in front of the Memorial Building. Among the rows of white crosses honoring dozens of Tulsa's sons was a cross for Bill Lewis. At the American Battle Monuments Cemetery in Luxembourg, the name of Lt. William M. Lewis was inscribed on the Tablet of the Missing. In February of 1947 Eleanor received a letter from Robert Patterson, the Secretary of War. The President had authorized the award of a posthumous Purple Heart, which was to be sent shortly. Patterson wrote; *"The loss of a loved one is beyond man's repairing, and the medal is of slight value; not so, however, the message it carries. We have all been comrades in arms in the battle for our country, and those who are gone are not, and will never be, forgotten by those of us who remain. I hope you will accept the medal in evidence of such remembrance."* [32] All these events were the closest Eleanor and Nola would come to closure.

The medal arrived, and was placed in the trunk, there to remain along with pictures of Ted, Nola and her former husband, Bill and Eleanor, two pairs of pilot's wings, one for Bill and another for Ted, various military records and personal letters, the assorted memorabilia of two young and shattered lives. The good memories contained within its confines were overshadowed by the recall of great loss. The trunk was kept in the home of the Powless's, Eleanor's parents, for many years and Sharon took it home with her after they died. After the discovery of the trunk in 1974 and Nola's death in 1997, more pictures and letters were added to the trunk. Its contents would remain essentially undisturbed until January of 2001.

Searching

"Show me the manner in which, a nation or a community cares for its dead and I will measure with mathematical exactness the tender sympathies of its people, their respect for the laws of the land and their loyalty to high ideals."

Gladstone

Houston, Texas
June 3, 1983

It was a bright, clear summer morning. I sat around the kitchen table having a second cup of coffee after breakfast with my wife Yvonne, our daughters playing contentedly nearby. I had finished reading the first section of the newspaper when a headline caught my eye. It was something like *"remains of several Vietnam casualties returned to US for burial."* There, among the names of the fallen, was an acquaintance of mine. I remembered the day it happened, July 9, 1967. As a junior officer aboard the aircraft carrier USS Constellation, I was asleep after a 0400-0800 watch, undisturbed even by the loud banging of the ships catapults as they launched aircraft. The ship's public address system blared the alert. *"Launch the search and rescue helicopter."* I remember waking on hearing that news, and going immediately down to the Combat Information Center to ask what happened. An A-4 Skyhawk had gone down near Haiphong, North Vietnam. The pilot was Charles Lee, a 26 year-old Navy Lieutenant and Annapolis graduate. I didn't really know him well, but when the Chaplain would have Catholic services, Chuck would often join me as an altar server. I had some conversations with him, but little more. He was lost on that day, and now a US Army team had recovered and identified his remains some 16 years after his death. There was an instant understanding of his loss at that moment. It was something that had eluded me at the instant it happened in 1967, though I was saddened by it. At that moment, I viewed more clearly the true cost of the war. I had a wife, children, and a home. He was forever young, and would know none of this. Despite the clarity of this understanding, I had no knowledge of how his loss would affect me in years to come.

Houston, Texas
January 2001

The search regarding the circumstances of the death and disappearance of Lieutenant William Lewis began casually. In all the years that my wife and I had known Sharon Cross and her husband, she had only briefly talked about her biological father. It was after she had seen the movie "Saving Private Ryan" that her thoughts often turned to her father and the circumstances surrounding his death. The movie had affected her greatly, and as she began to reflect on the fact that she had a legacy of that war, she resolved to learn more about her father. When she first mentioned it to me, I thought that it would be an interesting challenge to help her learn more, and in the process learn more myself, since I had an interest in the history of that war and those who fought it. I understood the story, and I could relate to it from personal experience. With my familiarity with military records and administrative practices, and knowledge of operations and how to interpret the data from them, it seemed that I might be in a position to help. I had no idea that the search would become such a personal challenge, nor of the experiences it would bring.

I started the search the second week of January 2001. Since

For years, Sharon's only knowledge of her father consisted of a few photographs, documents, and an empty grave in Tulsa.

I would be on the road and traveling for most of the next several months, using the Internet in the evenings seemed a practical way to start. The first weekend, I went to visit Sharon, and we opened the trunk that had contained Bill's belongings. In it were the fondly remembered treasures of a shattered family. While it was sad to read the letters, the trunk also provided us with a picture of the married years of Bill and Eleanor, and gave meaning to the search. The newspaper clippings were especially poignant. They reflected the hope Eleanor and her mother-in-law Nola must have had. We save things that mean something to us, and the collection of news items clearly spelled out the desperate hope she possessed. It would have been impossible to dig in to that collection of cherished memories without becoming involved, and that is how the search began.

I wrote down what I thought I would need to get started, basic things such as his full name, service number, squadron, and began the search. Making an official request through the Army Personnel Command was also an option, but that would come later. I felt certain that using the Internet would be quicker. At first I was able to find a few basic details about Bill Lewis. One Web page, established by Peter Randall in England called "Little Friends" was very helpful. Little Friends was the term that the Bomber crews used to refer to their fighter escorts. From this page I learned about the 55th Fighter Group and its three squadrons; the 38th, which was Bill's; and the 338th and 343rd. From "Little Friends" I also learned the date of Bill's crash, September 11, 1944, and the serial number of his airplane. The 55th Fighter Group's insignia was a green and yellow checkerboard just behind the propeller and on the nose of the planes.[33] The individual squadron designation for the 38th was the letters "CG" on the fuselage aft of the cockpit. These were part of the "QIM" or quick identification markings that pilots used to identify the people with whom they flew, especially while in the air. The individual squadron mark was a white triangle bordered by green on the tail of each aircraft.[34] The group collective radio call sign and the squadron call signs were available on the "Little Friends" web page also. More information was presented about the physical location of the squadron, Wormingford, also called Station 159 from where all the Group's missions were flown.

It would seem unimportant now but most of these small details were to prove critical in the months ahead. About Bill, there was only the statement that flying P-51D, serial number 44-14176, 2nd Lt. William M. Lewis was missing in action beginning September 11, 1944. The American Battle Monuments Commission listed the name of Lieutenant William M. Lewis on the Tablet of the Missing at the

American cemetery at Luxembourg. I could find little else. I had started the project looking forward to a challenge, and this was proving to be all of that. The location of his death was unknown, and there was no evidence that he might have been buried in a US military cemetery in Europe, possibly after the war ended. After 57 years, he was still Missing in Action. When I began this search, I felt that it was possible that Sharon's mother had known of the circumstances, but after her marriage to Nelson and the passage of years, she had simply chosen not to tell Sharon. Now I felt that it was possible that Bill Lewis's loss was a mystery that even the Army Air Forces, with all their resources, had failed to solve. All of these discoveries, interesting as they were, were just background. There had been no real progress in learning what had happened to Bill. My confidence was waning. The Lieutenant had flown away and never returned. I knew little more than Sharon had known when we started the search. That was all the information I could find. There was a nagging and persistent doubt that maybe we would never achieve anything more than what we already knew. Frustration was setting in.

The Czech Connection

I was certain that September 11, 1944 was the correct date of his crash. The "*Little Friends*" website had the 55th Fighter Group database which listed the date of Bill's loss, his name, and the aircraft serial number. Sharon had the original telegram sent to her mother as proof, and the American Battle Monuments Commission information seemed to fix the date of Bill's death on September 11. I decided that I would just research that day, and everything that happened that had been recorded that day. It was a little like the proverbial needle in the haystack, but it was a place to begin.

The Internet is a great tool. It is especially useful in that it allows people with specific interests to communicate with each other at great speed and low costs. It is also a good place to find certain databases that relate to those specific interests. It is not a replacement for basic research in primary sources, and it does not replace old-fashioned persistence. Most of the work that enabled the success of this effort did not come from the Internet, but it is still often a good place to start, and that is where I began.

The next logical step was to try to find information about the bomber groups on the Internet and to see if I could find mission logs, debriefs, anything pertaining to September 11, 1944. If the P-51s were escorting bombers, the name of the mission and target on that day might be found in the bomber unit mission histories. This might prove to be a daunting task, however. I did not know which bomber groups flew missions that day, so the challenge would be to look through all the mission reports available.[35] If the weather was good over the continent that day, there might have been several thousand planes aloft, each with several squadrons serving as escorts. It was possible to eliminate only those squadrons flying from bases in North Africa or Italy. Mustangs from England would probably only escort bombers from England. One bomber group in particular had a published mission log indicating the target that day was a mission deep into eastern Germany, close to the Czech border. From the information found in the unit histories, that particular mission was a large undertaking, a maximum effort, with several hundred planes flying. The target was the synthetic oil plant at Ruhland, with many secondary targets and targets of opportunity. It was a little bit more than I had when I started, and maybe there was a connection.

While I was pursuing the bomber connection, I became interested in the various Eighth Air Force bulletin boards that are found on the Internet. Many of these contain requests for information from the children, nieces, or nephews of deceased airmen. Aviation enthusiasts and researchers support these bulletin boards, and many contain official documents obtained since the war through the Freedom of Information Act. Some offer these documents for a fee. Others, such as *"Little Friends,"* ask for nothing and derive much information from material sent in by surviving veterans and family members, and US military archives. Many of these are very extensive, and contain ongoing discussion of specific inquiries.

One evening, while searching one of these, I found a request for information of any kind regarding a battle over the town of Kovarska, now in the Czech Republic but in 1944 part of occupied Czechoslovakia. The request had been on the web site since March of 1999; someone named Jan Zdiarsky in the Czech Republic had placed it. The date requested was for September 11, 1944. Encouraged but not really optimistic, I had nothing to offer the requester but more questions. What were the chances of him providing information regarding one airman of whom even the US military knew nothing? I had confidence that the military would know all that there was to know about his loss. After all, Bill Lewis was one of their own. Someone in another country would hardly be expected to have information that even the US military did not have. The same day was all we had in common. I e-mailed him that I had read his request, and was sorry that I had no answers but questions. Did he have any information about a USAAF 2nd Lieutenant named William M. Lewis who was flying a P-51 and was lost on September 11, 1944? What did we have to lose? Nothing ventured, nothing gained.

That same evening as I searched the Internet, I found a web page dedicated to the *"Museum of the Air Battle of 11 September 1944."* It was a site dedicated to airmen of both sides who had perished in the air over and around the village of Kovarska, a village of 1,500 people in the Czech Republic, close to the German border. From this site I learned that many of the American bombers had been shot down, along with some of the fighter escorts and German Luftwaffe defenders. One of the targets was Ruhland. Four P-51s had been shot down that day, with three pilots killed, one taken as a POW. As I researched the various pages of the site, I discovered the name of Jan Zdiarsky, the very same person who had placed the inquiry on the Historic Wings bulletin board in March of 1999, requesting information on the events of September 11. Jan was a founder of the museum and currently its director. The possibility of knowing what had become of Bill Lewis loomed a little larger, but it was still distant, and far from complete. I composed another e-mail to Jan that same evening.

As I waited for information, I found a picture of Bill from Sharon's box of records, digitally scanned it and sent it in to the *"Little Friends"* website. Peter Randall placed it on the website, and now at least we had a picture of Bill in the photo gallery of the 55th Fighter Group, noting his name and the date of his loss. It was a small act, but the process of honoring Bill in our generation had begun.

Plano, Texas – Prague, Czech Republic
January 12, 2001

I had a full day at the company offices, and went straight from the company campus in Plano to a restaurant right after work. It had been a tiring day, and I was going to turn in early. I thought I'd check my e-mail first. The first e-mail I looked at was from Jan Zdiarsky in the Czech Republic, to whose inquiry I had responded with a question. I was surprised and very pleased that he'd replied so quickly. My e-mail, he said, was a very big surprise for him. The name of William M. Lewis was very familiar to him. William Lewis was the only remaining airman of more than 140 killed, captured or missing that had never been found during an air battle that he had been researching for many years. He had another startling revelation for me. Only this past summer, in June of 2000, someone with whom he had been working had discovered a crash site in Germany that Jan believed to be that of Lt. William Lewis. Perhaps more importantly, he had gathered historical documents that seemed to confirm this site as the place where William Lewis had crashed. He had been trying to determine the location of any of Lt. Lewis's family members since 1999. That was pretty exciting, and I called Sharon to tell her.

Sharon remembers:

The first emotion I had was absolute shock and disbelief. How would someone halfway across the world have known anything about my father? After that was the sentiment that made me wonder why had I not pursued this effort while my mother and grandmother were alive. Now, I was learning about my father and his death, and there was no one alive to share it. I was pleased though, to think that someone knew of my father and appreciated his sacrifice.

I had a range of emotions. There could have been a mistake, especially after 57 years. But of all the emotions, I hoped that it would really happen, that my father would be brought home after all these years.

I felt an obligation to him, an obligation I had really always felt. I never thought there was anything to pursue. My step-father had known my father, had attended the same schools and church as both my parents. I had heard of something that happened after the war was over. My stepfather had come to visit my mother. He was still in uniform as he stood at the front door. I had heard that my father was a soldier of some kind, and I looked at him and shouted "My daddy, my daddy." I can only assume that my mother was shocked at this. Later, after their marriage, my stepfather seemed to block out discussion of the past. My grandmother would visit and mention my father, and I think my stepfather was uncomfortable with these visits. My grandmother would begin to discuss it, but she could never sustain a lengthy discussion. The bitter memories of both her dead sons were too much to remember. As a consequence, my mother and I rarely spoke about him. As a teenager, I tended to discuss it more with her, and she emphasized the time in which she married was different, and reminded me that circumstances accelerated their relationship. All of my mother's mementos relating to my father were packed and remained with her mother. They did not accompany us on our moves and travels over the years. The trunk remained essentially unopened until I was in my late twenties. I was at my grandmother's with my children and mother. There was a second shelf above the closet, and there was an old cardboard suitcase, covered with dust. "That is Eleanor's. I think it is Bill's things." My mother claimed no knowledge of what was in the case. When I opened it, she seemed stunned and had to sit down. She trembled and stared for a few minutes, as the memories seemed to overwhelm her.

In the meantime, Sharon and I were examining some of the material we had gathered from the trunk at her house. There was an old picture of several pilots in front of a P-51, probably taken in England. On the back were some names. Sharon said that one of the names was someone she recognized. David Jewell had been a high school friend of Sharon's father and her mother, Eleanor. He was from Tulsa, and as a child she remembered her mother talking about David or "Buddy" as she called him, and his wife, Helen. I went to an address finder on the

Internet and looked up David Jewell. There was one in a Tulsa suburb. This address looked promising, since David had joined the Army from Tulsa, and I composed a letter telling him about our search and mailed it the same day.

The search had found something else that might be valuable in learning more about Sharon's father. It was a book published by John Gray called "*The 55th Fighter Group against the Luftwaffe*," and I ordered a copy. John Gray is the son of a career Air Force Officer and served on active duty as a US Army Officer. Having grown up around Air Force bases, and studied history in college, he developed an interest in the USAAF of World War II, and decided to research the history of the 55th and write about it. Gray had researched the 55th Fighter Group extensively in preparation for his book, including interviews with surviving veterans, reading published and unpublished manuscripts, and poring over old photo collections. The book is excellent, and provided several more links to pursue. Among the more interesting items were several detailed descriptions of the Group's missions in the months of July and August. By comparing these with Bill's logbook, I was able to link those descriptions to his logbook and learn much more about those flights. Since John was in contact with several members of the 55th, I decided to write to him, tell him about the search and ask him for help. It wasn't easy. His publisher would not give me his contact address, but did say that they would forward my letter through them. At the same time, I decided to pursue one of the references in Gray's book. One of those was a book published by Lt. Col. Robert Littlefield, a retired US Air Force officer. Bob Littlefield was a member of Dog Flight of the 38th Fighter Squadron, one of the men in the original aging photo found in the trunk. He had published a book called "*Double Nickel, Double Trouble*," the "Double Nickel" a reference to the 55th. I made some trips to libraries and a couple of bookstores, searching for his book without success. It became even more frustrating when, after an evening at the bookstore, I found Bob's book referenced in several other books about World War II fighter pilots, but no trace of how the book could be acquired. I felt strongly that I needed to contact someone who had flown with Bill on the Ruhland mission in order to learn more of what happened. When I checked my e-mail the next morning, there was a message from Jan Zdiarsky. We had been communicating now for several weeks. He said that it might be useful for me to communicate with someone named Robert Littlefield! The e-mail contained his address and phone number in California. I wrote a letter and mailed it the next day. Over the next few weeks, I communicated with Jan in Prague, and waited to hear from Bob Littlefield and David Jewell. On February 19th I received a letter from Bob Littlefield. He lived in northern California. He told me that he would be glad to talk, and that his book was self-published and how I could buy it. He also offered that there were four members of Dog Flight who survived, and told me where they lived, but he had not flown on the escort mission to Ruhland. In fact, he had been shot down and was evading in France at the time of the September 11 mission. He would return to the squadron sometime after the Ruhland mission. I realized then that the David Jewell I had sent the letter to in Tulsa was the wrong one, and found the correct David Jewell in the Dallas area. I sent him a letter that week, gave him Sharon's address and phone number, and on Saturday, March 10 he called Sharon. "*Sharon*" he said, "*this is David Jewell.*" Sharon says that the only thing she could say for a minute or so was "*Oh my God.*" He asked her who I was and how I found him, and told her about how he and his wife had wondered what had happened to little Sharon, and what had happened to Bill. Sometime later she received a letter from David, and in it he had enclosed another picture of Bill with several pilots of the 38th that we had not seen before. The disappointing news was that he also had not flown that day, and therefore had little to offer about what might have happened to Bill. Still, it was good to know that someone who had known Bill since his youth was so close by, and we felt good about the contact. Within a few days after Sharon heard from David Jewell, I received a phone call from John Gray. His publisher had forwarded the letter, and he had found it interesting. We talked at length about the search, and John offered to help in any way that he could. Finally, the search was gaining momentum.

After the initial contact with Jan, I found several other Internet sites that looked promising. On one of these sites was another inquiry written by John Carroll. John said simply that he was seeking communication with other pilots of the 38th Fighter Squadron from the World War II era, and former Prisoners of War from a specific camp. I thought this might be another stroke of good luck. Could John Carroll have known Bill Lewis? I e-mailed John asking if he knew anything of Bill. John's reply was gracious, and said he wished he could be more help, but he had been flying P-38s when he was shot down on November 29, 1943, over Bremen; well before Bill had joined the 55th. As John put it "*it was a bad scene.*" I went to John Gray's book to get a full description. There was a chilling narrative of what happened on that mission. John's words were an understatement, but that is what I have come to expect from these men. They do not seem to brag or over-emphasize anything, they just state the simple truth. The November 29, 1943 raid on Bremen was conducted by 306 B-17s and B-24s supported by 352 fighters. In a twenty-one minute span between 1429 and

1450, 457 tons of bombs were dropped on Bremen industrial targets. 13 bombers and 16 fighters were lost, including 7 P-38s of the 55th. As John had said, it was a bad scene.

Kovarska, Czechoslovakia
March 19, 1982

Kovarska was not always known by that name. For centuries, the little village nestled in a wooded mountain range was known as Schmiedeberg. In political maneuvering which mirrored the history of the country, Kovarska had been caught up in the Sudeten compromises of 1938. The area had been part of a larger controversy since 1918, when the Czechoslovak Republic was first recognized. Even then, the German speaking Czech nationals, the residents of the Sudeten in the south, wanted to join with Austria, and the region of Slovakia was not officially a part of the Republic. Among the decisions of the treaty of Versailles was that the territory acquired by the Czech government would remain under Czech national control. The region had been historically a part of the Czech Kingdom for many centuries. The Germans in the Republic did not forget. When Hitler began his territorial moves in 1938, among his first acts was the declaration of the Sudetenland as German territory. Czechs then sparsely populated Kovarska. A small town of about 1,300 in the mining region, it would now be subject to German control. The autonomy demanded in 1919 took nearly twenty years to come about, but Hitler had won one of his first victories without firing a shot. British and French concessions of the Munich agreement established a German "protectorate." Prague came under the heel of Hitler's troops on March 15, 1939, and the years of wartime occupation began. At the end of World War II, General George Patton reluctantly agreed to the conditions of Russian control, and the Czechoslovak Republic simply passed from the control of one occupier to another. It was in 1947 that Schmiedeberg became known by its recent name, Kovarska.

In March of 1982, while repairmen were working on the Kovarska School, events long forgotten began once more to change the lives of people half a world away. Roman Zdiarsky, Jan's brother, was fourteen years old at the time. Roman and his classmates were helping the workers repair the school in Kovarska.

We were in eight class, when we, a few boys, helped with tidying one of the rooms, where the electricians worked that

*moment. One of them cut a big hole in the wall in the place
where was the upcast and made gaps to place some cables in.
When he was cutting upon that hole, we heard something falling
from the upcast and from the hole flowed clouds of dust. When
(the) dust fell off, we saw (a) dusty and dirty package of something lying on the floor.*

From this package they learned that the items had been the property
of Staff Sergeant John C. Kluttz. They learned also that he was married
and lived in Dallas, Texas before the war. There was an equipment
list, Army Air Forces form # 121, itemizing the equipment issued to the
Sergeant, and an identification picture taken in civilian clothes to be used
for escape purposes. To the local schoolboys, these items were a strange
appearance of the evidence that something had happened here long ago.
Some of the old villagers were asked about the clothes. *"Ja, it could be
something from that airplane that crashed into the school during the war,"*
they had replied. It could have ended there, but Jan was particularly interested in the package. He wanted to learn about the people who flew these
planes, and what happened on that September day so long ago.

The task was not easy. There was a vague oral tradition of the
history of the village and the war, but as Jan worked to chronicle the
events, he found little factual evidence. His search was made more difficult by the fact that the demographics of the little town had shifted
dramatically. Jan's research indicates that in 1938 the town of Schmiedeberg contained only about 10 percent Czech population, and by
1944, there were no Czechs remaining in the town. At the end of the
war, some Czechs returned, but the German population immigrated
to Germany. Many of these people were forcefully removed due to
international agreements relating to the original appropriation of the
Sudetenland. Now, Jan says, the town has regained perhaps 5-10
percent of its original German population.

Petr Frank, a resident of Kovarska whose father was a witness to
the events of September 11, 1944, joined Jan in the efforts to learn the
facts and became a member of the museum. Petr's family was among
the original Sudeten Germans of Kovarska.

Jan pursued the facts with diligence. The eyewitness accounts were
few, and there was the usual conflicting information from persons who
saw the same event but reported it differently. Early accounts of the
bomber's tail section that struck the school were far from accurate.
That wreckage was reported to have come from a single-engine two-
seat fighter from which the pilot, a black man, was removed and killed
by angry German civilians.

In my conversations and correspondence with Jan, I am struck by his admiration and appreciation of the sacrifices of the men who fought the war in Europe. It was curiosity that drove him to the truth about the battle of September 11. It was an understanding of the precious cost of freedom that drove him to do even more. As he viewed the papers of Sgt. Kluttz, he thought of the man and his family, and wondered if he were still alive. He thought especially of the men who died in his town, protecting his freedom so far from their own homes.

By 1994, a great deal of documentation had been gathered, and the facts of the battle were slowly revealing themselves. Another thought had come to Jan. It would be appropriate to erect a small memorial to the airmen of both sides who perished in the battle of September 11, 1944. On the 50th anniversary of the battle, and at the approximate time the fight over Kovarska began, the memorial was dedicated. There was a flyover of jets by the Czech Republic Air Force. The school into which the tail section fell was renamed the *"The Basic School of Sgt. J.C. Kluttz."* Later, in 2000, the street on which the museum stands was renamed *"Albert E.Trommer Street,"* in honor of the ill-fated pilot and his crew whose B-17 exploded over the town.

But the event for which Jan and his friends are probably the proudest is the meeting of the former enemies. Representatives of both the USAAF and the Luftwaffe met as friends. Jan has remarked of the "rare and unusual meeting" that took place that day, and the genuine warmth the former opponents felt for each other. That friendship, he said, portrayed the absurdity of war and the battle over Kovarska. Every year since 1997, these international meetings are held in Kovarska on the weekend closest to the anniversary date of the September 11, 1944 air battle.

With the ceremony in 1994, Jan had begun a new chapter in his life and that of Kovarska. He was 22 years old, and already he had invested ten years researching the air battle. But he says, as he later discovered, most of the knowledge of the subject was yet to be revealed. The memorial was the beginning of a rigorous pursuit of the truth about September 11, 1944. The first step was the founding of the Air Historical Association Kovarska, and the next was the establishment of a cooperative effort with a group of aviation researchers and historians in Pilsen called "Slet Pilsen."[36] Over the next six years, Jan made remarkable strides in his research. Crash sites were located and mapped, and artifacts dug up from the earth. As the collection grew, the idea for a museum evolved, and on September of 1997, the Museum of the Air Battle of 11 September opened with a large complement of the survivors of the battle in attendance. Wayne

Rosenoff of the 55th was there, so was Donald Lienemann of the 100th Bomb Group, and Paul Kramp, Ferdinand Herres, Donald Farley, Arthur Edmonston, Luther Bennett and Jack Moore. Major General Francis Gerard, USAF Retired, attended as a representative of the 339th Fighter Group. Werner Dehr of JG 4 attended along with Manfred Kudell, Heinz Zimmer, Gunter Kinner, Hans Klaffenbach, and Oskar Butenopp.

The story of Donald Lienemann's return to Kovarska is especially compelling. His 1997 trip was his third to the region. He felt a strong urge to return to the spot where he as he put it... *"got a second chance at life ..."* He had attempted to find the exact place, but thought it much like the needle in the haystack. Through a friend who was active in Nebraska politics, he finally found a German Exchange student, Lutz Ammann, who had studied at the University of Nebraska. Ammann had returned to Germany and was now at Police Headquarters in Berlin. With Ammann's help, they located the mission maps and placed the area in the Erzegebirge. In October 1994, Lienemann felt that he had gathered enough information, and set out for Germany and the Czech Republic to find his place of redemption. He remained in the area of the battle for several days and searched with no success. Lienemann had not yet met Jan Zdiarsky, and had no idea that a monument had already been erected to his fellow crewmembers. On the evening of his last day of searching, he told his companions that he felt certain that

The memorial to the fallen airmen of both sides in Kovarska.
It was dedicated on the 50th anniversary of the battle.

he was close to the crash site. What he did not know was that Schmie-deberg/Kovarska lay just a few miles distant, beyond a small mountain. He resolved to return, and with more help, locate the site. He had just missed the 50th anniversary of the battle, but widely disseminated news of the event reached his German friends, and in 1995, armed with the knowledge of the Kovarska Memorial and Jan's research, he returned. Lienemann was astonished at the discovery of artifacts from his airplane, and understandably emotional. After a lunch in the town, with the Mayor and others, they left for the place where the B-17 had fallen. The piles of twisted aluminum were the only remains of his ship.

After finding the crash site, the small group dispersed, looking for the place where Lienemann had concealed his wings and insignia and other identification. They were unsuccessful but Lienemann left satisfied. The warmth and sincerity of the Czechs overwhelmed him, and he thought it an unbelievable experience. At the time of his second visit, he was writing a book about his wartime experiences. After the visit to Kovarska, he decided to add one more chapter. He would call it "*Unbelievable Discovery.*"

Jan was really only just beginning. With the establishment of the museum, he plunged into learning more details of the battle. To that end he traveled to America in 2000, and visited the US National Archives to find some very specific German documents he believed might be there, and which if found would be very helpful to his research. It was primarily because of his exhaustive research that we now know anything about not only Bill Lewis, but of many more young men and how they spent the last hours of their lives.

It was into this already functioning and well run operation that I fortunately stumbled during the second week of January 2001.

La Longueville, France
February 2001

The *Houston Chronicle* carried an article reporting the discovery of the remains of an American P-51 pilot found by a farmer draining a field in France. His name was William Patton, and by a remarkable coincidence he had also been a member of the 55th Fighter Group. He was a former bomber pilot who had been assigned to the Scouting Force, whose planes, and some of their pilots, the 55th provided. Their task was weather reconnaissance and navigation for bomber missions. He had been missing since January of 1945, when he was lost on a weather reconnaissance mission. When the remains were discovered, his Dog Tags were still around his neck, and his uniform items were in remarkably good condition. It is almost as if this were a message to keep trying.

By the last weekend in March of 2001, I was convinced that Jan had found the site of Bill's crash and that his research was of superior quality. Our daughter Claire had been in France completing her final college year studying for the French National Language Exams. She had proposed that we visit her and take a trip to the Normandy landing beaches. It was a good idea, and I made plans to visit in April, notifying Jan of our plans and telling him that we intended to visit the crash site. Claire had also studied for a year in Oberursel, Germany as a Bundestag Scholar, and her German was as good as her French. She would be an excellent companion if we ran into language difficulties. She agreed to visit Prague, with the idea that we would make a quick trip to meet Jan, visit the crash site, take some pictures, and then go to Normandy.

Houston, Texas
March 28, 2001

I will leave for Europe in a little more than a week. Sharon is leaving town to take care of her ailing mother-in-law, and I will give her a ride to the airport. We agree that I would come early and take another look at the contents of the big trunk. We go through a large group of letters, clippings, and Army Air Force documents and pictures, and I select some that I have not seen before and put them inside a manila folder before I take Sharon's luggage to my car. Later that evening, after supper, I began to go through the material. There is one item, a letter that I have not seen before dated October 30, 1946.

30 October, 1946

Mrs. Eleanor P. Lewis
1415 South Rockford Street
Tulsa, Oklahoma

Dear Mrs. Lewis,

I am writing you relative to the previous letter from this office in which you were regretfully informed that a Finding of Death had been made in the case of your husband, First Lieutenant William

M. Lewis, Jr., 0763247, Air Corps, and that the presumptive date
of his death had been established as of 12 September, 1945.

Since that time a revision has been made in the Missing Persons
Act which enables the War Department to fix an actual date and
issue an official report of death in any case where circumstances
lead to no other logical conclusion. Lieutenant Lewis was the pilot
and sole occupant off a P-51 (Mustang) fighter plane which failed
to return from a bomber escort mission to Ruhland, Germany on
11 September 1944. Translation of captured German records
reveals the crash of a Mustang fighter plane three and one half
kilometers northwest of Oberhof, Germany on 11 September
1944, the pilot of which was dead. ... it is logical to conclude that
he was killed in action 11 September 1944 ...... the records of the
War Department have been amended accordingly ......

My continued sympathy is with you in the great loss you have
sustained.

Sincerely yours,

EDWARD F. WITSELL
Major General
The Adjutant General of the Army

This is a surprise. This letter seems to confirm exactly what Jan
and Petr Frank have been thinking all this time. If I had doubted Jan's
research when I first heard about his discovery, those doubts were now
dispelled, completely and finally. The crash site seems to be in Oberhof,
right where they have been looking. This seems to fix the place of Bill's
death accurately, but it also begs more questions. If the Army knew
where he died, why did they not search for his body? One speculation
is that this place must have been in the east, the DDR during the time of
the Berlin Wall. The Deutsche Demokratische Republik, more commonly
known to Americans as East Germany, was one of the states the
Russians would have used as a buffer in the event of a war with NATO.
It is possible that even if the Army had wanted to investigate there, they
would not have been allowed to do so. Then too, with nearly 70,000
total unknowns for all the theaters of World War II, there may not have
been the resources to search for all of them. Still, it seems strange, and
somewhat disturbing. They knew that it was highly probable that Bill had
gone down in the Oberhof area, and he may still be there. We owe him a
great deal more diligence in the search.

The pictures from Jan Zdiarsky arrived today. On the 30th of March, just days before I left on the trip, Jan and Petr Frank, his colleague at the museum, searched for and found the crash site. They had never visited it before, and took the chance that they might not find it after traveling 200 kilometers or more to a different country. But after several hours, as Jan describes it, "*a miracle ...*" The airplane was in pieces, and few were much larger than a foot or less square. Most were twisted. Only the breech mechanisms of the .50 caliber Browning machine guns were identifiable, rusted by the elements. They also found some aluminum pieces, which still bore the paint applied by the squadron, the checker-board yellow that decorated the cowling of the engine clearly identifiable. There can be no doubt that this was a P-51 Mustang from the 55th Fighter Group. They found what appeared to be the sole of a flight boot; pieces of the tire with tread markings, and a piece of hydraulic tubing with fittings. Some small pieces of the engine were found, and a somewhat larger section of aluminum which turned out to be the section of anti-glare paint just in front of the cockpit. Soon after Jan and Petr returned from Oberhof they contacted some experienced aviation archaeologists in England. They had retrieved some part numbers from the wreck site, and sent these to the British contacts. The part numbers carried the typical prefixes for the parts found on the North American P-51D series 10. They had a match for the type of airplane Bill flew on the day that he was lost.

It is sobering to see these pictures. It is also perplexing that such small and fragmented amounts are found, with no sight of the wings, tail or horizontal stabilizers. Even the once mighty block of iron that was a Merlin engine is shattered. Jan feels that the next search should be made using a magnetometer, which will reveal the presence of larger masses of ferrous metal buried all these years. They were now certain that they had found the exact site where Bill crashed and where he died. But the discovery only generated more questions. What had happened to Bill's body? Was he buried here? In the confusion of the war was his body removed from the site and buried at one of the American military cemeteries as an unknown? Did his remains rest in a local cemetery?

For months I have been pursuing this search for Bill's remains and the answer to the riddle of his disappearance in the abstract. It has been an exercise of the mind, a detached investigation, and an analytical process. But as I pursued the answers, slowly I developed an affinity for the Bill Lewis that emerged from the search. He had become real to me. Now, as the first physical pieces of the puzzle emerge, there is a visceral sense of what happened. The force of the crash must have been enormous, the damage so complete that only an experienced searcher can determine that this was in fact an airplane. The sole of the flight boot found in the wreckage is perhaps the most unsettling piece of evidence. The mind wants to reject what happened to the living being who wore that boot. I am surprised to find myself in denial, the same process of denial we exercise for the living, and in the stages of our own life and death. It is surprising because I have never known him alive, yet have the occasional flight of fantasy that we can find him alive. But for me, Bill Lewis is a brother in arms, one who took the same oath, wore the uniform, took the ultimate risk, and lost all he possessed; his wife and daughter, his life. I need to pursue this to the end. It is my privilege to honor him in this way.

As I traveled to Europe to meet Jan Zdiarsky, Sharon waited for our news.
In Tulsa's Memorial Park cemetery, the headstone and Bill's empty grave
only marked the beginning of the story.

Oberursel – Prague – Oberhof
April 2001

Atlanta, Georgia
April 7, 2001

I will leave for Frankfurt in a few hours. There I will meet Claire, and we will drive to Prague on Monday or Tuesday. Before leaving, I had researched the German Stalag system. I found an interesting item that referred to Oberursel, the small suburb north of Frankfurt where Claire had spent her year in Germany. The US Military had appropriated the property, which served as the German Luftwaffe Interrogation Center during the war. It was still a US Army Facility, now called Camp King. Remarkably, it was just a few blocks from Claire's host family, the Welteke's in Oberursel.

As I flew over from Houston, I read the Mission Reports of the 390th Bomb Group for the Bohlen-Ruhland mission. I compared them with the weather outside from 30,000 feet. It must have been a day much like this — a high thin wisp of cirrus at our altitude, with small bunches of cumulus forming at 3,000 and rising to between 5 and 7 thousand feet, a beautiful day to fly.

Now, waiting for my flight in Atlanta, I am curious about a crowd gathering excitedly at the arrival gate. In their 50s and 60s, they are active and retired Delta pilots who are signing a large poster sized picture of a Boeing aircraft. It will be presented to a Captain arriving from Frankfurt who is flying his last flight. I strike up a conversation with one and tell him about my trip, which also involves a last flight. His uncle was a World War II aviator who was lost on the Ploesti raid. His uncle's aircraft was recovered a few years ago, but there were no remains inside. He seems interested in my story, and graciously wishes me good luck, quite a difference between that happy event and Bill's last flight.

There are still two more hours before my departure, and another aviation event makes the news. A helicopter searching for Vietnam war MIAs has crashed and all aboard are dead.

Oberursel, Germany
April 8, 2001

When Claire was a student in Germany, she was a guest of Silke Welteke and her children. She became a member of the family, going to a German school and learning the language. Now, we will be their guests once again. In the evening after the traditional "*Abendbrot*," we related the story of Bill and our search. Silke was interested, and she graciously offered to loan us her car to drive to Prague, and we gratefully accepted.

In the afternoon, we walked over to Camp King. The property has been turned over to the German government, and the quaint old stone buildings are being demolished. The pictures and map I found on the Internet were helpful, and I can distinguish some of the old buildings where the Luftwaffe interrogators once grilled the American and Allied pilots. Later, we drive by the train station. It is essentially unchanged from its wartime appearance. This was the first stop in the Stalag system, and thousands of young aviators entered the German POW system from this place. The place was originally a farm then in the northern suburbs of Frankfurt. During the war, it was known as "Auswertstelle West."

In the morning after a hearty breakfast, we left in Silke's car for Prague to meet Jan Zdiarsky and discuss his findings, learn more about his research and plan our next activities. The roads were excellent, and we made great time, stopping occasionally to view the rolling hills and forests. We took the Autobahn southeast out of Frankfurt, then past Nuremberg to Regensburg and on to the Czech border. It was a beautiful spring day, clear and chilly, and the rolling hills and forests were awash in shades of green.

The train station at Oberursel. Most allied flyers came through this station for interrogation and later transfer to POW camps.

Prague, Czech Republic
April 10, 2001

We met Jan for lunch in a restaurant adjacent to the University campus. I gave him the documents I had prepared for the exhibit they will create for Bill at the museum, and we discussed some details about the search. He told us that he had prepared an extensive document for us that he would bring when we went to dinner that evening. He offered to give us the tour of Prague, and we spent the evening hours until sundown in the Golden City.

We finished the tour and spent a little while in our room at the College Hotel before we met Jan and his girlfriend Martina for dinner. During dinner, Jan presented some of the results of his work. It was meticulous, organized and informative. He had created a picture of the battle with great detail. It is all there — the initial operation order, weather, pilot reports of the combat, German KU reports; a mosaic of the actions of a massive coordinated effort that took place nearly sixty years ago. He reviewed the details of how he determined the crash site to be that of Bill Lewis, and described some of the aircraft parts found in the ground surrounding the impact crater. As Jan flipped through the pages of his work, he described each piece. But he kept a surprise

The author with daughter Claire on the Charles Bridge in Prague, April 2001.

close. When the dinner was nearly over, at about 10:45, Jan told us that they had found something else in the woods; something more than just the wreckage of Bill's plane. It is something, he said, that assured him that this crash site is indeed the place where Bill Lewis died. Until this time he had used the logic of elimination to determine the identity of the airplane and its pilot. Of the Mustang pilots gone missing that September 11th, the only plane and pilot still unaccounted for was Bill Lewis.

Jan turned to the last page. There it is ... a digital photograph of a small wooden cross in the forest. It is perhaps a foot high. Made of what seems to be finished wood, it still bears a yellow coat, now flaking, and the bottom of the cross, which had been driven into the ground, is now rotted. On the arms of the cross, written in red are the words ...

"W Lewis USA gef. 11.9.44"

Jan told us how he felt when they found the site and the cross. *"When we find the plane and this cross, I know this for sure it is him, and I tell him, I speak to him on that place. I tell him that his daughter is a big girl now, and that she is thinking of him."*

Jan and Claire agreed that the abbreviation "gef" refers to the German word "gefallen." Someone knew the identity of the American flier who perished so long ago on this tranquil wooded slope in Thuringen.

We were stunned by the development, and the sense of emotion was high. Despite the terrible condition of Bill's body *"through explosion in countless small pieces"* as described in the German KU report, it now appeared that someone knew his identity. Perhaps all these 57 years, they knew. Perhaps every few years the cross was taken down, repainted or replaced as weather wore away the wood and paint. What else would explain this? Before we leave, Jan gave me some pieces of the airplane, which are unique. One is the twisted piece of nose cowling painted with the still visible green and yellow checkerboard, the symbol of the 55th. Another is a small strip of heavy aluminum with the lettering "ALCOA ALCLAD." Jan told me later that this was an item found on most American airplanes. We agreed to meet Jan at 7:30 in his office the next morning.

The picture of the cross with Bill's name and date of death created a surge of emotions. Sudden and unexpected, it told us that from far away and through the years, someone had made the discovery and left something to honor the memory of the young airman. It was simply overwhelming. We had no idea that such a simple discovery could have an effect so powerful. We now knew that we had always had an ally in our search.

The cross fashioned by Adelbert Wolf. It remained here until its discovery in March 2001.

Neither of us could sleep as we sat and talked in the dormitory room until perhaps 2:00 AM. We decided to abandon our plans to visit the Normandy beaches. We would continue the search in Oberhof. We discussed possible explanations for the cross and fell asleep only to wake about 4:30, our minds buzzing with possibilities. Perhaps we thought we would be the ones to begin the process of discovering Bill's resting place and honoring him. Now it seemed that a former enemy had made the trip into that quiet forest and performed the simple and fitting act of placing the cross there. We feel humbled and grateful, but we are also puzzled. Who could have done this, and why? How was Bill identified?

When Jan received my e-mail on January 11, 2001, he was surprised and happy. His research had determined that the only remaining MIA from the battle was Bill Lewis. Now, from across the Atlantic, this E-mail had told him that someone was looking for Bill Lewis, and knew his daughter. Jan and Petr Frank had wondered for some time if Bill Lewis was survived by relatives, and had been searching for some years for anyone connected to the remaining MIA. Even if they had known that Bill had survivors, it would have been nearly impossible to trace them because of Sharon's adoption, some address changes and the subsequent marriage and divorce.

Once we notified Jan that we were coming, he decided that it was necessary for him to go to the crash site himself. He would not have wanted us to come so far and have it be the wrong site. Jan's research had been impeccably thorough and painstaking. He had felt for some time that this site held the clues to Bill Lewis's status. Now it was time for him to confirm his hunch, and he and Petr left for Oberhof on March 30. Searching on the hills still partially covered with snow and at the end of the day in waning sunlight, they found the site after an exhaustive daylong effort. The cross was only the confirmation of their work, a sort of unexpected reward.

The early efforts of the Museum concentrated on the bombers role. After all, they had experienced the largest numbers of casualties except for the Luftwaffe defenders; well over 140 missing. In 1997, they began to investigate the role of the 339th Fighter Group and later the 55th Fighter Group in the battle. They also determined that the II Sturm and III Gruppe of Jagdeschwader 4, based in Alteno and Welzow in the Cottbus region opposed the US fighters and bombers. Further, they determined each of the serial numbers for the P-51s involved, and the corresponding MACRs (Missing Aircrew Report). Among the four fighter aircraft of the 55th that were downed that day, there was only one survivor, and there was only one remaining

The wreckage of Bill's plane as found by Petr Frank and Jan Zdiarsky in March 2001. Note the cross on the tree in the left background and compare this site with the historical photo on page 167.

MIA. The crash sites for Williams (KIA) and the survivor, Rosenoff had been found by the museum between 1998 and 2001. The general area for Kenneth Crawford's crash site was also already known. Only Bill Lewis's crash site was still a mystery.

Jan's next step was to acquire the pertinent MACR's and develop information from them. In one, the MACR 8684, he cites a report of a Lt. W. J. Ingram of the 338th. Lt. Ingram stated that he observed an unidentified P-51 on its back and smoking during the combat south of Gera, but no other information was given except that Ingram believed that this plane was from the 38th. This was a start. During this early effort, Jan and his friends believed that Bill had gone down near the town of Gera. They did not yet have the more detailed records that would tell them that this was a mistake. The town near where Bill was last seen was in fact some sixty miles west of Gera, and was Gotha, north of Oberhof.

His next effort was of a much larger scope, and much more labor intensive. He obtained a roster of every P-51 casualty of September 11, 1944. Comparing this to scores of other data such as unit histories, MACRs, eyewitnesses and local historians enabled him to develop some conclusions:

- *24 P-51s of the Eighth AF were lost over Germany or occupied*
  Europe on September 11, 1944
- *An additional three were lost or significantly damaged in Ukraine*
- *One loss occurred in England*
- *One made a forced landing in friendly territory*

What Jan wanted to do now would be more ambitious and expensive. Jan believed that there were original sources that could reveal in great detail the events of the aerial battles over Kovarska and Oberhof. These documents were held in the US National Archives in Maryland. After communicating with the personnel from the National Archives, Jan and his girlfriend Martina made a trip to Maryland in 2000. He was successful in acquiring the records of most of the units involved in the battle. Many of the original German documents had never been opened. Some were still stapled or taped shut. As they opened them, they found personal effects of deceased or captured pilots; such things as photos, identity cards, and other items the pilots were generally forbidden to carry on combat missions. From this visit, he was able to eliminate 22 of the 24 Mustang losses as possible sites for Bill Lewis.

For the 22 reports that he eliminated, either the name of the pilot or the serial numbers of the plane were distinguishable. This left only two reports. One was in the vicinity of Oberhof, 3.5 kilometers northwest of town on the Tambacher Strasse. The other involved an unknown pilot shot down near the village of Hochelheim in the Marburg area, north of Frankfurt. The times and location of the Marburg report did not fit the occurrences of the battle south of Erfurt. This loss was later determined to be a pilot of the 355th Fighter Group, Captain Kevin G. Rafferty. Only KU report # 2087 remained.

It is translated here from the German:

Place of accident: *3.5 kilometers northwest of Oberhof in the forest section Greifenberg, on the Oberhof to Tambach Road*

Time of accident: *11.9.44, between 11.30 and 11.40 hours*

Type of airplane: *P-51D*

Distinguishing marks: *Unable to be determined*

Fate of airplane: *Destroyed through explosion*

Fate of pilot: *Through explosion, in innumerable small pieces*

Identity of pilot: *Unable to be determined*

Condition of airplane: *99 percent destroyed*

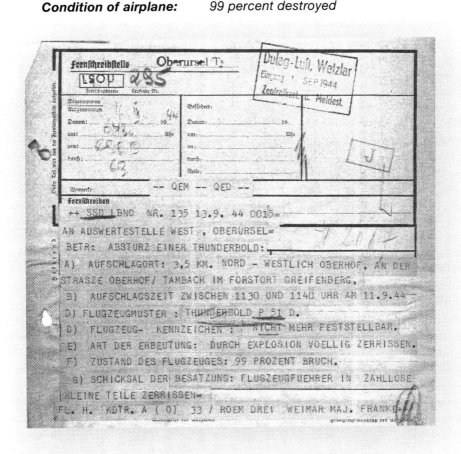

After Claire read this and translated it, we could only wonder even more about why the cross had Bill's name on it. There were some other questions as well. If the airplane was "*99 percent destroyed*" how were the investigators of the KU report able to determine that it was a P-51? The answer to this question may lie in the fact that Luftwaffe Intelligence probably determined that the American fighters seen at 1130 hours around Oberhof consisted of a force of P-51s. Another question involves the use of the term "explosion." Bill probably was carrying nearly 60 percent of his fuel load at the time of the crash. There was no external ordnance such as bombs aboard the Mustang at the time of the crash. It is possible that the damage viewed was the result of a near vertical dive and subsequent fire.

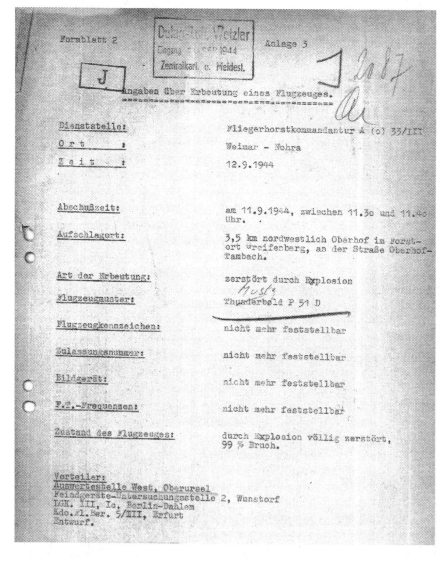

Formblatt 2   Dubas... Metzler   Anlage 3

Eingang ... 1944

Zentralkart. u. Meldest.

J

Angaben über Erbeutung eines Flugzeuges.

Dienststelle: Fliegerhorstkommandantur A (o) 33/III

O r t   :   Weimar - Nohra

Z e i t   :   12.9.1944

Abschußzeit: am 11.9.1944, zwischen 11.3o und 11.4o Uhr.

Aufschlagort: 3,5 km nordwestlich Oberhof im Forstort Greifenberg, an der Straße Oberhof-Tambach.

Art der Erbeutung: zerstört durch Explosion

Flugzeugmuster: Thunderbold P 51 D

Flugzeugkennzeichen: nicht mehr feststellbar

Zulassungsnummer: nicht mehr feststellbar

Bildgerät: nicht mehr feststellbar

F.T.-Frequenzen: nicht mehr feststellbar

Zustand des Flugzeuges: durch Explosion völlig zerstört, 99 % Bruch.

Verteiler:
Auswertestelle West, Oberursel
Feindgeräte-Untersuchungsstelle 2, Wunstorf
LXX. III, Ic, Berlin-Dahlem
Kdo.Fl.Ber. 5/III, Erfurt
Entwurf.

Haus "Vergissmeinnicht,"
Oberhof, Germany, April 10, 2001

It has been a long drive in rainy weather. We took turns driving, but now we are both tired and cranky. The map we are using does not seem to have enough detail, and once we left the Autobahn for the rural roads, finding Oberhof became more difficult. We were close, but didn't know which direction we should pursue. Claire went into a gasoline station and asked for directions. While she was talking to the lady at the counter, she felt a tap on her shoulder. A German gentleman had overheard and said that he was going toward Oberhof. He invited us to follow him. After a while, he left the road and pulled over to give us some last minute directions. Claire thanked him, and we talked about our good fortune as we drove on. The road up the mountain winds and switches and the shoulders are steep, almost vertical. As we neared the town, a beautiful rainbow appeared just over the road, forming a portal through which we passed, and we were finally in Oberhof. The tourist center was still open, and Claire asked them if there were any hotels or bed and breakfast places open. Oberhof is a town which hosts winter sports and ski events, and we were not sure if we would find a place to stay. The tourist office personnel were very gracious, and made a phone call to find a place for us. The Vergissmeinnicht had vacancies, and we reserved a room there for the night. Claire listened to the woman making the arrangements, and then told me, *"We are staying at a place which in German means 'Forget mine not.'"* She emphasized the *"forget mine not."* An interesting coincidence, just as the rainbow was, and the welcome help from the stranger. We felt that we were in the right place, and we had a sense of purpose.

Catholic Cemetery, Oberhof, April 11, 2001

"Ich hatte einen Kameraden..."
German Army song

Based on our discussions with Jan, none of us could be certain that the cross indicates the resting place of Bill Lewis. Jan thought that we should both visit the cemetery and inquire about church records in Oberhof. He had also told us that we would find the graves of some of the Luftwaffe airmen who died in the battle over the Thuringer Wald. The church records might also indicate that a burial of an unknown American took place. There had been at least two burials of Americans in the month of September 1944, first Lt. Kenneth Crawford on the 11th and on the 13th, Lt. Carl Heleen. Perhaps they had cared for Bill in this way also. After breakfast at the Vergissemeinnicht, we headed down the street to the little Friedhof, the cemetery. The tranquil little church, really small enough to be a chapel, is surrounded on all sides by grave markers. We had hoped to be able to meet someone from the church here, but it is closed, and we decided to search the cemetery instead. We searched the whole area, but first looked closely at what we know to be German military headstones, small uniquely shaped stone crosses made from what looks like granite. There, as Petr and Jan had said, we found the graves of the Luftwaffe pilots fallen on September 11 of 1944; Jakob Cryns, born 27.9.1923, Gunther Mechau, born 15.10.1924, and Johann Roth, born 4.12.1921. These were very young men, as are mostly all who are called to war. All are pilots like Bill, and I can't help but wonder if perhaps he shot one of them down, or if one of them shot him. They certainly saw each other in the skies on that last day for each of them. We completed the search. There were some unknown graves there; one said *"Drei unbekannte KZ Haftlinge, April 1945"* (Three unknown concentration camp prisoners …). We found another stone for a Russian soldier and some German military graves from April 1945. But there were no more unknowns; no Americans, and we set out along the Tambacher Strasse to search for the crash site.

Claire Breaux on the foggy morning of April 11, 2001 when we visited the cemetery in Oberhof. Pilots of the Jagdgeschwader 4 lost in combat with the 55th Fighter Group on September 11, 1944 rest there today.

Tambacher Strasse, north of Oberhof
April 11, 2001

As we left to search for the site armed with Jan's map, we felt confident that we could find the place where Bill came to earth. What we did not realize was that there were two Tambacher Strasses in the Oberhof area. There was the new, modern road, which was inside the town, and the Alte Tambacher Strasse. The Alte Tambacher Strass was outside of the town and led to the town of Tambach to the north. We had misinterpreted Jan's map, and spent several hours of the morning trudging along the steep and wet hillsides along the new road with no success. Claire suggested that we go to the Forstamt Office to ask for directions. Maybe the forester had seen the crash site and could guide us to it.

Forstamt office, Oberhof, Germany
April 11, 2001

In Germany, foresters manage the lands adjacent to the small towns. They take flora and fauna surveys, enforce no trespassing regulations, and in general act as managers and protectors of the land. If you have a question about the forest, they are the first source of information. The forester in Oberhof was helpful, but he said that if the crash site was where the map said it was, then that Forest was under the supervision of another town, Crawinkel, some 20 kilometers north. He made a copy of the large map found in his office, and told us where

the Greifenberg, the place mentioned in the crash, was located. He told us how we could find Herr Jurgen Neupert, the Crawinkel Forstamtleiter, and we set off again.

Forstamt office, Crawinkel, Germany
April 11, 2001

Herr Neupert was interested, but he had never seen the crash site. In fact he was the Forstamtleiter, the senior forester. Perhaps Herr Klaus-Roland Müeller, the forester who was responsible for the woods north of Oberhof might have seen the site. We showed Herr Neupert the photograph of the cross, and he called for Herr Müeller to come down right away. Herr Müeller arrived, and Claire told him the story, finishing with the picture of the cross. He was visibly surprised. He had never expected two Americans to come looking for the site. "*Das ist die Grabe*," he said. ("*This is the grave*") Yes, he said, if this was what he had seen, he knew where it could be found. He had come upon the site in 1997, had seen the words on the cross and the piles of debris arranged in a rough square at the foot of the cross. He thought it must have been a grave, and he wrote the inscription from the cross into the record book he kept on his surveys. He was able to find the date of the discovery, and found the actual record tucked in between pages of a botanical survey. He gave us a copy of his record, and said that he needed to go in that direction, then offered to show us the site.

Before we left, Herr Mueller told Claire that when he first saw the site there was a steel helmet there. We were confused by this information, because pilots of that era did not wear steel helmets. We wondered how it came to be there at the site of Bill's crash. This fact would surface again as we pursued our investigation, and we would be surprised by the results of this discovery.

We departed again, in mid afternoon, following Herr Müeller in his official car. We were excited. Finally, it seemed, we would soon be viewing the crash site. He turned and led us down the first road we started out on, then stopped and told Claire that we would go onto the road which branches off to another, smaller road. This is the Alte Tambacher Strasse, the old road through the forest, which is closed to automobiles. There was a gate blocking the entrance, and he stopped to unlock it. He drove for a couple of kilometers, and then stopped. This is the area, he told Claire, but it may take a while to find the exact spot.

We spread out to search. I took the eastern end of what we later determined to be the crash site. There were some promising pieces of debris visible from the road, and I started down. I quickly found an old leather fingerless glove, probably a driving glove, and not far from this what looked like an automobile headlight. I surmised these pieces may have come from an automobile accident, and left them. I would later regret this action.[37] About a half-hour later, we heard Herr Müeller calling. He had found the site, and we walked as quickly as possible toward the direction of his shouts. This was it. The larger parts of the wreckage were in a neat pile, the cross now hanging from a tree nearby. We examined some of the parts. The amount of debris and its size was discouraging, but Herr Müeller had told us that when he first saw the site, there was a great deal more wreckage. He said that during the days of the DDR, the east was hard pressed for things such as aluminum, and he thought scavengers had carried off all the larger parts. We looked around and determined that there were many small pieces of wreckage scattered over a large area, perhaps several hundred feet in diameter. As we examined the area more closely, what seemed to be an impact crater was visible. It was littered with several small pieces of aluminum, each perhaps two inches square. There are no trees around the crater, and Jan had told us that when they first saw the site a few weeks ago, they dug deeper and found a layer of ash several inches beneath the soft soil.

*Crawinkel Forstamt Klaus-Roland Müeller and Claire Breaux
examine the wreckage.*

I found the pattern of wreckage interesting. For maybe a hundred feet around the crater, there are small pieces of aluminum, and it is evident that no large trees have grown up around the crater itself. Having lived in the subtropical South all of my life, I did not fully appreciate the short growing cycle and long winter in more northern latitudes. Had this occurred in the southern United States, the site would have been impossible to find after only a couple of years, but on the Greifenberg there was an absence of undergrowth that we would expect in a southern forest. The land on the slopes of the Greifenberg had an appearance similar to a garden or park, and seemed manicured and cultivated compared to American forests. I found myself thinking that this must have looked almost the same the day the crash occurred.

One of the primary rules in aircraft accident investigation is a quick visual survey. The investigators look for four points of the aircraft. If they find the nose, tail, and left and right wings in close proximity, they conclude that the aircraft did not break apart before hitting the ground. None of this was possible in the survey of the crash site of Bill's plane when we found it. Nor did we have the time or abilities to do what the professionals would later come to do. The parts had been crumpled badly, and if any pieces other than the nose were identifiable, we were unable to locate them. I felt this was important, since we discovered that some P-51 crashes had occurred after high-G maneuvers. Another possibility in a dogfight between so many airplanes was that of a mid-air collision.

There is really not much to see, once you realize that this is most certainly the place where Bill Lewis died. The cross is there though, and it is a hopeful object among all this debris and destruction. I have some real doubts now about whether Bill's remains may ever be recovered, and the cross beckons. It is a sign of respect accorded by a former enemy. It loomed meaningful and attractive, and Claire talked with Herr Müeller. We wanted to show respect for what is German, including this site. To take it without asking would be presumptuous. He offered a suggestion; the debris has been diminishing, so maybe the cross will disappear. We should take it, he said. I was grateful and relieved. Sharon will appreciate this; it is very unique and unlike anything we could have brought back. We looked around the site one last time and began to climb the steep slope leading up to the road, the cross in hand. We placed it in the trunk gently, and began the long ride back to Frankfurt and Silke's house.

Luisenthal, Germany
April 11, 2001

Herr Müeller had found it strange that no remains were reported buried in either Crawinkel or Oberhof. He thought it possible that the Revierleiter responsible for both Crawinkel and Oberhof may have made the decision to bury the unknown American in Luisenthal, which is where the Revierleiter (senior forester) for the overall region lived. We checked the map and it seemed practical to stop at the Friedhof in Luisenthal to walk among the headstones in search of an *"Unbekannte Americanisch."* It had begun to rain, not heavily but a cold, slow, penetrating mist. Luisenthal is situated on a narrow defile in the mountains, and the houses fanned out only a short distance before the mountainsides were too steep for them. We passed the church, and the gravestones of the Friedhof were barely visible on a steep bluff overlooking the road on the left. We parked the car and walked the steep path past iron cemetery gates. At the very first row of graves stood seven German military headstones from 1944-45.

There are six stones, then an empty space, then the seventh, all German military personnel from various regions of the country; they had been buried where they fell, and most of these graves it seems, are from April 1945, just days before the end of the fighting in this area. This was just as we found in Oberhof, and as in Oberhof, there are no markers for German military which state they are from Luisenthal. Perhaps their custom is as the British, who buried their soldiers where they fell. Who could have been in the seventh plot? Had this been the son of a German family who brought him back to his own region after the war? Or was this perhaps an unknown American who had been reburied at one of the larger cemeteries in Belgium, France, or Luxembourg? If there was an unknown American here, his resting place was not marked.

Over the next day or so we pondered the German graves dated April 1945, and the Russian soldier and the three unknowns from the concentration camp. I was curious for two reasons. The first was that the towns of Luisenthal and Oberhof seemed too small for strategic importance, and in April of 1945 much of the fighting had diminished. Why and how had these young men died in such a remote and militarily unimportant locale?

The answer came later as I researched the waning days of the war. The VIII Corps of the US Army was ordered to consolidate *"along the general line Gotha (J-0965)-Oberhof (J-1138) and, on Army order, continue to advance to the East and Southeast in Z."* As the 89th, 87th, and 65th Infantry Divisions with their supporting and attached units carried out their orders, they were subjected to occasionally intense and lengthy resistance from the retreating German units. At Oberhof, Tambach, Dietharz, and Luisenthal, German units had set up roadblocks, and while the Americans were busy clearing these and the opposition, they were shelled by light and medium artillery. Oberhof itself was subjected to attacks as the Germans attempted to reclaim the town. As the forces advanced deeper into Thuringia, there were more surprises. In Ohrdruf, the Americans liberated the first concentration camp. In the same general area, the soldiers discovered the gold reserves of the Nazi government in a salt mine near the village of Merkers. It is believed that the tunnel complex consisted of several hundred kilometers in length filled with gold, paper money, jewelry, and art treasures. This complex was part of a huge area of underground tunnels and command and control centers. They were lavishly furnished with entertainment and recreation facilities, beautifully decorated and with all amenities. Concentration camp laborers, such as the ones whose graves we found in Oberhof, had dug them. The Buchenwald and Sachsenhausen camps were nearby also.[38]

There was a great deal to consider as we drove toward Frankfurt and the setting sun. The first issue was how we might approach the recovery of Bill's remains. Jan felt very strongly that the museum should lead that process. His concern was that he must first obtain permission to go to Germany and excavate. At first, I was unsure how to deal with this. As I gave it more thought, I tended to agree with his position. The US military is believed to have known of his crash site in 1946. No effort had been made to determine the exact location of the crash site and recover his remains, or at least there was no documentation to that effect. I decided that I would call the US Embassy in Berlin, and attempt to reach the Air Attaché. Surely the Air Attaché would have an interest in the repatriation of a fellow flier. I was able to call them from Frankfurt, and obtained the name of the Assistant Attaché. I then composed an e-mail message outlining the specifics of Bill's case and sent it off, requesting advice on how to proceed. In all these contacts, I had been asking for permission for Jan and the museum to begin the excavation for remains. In all these efforts though, we were talking to the wrong people. There were secrets in our search that would not be revealed for nearly one more year, and in March and April of 2002, we would begin to find answers from new and unexpected sources.

Brussels, Belgium
April 16, 2001

My mind was anywhere but on the security questions the ticket agent was asking as Claire went with me to check in for my flight from Brussels to New York. When he asked me if I was carrying anything that might be interpreted as dangerous by the X-Ray machine, Claire said that she thought I'd better tell him about the parts of Bill's plane in my suitcase. Ten pounds of irregularly shaped aluminum and iron might get someone's attention. We did, and it did get his attention. He was mildly interested, and said he should go and alert the technicians that it was just parts of an old airplane from the war in Germany.

I was surprised to find the seat to my right empty, both from Brussels to New York, and then from New York to Atlanta. I took the cross out of my bag and placed it on the seat next to me for most of the trip. It was wrapped in plastic and in a small thin box. At some point, one of the stewardesses asked me if I had enjoyed my trip to Europe. I told her yes, and launched into the story of the cross. After a few minutes, she began to ask questions. I told her as much as I knew, and after a while, I glanced behind my shoulder. The three people in the seat behind me had leaned forward, and were listening to the tale of the cross, and another stewardess had joined the first one. Someone in the seat behind me asked if I planned to write this story down. She thought it might be interesting. Neither she nor I had any idea just how much more interesting the story would become. I had not set out to write a story, only to find what had happened to Bill Lewis, and if possible to bring him home. But the story had found me, and it would not relinquish its grip for more than two years.

Houston, Texas
Monday, April 16, 2001

We had called Sharon and told her that we were bringing something back from the crash site that was truly unusual and remarkable. She had agreed to come over for breakfast with Villere, and together they would be able to see what we had discovered. We tell the story, and show Sharon the pictures that Jan took on his first visit to the site. We save the picture of the cross for last. She must have felt the same surprise we felt when Jan showed it to us. She must also feel something else, which only a daughter could feel. She still does not know that we have brought the cross with us, and we present it to her after the story is told. From thousands of miles away, this small, painted cross with her father's name has now come to rest in her hands. My thoughts must be different from hers; I am thinking mostly of the maker of the cross, and why that person chose to do this. I am wondering if they ever thought that someone one day might come searching for Bill, and because of this act, they would know so much. I am thinking that I would really like to meet the maker of that cross.

Sharon remembers:

That early morning breakfast at Ken and Yvonne's that my husband Villere and I went to was emotionally charged, to say the least. I wanted to see the pictures and hear the stories of Ken's trip to Europe; to see the pictures of the woods that held so many secrets. He had told me that he had a great surprise for me but never could I have imagined what he brought back. The pictures of the forest seemed somber, the pieces of the airplane were cold. They were mangled, twisted, and still strangely comforting. To have something tangible to hold that really could have held a father I never knew was emotionally staggering. I was quiet and on the verge of tears. I cry easily anyway, and this was almost too much to bear, but when I saw the next treasure, the cross from the tree with "W Lewis gef. 11.9.44" the floodgates opened. Someone, thousands of miles away cared. Someone, maybe a father, brother, mother, cared enough to build a remembrance for someone they would never know. They did this for someone who had a beautiful wife, a daughter, and every reason to resume his life when the war ended. They did it for someone who died alone in a forest so far away from his own home.

Whoever that someone was, he took the time to bury what remained after the crash, and to make that cross. I wanted to know about them. Why did they take the time to do these things to honor someone they would never know, especially in the middle of a war. What did they find to identify him? Dog tags, other identification, what was it? I wanted to know who had cared for my father. I wanted to let them know who he was and what that act meant to me, his only child, after all these years. God must have sent someone to take care of him, and I need to thank them. I still need to know all that I can to finally answer the mysteries that have always been there. I thought that someone might have risked their life to honor a life so quickly gone. Was there a prayer? Was there a small ceremony? Did they wonder about his family — who had he been? Were they fearful that the cross and their actions would be discovered? I had so many questions, and no one to answer them for me.

What would I give to be able to say thank you to the family of this brave soul? I will always keep them in my heart as brave and loving. If only my mother and grandmother, now gone for some time, could have had their questions answered. It would have been such a comfort for them to know that someone had taken care of their Bill, thousands of miles across the world. But now I realize that they do know, in my heart I know the answers for them have finally come. They know.

Delta Airlines Flight 120, Baltimore to Houston
April 20, 2001

The man sitting next to me was wearing something I had not seen in a long time. It was a POW-MIA bracelet from the Vietnam era. I struck up a conversation with him and learned that he was a retired Air Force Officer, and the bracelet he wore was for another Air Force Officer from Pennsylvania, missing since 1968. We shared Bill Lewis's story, and he wished me luck on the continuing search. The MIAs seem to be at the front of my consciousness, no matter where or what I am doing. *Vergissemeinenicht.*

Houston, Texas
April 21, 2001

Sharon's birthday is on the 21st, and we were invited to come over and tell the story to her daughter, Lauri, and Lauri's husband and children. Sharon got everyone's attention before dinner, announcing that this was her birthday, and that she wanted everyone to hear the story of her father and what has happened over these last four months. Even the little children were quiet as we related what we have done, and finally we presented the cross. One of the questions that we all had was who made the cross, and how did they know that this was where Lt. Bill Lewis died. The date on the cross is not a mystery, but the name is. No one in the town, only three kilometers distant from the forest, could have missed the explosion and fire that must have accompanied the crash. Lt.

155

Kenneth Crawford died on that day as well, and another American pilot, Carl Heleen, on the 13th. In three days of September, the little town on the mountain had seen a great deal of young men die. Surely these events were a part of the collective memory of Oberhof. Oberhof had buried not only two Americans, but also three sons of Germany killed on the 11th of September and several other young German soldiers or airmen during 1945. But if the German military report is correct, there was no way to identify the remains. Ashley, Lauri's daughter, offered a thought. Maybe someone comes every year, on September 11th. That is when we should go back, she said. Perhaps we could hold a ceremony on that date, or perhaps the maker of the cross would return then. It was an interesting idea, both for the possibility it held and the symbolism of the date itself. All the tourists will be gone then, the town will be more placid. It would be a good time to go, and I thought that Sharon might consider it.

A Soldier's Resting Place

"May you find a soldier's resting place,
beneath a soldiers blow"
Benny Havens, old Army ballad

Just as in the ballad, Bill had fallen beneath the blow of another soldier, and had rested there for nearly sixty years, his place of death known only to Adelbert Wolf and a few in whom he confided.

What should we think regarding the letter of October 30, 1946? At first glance it is disturbing that the Army did not pursue the issue of recovery any further. In 1942, two months after Pearl Harbor, the US Army Quartermaster Depot in Kansas City allocated more than 200,000 square feet of space in their warehouses for the disposition of personal property of captured and fallen soldiers. This is what Bud Jewell referred to in his letter to Eleanor when he told her that Bill's belongings would be sent first to a place in England and then to Kansas City. Two years later, in 1944, General Dwight Eisenhower put in place procedures for identification, burial, and disposition of personal effects of service members. As the Allies advanced across formerly German occupied territory, they established cemeteries. The task they faced was huge. Never before had war been conducted on such a vast scale, involving so many countries and thousands of square miles of geography. By late February of 1947, only 471 soldiers were known to be buried in isolated locations. There were many more than this of course, but information was only coming in slowly from across the many battlefields. Another 17,858 had been located but unidentified, and 26,117 were not yet located. At war's end, there were 353 American cemeteries dispersed across the landscape of the hostilities. Most of these were temporary, and after the war, they declined from a total of 61 to the 14 that are maintained today by the American Battle Monuments Commission. No Americans would knowingly be left in the country of a former enemy.

At the end of hostilities, the recovery program for the MIAs began. German military burials of Allied personnel numbered more than 12,000. Civilians, such as the church in Oberhof, interred another 6,000.[39] Many of these were aircrews who fell to their death miles from major land battles or soldiers who were killed in small skirmishes. And while the majority of the Americans killed in action would be found in Western Europe, many airmen fell in countries in Central and Eastern Europe. Many of the countries where they fell would come under Communist control after the war, and access to their burial sites was not granted. Presumably Bill's death falls into this first category. The procedures to establish identity were spelled out in the regulations:

  - *An identity or "dog tag" is proof only if found around the neck of the deceased*
  - *A soldier's or airman's pay book is considered proof*
  - *Emergency Medical tags*
  - *Identification bracelets on wrists*
  - *Signed statements of identity*

As we searched the documentation for any clues of what had happened to Bill Lewis, another possibility came to mind. The translation of the German KU report indicated that no identification was found, and also tells us that the condition of the remains may have made recovery difficult if not impossible. The Army, faced with legions of MIA cases, and the increasing difficulty of gaining access to Russian controlled regions after the war, may have opted to withhold the details from Eleanor. It would have served no purpose to give her all of the information contained in the KU document. There are no records of her asking for recovery of her husband's remains. Perhaps she was resigned to the fact that having him buried in his home made little difference. All of these things were speculation, and the truth, when it came, would be far more fascinating.

In his analysis of the documentation, Jan had discovered an item in the files that referred to an International Red Cross document called simply P.O.W. list US2394/Casualty Message No. 293188. This document itself was never found by Jan or myself, despite requests to various agencies. It was said to refer to the recovery *"of an unknown deceased pilot from a Mustang aircraft, which was shot down on 11 September 1944, at approximately 11:35 near Oberhof, Germany."*

On October 18, 1944, the German Government sent this document to the International Red Cross. Again, tantalizing clues to the possible identity of the pilot, and an exact location, but no further progress toward Bill's recovery.

Jan and I had the idea that remains might have been recovered from the wreck, and later transported to an American Military cemetery in Europe, where they could have been buried as an unknown. This document, had it ever been found, might have told us more than we knew to date.

Some months before, Jan had suggested that I order the Individual Deceased Personnel File (IDPF) for Bill Lewis. The IDPF is a special document that details the process of the search for MIAs. It also gives the details of the reburial and the steps taken to carry out that part of the process. An IDPF existed for every missing and recovered member of the US military. We did not believe that having access to this document would tell us any more than we knew about Bill's status as an MIA, but we wanted to read it to find out just what might have occurred during the post-war years and how the process worked. We felt it might be useful to know the steps involved, and possibly to determine why Bill's resting place was not found in the years after the war.

In August of 2001, the long awaited letter in response to the request for Bill's IDPF finally arrived. The news was bad. There was a file with Bill's name on it in the IDPF section, but the file was empty. The young lady who worked for the Army Personnel Command called me within a few days to explain. They had no idea where his file might be located. There were some handwritten notes in the file, with the notation, *"local request, Edward Giller"* and the date, 1979. Later, I searched the database of World War II missing and dead in the American Battle Monuments Commission database on the Web. This search revealed that there were 26 service members with the name William Lewis killed during World War II. One of these was an Army Air Corps pilot with the name of William Martin Lewis, killed in January of 1945. Was it possible that someone had removed the information in our Bill Lewis's file and mistakenly replaced it in another? The missing file, and the possibilities it represented, would continue to vex us for a long time.

At this point in our search, we were thoroughly frustrated. It seemed that although we knew much more, we were unable to progress any further. Our research efforts were at a dead end. Without help from a government agency, we had little hope of achieving our goal. We were certain that a recovery of Bill's remains could be accomplished, but we were helpless to move things forward. We simply had run out of ideas.

We waited for any response from the Air Attaché at the Berlin Embassy. After several months with no response on obtaining per-mission for an excavation in Germany, we turned our efforts to other directions. One of the items that seemed promising was the shoe found in the wreckage. Jan had planned to bring the shoe on his trip to the US in September. He would be visiting the 100th Bomb Group for

The shoe sole found by Petr Frank and Jan during their first visit to the crash site.

their reunion. We wondered if the shoe might be a way to identify the crash site as authentic.

As in the other moments of breakthrough in the search, the next breakthrough came suddenly, and was quite unexpected. My wife, Yvonne, had noticed an article in the Houston newspaper. This story concerned an Air Force group in San Antonio, Texas. This group was assisting the US Army Central Identification Laboratory in Hawaii with identification of Korean War and Vietnam MIA cases. They specialized in flight equipment, items such as life vests, parachutes, boots, and survival kits. When these items were found in the vicinity of a crash or with remains, this group verified their authenticity. They had acquired remarkable amounts of information on suppliers of this equipment, construction, and specifications. My wife suggested that I send them an e-mail and tell them of our search. I rejected this at first, assuming they would be only interested in Korea and Vietnam era searches. She made the suggestion again, and this time I agreed. I fired off an e-mail, expecting nothing. When the phone rang a few days later, I was pleasantly surprised. The caller identified himself as Elton Hudgins. Hudgins was one of the principal investigators at the USAF Life Sciences Laboratory, and he was interested in Bill's case. He cautioned that he would not proceed unless he first obtained permission from CILHI, the US Army

Central Identification Laboratory in Hawaii. I contacted Jan, telling him that this was the most promising thing that had happened yet. More importantly, it came at a time when we were all at a psychological low point, and it gave us a renewed sense of purpose and hope of finding Bill's remains. CILHI had standing agreements to excavate in most of the countries where World War II missing could be found. They did not require the permission we had sought. They had several teams in Korea and Vietnam, but since the fall of the Communist bloc countries, they had increased their activity in Central and Eastern Europe and now spent a significant amount of their efforts on World War II recoveries in those areas. Elton passed on my e-mail to members of the CILHI Headquarters in Hawaii, and I forwarded all the pertinent items of the search for Bill to them.

CILHI is the field branch of the Total Army Personnel Command responsible for Casualty and Memorial Affairs Operations. Their mission is to search for, identify, and repatriate the remains of American military that are missing in action. Their scope is worldwide, and they work on behalf of MIA's in World War II, Korea, Cold War combat actions and Vietnam. At the time of their involvement in Bill's case in the fall of 2001, they had been making arrangements for a spring conference in 2002, to be held in Strasbourg, France. The purpose was to meet with the numerous aviation and military researchers in Europe and enlist their capable help in searching for World War II remains. (Before this book was printed, CILHI was absorbed into the Joint POW/MIA Accounting Command and is now a part of that larger organization.)

All this time, I was curious about the name of Edward Giller in the single piece of paper in Bill's IDPF file. I went back to Peter Randall's excellent database of the Eighth Air Force, which I had found on the Internet earlier. Edward Giller was a Major during World War II. He had flown in combat with the 55th Fighter Group during Bill's service. One evening, I decided to do a search for his name on the Internet. I came up with a biography of Major General Edward Giller, outlining his early service in the 55th and his training toward a Ph.D. in Engineering after the war. He had retired in New Mexico as head of the USAF Special Weapons Program. The website at Switchboard.com provided the next surprise. There was an Edward Giller in Albuquerque. I told the voice on the other end of the phone that I was looking for Major General Edward Giller. *"Speaking,"* he boomed back. Unfortunately he was unable to spend much time with me, since he was on his way to visit his wife, who was recovering from heart surgery. But he did want to hear my story, and offered to talk in a few days. When he called back, I asked him if he remembered requesting Bill's file. He said that he had no reason to request it, and could not remember having done so. He also said, *"People have been trying to find Bill Lewis for a long time."* He had been on leave during the time of the September 11th mission. When he returned, his squadron mates of the 343rd told him that he had missed a big fight, with lots of claims of Me 109s shot down. I told him what I was doing and with whom I had been communicating, and he said they were the right people — they knew the details and could provide help.

During the wait for Bill Lewis's IDPF file, I had obtained another file, the IDPF of Lt. Kenneth Crawford, who flew in Bill's squadron and was killed on the same day. Our logic in requesting this file was because we thought that somewhere in the document there might be a reference to an unknown airman killed in the area on the same day. Jan had recommended that we obtain this file to cross check and make certain there could have been no confusion of the identification of the remains. It was through this file, and another requested later on an unrelated case, that I came to a much better understanding of the process of post-war identification and recovery. The US Army Quartermaster Corps is the branch responsible for the logistical support of its members. It is also the branch responsible for the final act of an Army for its members.

The Quartermaster Branch was very busy in postwar Europe. With nearly 500,000 dead, and another 78,000 missing worldwide, a prime objective was recovery and identification of the remains. The first part of the process began with the names of the known missing. Even something so seemingly simple had to be checked and double-checked. Men with the same names had to be carefully eliminated. The Army serial number became the key identifier in establishing status, and finding of Dog Tags was often the only available method in proving a soldier's identity. In areas where there were multiple casualties in the same terrain, special care would be taken to make sure the remains were not commingled. The Quartermaster Branch established a presence in the occupied and liberated areas. One of their first tasks was to either employ native speakers of French, German, Czech, etc., in the various countries, or to assign soldiers who spoke that language to the various Quartermaster Corps units. As these people were assigned, their task was to canvass the churchyards and cemeteries all over the continent, looking for graves of soldiers. Requests were sent out through the Army of Occupation to every village and town in all of the European Theater and to the governments of the countries involved. As many of these graves were found, the MIA cases were resolved, since many men had died with their identification intact, or had been buried with complete identification. A file was assigned to each of the nearly 600,000 killed and missing. Even if the soldier had been buried as identified, the next step was exhumation and examination of remains. In some cases, the equipment on the bodies provided further identification.

This process was a necessarily lengthy one, and well into the late 1940s and early 1950s the repatriated bodies of American fighting men were being returned to final resting places in the United States or at least on American owned soil in the US Military Cemeteries in Europe.

The IDPF files gave us a remarkable look at the detail of the attempts to identify US MIAs. They included dental charts, physical descriptions, expected articles of clothing, in general, anything that might be useful in determining the identity of the unknown. Boots of fliers were different from those of Infantry, and clothing was also a useful aid. Laundry marks found on the clothing were noted. Personal items such as rings or watches were sometimes used. The caretakers of cemeteries, physicians, priests and ministers, former German soldiers, were all interviewed in their own language and the files populated with both versions of the interviews, both the native language and an English version. Particular attention was given to the dates of discovery and burial. In the circumstances of single engine airplanes, the time and location of the crash was often the factor that made identification certain. With the crews of bombers, it was of course much more difficult. In the review of one file, I came across a chilling account. A young bomber crewmember had been captured by the local German garrison and was being detained by a corporal in a small town. He had been identified by his Dog Tags as Jewish. When this became known, two SS officers took him by force from the corporal. His body was found days later with a gunshot wound to the head. The file also contains the result of the investigation; the SS officer was identified and located. He was later hanged for his crime.

As these remains were recovered and identified, they were removed from Germany and either repatriated to their relatives in the United States, or buried in one of the American Battle Monuments Commission (ABMC) cemeteries in Holland, Belgium, Luxembourg or France. Many victims who died in the Italian campaigns were buried in the ABMC cemeteries in Italy. No soldier or airman was to be left behind in a country of our one-time enemy.

We know from existing records that the US Army visited Oberhof in 1945-46. We know, too, that they completed the identification of the remains of Lt. Kenneth Crawford, who at that time was buried in the Friedhof in town. We also know that one of the requirements of the process of identifying remains was to convene a board if remains were to be declared unrecoverable, and issue a finding of such. Without a Deceased Personnel File for Bill Lewis, we cannot know if such an event occurred. But it would be odd if the letter of October 1946 to Eleanor Lewis was not known to the search teams, who when they discovered the well marked grave of Lt. Crawford in the Wald Friedhof were then only 3.5 kilometers south of Bill's crash site, and most likely were aware of the action of the 55th over the skies of Oberhof that day. It would be odd, but later events would seem to prove that the searchers who returned for the bodies of Kenneth Crawford and Carl Heleen knew nothing of the crash of Bill's P-51 north of the little town.

It was at this time in the search for Bill Lewis that the events of our own September 11, 2001 tragedy unfolded. I was unable to resist the comparison of the events. Different in scale they may have been, but the eyewitness accounts of the Kovarska incident were eerily similar; planes falling from the sky, bodies and body parts, the sky on fire.

In late October of 2001, Jan mailed the shoe that he and Petr had found at the crash site in March of that year. Jan had commented earlier that the shoe was evidence that the pilot of the Oberhof aircraft was in the plane at the time of the crash. I concurred and sent it to Elton Hudgins, and told him that I had found the numeral "10" stamped into what appeared to be the middle of the sole. The "10" seemed to me a certain indication that the shoe was from an American, since the European sizes use metric equivalents. CILHI contacted me directly later, and said that they wanted the shoe sent to them instead, and that they may not need to do an analysis just yet. I took this to mean that they may be able to use the documentary evidence as proof enough to begin a search.

Though there had been a great deal of progress in a short time, we still had far to go. And there was still a nagging question. Who found Bill's identification and made the cross? Jan had first learned of the site from a former museum cooperator in Germany. That man had told Jan that he believed it was made by an old man who had since died. But he offered no name or contact information. After we returned from Oberhof, Claire and I composed a letter to be sent to several people in the town. These included the Catholic Church, the mayor, the mountain patrol, and others. The letters told of the cross, and the great sentiment we experienced when it was discovered. We were grateful for this act, and the family of Lt. Lewis wished to thank the person who might have done this. Jan and Petr then mailed the letter as an official museum request to at least 20 subjects in the Oberhof area. Only the Catholic Church, which maintained the little chapel and the surrounding Friedhof, responded. They would like to help us, the letter said, but it was not until some time after the war that they took over the management of the cemetery and the chapel. They had no records of any burials there. The mystery deepened; instead of answers there were more questions.

At this point in our efforts, we were truly frustrated. We had written to the military and the state department, contacted many people who might have helped, and we still had only the cross to show for our efforts. But just as in other junctures in our search, we were about to receive a tremendous surprise. Jan and I continued our efforts, telling the story to anyone who might listen, and sending letters to Senators, Embassies, and other government agencies that we thought might help. We were close, but success was elusive.

In early March of 2002, the Individual Deceased Personnel Files for Lts. Kenneth Crawford and K.T. Williams arrived. We had hoped that we might learn more of the events surrounding their discovery and burial, and in doing this, learn if there were any sources of information that we might use to learn what happened to Bill Lewis. Unfortunately, there was no information in those files we might have used to learn more of Bill's crash. There had been a German Army hospital in Oberhof during the war. One of the nurses, named Annie Goetz, had been interviewed after the war. She recalled Lt. Crawford, as he had been brought in to the hospital in critical condition. There was another American, an Infantry soldier, brought there in April of 1945, as the war was waning. But there was no mention and apparently no knowledge of the crash of Bill's plane, which had occurred just 3.5 kilometers from the center of the town. The files did seem to confirm an earlier belief that access to the area would have been difficult in the postwar years. Even the simple act of disinterring graves clearly marked as those of American military personnel was a time consuming process. American military personnel investigating the MIA's were not given free access to conduct those searches. Even the interview of Miss Goetz had to be arranged with Soviet bureaucrats, and took several months before permission was granted. When it did occur, it could only take place in the presence of two Russian officers.

Houston, Texas – Strasbourg, France
March 22, 2002

In early February, I received an e-mail from Paul Patist in the Netherlands. Paul is a Police Officer in the coastal town of Castricum who has an abiding interest in the history of World War II, and especially aviation. He has worked diligently to assist families in the recovery

The table containing the file in Jan's room at the Hilton Strasbourg.
He copied nearly the entire contents of the file that evening.

of their loved ones, and I connected with Paul originally through Jan. He quickly proved helpful in the Lewis case, and we began a collaborative effort on a case he had been working on for some time, involving Adrian Caldwell of Tupelo, Mississippi, the daughter of a B-17 crewmember lost off the coast of Grevelingen Bay in Holland. The e-mail concerned a conference to be sponsored by CILHI, to be held in Strasbourg, France beginning March 22nd. Paul had wondered if I might be interested in attending. It proved impossible because of work, but I wrote to the Army Major planning the conference and suggested that CILHI invite Jan in my place, thinking it would be easier for him to attend. Generous support from the 100th Bomb Group Foundation allowed Jan and Petr Frank to attend the conference. It was planned that Jan would provide CILHI with the complete results of his research on Bill's case and explain to them how he found the Oberhof crash site. The conference would begin on March 21 and conclude on March 24, 2002. Late Friday afternoon, the 22nd of March, I was preparing to leave my office when the e-mail came through. It proved to be as sudden and stunning a development as we had ever had in the search. Jan wrote, *"Things are much more clear and (there is) also much more "fog" than before."*

Among the attendees at the conference was the civilian director of the US Army Memorial Affairs Activity-Europe, Mr. David Roath.

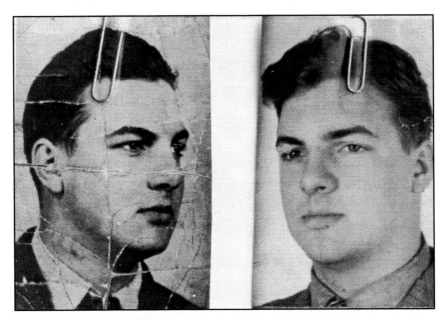

Bill Lewis's escape photos. Jan was stunned to discover these in the first page of the file loaned to him by David Roath. He had been certain that the file must have been that of another airman named Lewis.

A significant historical photo. The wreckage pile at Bill Lewis's crash site was photographed by Adelbert Wolf in the first few years after the crash. Note the amount of wreckage and the cross resting on the tree.

Paul Weiß   DDR 606 Zella-Mehlis/Thür., am 16. Mai 1972
                                               Kohlenmagazin !

     Herrn
     LeRoy J. Schindler
0-6000 Frankfurt/Main

     Homburgerlandstr. 75

          Sehr geehrter Herr S c h i n d l e r !

Ihr Schreiben vom 18. 4. d.J. erhielt ich am 25. v.M. Kaum eine
Stunde später war ich schon bei Herrn Adalbert Wolf, um die von
Ihnen gewünschte Auskunft zu erbitten. Herr Wolf ist 72 Jahre alt,
ein großer Naturfreund, verbrachte den größten Teil in den Wäldern
und kennt die ganze Gegend wie seine Westentaschen. Da es Herr
Wolf sehr genau nimmt, und von jedem Lichtbild, welches Sie sehr
interessieren dürfte, nur eins hatte, gab er diese zu einem
Fotografen zur Neuanfertigung. Diese soll er heute erhalten, so
daß ich hoffentlich noch heute diesen Brief absenden kann. -
Aus diesem Grunde konnte ich nicht früher antworten, entschuldigen
Sie bitte die Verzögerung.-
Herr Wolf konnte mir folgendes mitteilen:
Am 11. September 1944 (es war ein Montag) hörte ich,daß in der
Gegend von Oberhof ein Luftkampf stattfand, auch konnte ich sehen,
daß zwei Mann mit Fallschirm absprangen. Ob es sich dabei um
Amerikaner oder Deutsche handelte, weiß ich nicht. Mehrere Tage
später durchstreifte ich die Gegend, wo der Wald ca zur Hälfte
mit dichten, halbhohen Bäumen bewachsen war, so daß genaues Durch-
suchen unmöglich war. Erst in den 50er oder 60er Jahren wurde der
Wald durch Ausforstung lichter.
Ich fand unter einer Platte einen Fuß, Knochen, Fleischreste, eine
Armbanduhr, eine Antenna-Mast Nr. 104-A und viele Flugzeugteile.
Die Uhr stand ca 20 Minuten vor 12 Uhr (11.40 Uhr). Zuerst nahm
ich diese Uhr an mich, habe sie aber dann weggeworfen, da ich im
Elternhaus selbst Amerikaner hatte und Unannehmlichkeiten zu
fürchten hatte.- Das Armband fand ich ca 8 Tage später. Ich habe
damals die menschlichen Reste in die Erde gebettet, Steine darüber
gelegt, die Flugzeugteile auf einen Haufen gelegt und Lichtbilder
davon angefertigt. Vor ca 14 Tagen konnte ich mich davon überzeu-
gen, daß die Teile noch so liegen. Ich habe versucht, Blumen dort
anzupflanzen, aber sie verdorrten alle, sicher war an der Stelle
sehr viel Benzin oder Öl ausgelaufen.-Auch ein Versuch im letzten
Herbst, Lubinen wachsen zu lassen, mißlang.-
Ein Naturfreund von mir fand später die Erkennungsmarke mit dem
Namen William Lewis jr. (Chikago kann ich nicht beschwören).Diese
Erkennungsmarke wurde auf der hiesigen Polizei abgegeben. Der
fragliche Naturfreund ist inzwischen verstorben.- Der Name
William Lewis ist mir - trotz der verflossenen 28 Jahre - nicht
aus dem Gedächtnis gekommen.-Eine Kopie des damals gefundenen
Lichtbildes habe ich an das Internationale Kreuz in Genf per
"Einschreiben" geschickt, die Quittung der Post besitze ich noch.
Aus Flugzeugmaterial u. Flugzeugglas hatte ich einen Rahmen dazu
angefertigt. Ich bat das Rote Kreuz, mir nicht direkt zu schreiben,
sondern sich bei Verwandten in der Schweiz nach mir zu erkundigen,
Letztere gaben mir Nachricht, daß mein "Einschreiben" angekommen

*One of the letters found in the folder provided by David Roath. It was written in 1972
by Paul Weiss, a friend of Adelbert Wolf from Zella-Mehlis. Addressed to US officials,
it provided answers to the questions about the cross and how Bill's identity was determined after the crash. This message was the first official contact between Adelbert
Wolf and US military authorities.*

This group is responsible for mortuary services of active duty members of the US military killed in Europe, often in training accidents. A collateral duty of the group is to assist in the recovery of remains from World War II. Jan said that David Roath approached him the first day of meetings and told him that he had information about William Lewis. Jan's first reaction was that the information concerned the other pilot named William Lewis who was still missing. Still, he thought he should pursue it further just to make sure, and they met after the day's formal sessions in the hotel bar. David presented the folder to Jan and Petr. The first thing they saw was a small photo of a man in civilian clothes that they recognized immediately as Bill Lewis. Another photo showed the crash site and the cross, clearly visible on a tree, just as they had seen it on their visit to Oberhof. A third photo showed an older man. The pile of wreckage was clearly visible, though much larger than Jan and Petr found on their visit. Clearly, this was a breakthrough. Jan and Petr's spirits were lifted. All of their efforts had been suddenly and dramatically rewarded.

Clarksville, Arkansas
November 1971

Jesse Thompson, the retired fighter pilot and the first American to learn of the Lewis crash site in detail. He worked for many years to repatriate Bill's remains.

In the town of Clarksville in Northwest Arkansas, Jesse D. Thompson was making preparations for a trip to Germany. The 54 year old retired fighter pilot and West Point graduate was pursuing one of his keen interests. Born in 1917 in Durwood, Oklahoma, he had begun a lifelong interest in flying while a young boy, helping barnstorming pilots to maintain their airplanes and often flying along as a helper on their trips. He had long been interested in another pursuit, that of target shooting. To that end he would travel to Germany to interview a man named Paul Weiss, a former employee of the famous Walther pistol factory in Zella-Mehlis. An avid reader and collector of books both on aviation and weapons, his interest now was in compiling a manuscript describing the history and craft of German target weapons.

Houston, Texas
April 2002

Some weeks later, I had the opportunity to view the archival information provided to Jan by David Roath. The documents in the folder revealed some things we could never have imagined. This folder had been in existence since 1971. Its contents proved as remarkable as anything we had yet seen in our search for Bill Lewis. At 2400 hours on November 11, 1971, the duty officer at the US Army Mortuary System received a telephone call from Jesse Thompson. Thompson was returning via military aircraft from Frankfurt, and he wished to report something that had happened in Zella-Mehlis. Mr. Weiss stated that he wished Lt. Col. Thompson to meet a man named Adelbert Wolf. Wolf had a story to tell. He had been walking in the woods after the air battle and discovered the crash site. He and a friend had recovered the airman's ID card, which stated that his name was William Lewis or Levis. He had also found the watch the pilot was wearing at the time of the crash, which had stopped at 1140 hours, and some escape photos of Bill Lewis in civilian clothes. He had later buried the scattered remains, and had taken care of the grave ever since that Monday in September, 28 years ago. He had notified authorities, he said, but nothing had been done. Born July 17, 1900, he was getting old, and he wanted the Americans to come and give the young airman a proper burial in his own country. Thompson did not visit the gravesite, and Wolf told him that he was the only one who knew its location. Cor-

Adelbert Wolf's identification photo, taken in 1943 and 1972.

respondence for Herr Wolf was arranged through Paul Weiss, who spoke and wrote English quite well. The follow-up reports were sent directly to the Commander of 7th Army in Europe and the Commanding General of US Army, Europe. It was formally requested that a team visit the area with the objective of effecting a recovery of remains. The documentary trail shows clearly that three investigations had been carried out in the Oberhof area since the end of the war in 1945, with negative results. No one seemed to know of the existence of the wreckage just 3.5 kilometers north of the town. In 1953, the forester who claimed to be a witness to the crash was interviewed. He stated that he had indeed seen the crash site, but there were no recognizable body parts except perhaps bits of flesh and blood, a portion of a finger and toes. There was nothing he said, to be buried.

In 1972, as the dialogue between Adelbert Wolf and the US military continued, the Army anthropologist in Frankfurt prepared a letter with questions for Paul Weiss to relay to Adelbert Wolf. He asked him very specifically what the remains he buried looked like, how large were they, and whether or not he saw any dental remains which could be useful in establishing an identity. Adelbert Wolf replied a month later through his friend Paul Weiss. This letter clarified the events and provided more detail. He had not seen the crash when it occurred, but he did see two parachutes descending in the general area around Oberhof. It was several days later that he found the wreckage, and with it, scattered over a large area, several remains. The watch, he noted again, had stopped at 1140. About eight days later, he returned to the site and buried the remains, laying stones on top, and collected the aircraft parts in a pile and took pictures. He had tried to grow Lubinen flowers on the grave, he said, but nothing would grow there. Later, a friend of his found the Dog Tags, and gave them to the local police. For 28 years he said, he did not forget that name. He even sent a copy of one of the photographs he found to the Red Cross in Geneva, by Registered Mail. He had relatives in Switzerland, and he requested the Red Cross contact them. He kept a copy of the receipt framed in his house, but no one ever came to look for the grave. He was unaware of the recovery operations and the visits to the Oberhof area by the US Army that took place in the 1940s, just after the war's end.

A subsequent letter revealed that the aluminum fragments collected over time were close to where Bill's remains had been buried, if not the precise location of the grave of Bill Lewis. And there was a puzzling statement. He wrote that the pictures, when found, seemed to have a bullet hole *"on the right side."* Neither the translator at the time nor anyone who recently viewed this statement can understand what he meant. The pictures do seem to have a circular defect or flap, which could have been caused by a small caliber bullet. It is possible that he surmised the pictures were carried in the left pocket of a uniform shirt, and the small hole in both pictures indicated they were in the same pocket. He also revealed that he and Mr. Wolf had found a number of cartridge cases, which seemed to be about 20 mm in diameter at their base. These would almost certainly be from a Browning .50 caliber machine gun of the type used in the P-51, and recent research indicates that these cartridges had been manufactured in the Des Moines, Iowa munitions plant during World War II. Subsequent discoveries of cartridges at the crash site indicated that some were also made in the St. Louis munitions plant.

Herr Adelbert Wolf had added a poignant comment. Would it be possible for someone to send him a photo of the home where the Lewis family lived, and maybe he could contact them to tell them how he had cared for their son?

Over the next months and well into the winter of 1972, there was a flurry of activity. The US State Department made a formal request to send a recovery team into the woods above Oberhof, again with no results. The Commander of the US Military Liaison Mission in Berlin became involved, and the process continued into 1975 with no action taken. Jesse Thompson must have been frustrated. Here was compelling evidence of the grave of a lost flier. He contacted the Air Force Museum and also his Congressional Representative, John Hammerschmidt, who in turn contacted the Army again. This went on for some years with no apparent results. It was in 1978 that the contact with Adelbert Wolff was apparently lost. Letters to him were returned. He had apparently died in the winter of that year, or so we thought. Adelbert Wolf actually died in 1984, but there were other reasons why the letters may not have been answered. In addition to the file documents and pictures, there exists a picture of three men, one of whom is certainly Adelbert Wolf, a second man who appears to be a US Air Force Lt. Colonel, and a third man in the uniform of a US Air Force Captain. The picture was taken in the winter, as there is an abundance of snow in the scenes. We know clearly from these pictures that the site was identified and that the US Military knew of Bill's crash site. They also knew that remains were recovered from the wreckage. Later investigation would determine that the picture was taken in November or December 1979, when the United States Military Liaison Mission in Berlin sent a team of investigators to the site.

The US Military Liaison Mission (US MLM) was a small and unusual unit. In postwar divided Germany, zones of control were established between the Allied powers and the Russian military. By formal agreement, the United States and Soviet missions were established in April 1947. In the early years, their functions were essentially to keep track of the disarmament of the German military. That objective established, the units began to keep track of each other's military. In a sense, they were *"legal"* spies. The actual document establishing the missions states that *"each member of the missions will be given ... permanent passes ... permitting complete freedom of travel, whenever and wherever it will be desired over territory and roads in both places, except places of disposition of military units, without escort or supervision."* That was the theory at least, but as the Cold War developed, it became more challenging for the members to travel in East Germany. Each zone, east and west, had a liaison mission. The Soviet mission was established in Frankfurt, in the American zone. The American mission was given quarters in Neu Fahrland, near Potsdam in the Russian zone. From 1951 through 1957, the USMLM was involved in recovery of many missing Allied soldiers and airmen from World War II. Over 130 sites were investigated, with a substantial number of these resulting in recoveries of American soldiers and airmen. All this changed in April of 1957. At that time, the Soviet mission ceded authority to grant MIA searches to the East German government, citing their status as a sovereign power. Thus it happened that when the issue of recovery of the remains of Bill Lewis came about, precedent had already been set. Despite the attempts by the USMLM and other agencies to obtain permission, only two visits were allowed. The Commander of the USMLM at the time even notified the Russian Mission Commander that it was not necessary for a US team to make the recovery. A qualified Russian team would be acceptable to the US. This did not occur. Despite the fact that the document record does not indicate any further contact after the initial series of communications, there was clearly communication between Adelbert Wolf and someone from the US military, and that contact resulted in a visit. It is almost certain that Germany's Internal Security Police (STASI) monitored the meeting.

It is also possible that letters to Adelbert Wolf from the US Army were intercepted. The recently declassified mission history of the USMLM indicates that the Oberhof issue had been escalated to the Ambassador level in the State Department. But from the time of that visit in November of 1979 until March of 2001, for another 22 years, the case languished among the mountains of paper in the archives. The East German government never granted permission for the team to conduct a proper investigation and recovery of remains.

"Duty, Honor, Country"

Most people who encountered what Jesse Thompson did would have made the report and let the matter fall. Jesse Thompson was not to be deterred. The former fighter pilot had an unfailing sense of duty and an enduring persistence. The file found in the US Army Memorial Affairs Activity (USAMAA) reveals a trail of intense activity on the part of Jesse Thompson. Had he not been so committed in his actions, the file would have ended with his phone call to the USAMAA facility in November of 1971. Most people would have made the phone call and considered their duty done. Instead, his determination and persistence created an undeniable trail of evidence and kept the matter alive, which resulted in the official visit by the Army to the crash site in November of 1979. For Jesse Thompson, the United States Military Academy motto of *"Duty, Honor, Country"* was more than a slogan.

Jesse Thompson was probably not alone in his frustration. Adelbert Wolf had waited 27 years, from 1944 to 1971, to make contact with the Americans. Then from 1971 to 1979, he waited eight more years. In 1979, when the visit with the official American group finally occurred, he was 79 years old. He must have been told of the difficulties in obtaining a recovery of Bill Lewis's remains. It may have been then that he made the cross, as it appears in the photo, and placed it above the wreckage in the hopes that someone might be able to find the crash site after he died.

The strange case of the disappearance of Lt. William M. Lewis and the even stranger discovery of his crash site had more in store for us, however. I had found an address for Jesse D. Thompson, who along with Adelbert Wolf had worked so faithfully and diligently during the 1970s to bring a fallen comrade home. I wrote a letter to the address, and a few days later, his wife Dorothy telephoned me. Jesse Thompson had been stricken with Alzheimer's disease and could not contribute any more to our knowledge of the case, but she said he had been a fighter pilot in the 55th Fighter Group. She thought that he had been in a different squadron than the 38th, and had not known Bill. This was a surprise. But later, as I checked my 55th Fighter Group rosters and reference documents, there it was. Jesse Thompson had in fact been a member of the 38th Fighter Squadron, in the same Group and Squadron that Bill flew in when he died. Jesse himself had been shot down in March of 1945 over France. Serendipity? Coincidence? Something greater?

Jan recalled that on the evening of March 22nd in Strasbourg, he was overwhelmed and shocked by the discovery of the file. I quickly e-mailed him and told him that I could think of no better person to represent the family of Bill Lewis, and congratulated him on the finally realized fruits of his efforts.

Now, we had finally learned the name of the mysterious person who made the small cross for Bill, but we had also learned that Bill's remains might be in the area. We were excited at our progress and with the many answers we now had, but were also aware that there were still many questions to be answered. Claire was home when I returned from work, and we decided to call Sharon right away. She was speechless when she heard the news, and somewhat quiet after she was told. A few hours later she called again, and this time she was crying and troubled. She clearly understood the meaning of this discovery. The remains of her father had been found and clearly identified, and their resting place well marked. In 1972, both her mother and grandmother were alive. Sharon was grieving for them. She spoke through tears as she related her feelings to me. *"The Army knew where he was, but someone made a mistake. I can't imagine how my grandmother felt, with Ted gone, and knowing Bill would never come home, but never knowing what had happened to him, and where, and how. All these years he could have been brought home, and given the honor of a burial."* I understood how she felt, but also felt that unless we had a chance to see the file, we could not be certain of the events surrounding the mistake and how it happened. As we discovered what had transpired in the search for Bill, we realized the irony of the situation. Bill Lewis had been truly lost for only two days, from the time of his crash until September 13, 1944. Since Adelbert Wolf took his walk in the woods along the slopes of the Greifenberg, the whereabouts of the remains of Lt. William Lewis had been known. It was a sad revelation.

Claire had another perspective, which no one had thought of. The situation in East Germany in 1971-1972 was one of oppression. The maker of the cross, when he decided to contact the US Army, took a huge risk. Such things were not done in the East, and getting such a document out would have been difficult and dangerous.[40] The East German internal security police (STASI) built a huge network of formal and informal spies, many of who kept watch on neighbors and even their own family members. It was very likely that Adelbert Wolf had risked much to attempt to honor this American pilot and close the circle of loss for his family.

I thought that Claire's idea was probably correct. The documents in the file indicated that Adelbert Wolf made several attempts to get the US Army to visit the site. The East Germans denied permission, and his repeated attempts certainly placed him in danger. It is very possible that the file was limited in distribution to those with a need to know so that his identity was protected. Although some official diplomatic efforts took place, the final notes in the USAMAA file indicated that if no permission would be given, the case was to be closed as *"non-recoverable status."* That is precisely what happened. Despite the knowledge that the case could have been pursued with probable success, and the intense efforts by Adelbert Wolf, Jesse Thompson, and Paul Weiss, the case was finally abandoned.

Immediately after the Strasbourg conference, Petr Frank and Jan went to the American Military Cemetery in Luxembourg. They viewed the Wall of the Missing, where the name of William Lewis was inscribed, and where some of the airmen killed on the Ruhland mission were buried. They returned to Strasbourg several days later to meet three CILHI officers who would accompany them to Oberhof to view the crash site. The senior of the officers, Captain Octave MacDonald, took GPS positions and photographed the site. He was able to tell Jan that as a result of the research Jan had presented, and upon viewing the site, he felt there was a high probability that an attempt at recovering the remains would be made in the near future. During April and May 2002, the CILHI researchers in Hawaii went through the documentation concerning the loss of Bill Lewis. They reviewed the information in the old file held by David Roath, and compared it with the information contained in Jan's research. It was during this time that Captain Octave McDonald notified Jan and me that the CILHI mission was finally confirmed, and his team would arrive in Oberhof in late June or early July to begin the recovery operations. In just a little more than 17 months, it seemed that we were finally about to reach our objective.

Kovarska, Czech Republic and Oberhof, Germany
June 2002

On June 3rd of 2002, Sharon and her husband Villere left for France, Germany and the Czech Republic. Their plan was to visit Paris first where they would observe their 20th anniversary, then meet Jan and Petr Frank in Kovarska, visit the Museum, and then follow them to Oberhof, where Sharon wished to see the site before CILHI and the Army team and the Museum volunteers would begin the recovery mission one month later. Villere's son Casey had completed a semester in Spain and would meet Jan in Prague and then go with him to Kovarska to meet Sharon and Villere. They arrived at the Museum in

Sharon and Casey Cross talk with Jan during their visit to the museum in Kovarska.

Kovarska on June 8th, where they learned a great deal about the battle in general. The following day, they traveled to Oberhof, some 100 miles to the west, to visit the site where Bill died. It would prove to be an emotionally charged occasion. I would have the first hint of how emotional it was in an e-mail from Jan.

"I am unable to tell you what I have in my soul and heart after days spent with Sharon and her family. It was so wonderful time, often so sad, but great. I am so thankful I had the opportunity to meet Sharon and again-to be included in this great story. Sharon is so beautiful lady and Petr and me naturally were 'hit' by her charisma. We so much understand each other, also as with Villere and Casey. I can tell you what happened, but I am unable to tell what I have in my thumping heart ..."

Sharon's anxiety at visiting the site was relieved as she contemplated the setting. *"If you had to die in a horrific crash, that would be the place, because it's just beautiful."* She completed her visit by placing flowers and an American flag at the site.

Sharon and Villere came over for dinner a few days after they returned. She had called to tell me that the trip was *"a high point of my life."* Her experiences were much as Jan had described, very emotional,

Sharon in a moment of reflection while at the museum. She was troubled by the fact that she had known so little of her father in childhood, and that her mother and grandmother had died without knowing Bill's fate.

but also very satisfying. They went first to Kovarska, where they toured the museum and the area around the town where the planes fell on September 11, 1944. Sharon had paused before an exhibit dedicated to Bill. There was a picture of Sharon and Eleanor, and next to it a picture of Bill in uniform. Petr and Jan had discussed what might happen at this moment. They understood what this might mean for Sharon. Their emotions ran high as they anxiously watched her standing before the exhibit. As she viewed the photos taken in the Greifenberg forest and the torn pieces of the airplane her father flew, the tears began.

After the group had been there for some time, two small Czech boys came into the museum. Jan told Sharon that they often came and worked around the museum, helping in various chores. She asked Jan to tell them that the baby in the picture was she, and the man and woman were her father and mother. The boys listened intently, then left. One of them, Jan Jelinek, returned, and came up to Sharon and touched her arm, then held out his hand. He had come back with a gift. It was a tiny carved wooden airplane, so small that it fit into the palm of his hand.

The next event was a dedication of the day to Sharon, and she was asked to speak before reporters and the Mayor of Kovarska, who presented her with a gift. It was a pair of cups and saucers, made of Czech porcelain. When Sharon returned home, she deliberated about where she could put them. Some years ago, her stepfather and stepmother had given her a porcelain coffee server and cream and sugar bowls. She thought they looked similar. When she placed them next to the coffee server, she found the pattern was identical. On the bottom of all the objects was the stamp, *"made in the Czech Republic."* The same company that had made the coffee server made them.

Sharon composed an open letter to the volunteers and read it to the assembled group in Kovarska. It reads in part:

> *How do I thank someone who has reunited me with my father after 57 years? How do I express my gratitude to people who have honored my father as a hero, although virtually unknown to them, except for one brief moment in history?*

June 9, 2002: Sharon places a flag and white roses at the crash site. Though the site had not officially been confirmed as the place where Bill had been killed, Sharon was certain that this was the place her father perished.

Casey Cross, Villere and Sharon examine .50 cal. ammunition found in the crash crater.

I never knew my father, Bill Lewis. I was only six months old when he was lost. I have no memories except those given to me by my mother and grandmother. I only knew as a child growing up that my daddy had been killed in the war. Now, I am the only one left. Both my mother and grandmother are gone too. The always-present question of what happened to him has now become a reality, because of all of you.

What a priceless gift.

My children and grandchildren will now learn about a grandfather and great grandfather that was here only for a short while, but whose life made an impact on people across the world. They will learn about people coming together with different backgrounds and beliefs but caring enough to help someone lost so far from home.

I understand a man by the name of Adelbert Wolf found my father's wrecked plane and what remains were left. Together he and a friend Paul Weiss cared for the area for years. I don't believe they are still alive, but to the families of these brave men, I say thank you, thank you. I only hope that one day I can thank them in person for what these wonderful men did for my father.

And then there is my friend Jan Zdiarsky. I'm not sure what you say to this man either. What a remarkable man to follow his heart and dedicate so much of himself to a generation of lost men and brave heroes. His love of history and freedom is remarkable. He really cared about finding a family for Bill Lewis. I will be eternally grateful to him for his love and dedication to these men. Jan — you are my hero.

My love forever to my husband Villere, who has helped me to achieve a life long dream, to find my father. He has been with me through it all, sometimes in the back, but always there to hold me together when the emotions ran almost too high. I love you.

And to all of you here today and yesterday, who had something to do with this miracle, I thank you from the bottom of my heart. I can never know all of you, but I know that your hearts were in the right place and with people like you in the world there has to be Peace for all of us. I am so honored to be here today, you are all Heroes to me.

Sharon, alone with her thoughts at the end of a day of discovery and emotion.

Recovery Element One

Oberhof, Germany
July 5 – August 10, 2002

USACILHI
Recovery Element One
02-1 Germany

Mission

In conjunction with the government of Germany, Recovery Element One conducts excavation operations in Oberhof, VIC 48Q XD 436555 from 5 July 2002 to 10 August 2002 to achieve the fullest possible accounting of Americans unaccounted for as a result of worldwide conflicts.

Site Information

Possible P-51D crash in 1944. Site identified by deceased local witness. Investigated four times immediately following WWII. Site never located. Information linking site to unresolved WWII case.

Loss Information

Possible crashed aircraft was flying as a bomber escort. Aircraft was reported missing 11 September 1944. A local resident reported the site and subsequent remains of a supposed U.S. serviceman and buried in an isolated plot. A significant amount of wreckage was reported at the site.

Such was the introduction to the briefing conducted by Captain Octave MacDonald, a US Army Quartermaster Officer who would be the mission leader, and Sergeant First Class Andrew Garate as they addressed the assembled group of German and Czech volunteers and other government officials prior to starting the physical work. The two young men, both in their early thirties, nevertheless had almost thirty years of military service between them. MacDonald had entered the Army after a year in college at Louisiana State University, dropping out to become an enlisted Medic and qualifying in the Airborne. He returned to college and graduated in 1994, commissioned through the Army Reserve Officer Training Corps at the University of Louisiana in Lafayette.[41] Sergeant First Class Garate had entered at seventeen years of age, right from high school in Arizona. He had served with the 82nd Airborne during Desert Storm, and after the final recovery mission of 2003, he would receive orders back to Fort Bragg, again to the 82nd. Their levels of experience indicated just how much importance the military attaches to recovery missions. The two experienced leaders and their teams would deploy to locations all over the world to find and recover remains of US military personnel. They would operate independently, almost always in places where they did not speak the language, and would have great latitude in the day-to-day utilization of their teams. They would be required to interact with local volunteers, government officials of the country, and media representatives. They must be physically fit, have the sensitivity of a counselor, and the planning skills of a manager. There are few occupations either in the military or in civilian life in which such a combination of skills would be demanded. Captain MacDonald's team would consist of a civilian employee of the Army, Dr. Mark Leney, an anthropologist who would function as Recovery Leader; five Army Mortuary Affairs Specialists; an Army photographer; an Explosives Ordinance Disposal Specialist; a team Medic; and a German civilian who would serve as linguist. Jan Zdiarsky and Petr Frank led a large contingent of Czech volunteers. Included was Milan Duhan, who was the mayor of Kovarska, along with a German volunteer group.

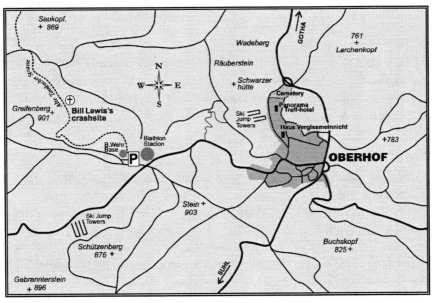

Map of the Oberhof area. The Alte Tambacher Strasse is marked by the - - - - - - - style. The author and his daughter Claire stayed at the Haus Vergissmeinnicht during their April 2001 visit, and Villere and Sharon stayed there on their trip of June 2002. The Panorama Treff was the base for the CILHI recovery team and Czech volunteers during the July - August 2002 recovery operations.

The mission briefing had essentially three objectives. The first was to acquaint the team with the mission in a structured manner familiar to them as military personnel. The other two were to find and recruit volunteers and interview eyewitnesses. Captain MacDonald acquainted the volunteers with the CILHI mission and the procedures they would use and talked with local leaders about the mission, and the linguists/translators were introduced to the assembled team.

If the orders detailing the mission were dry, precise, and bureaucratic, the recovery mission itself would prove to be something perfectly opposed. Some time after the mission had been completed, I received an 18 page single spaced letter and two CDs full of photographs from Jan. The letter had been composed in the weeks after the mission, and instead of technical details of the recovery, it was a journal of the emotions and feelings of the group as they pursued their common goal.

The premise is fascinating in itself. A United States Army team, operating in a foreign country, and a team of volunteers, few of whom know each other, commit to a strenuous work schedule, digging, moving rocks, carrying buckets of dirt and sifting them for clues, to search for the shattered remains of a man none of them ever knew, and who died 58 years earlier.

Jan though, did feel a sense of closeness with Bill. His museum efforts had brought him into contact with survivors and veterans, but this was different. In his efforts, he had come to feel that he knew Bill. In an earlier letter to me, he remarked, *"I can see his eyes, looking at me from Sharon's face."* He had studied the pictures of Bill, and for him this connection was almost tangible. The Museum work had occupied Jan for several years, and his contacts with the veterans had given him an appreciation of their sacrifice that few people of his age would understand. The recovery though, would mark a high point in his efforts to commemorate the men who had fought in World War II.

The volunteers met with Captain MacDonald and his team on the 5th of July and helped them unload the truck with their equipment. Here *"Mac"* introduced his team to the volunteers. Dr. Mark Leney and Sergeant Ken Miller began the first work. Leney would divide the site into archeological grids and establish the *"Datum"* or point of reference to which all other discoveries at the site would be linked. Ken Miller, the Explosives Ordnance Disposal specialist, would begin his searches for ordnance with a metal detector.

On the 6th of July, the briefing was held. Captain Mac was responsible for the overall mission, including liaison with local officials, logistics, and lodging. Sergeant First Class Andrew Garate, a Navajo Native American, would be the work leader. He would oversee the schedules, breaks, team tasks and the daily routine of the group and supervise the work efforts of the volunteers. Mark Leney, a British born PhD, would function as recovery leader. He would supervise the excavation efforts, identify the aircraft parts with assistance from volunteers, and attend to the scientific detail and rigorous protocol required in the recovery. His efforts would include pinpointing the impact crater, determining the distance and depth from the crater that would be excavated, and separating all non-natural objects such as stones and dirt from the diggings and identifying them. To accomplish these tasks, he would employ classical archeological methods. After establishing the grids and datum point, he would examine such things as the strata, or levels of the ground. He would look for evidence of a disturbance in the natural state of the site, such as a layer of ash several inches deep that would indicate a fire. He would establish the dimensions of the debris field, stretching some 300 meters in diameter from the center of impact, and finding ammunition from Bill's .50 caliber machine guns that still ignited after all this time. It was he who would be responsible for writing the scientific report of the effort and proposing a conclusion.

Sgt. Benjamin Bond would serve as team photographer. Sgt. Brandy Anderson would be the only female CILHI team member. Air Force Master Sergeant Dennis Shields would be the team medic. Additional members were Sgts. Travis Ruhl and William Hagins and Specialists Rolando Garcia and Steven Robles, both natives of Puerto Rico.

Matthias Leich, a young German who had been involved in assisting Jan and Petr earlier, would join them for several days of the search. Matthias had helped secure the site from souvenir hunters and would also help in the excavation.

After the briefing on the 6th of July, the physical work began in earnest. Mark Leney instructed the volunteers. One of their first tasks was to dig several small shallow test pits. A total of 15 such pits were dug around the crater made by the impact. The purpose of these was to determine the location of the wreckage field and its limits, and to confirm the presence of disturbed soil layers. Few of these delivered much if any wreckage, and the crater was confirmed as the primary site of debris. As the site was excavated and earth passed down the line to the screens in buckets, they were to set aside any item other than dirt, grass, wood or stones. These would be placed in a single bucket. Jan, along with another US Army Memorial Affairs employee coincidentally named Kenneth Crawford, would attempt to identify

P-51 parts. Jeff Sweffling from the UK had provided a P-51 parts catalog, and this would be used to assist in identification. Paul Patist, who had already made a recovery and identification of a crashed P-51 in Luxembourg, would also assist in the identification of parts, often conferring with Dr. Mark Leney by e-mail as items were recovered. The screens were constructed of a 4-millimeter square mesh. That size would retain any unattached dental remains, which could prove critical in identification of the missing.

The end of each workday involved a session on the road above the crash site for debriefing. Here the assembled group would talk about successes, problems, and logistics such as where to get laundry done, or any other item the team leaders wished to discuss. Back at the hotel, they relaxed at the bar or by swimming in the pool.

The long, arduous days of physical effort and shared hardships, along with the casual evenings over meals and drinks or at the hotel pool, brought the ad hoc coalition together. It was in these sessions that the volunteers and Army personnel learned of each other's personal lives and formed remarkable friendships. It was in these sessions that the group assigned nicknames to each other. The diminutive Jan was dubbed *"Frodo"* by the American team. The Czech's nicknamed Sgt. Andy Garate *"Volodja"* and assigned Russian nicknames to other team members as well. The necessity to communicate between group members who spoke three languages provided some interesting moments. Some spoke only German, others only Czech, others only English. Soon, team members learned who could speak which languages and developed an unofficial protocol for communications.

From the beginning of the physical work, it was evident to the volunteers that the two Army leaders knew both how to work hard and how to have fun doing it. MacDonald and Garate each possessed a sense of humor that meshed nicely with their work ethic.

This mission was different in many ways from the typical missions the team carried out. In Southeast Asia, the missions were more structured events. Host governments often recruited farmers in large groups to work at the sites, and there was typically little contact with the workers. Here though, media coverage in advance of the event alerted people in the towns of Oberhof and Zella-Mehlis and some of the outlying villages. The *Los Angeles Times* sent a reporter to cover the recovery mission and so did the German press and television groups. Captain MacDonald said that one of the curious things was the presence of young people dressed as if they should have been in a punk rock band gathered at the site to ask how they could help as the team approached each day. People in the area were curious. Where

Andy Garate, at left in the crater, supervises the team in the removal of rocks. Each of the large rocks had to be removed manually as the team went deeper into the site.

Buckets of dirt from the crater were carried to the screen and sifted through a 4 mm mesh for artifacts.

did the team come from in America? Why were they here so many years after the war? For whom were they looking? It was all very refreshing to the team to see so many interested in what they were doing. Sergeant First Class Garate noted that though all recovery missions were fulfilling, this one was somewhat supercharged. The teams always study the files regarding the mission's recovery subject. But in almost every case, save a slight few, the families of the MIAs do not know their relative is the objective of the effort. The fact that Sharon had visited the site was not lost on the team. The team all had thoughts about Sharon, and at different times all expressed the interest that if they ever had the chance, they would have liked to meet her. *"We felt that what we were doing was the least we could do to honor Lieutenant Lewis."* Sergeant Garate talked of

Jan Zdiarsky and Jaromir Kohout from the Czech team work to identify an artifact from Bill's P-51.

the gatherings of people each day at the crash site and how they often brought bouquets of flowers. *"It reminded me of the movie 'Field of Dreams.' People just came, non-stop."*

Many of the volunteers were staying at the same hotel in Oberhof, and evening meals were typically spent together as the CILHI soldiers, Czech and German volunteers shared beers and food and planned strategy for the next workday. *"It was a rare opportunity for us to connect on a personal level,"* he said. The energy of the Czech and

Captain Octave "Mac" MacDonald, US Army.
He was responsible for the overall team leadership on the Oberhof mission.

Sergeant First Class Andrew Garate, US Army.
His responsibilities encompassed logistics and work schedules.

German volunteers and curiosity of the local people gave all the team a little extra energy, he recalled. The CILHI team members gave the Kovarska volunteers an honorary nickname. It was "CILKO," for Central Identification Laboratory-Kovarska. All the troops felt the mission was a very positive experience, and knowing the story of Bill Lewis was a personal motivator for each of them.

It was during a working day that a woman and her husband came up to the site. Someone remarked that this woman was an eyewitness to the crash. Jan attempted to practice his German with the lady as she told him, *"My uncle buried someone on this site."* Jan said *"Adelbert Wolf?"* Surprised, she answered yes. Jan showed her his folder with the picture of her uncle as tears began to flow. She came again the next day and brought her own pictures as they shared her memories of her uncle. Later, we would correspond with her in writing and by telephone as she told us more about that September day in 1944 and the events that followed.

One of the elements of such an investigation is to seek out and interview eyewitnesses to the incident. After such a lengthy period, it would seem that few eyewitnesses would present themselves. This was not the case. From the initial work, people came forward in numbers. Some claimed to know where Adelbert Wolf buried the larger remains, others claimed to have seen the crash. None of the reports proved correct. Eyewitness accounts are seldom completely accurate, but taken together, they can often synthesize into a coherent whole by verifying those elements of the story that are correct. The team was obligated to listen to these accounts and record them, no matter how unreliable they might seem. It was during the collection of these accounts that a German man came forward with another story. He knew of a Russian memorial to Bill Lewis. It consisted of a Russian military helmet, a cross of wood, and a Russian military emblem. He had seen this in 1950, about the time the Russians had begun to establish a large military presence in the Oberhof area. The cross was adorned with a white-painted US star, and the helmet was inscribed with Bill's name, a small painted cross, and Bill's date of death. Beneath the cross was what appeared to be a plastic pouch with documents inside, and below that a Russian star with a hammer and sickle emblem, probably from a Russian uniform. This must have been the helmet that Herr Klaus-Roland Müeller described in our initial meeting. None of those items remained when we visited the site with Herr Müeller. This witness proved to be reliable. In fact he had a picture of the small memorial, which he provided to the team. It was another element of the story. We obtained some more facts, but also more

Matthias Leich with Regina Wolf and husband Klaus.
Matthias provided early security for the site.

Petr Frank giving an interview to a German TV station during the recovery operation.

mystery. How did the Russians know these details? Was Adelbert Wolf's cross already in place when the Russians discovered the scene? What happened to the helmet, cross, and emblem? It seemed that every new fact was accompanied by new mystery.

One workday, a German man presented himself to the linguist, Peter Drespa. He identified himself as a former member of the STASI security police in the area. He was aware of the case, and wished to help in any way that he could. STASI officials were aware of the site, he said. During the 1950s, they had expressed concern that the site would become a memorial to the American airman, and were not pleased with this development. They discussed removing the remains, but he did not believe they acted on this.

One of the elements of identification of aircraft from the World War II era is the discovery of the machine guns. Each gun of the six aboard the P-51 had a unique serial number. The contents of the MACR, or missing aircrew report, always included these serial numbers. There was no doubt that this site held the remains of a USAAF aircraft, but it would not be until the discovery of the machine guns with their serial numbers intact that the team could say with certainty that this airplane was the one flown by Bill Lewis. Around

This photograph was provided to the recovery team by a German civilian. The memorial may have been made by Russian soldiers. The Russian emblem is visible just in front of and below the plastic pouch.

the time that the machine guns were found, the serial plate bearing the aircraft serial number was discovered.

The analysis supervised by Mark Leney would reveal a great deal about how the plane crashed, and the last moments of its pilot. At the very center of a compact, compressed mass of metal, the team would find the propeller reducer of the P-51. Weighing perhaps a hundred pounds, the reducer had been shorn of its four propeller blades and lay at the very bottom of the crater. To the left and right were the machine guns, facing nearly vertical downward in the soil. Fragments of the canopy material lay just a few feet from the propeller reducer, indicating the canopy was in place at the time of the crash. Bill had not bailed out or released his canopy in an attempt to bail out. Pieces of each wheel were found in the remains of their respective wings. From this pattern it was clear that the airplane descended nearly vertically, the left wing facing southwest, and impacted with the leading edges of each wing relatively parallel to the earth. We had speculated that Bill might have been killed in the first contact and fallen with his stricken plane from a high altitude. The discovery of some .50 caliber machine gun ammunition seemed to disprove that, however. A spent .50 caliber case was found very close to the crater, and its firing pin was indented. While it was possible that the firing pin could have been struck at the moment of impact, it was also possible that Bill might have been firing his weapons at the time of the crash.

After talking with the recovery team and looking at evidence from other crashes, we decided that some of the ammunition in Bill's plane had fired on impact with the ground. He could not have been the pilot of the 55th who indicated that he was out of ammunition and motioned for another 55th pilot to take over his pursuit of a German fighter. It is likely that this pilot was Kenneth Crawford of the 38th.

Meanwhile, the search for remains continued. The team sifted through the buckets as they came up from the increasingly large and deepening excavation. As they pursued the search in the center of the crater, they began to find bone fragments shattered by the tremendous impact as the P-51 met the earth. The team found remnants of Bill's flight jacket, his life preserver, and a survival compass. Fragments of gun camera film, a military shirt, and a pocketknife were unearthed as the crater yielded its clues. Everything was catalogued, numbered, and photographed for inclusion in the final report.

The site was declared a restricted area, protected by German law. In order to keep it secured during the night, the German Army provided a three-man security team to spend each night protecting the site.

A view of the crash site looking from the cross to the West. The empty space in the foreground was created by the explosion. The impact crater is at the edge of the near tree line, and the Alte Tambacher Strasse is the elevated area in the distance.

The crater as seen from the road, looking down slope. These photos were taken one day before the recovery mission began in July 2002.

Nearly identical view as the previous page, with the mission in full progress.
The team covered the impact crater with a tarpaulin due to rains.
The screens are in the distance behind the flag placed by Sharon.

Looking North toward the crater. In this area and to the right were found
large amounts of the airplane's shattered canopy.

*Andy Garate giving instructions. To his right are Petr Frank,
Steven Robles, and Dennis Shields.*

*Relaxing after a hard day. From left – Andy Garate, "doctor D,"
Brandy, and Mac with new German friends.*

Forensic archeology plan of the Oberhof Recovery Mission
July - August 2002

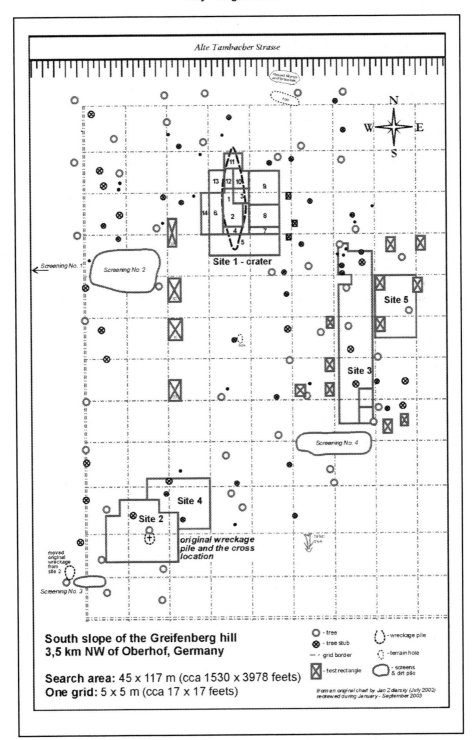

Alte Tambacher Strasse

N
W ● E
S

Site 1 - crater

Screening No. 1
Screening No. 2

Site 5

Site 3

Screening No. 4

Site 4

Site 2

moved original wreckage from site 2

Screening No. 3

original wreckage pile and the cross location

South slope of the Greifenberg hill
3,5 km NW of Oberhof, Germany

Search area: 45 x 117 m (cca 1530 x 3978 feets)
One grid: 5 x 5 m (cca 17 x 17 feets)

○ - tree
⊗ - tree stub
--- - grid border
⊠ - test rectangle

◠ - wreckage pile
◌ - terrain hole
⬭ - screens & dirt pile

from an original chart by Jan Zdiarsky (July 2002)
redrawed during January - September 2003

197

The impact crater at the completion of the mission.
No parts of the airplane were found below these levels.

Each morning the German soldiers watched the recovery team and volunteers negotiate the steep slope from the road down to the crash site. One morning as they arrived, the recovery team and volunteers were surprised to see a gift from their German security team. During the night, the German soldiers had fashioned a staircase made of wood forms filled with dirt. Now, after a hard day of digging the team could make their way up the slope more comfortably. *"Eine Höflichkeit des Herzens."* A courtesy of the heart.

By late July, the work was nearly complete. The archeological technique had exhausted the possibility for further discoveries. The team would replace the dirt and stones and the forest would eventually return to its natural state. Only the cross placed by Jan and Petr would mark this place as a memorial.

Jan remembers the final days as charged with emotion. In a little over a year, and especially in the few months since March of 2002, he had come full circle with his search. Now, as he looked around the site and thought of the successful effort and the friendships he had formed, he was filled with pride and satisfaction. This was something he would never forget.

British-made survival compass found in the wreckage.

All three left wing machine guns were recovered at the west edge of the impact crater.

The propeller spinner in the same position as it was recovered, from the deepest part of the crater.

The team members of Recovery Element One would undertake three more MIA recovery efforts in Europe before returning to Hawaii. After leaving Oberhof, they traveled to Bulgaria, and then on to Luxembourg to search for more World War II MIAs. They parted with their new German and Czech friends as they prepared to search for other missing US casualties. It is an impressive event, this searching for the fallen. Carried out by young soldiers who are ambassadors of the US at the grass roots level, the process can only impress the citizens of those countries in which they search. There is a strong message, too, for those who serve in our military. We will find our fallen and bring them home, no matter where they fell, or how long ago they have been lost.

Houston, Texas and Oberhof, Germany
July – September 2002

July 12 was a Friday, and late that afternoon I received an e-mail message from an Associated Press reporter in Frankfurt, Germany. He was doing a story on an American pilot, William Lewis, and the recovery efforts for his remains. Would I be able to give him some

The radio call plate found in the crashsite. It was undeniable proof that this was indeed Bill's airplane.

**Situation on the Greifenberg slope at the moment of Bill's crash on
September 11, 1944 as reconstructed from terrain research in 2001-2002**

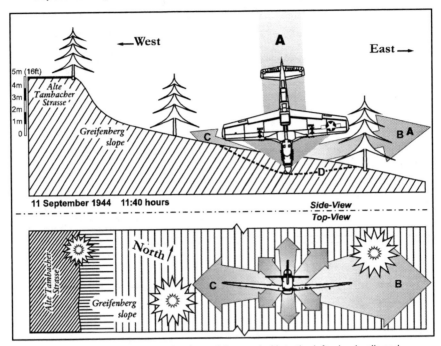

A. Orientation of Bill's airplane at the time of the crash. Note the left wing is aligned
to the West, and the crash is vertical or nearly vertical.

B. The force of the impact distributed the greatest amount of wreckage in this direction.

C. Smaller amounts of wreckage were found in this area.

D. The engine, wings, and explosion excavated the original site to a depth.
of about 1.5 meters (5 feet).

E. Left wing guns were found here, almost intact, but bent (2002).

F. The right wing guns were found here, totally destroyed (2001 / the site of the cross
and wreckage pile).

G. Location of the propeller spinner
and gears (2002).

H. Most of Bill's personal effects
were found in this area (2002).

I. The tips of trees in the impact area
had been shorn off by the explosion
and wreckage debris.

J. Soil level in 2001-2002.

K. Soil level after the crash, Sept. 11, 1944.

background information? The next morning many papers in the United States carried the short, concise piece telling of the recovery of the remains of the pilot, believed to be William Lewis, aircraft parts, and a life preserver. Our success was now assured. The courtesies of the heart begun by Adelbert Wolf and completed by the US Army team and Czech and German volunteers in Oberhof signaled the end of the mission to honor Bill Lewis. He was coming home at last.

Over the next few weeks as the search unfolded, I was fortunate to be able to communicate with Mark Leney. He was satisfied that the airplane had not broken apart in midair, either from a collision or a wing loss. Significant parts of the tail, nose, and both wings were found, indicating the plane was intact when it hit the ground. The pieces of six different machine guns, Browning .50 caliber, indicating that both wings were intact at the time of the crash, were also found at the scene. Some still contained rounds in the chambers, indicating Bill had not expended all of his ammunition, just as we believed. The extruded powder found in the shells was intact and still retained its potency. The team tested remains of the powder and found that it readily ignited. Dr. Leney also said that the anthropological evidence and crash pattern indicated the crash was near vertical. The engine parts and some cockpit items were found some eight feet deep.

In late September of 2002, the team that had performed the excavation at Bill's crash site had finished their tour in Europe. They made one last visit to Jan's museum in Kovarska.

The CILHI and Kovarska Museum team members conducting the Bill Lewis recovery mission in Oberhof July 5, 2002 - August 2, 2002

CPT. Octave V. MacDonald
"Mac" – Mission Leader

Marc D. Leney, PhD.
"Doctor" – Anthropologist

SFC. Andrew Garate
"Volodja" – Team Sergeant

SSgt. Kenneth Miller
"Ken" – Explosive Ordinance

Sgt. Brandy Anderson
MA Specialist

SSgt. Dennis Shields
"Doc" – Team Medic

Sgt. Travis Ruhl
"Bručoun" – MA Specialist

Sgt. Steven Robles
MA Specialist

SPC Rolando Garcia
MA Specialist

Peter Drespa
"Delta" – Team Linguist

SSG. William Hagins
"D" – MA Specialist

SSG. Benjamin R. Bond
"Ben" – Team Photographer

Milan Duháň
"The Mayor"

Petr Frank
"Dimitrij" / *"Wacuments"*

Vašek Holeček

Jana Jiránková

Jaromir Kohout
"The Last Mohycano"

Martin Kohout
"Macek" & wife

Jaroslav Král
"Team Playboy"

Jan Král
"Yardoo"

Radek Kučera
& wife

Matthias Leich
"Sergej"

Veronika Medvědová
"Verča"

Lenka Nemešová
"El Buggy"

Jan Zdiarský
"Sabáka" / *"Frodo"*

Jaroslav Vlachý
"Beer Buddy"

Kamil Vik

Kirsten Fuhrmann
(local German volunteer)

Mandy Kaempf
(local German volunteer)

Ulf Rempel
(local German volunteer)

The Legacy of Duty

Houston, Texas
October 2002

In late October of 2002, we received a phone call from Regina Wolf of Zella-Mehlis. When the news of the American recovery team in Oberhof became known, she had realized that this missing American airman was the pilot whose remains her uncle had buried. Adelbert Wolf was the twin brother of her mother. A precision machinist who made custom hunting rifles and worked independently, he never married, and lived with his sister and her children. Essentially a private person, he never embellished the story of the young airman. She related to us that the story of Bill Lewis was something to which he returned often, emphasizing that once he was gone, they should attempt to find Lewis's family and have his remains returned. He told her that this might be possible if East Germany were free, and in that circumstance, they should try to contact the Americans. He was deeply concerned that no family had been identified to claim the remains, and his efforts to get the Americans involved had brought him to the attention of the STASI, the German security police. Since Bill's remains could not be repatriated, Wolf told his family that now Bill was *"Bekamm wie familie."* He had become as family to them. When the news of the American team was published in the local newspaper, the emotion that she might finally be able to fulfill her uncle's wish was overwhelming.

I think of the remarkable network of events that brought us as far as we have come. The first was Sharon's declaration that she wanted to know more. The remarkable discovery of Jan Zdiarsky's message on an aviation researcher's bulletin board was the next surprise. One of the great breakthroughs in the search came from my wife, when she discovered the existence of the Army Laboratory in San Antonio, which subsequently brought us into contact with the CILHI group and greatly accelerated the process of recovery. Had Jesse Thompson not met Adelbert Wolf, the link would have been lost forever. The meeting of these two men through Paul Weiss had built the bridge that would connect the family of Bill Lewis with younger, modern day searchers, and enable them to complete the search for Bill Lewis successfully. These were three remarkable men with a sense of duty that compelled them to act without expectation of reward. The fact that my daughter Claire was in Germany at the time and spoke the language was the primary enabling factor in my continuing the search. The fact that the cross was still visible, and was discovered by Jan, along with his remarkable dedication, were huge factors in the process. None of this communication would likely have occurred without the utility of the Internet. It enabled us to span the miles and the years and come to a remarkably rapid resolution. It gave us the means to access a bridge backward into time, and to uncover a story rich in meaning and hope.

In the final analysis, the recovery of remains is largely symbolic. Indeed, as a result of war the amount of remains is often terribly small. But in the case of Bill Lewis and those like him, the journey toward recovery is likely to provide much more information regarding the life of the fallen. People come forth with information, and documents reveal much of the lives that soldiers and airmen led. It is this quest that is most compelling and revealing.

Among the great philosophers and writers of Europe, one in particular seems relevant to the core of this story. It is Immanuel Kant, the German professor from Konigsberg who lived in the early 1700s. Kant was a student and teacher of the philosophy of morals. His greatest legacy may be that he advocated a concept of duty for the sake of duty. Duty existed and flourished in Kant's concept simply because it was duty, with no expectation of reward. Duty, he said, was its own motive. As I wondered about Adelbert Wolf, I found myself comparing his dutiful act to Kant's concept of duty. We know very little about Adelbert Wolf, except what the legacy of his duty left us. The gift of his efforts and the symbol of the cross are gifts that waited for years to be claimed. An unknown American, his body torn apart, identifiable only by a pair of pictures found on the forest floor in the midst of a tangled and smoking pile of aircraft parts, and Adelbert Wolf's sense of honor and duty led him not only to bury the remains, but to care for the lonely grave for 28 years. We cannot know if Adelbert Wolf read the philosophy of Kant. We know something more important; he practiced it.

The Parting Gift

Jan commented once that Bill Lewis had given many people a gift. In the search to find Bill, a small band of people had come together in a common effort. Across the globe, from Hawaii to Texas in the United States and in England, the Netherlands, Germany and the Czech Republic, people focused on the effort to find Bill's remains and to honor him. Each delivered their own courtesy of the heart; and each in turn became members of a society of the heart.

On one remarkable evening in October of 2003, a gathering of this society occurred. Jan was in town for the bi-annual reunion of the 100th Bomb Group, and Sharon and Villere Cross organized a dinner around his visit. Grant Fuller, who flew the September 11, 1944 mission to Ruhland as a copilot attended with his wife Mary. Bruce Nichols, the author of a *Dallas Morning News* article on Bill Lewis, was also there. Virginia Wallace, who was a high school classmate of Bill and Eleanor, came for the evening. Friends and neighbors who had followed the adventure completed the gathering.

As I looked out at the group, I was struck by the fact that only a few of us had known each other before beginning the search for Bill. It was improbable that any of us would have met the other in normal circumstances. Yet here we were, all because of a man who died many years ago and far away. We gathered as a result not only of a death, but also because of the solitary and gracious act performed in September of 1944. The courtesies of the heart of Adelbert Wolf gave rise to our own courtesies, performed later, under much more comfortable circumstances. At the center of our society was the courtesy he offered without hope of reward.

We often form ad hoc coalitions for reasons of business, school, church, and mutual support. We are asked to contribute for the sake of a team, the members of which we rarely know. Once done, we usually melt back into our own routines. This assembly has been different. There was no membership drive. The help we sought materialized from sources, people and places often unknown to us. The courtesies extended to us came freely, from the heart. The society formed is one of caring and support, with no expectation of reward, yet the experience has been most fulfilling and incredibly rewarding.

In November of 2003, Sharon Cross was notified by the US Army that the opinion of the Central Identification Laboratory staff was that the remains recovered in Oberhof the previous summer were that of her father. The initial casualty visit, in which a pair of US Army Officers would present the findings of the case and outline the procedures to follow, was to take place in Houston on March 2004.

During the winter of 2003, I had begun to search actively for the personnel involved in the November 1979 visit to Oberhof. I placed an inquiry in the member exchange pages of the monthly magazine of the Military Officers Association of America, asking that any USAF Officers who were attached to the USMLM and visited Oberhof in 1979 contact me. Months went by, but in early March I received a phone call from a former USMLM officer named Bill Burhans. Burhans was aware of the trip to Oberhof but cautioned me that former MLM personnel often declined to talk with people seeking information of their activities. Much of their mission tasking was then secret and some information is still classified. Bill Burhans was the president of the MLM Association, and he offered to help in that capacity. He had a members' mail list and e-mail addresses for most members of the association, and he offered to send an e-mail to the people involved in the trip to Oberhof. I decided to wait a respectable time before contacting any of these people. These men had worked under immense pressures in East Germany at the height of the Cold War. They needed to feel comfortable talking with me, and if that meant taking a little longer to contact them, I certainly understood. Several days after I spoke with Bill Burhans, I received a phone call from a retired USAF colonel, James Tonge. He had taken the time to check me out before talking to me, he said, and now he wanted to help me in reconstructing the events of that November visit in 1979.

In late November 1979, Jim Tonge and Sergeant Larry Raney, who would serve as driver and German linguist, left for the drive to Zella-Mehlis, where Wolf lived. Arriving in Zella-Mehlis, the two set out to inquire about where they might find Adelbert Wolf. The Russian-American agreement governing such searches was clearly set out. The MLM members could speak with ordinary citizens but were not allowed to approach government, military, or municipal officials. The first person they spoke with referred them to "the Doctor Sisters." The Doctor Sisters were two elderly women who were either PhD's or Medical Doctors. *"The Doctor Sisters know where everyone in Zella-Mehlis lives,"* they were told. When they arrived at the home of the two women, one of the sisters asked if they had come to pay the ladies for the damage caused during the war when an American officer who was quartered in their home damaged a valuable wooden chest. She was disappointed in their answer, but soon relaxed and told them how to find the house of Adelbert Wolf. He was not at home when they arrived, so they decided to take dinner at the local Gasthaus.

It was during dinner at the Gasthaus that an event occurred that might have resulted in a serious setback for their efforts. The presence of Americans in military uniform was sure to generate curiosity in the small village of Zella-Mehlis. The men entered a restaurant and sat down to wait for their meal. A gathering of local patrons sat at the Stamtisch, a table informally reserved for people of the town, and they cordially invited the two men to join them. A restaurant patron asked them what they were doing in the town. When he learned of their mission, he began to object loudly. *"We lost millions in Russia, and we are not going to Russia to get them back. There might be someone at this table who found your Lieutenant and killed him. In fact, they might want to kill you too."* The tension increased as other patrons began to argue with the man while the distressed restaurant owner began to lower the shades and close the curtains. The Americans were relieved when the man left, and the remaining patrons began to talk with them. One said, *"We are mountain people. We live in difficult terrain, and we are used to helping people in trouble in our mountains. If we had found Lieutenant Lewis, we would have given him help and not harmed him. This man does not speak for us."* The courtesies of the heart evidenced in 1944 were still in place in the small mountain community of Zella-Mehlis in 1979.

Jim Tonge recalls that Adelbert Wolf was hesitant and quiet during their first meeting. On December 26, 1979, a clear and cold day, Jim Tonge and Captain Wayne Boddie made their second visit to Zella-Mehlis and Adelbert Wolf. Tonge says that Wolf was a true gentleman, and absolutely fearless. As a youth, Wolf had been an Olympic caliber cross-country skier, and he knew the mountains north of Zella-Mehlis well. As the Americans accompanied him up the slope of the Greifen-berg, Tonge says they encountered East German military vehicles along the road. The Americans listened as Wolf voiced his criticisms of the authorities. In 2004, 25 years after this event, Jim Tonge recalled his concern for Adelbert Wolf's safety. *"I felt we had placed him in great danger. That, as well as his lack of fear, has concerned me all these years. I have often wondered if he survived. I am relieved that he did."* More than anyone, the former members of the USMLM understood the danger an inquisitive citizen of East Germany might face in 1979.

On this visit, they accompanied Wolf to the crash site. The two Air Force officers were convinced of Wolf's sincerity and the authenticity of the crash site. He related how he had marked the site and returned to it often. They offered a prayer at the site and took pictures, then thanked Wolf and returned him to his home in Zella-Mehlis.

Jim Tonge was transferred out of the USMLM a short time after his meeting with Adelbert Wolf. Subsequent documents detailing the visit indicated that

Lt. Col. James Tonge and Adelbert Wolf at the crash site, December 26, 1979.
[photo: Jim Tonge collection]

*Lt. Col. James Tonge and Adelbert Wolf
examine a piece of wreckage.*
[photo: Jim Tonge collection]

*Capt. Wayne Boddie and Adelbert Wolf. Wolf
is holding the cross he placed on the site.*
[photo: USAMAA-E]

The cross, as found by Jan and
Petr in March of 2001.

Bottom right: Silver replica of the cross given
in 2002 by Sharon Cross to four friends related to
the search for her father — to her husband Villere,
author, Petr Frank and Jan Zdiarsky.

diplomatic communication had begun toward recovering the remains and repatriating them to the Lewis family. All the necessary people had been informed, and everything seemed in place for a successful recovery.

Houston, Texas
March 22, 2004

Lt. Col. Ron Long, the Chief of Mortuary Affairs and Casualty Support, would be the senior officer in the notification process. Major Scott Erdo, a local officer who would be responsible for contacting Sharon after the visit and following up on details, would accompany him. The Casualty Notification process is a rather structured event. Much of the process focuses on the report of death. In the cases such as Bill Lewis's, where the identity of the service member could be disputed, the CILHI record becomes the central document. It describes the recovery effort, and reveals all the findings, including the pictures of bone fragments found and their origin. The reports of all possible witnesses are included. Each item of equipment found is described in the report. Finally, the report is submitted to an independent anthropologist for verification. The family is given the opportunity to challenge the finding through an Armed Forces Independent Review Board.

The last part of the process concerns the details for return of the remains and allowances for expenses. Bill would be buried with full military honors, just as if he had died in Iraq. An Army Chaplain from Fort Sill would preside.

The report contained few surprises. The witness interviews revealed little information that we did not know. The most intriguing possibility was that we might learn what happened to the remains buried by Adelbert Wolf. Several of the witnesses claimed to have met Herr Wolf and inferred that they knew of the secondary burial site. None of these accounts generated any knowledge of the site or the disposition of the remains. Among the witnesses were two STASI officials. They verified the STASI interest in Herr Wolf's activities. There was a report in the STASI archives of an interrogation of Herr Wolf by a Russian Colonel who was the head of Military Intelligence for the East. We also learned that the MLM team had been under constant surveillance from the time they left their headquarters until their return.

The report is a very impressive document. It portrays an exhaustive effort governed by excellent scientific and investigative procedures. It also emphasizes the attention given to establishing the conclusive identity of the MIA's remains. A three and one half year effort had been concluded successfully. All that remained was to render final honors for Bill Lewis.

Closure and Commemoration

Sharon Cross had traveled to Tulsa with her son and daughter
and their children to prepare for the funeral of her father. She visited
the funeral home to review the details, sign the necessary paperwork
required by the US Army, and spend a quiet moment before the
casket. She placed her hand over the uniform of a US Army First Lieutenant that bore the insignia, ribbons, and pilot's wings of her father.
It lay over a folded Army wool blanket that contained his shattered
remains. She wept quietly, aware of the closeness that had eluded her
over the years as she realized that this touch was as close to her father
as she could come in this life.

Friday, May 28 was a workday, warm and humid under a brilliant
sun and a sky dappled with clouds. Memorial Park Cemetery in Tulsa
sits on an expansive stretch of land set on gentle rolling hills, and the
services would begin in the distinctive stone chapel of the Park. With a
gentle, almost loving precision, the casket bearing Bill Lewis's remains
was borne from the hearse by a team of soldiers from Fort Sill, all volunteers, many of whom had seen combat in Iraq. In the chapel, Army
Chaplain Colonel William Broome, a former helicopter pilot in Vietnam,
presided over a religious service, recalling his own experiences as an
airman in Vietnam on a day of combat which must have been much like
the one on which Bill Lewis had perished. Bill's great-granddaughter,
12 year-old Taylar Williams, sang "God Bless America." Sharon Cross
spoke of the father she had come to know and the remarkable events
that had swept her along on this journey of discovery.

At the grave, the team of soldiers folded the flag and placed the traditional three spent cartridges inside. Sixty years and one month after
he left Tulsa for combat, Bill Lewis was laid to rest next to his mother
and his younger brother Ted. A group of veterans from the 100th Bomb
Group, whose planes Bill and his fellow pilots escorted on the day he
was killed, presented a wreath and a 100th flag to Sharon. There was
a brief period of silence as the formal activities came to an end, but
there was one more event to mark the already memorable day.

A flyover of World War II airplanes, four T-6 trainers flown by a
group of Tulsa volunteers, thundered across the cemetery from the
south, their big engines audible long before they could be seen. As they
crossed the cemetery, one soared upward to leave his comrades in the

symbolic missing man formation. Seconds later, two F-16 Falcons of the Oklahoma Air National Guard roared overhead in a remarkable display of technology. It was a remarkable honor, and offered a unique symbolism of the time that had passed in the search for Bill Lewis.

What had moved one hundred and fifty people, mostly strangers to the Lewis family, to leave the comfort of their homes on this day to attend these ceremonies? Few spoke to the family, few even came forward to identify themselves or claim knowledge of Bill Lewis. Among those who did was a former neighbor from childhood, another was a woman Bill Lewis had escorted to the high school prom.

But most were like the retired Air Force General I spoke with briefly. He, as most of the others, had not known Bill but simply wanted to pay his respects. They stood silent and at a distance from the burial site, yet their simple presence gave strength to the gathering. The confluence of events had brought many to the manicured grounds of the cemetery. It was Memorial Day weekend, the same weekend the World War II memorial was to be dedicated in Washington, D.C., and at a time when American troops were engaged in Iraq. Tulsa is a town with mainstream values, often reflecting the experience of the war years of the 1940s when women worked in the aircraft plant while the men were away. This day would allow them to remember and reflect as they came to honor one of their lost sons.

Each was likely to observe the event through their own prism, coloring and shaping it as a result of their past experiences. The many veterans of World War II who attended remembered others lost decades ago. The Korea and Vietnam veterans had their own similar experiences. Many of the young artillerymen from Fort Sill who bore the casket of their brother-in-arms wore medals from the Iraq war. Each had his prism, each filtered his observations, but all had their humanity.

David Jewell, Bill's boyhood friend, attended the funeral along with his brother Clifford. Kathleen Morrison, Bill's first cousin, was there. Jim Tonge, the retired Air Force Colonel came out from California with his wife, Shirley. Jan Zdiarsky came from Prague. It was as the ceremony ended that I received a personal surprise. Larry Wolverton, a Tulsa resident with whom I had served in 1969 when he was a Marine First Lieutenant, came up and introduced himself. He had read of the events in the local paper, and felt that I must have been the same Kenneth Breaux he had known as a Naval Officer more than 30 years ago.

On this day, those who gathered had made a decision to stand together in the unity of their sentiment. They chose to witness the

Bill's casket is brought into the chapel by the honor guard.
[US Army photo]

Sharon delivered the eulogy for her father.
[US Army photo]

The people of Tulsa turned out in numbers to honor one of their own.
[US Army photo]

From across the Atlantic, then the Pacific, Bill Lewis is finally laid to rest
in Oklahoma soil. Bill's casket is moved to its final resting place. [US Army photo]

In Memory of

William M. Lewis, Jr.

January 18, 1922
September 11, 1944

*Remember me with laughter and not
with grieving tears.*

*Remember me with loving thoughts
that show how much you care.*

*Remember me forever and my life
will never end.*

*Keep alive my memory and
we'll never have to part.*

*For when you feel you need me,
I'll be here inside your heart.*

IN LOVING MEMORY OF

William M. Lewis, Jr.

Entered This Life	Entered Eternal Life
January 18, 1922	September 11, 1944
Tulsa, Oklahoma	Oberhof, Germany

Age
24 Years 7 Months 23 Days

Funeral Service
Invocation
Chaplain Col. William Broome
Ft. Sill, Oklahoma
The Army Air Corps Song
Rex Veron, Jr.
Grandson of Lt. William M. Lewis, Jr.
Sharon Lewis Cross
Daughter of Lt. William M. Lewis, Jr.
"How Great Thou Art"
Musician: Mrs. Billie Cortez
Soloist: Jeff Elkins
Speakers
Ken Breaux
Villere J. Cross
"On Eagles' Wings"
Closing Benediction
Col. William Broome
"Amazing Grace"
Bagpiper: Bill Tetrick
Military Honors
Fort Sill Funeral Honors Team
Presentation of Wreath 100th Bomb Group
Under the direction of
Moore's Rosewood Chapel

event in person rather than observe through the numerous media outlets of print and television that were covering the event. They did this as residents of a country in which they were free to move about. These were the things that Bill's generation fought for, to express themselves and to gather without fear. They stood as common members of the brotherhood of man, their freedom purchased long ago. Their silent presence formed an elegant and poignant statement. In one of the most fundamental acts of human compassion and in the awareness of our own mortality, we reach out, touch and connect. The connection is often startling in its intensity. It is simple, honest, and remarkable. It is what we do for each other.

Now the ceremony was over. The rendering of religious and military honors was complete. We had come together in a unique event filled with intense and varied emotions. After all the years that Bill Lewis had been missing and unaccounted for, the brevity, precision, and flawless execution of the ceremonies seemed all too sudden. We had closed the circle on an event begun more than sixty years ago, in the hours after Bill's aircraft had plummeted to earth. What had happened in those intervening years to bring us to this place was an intense and compelling story. Those few who really knew the story of how and why all this came about would be thinking of Adelbert Wolf, who had sought this day since he had come upon the wreckage of the P-51D Mustang flown by Bill Lewis. He had wanted to let Bill's family know, and in the tradition of the mountain spirit, *der Berggeist*, he would have been pleased beyond expectations. He would have understood the jumbled emotions of pride, awe, satisfaction and sadness with which we all struggled on this day. This was what he intended, and he understood it completely. For forty years, from 1944 until his own death in 1984, this good man and gentle man kept a solitary vigil over the place where he had found Bill. In many respects, this day belonged to him, a result of his sense of duty. In a sentimental fantasy, I imagined that he stood among the nameless in the crowd that day, or somewhere in the chapel, his satisfied spirit in quiet reflection. This story is as much about him as it is about Bill Lewis, and it is he who made Bill's story possible. Those of us who discovered him, beginning with Jesse Thompson, and Jim Tonge, and Jan Zdiarsky and the members of the Recovery Team, all were inspired by the example he left for us to follow.

*Veterans of the 100th Bomb Group came to honor their
"Little Friend" Bill for his sacrifice while escorting their mission.*

Folding the flag.

T-6 Flyover in the Missing Man Formation.
[photo: Charlie Cole]

Sharon receives the flag that covered her father's casket.

Bill's memorial service provided the opportunity for friends to meet.
Villere Cross, David Jewell, Sharon Cross.
[photo: Randy Finfrock]

Villere and Sharon with the two F-16 Falcon pilots who flew over Bill's casket
on May 28, 2004 — Major Scott "Krunch" Reddout (far right) and his wingman
1st Lt. Mike Scorsone from the 138th Fighter Wing.

Kovarska, Czech Republic
September 11, 2004

Sixty years later, at the exact minute the carnage began in the skies over Kovarska on September 11, 1944, four F-15 Strike Eagles of the US Air Force's 48th Fighter Wing based at Royal Air Force Lakenheath, England, thundered over the village and the assembled crowd below. No bombs fell, no airmen died, and peace blossomed in the Czech sky on this day.

The school named after B-17 tail gunner Staff Sergeant John Kluttz still bore the signs on its roof where the B-17's tail section had fallen. Speakers included veterans of the battle, German and American, and wreaths were laid at the small monument in front of the school. Eva Farnsworth Sage came from Dallas to place a wreath in honor of the older brother she saw for the last time as a teenager in 1944. Regina Wolf came from Oberhof, and despite our limited capacities in each other's language, each understood the sentiments of the other. Matthias Leich, who worked so hard and passionately to help bring Bill Lewis home, was there too. I finally had the opportunity to meet Petr Frank, Jan's museum colleague. Never before had so many I had never met seemed as old friends, but the goal of our common effort had made us so.

F-15E Strike Eagles of the 48th "Liberty" Wing on their flyover over Kovarska.
60 years after the battle, the American planes returned to the Kovarska sky.
[photo: Jim Tonge]

This area of the museum contains many of the items recovered from the crash site. The three machine guns from the left wing of Bill's P-51 are shown here at left center.

Nations have always sought to commemorate their war dead, but this ceremony had since its inception in 1994 done more than that. It actively brought the former enemies together, and the old men gathered with slow steps and time in their eyes to shake the hands of one-time opponents and share food and drink with each other. Jan Zdiarsky had always sought this as a goal, not just to commemorate a significant event in the history of his village, but to celebrate the peace.

Oberhof, Germany
September 12, 2004

On a hiking trail above the famed Rennsteig, a group of people gathered to commemorate the American and German fighter pilots killed around the town in the first battle of the day, as the bombers were still far from their target in Ruhland. There were prayers and Taps from a US Air Force bugler and band. A monument was dedicated by the Mayor of Oberhof, and afterwards there was a reception at the local German military barracks, and the veterans had one last time to gather before departing.

The display case contains many of Bill's personal items and airplane parts.

The museum exhibit showing items recovered from the cockpit of Bill's airplane.

This meeting was perhaps the last time that many of us would visit the site where Bill Lewis had died. Jan and Petr, Matthias, Jim Tonge who had been the first American to see the site, Regina Wolf and her husband Klaus, all of us now knew each other as friends. We had come together to see this effort through, and this was our final formal commemoration. We watched as the German pilots who had flown that day chatted amiably and posed for pictures with the B-17 crew members who attended the ceremony. How the world had changed in all those years. As Don Bradley and Helmut Detjens posed for a picture on the trail overlooking the Thuringer Wald I thought of what might have been and what was lost, but also of what we had made of it, and how the last few days had come together. It's a good feeling.

The author with wife Yvonne, Regina Wolf, and her husband Klaus. Taken at the beginning of the Alte Tambacher Strasse. The Greifenberg slope where German and American pilots died is in background. Oberhof, 12 September 2004.

Normandy American Cemetery
Colleville-sur-Mer, France
September 23, 2004

It seemed appropriate that before we returned home, we should spend some time at this place. My uncle had fought just miles from here in furious infantry battles, and my brother-in-law Daniel Fruge had been grievously wounded within a few short weeks after landing in Normandy. Below this sea of stark white stones lie 9,387 American men and women. The beach below this cemetery was the portal through which American, British, and Canadian soldiers began the liberation of Europe. We had been at both ends of the conflict, from the tiny mountain hamlet of Kovarska to the contested beaches of Ouistreham and Porte-en-Bessin, and the cliffs of Pointe du Hoc. As I walked through the cold mist drifting in from the ocean, I quickly found two graves from the 314th Infantry Regiment, the unit my brother-in-law had served in when he was wounded. As I headed back to the dry warmth of the car, the sound of Taps rang out and the flag was lowered. I paused with the others in the group as is the custom. It was time to go home and finish this story.

"Here rests in honored glory a comrade in arms known but to God." This cross marks the grave of one of the 78,000 missing or unknown from World War II. Our search was successful, but for the relatives of this unknown, only a legacy of mystery remains.

Reflections – The Children of War

What about the children and relatives of all the others lost that day? They live in Germany and the United States and carry on their lives. War has deprived them of their legacy. While we were able to learn more of Sharon's father than before, there are many who will never know this much.

For Sharon, it was a legacy found. She talked to men who flew with her father, read their letters describing him, learned of his life and her mother's love for him, and how he died. The long absence of knowledge and the silence of 57 years ended. From a distant hillside on the slopes of the Greifenberg in Germany, a simple wooden cross told her that even in that land, someone honored the father she had never known.

What do the families of Jakob Cryns, Gunther Mechau, and Johann Roth, Josef Proks, Kenneth Williams and Kenneth Crawford know of their legacy? Knowledge and closure are two different things, but they are related. As the knowledge of events such as Bill's loss increases, closure approaches. I am left with a lingering bittersweet melancholy. Of all the things we have learned about Bill's death, the waste of youth in war is the great over arching sentiment. We know about all that we could have sought about him. We know how, when, and where he died. We know that his cause was just, his effort courageous, his sacrifice supreme. The great unanswerable question that haunts us is what would have happened to his wife and daughter had he not perished half a world away? How many lives would be different had he grown to old age and spent his life with Eleanor and Sharon, and perhaps more children? Premature death of any kind deprives the dead of their futures and the living of their past. War does it often, and violently, and in great numbers.

It is estimated that there are as many as 180,000 American children alone who lost their fathers in World War II. Of that number, many thousands are the children of those still missing, the more than 78,000 fallen still unfound. For the orphans of the missing, their pain is unique. As the writing of this story progressed, I was surprised that as I related the story of Bill Lewis, people whose fathers and uncles were themselves lost in World War II would open up to me and relate their own sorrow and sense of loss. There was an effort on the part of the survivors, especially those women who lost their husbands, to move on. Most were young and remarried, such as Eleanor Lewis. As those survivors moved forward and picked up the shattered pieces of their lives, their children were left with only a vague legacy. Today, many of the children are searching for knowledge about their fathers.

In the Netherlands, the Czech Republic, Germany and England, groups of dedicated researchers have opened new lines of communication with the orphans of World War II. Many of these are themselves survivors, but there is an even more gratifying phenomenon in the numbers of people who are doing this work. They are people such as Paul Patist in the Netherlands, Peter Randall in London, Jan Zdiarsky and Petr Frank, Ruy Horta of the Netherlands, (who started the very successful air research bulletin board "12 O'clock High") and the many others in those countries that suffered the direct results of war. Perhaps it is because the remnants and artifacts of a long past war are nearer to them; constant reminders of the cost of war and the cost of freedom.

In Belgium, France, Luxembourg and Holland, and in England, groups of "Godfathers" have emerged. These people care for the graves of all those Americans who lie now in their countries, bringing flowers and flags on special days. Now many of these have continued into the second and even third generation. These people are determined not to let the memories of the sacrifices made in the 1940s die. They are committed, and their commitment is heartwarming. Through their work, they have given hope and honor to the generation of orphans of World War II. Their discoveries, and the honors they bring to the resting places of these men, now among the forever young, are a beacon for the children of the lost.

Despite the fact that we may never progress to the point where all the mysteries of Bill's loss may be known, I am nevertheless glad that we made the effort we did. As I look back on the critical events in this mosaic, I perceive a pattern. In the succeeding decades since the death of Bill Lewis, there have appeared caretakers, people who seem responsible for the guardianship of his legacy. Through the years since the crash and until November of 1979, there was Adelbert Wolf. Without his gracious act, none of the succeeding events would have been possible. Jesse Thompson took up the baton through the seventies, and left us with a documentary treasure of evidence. Jan Zdiarsky accepted the challenge in the decades of the eighties and nineties, first with the efforts to build a museum and memorial and later with research directly aiding the search for Bill. Paul Patist's contribution was his knowledge of the Strasbourg conference, without which the link to the deeds of Adelbert Wolf and Jesse Thompson would have been unknown. The e-mail from Paul Patist in the Netherlands regarding the Strasbourg conference was the key to opening the long forgotten file and ultimately the successful recovery of Bill Lewis's remains. Had Jan and Petr not known of the conference and been able to attend, our efforts might never have resulted in success.

Sharon's expression of interest in 2001 enabled the final chapter in the search for Bill's fate, and all these events would appear as gifts waiting to be claimed. I am most grateful for people like Jan, who made it all possible for us to know as much as we have, and the chance occurrences that placed us in contact with him. It is Jan Zdiarsky who made Bill Lewis come to life. Jan reminded us of Bill Lewis's sacrifice, and in this effort we came to understand so much more than we would have. We recognized the service and sacrifice of a young man who did his duty. In truth, we owe our freedom to him and his brothers-in-arms. The debt of his life cannot be repaid, but it can be stored away for the knowledge of future generations. They must know that events such as this are the bitter fortunes of war. War and adversity do not build character, but only reveal it. In the revelation of the darkest of the human psyche, war revealed its brightest counterpoint. Future generations must also know that this war had to be fought, as future wars might be. Those who love freedom and embrace it must face the troubling thought that war is sometimes required of them. The recognition of those who died is a weak and elusive shadow of what might have been. It is the best that we can do though, and must be done well.

As the children of the lost veterans of World War II age and contemplate what might have been, many have turned to active searching. Adrian Caldwell of Tupelo, Mississippi is an example of such searching. Her father was lost on the 4th of February 1944, just a few minutes short of the English Channel and safety as his B-17 bomber headed home. She has worked tirelessly in searching for the father she never knew, making a trip to Holland and dropping a wreath on the spot close to where his B-17 may have gone down. Her efforts have continued, and now volunteer divers in Holland have begun searching for her father's airplane with the hope of finding the remains of the six crew members who are still Missing In Action.

It was Adrian Caldwell who first introduced me to the American War Orphans Network (AWON). Founded in 1991 by the daughter of a World War II veteran killed in action, AWON provides a communications medium through their web site, which honors the lost of World War II. Their members provide support for each other, and encouragement in the search for the fathers they never knew. Founded in 1991, they locate, register, and provide assistance by familiarizing members with sources of government information necessary to pursue MIA or KIA information. They also provide support through meetings at the local and national levels.

With the advent of new technologies, there are new possibilities. DNA analysis allows for faultless identification of fragmentary remains, often all that is available as a result of combat trauma. Side-scan sonar allows the identification of submerged wrecks with near photographic quality. Ground searching radar distinguishes anomalies in earth indicative of foreign objects and disturbed terrain. Computer databases lend the information component a remarkable tool allowing the rapid comparison of reams of data resting in archives.

All these improvements in technology make the searchers' task somewhat easier, more definitive, and less prone to error. But in the final analysis, it will be necessary for dedicated people to seek out those answers with the aid of emerging technologies. The technology enables, but motivated people will enact. Persistence is invaluable in all these searches. It will be those dedicated young military personnel, such as Captain Octave McDonald's team, who travel the world in search of their missing brothers-in-arms, as they recovered Bill Lewis in Oberhof. It will be people like Jan Zdiarsky and Petr Frank, Matthias Leich who volunteered to provide security to the site while we waited for the Army team to arrive and who later worked with the recovery team, Lt. Col. Jesse Thompson, and above all, people such as Adelbert Wolf, who had such a beautiful sense of his duty. To them, and all those whose courtesies of the heart played a part in this story, we owe a great deal.

For my own part, there have been few things either as satisfying or as challenging as the search for Bill Lewis. I began the search to find a lost familial thread for a dear friend. I found much more than expected. I found honor in the face of unbelievable turmoil, new ideas of duty, and a renewed sense of what the human spirit can achieve. The character of others revealed in the search gave me a new sense of confidence, and my humility grew as I learned how deeply the sense of character was embedded in many of the persons involved in this story.

Sharon Cross asked, and she received the answers. Goethe, whose words provided the title for this book said this of initiative, "*Concerning all acts of initiation and creation, there is one elementary truth — that the moment one definitely commits oneself, then Providence moves too.*"

Gifts and Burdens

The story of Bill Lewis's loss encompasses tragedy and redemption. Overwhelmingly, the story is one of fulfillment and the random gifts of people committed to honor someone they never knew. It is on the surface a bright tale, replete with heroism, dedication, danger, and honor, which ends with a mystery solved. To tell only this part of the story would be incomplete, for within this story of discovery and human courtesy there is a darker component.

For Sharon Cross and all the orphans of war, the gift of recovery and its attendant knowledge brings with it an equally troubling burden. The gift of knowledge exacts a unique toll on its recipients. It is not an unknown feature of grief. All of us who lose parents and cherished relatives will experience the pangs of regret when some friend or relative remembers an obscure event that embellishes the life of the lost. We wish that we could have experienced that instant, and it pains us. In most of the losses we encounter in life, we have the personal recollections to strengthen our recall. We have our own memories, and the lives of the lost are constructed and enriched by these. In the lives of war orphans, though, there is not often any memory of significance. It is hard to mourn someone who was never there. The children of those men who were very young when they died have nothing but the recollection of others on which to build their images. Instead of a physical presence and remembered virtues, they rely on the words of others. The collected and often fragmentary reminiscences of friends and acquaintances form their vision. Each revelation becomes a small tragedy, each distant memory sharpens the awareness and pain of the relationship the survivor has never experienced. Some remembered that he was an outstanding fighter pilot. Others remembered his smile, more his gentle and happy demeanor, his Oklahoma accent. He was often airsick in flight training, and eager to do his part as a member of a combat squadron in England. David Jewell's most poignant memory of Bill Lewis is the devotion he expressed to his wife, Eleanor. Little pictures, joining to form a vision of the man.

Most of us will have the experience of losing a parent. Few indeed are those who experience the grieving process many decades after the loss. In this respect, the orphans of wars experience the many nuances of deferred loss. Their surviving parent sometimes adapts better than the child. Many picked up the shattered remnants of a relationship and moved on, marrying again. The child must adapt to a new father and changed dynamics in the relationship. Each successful recovery opens an old wound and restores the potency of a long dormant grief. Knowledge becomes a bittersweet compromise.

Mission accomplished! Sharon and the author at the reception following Bill's memorial service.
[photo: Randy Finfrock]

For the survivors, there is also the implication that there is a duty to mourn, and this in itself induces stress. Most of our histories will end with us. With the recovery of an MIA, the history commences anew and expands, and there is often an agonizing period of discovery before closure can begin and mourning can end.

The great goodness experienced in the recovery of Bill Lewis tells us much about our connections in the brotherhood of man. The multiple acts of kindness and courtesies of the heart reveal a desire for the performance of virtue by many. The death of a young man many years ago inspired and motivated many. In loss we all recognize our own mortality, and it moves us to connect in charitable ways, works of mercy. Sixty years after his death, a young man known only to a handful of friends and brothers-in-arms still inspires us to act with grace and love toward each other. Those things that Bill Lewis fought for are happening in ways unpredicted at the time of his death. This is the true legacy of Bill Lewis.

Acknowledgements

All of us who participated in this effort over several years owe a debt of gratitude to Sharon. Because of her desire to know more about her father, we discovered not only a brother-in-arms but the great gifts of each other as we searched for Bill Lewis. It has been a special and rewarding adventure. Sharon, thanks for asking.

As the discoveries of this adventure unfolded, there were several persons who aided the process. First on the list for thanks must come Jan Zdiarsky of Kovarska in the Czech Republic. Through his unflagging efforts, modest though he remains, he has given honor to many whose sacrifice and deeds of great courage would otherwise have been lost to posterity. Simply put, without Jan this story would never have been told. Thanks also to the other members of the Museum including Petr Frank of Kovarska, a Czech-German whose ancestors were Sudeten Germans. Regina Wolf of Zella-Mehlis Germany provided information on the efforts of her late uncle Adelbert. Elton Hudgins of the USAF Life Sciences Laboratory in San Antonio, Texas got the ball rolling for the US Army Central Identification Laboratory involvement in the search, for which we are truly grateful. David Roath of the US Army Memorial Affairs Activity-Europe was also instrumental in beginning the modern search for Bill Lewis and supporting the work of Jan Zdiarsky. Col. James Tonge, USAF-Retired, provided historical information regarding the efforts of the USMLM in the search for Bill Lewis, as did Dr. Larry Raney. For all the other aviation historians and researchers who helped; Paul Patist and John Manrho of the Netherlands, Peter Randall of London, John Gray in the United States, and Lt. Col. Robert Littlefield, 55th Fighter Group aviator and author, thank you. Dorothy Thompson, widow of Lt. Col. Jesse Thompson, provided information on the efforts of her late husband. The 100th Bomb Group Association, its veterans, especially Lt. Col. Jack Janssen, Grant Fuller, historians Jan Riddling, Mike Faley and Cindy Goodman provided contacts and information regarding the Ruhland mission. Credit is also due to the 390th Bomb Group Museum for their help in records retrieval for the Ruhland Mission. To the survivors of the 55th, Major General Edward Giller USAF Retired, Eugene Holderman, David Jewell, Al Koenig, John Carroll and Robert Rosenburgh, Robert Littlefield and Frank Birtciel, O.B.Clifton, and Joe Shea of the 357th, thanks for helping now and when your country called in 1944. In Oberursel Germany, thanks to Silke Welteke for her gracious hospitality, and to Herr Jurgen Neupert and Herr Klaus-Roland Müeller of the Forstamt of Crawinkel. Thanks go to Robert Caldwell for his initiative in arranging the flyover of war birds past and present. Reinhard H. Schumann-US Foreign Liaison Office, assisted the Recovery Team from CILHI in many ways. Villere Cross was there through it all as he supported Sharon in her quest. My sister, Katharine Breaux, provided proof editing and manuscript review, as did Jennifer Dykes Yates. To my daughter Claire, who served as capable translator and tour guide in two languages and search companion, and without whom I would not have made the trip, thank you. To the members of US Army-Central Identification Laboratory Hawaii, well done! To Herr Adelbert Wolf, the gracious and brave German we will always remember, Danke Schoen.

Kenneth Breaux
Houston, Texas
September 2004

"Lord guard and guide the men who fly
Through the great spaces in the sky
Be with them always in the air
In darkening storms or sunlight fair
Be with them, Lord, lest they despair,
For those in peril in the air."

Eternal Father
The Navy Hymn

Teams attending the recovery mission in Oberhof in July 2002

Recovery Element One-US Army
Central Identification Laboratory Hawaii
Octave V. MacDonald, Captain, US Army-Team Leader
Mark Leney, PhD. Anthropologist-Recovery Leader
Andrew Garate, Sergeant First Class, US Army-Senior Team Sergeant
William Hagins, Sergeant First Class, US Army-Mortuary Affairs Specialist
Dennis Shields, Master Sergeant, US Air Force-Team Medical Specialist
Kenneth Miller, Staff Sergeant, US Army-Explosive Ordinance Disposal Tech.
Benjamin Bond, Staff Sergeant, US Army-Photographer
Brandi Anderson, Sergeant, US Army-Mortuary Affairs Specialist
Travis Ruhl, Sergeant, US Army-Mortuary Affairs Specialist
Stephen Robles-Crespo, Sergeant, US Army-Mortuary Affairs Specialist
Rolando Garcia, Sergeant US Army-Mortuary Affairs Specialist
Ginger Couden, Public Relations Officer

German and Czech Volunteers
Milan Duhan-Mayor of Kovarska, Czech Republic
Jan Zdiarsky-Volunteer Leader (Museum Kovarska)
Petr Frank (Museum Kovarska)
Matthias Leich (Museum Kovarska)
Jaromir Kohout (Museum Kovarska)
Vasek Holecek (Museum Kovarska)
Jana Jirankova (Museum Kovarska)
Lenka Nemesova (Museum Kovarska)
Veronika Medvedova (Museum Kovarska)

Jaroslav Vlachy (Museum Kovarska)
Martin Kohout (Museum Kovarska)
Jaroslav Kral (Museum Kovarska)
Jan Kral (Museum Kovarska)
Radek Kucera (Museum Kovarska)
Kamil Vlk (Museum Kovarska)
Marie Kucerova (Museum Kovarska)
Martina Kohoutova (Museum Kovarska)
Kirsten Fuhrmann
Ulf Rempel
Astrid Gross

Agencies Providing Support

US Army Central Identification Laboratory Hawaii
US Army Memorial Affairs Activity-Europe
Museum of the Air Battle over the Ore Mountains on 11th September
    1944 in Kovarska, Czech Republic
City of Oberhof
Verteidigungs Bezirks Kommando
Hotel Treff-Panorama
Transport Battalion 133 Erfurt
City of Kovarska
Panzer Aufklaerungs Battalion 13 Gotha
Freistaat Thüringen

US Army Fort Sill Oklahoma (burial)
    Chaplain Col. William Broome
    SFC   Benerval L. Grimes – Casualty Assistance Officer   Williamsport, PA
    1LT   Matthew Snyder   North Hollywood, CA
    SSG Miguel Laguerre   Brooklyn, NY
    SPC Patrick Willingham   Mustang, OK
    SPC Isaia Siaosi   American Samoa
    SPC Vaughn Warriner   Sonora, CA
    SPC David Ramirez   Harlingen, TX
    SPC Christopher Amos   Cleveland, VA
    SPC Mike Mena   Orange County, CA
    SPC Jesse Askin   West Chicago, IL

Warbirds of America Squadron 10 (burial ceremony flyover)
- John Esposito
- Steve Campbell
- Jason Griffin
- John Loerch
- Mike Anderson

Department of the Army Casualty and Memorial Affairs Operations Center
- Lt. Col. R.W. Long Jr

75th Maneuver Area Command US Army
- Major Scott Erdo

138th Fighter Wing, Oklahoma Air National Guard (burial ceremony F-16 flyover)
- Major Scott Reddout
- 1LT Mike Scorsone

Moore Funeral Home-Tulsa
- Shirley Lawson
- Ken Adams

100th Bomb Group Foundation
- Charles "Hong Kong" Wilson
- John Luckadoo
- Gayle Leonard
- Grant Fuller
- Jan Riddling
- Cindy Goodman
- Ralph Bradley
- Michael Faley
- Randy Finfrack
- Eric R. Molbert

US Embassy Prague
- Col. Edward A. Gallagher USAF

48th Fighter "Liberty" Wing (F-15Es flyover on 11 September 2004)

Tulsa Memorial Reception
- Bill and Joanie Moore

Appendices

Appendix I.
Footnotes

1 *Roll is movement of an aircraft about its longitudinal axis while maintaining forward flight. Pitch is up and down movement under the same conditions, and yaw is movement from left to right.*

2 *A.P. was the designator the Army Personnel system applied to graduated cadets. They were now Airplane Pilots.*

3 *All early aircraft had fixed landing gear. These were always in the down position, and contributed to greater drag and decreased speed.*

4 *Bowyer, Michael J.F. Duxford Reflections, Duxford Diary, East Anglian Aviation Society, 1975.*

5 *Anti-G, or pressure suits, had been tested in October of 1942, at a simulated altitude of 60,000 feet.*

6 *Flak is an abbreviation for the German words "Flieger Abwehr Kannone." Literally, air defense guns.*

7 *Eighth AF regulations specified that two 1.6 ounce bottles of 86 to 100 proof rye or bourbon whiskey be dispensed by the flight surgeon "if such issue is medically warranted."*

8 *"Bruvver" was Bill's take on Ted's pronunciation of "brother" when he was a toddler.*

9 *Early crews carried ten men. Later in the war, the second waist gunner was removed and replaced by the radio operator.*

10 *At 700 rounds per minute, the rounds would last a little over two minutes if fired continuously. Pilot encounter reports indicate that pilots fired in ½ second bursts attempting to conserve ammunition and set up a target precisely. The barrels would also burn out if fired for more than a few seconds.*

11 *These weapons are still in service today, having survived with only minor modifications.*

12 *It was at this refinery that experiments were carried out on the gasification of powdered coal. US Intelligence agents visited the refinery and interrogated its management often after the war.*

13 *Britain suffered nearly 400,000 casualties, a high percentage of which* were civilians. This still pales in comparison to the Germans, who lost nearly 4,000,000 during the conflict. The exact number of Jewish casualties who lost their lives in concentration camps is unknown, but numbers in the millions.

14 Pilots flying out of Bodney called themselves "The Blue Nosed Bastards of Bodney." Their aircraft were painted with a distinctive deep blue around the nose.

15 Erich Hartmann of the Luftwaffe had over 350 victories in more than 1000 missions.

16 Jeschonneck, worn from constant political battles with Goering, committed suicide in August 1943. He left a note saying, "I can no longer work together with the Reichsmarschall. Long live the Fuhrer."

17 Jinking is a rapid evasive up-down movement.

18 A Lufbery is a circular pursuit in level flight. Originally it was a circular defense, which gave everybody a wingman. It was named for Raoul Lufbery, a World War I pilot and ace.

19 Waist gunner Thomas Kentes fell with the tail section, was injured but eventually recovered.

20 Original spelling.

21 Francis Gerard retired from the Air Force as a Major General.

22 Later evidence would establish the time of Bill's crash at exactly 1140.

23 The original German reads "zahllose kleinen teilen."

24 Self published by the author - Robert Littlefield, P.O. Box 3644, Carmel, California 93921-36444.

25 Eleanor's underline.

26 Francis Matney was a member of class 44-E, graduating with Bill Lewis and David Jewell in January of 1944.

27 Thorsen's underlining the "might" for emphasis shows his concern for Eleanor, and his reluctance to give her false hope that Bill might be alive.

28 Al Koenig was shot down 8 miles behind American lines on February 20, 1945 over Luxembourg. He felt he was safe when he saw a local filling his pipe from a tin of Prince Albert tobacco.

29 The Gold Star Mothers grew from the custom begun in 1918, when mothers were encouraged to wear a black armband with a gold star to signify their loss of a son in battle. It was incorporated in 1929, and granted a Federal Charter in 1984. It is open to all mothers of fallen soldiers.

30 The 55th was reactivated in 1947 as the 55th Reconnaissance Group. It exists today as the 55th Strategic Reconnaissance Wing, and deployed to the Persian Gulf in August 1990.

31 The disabled P-51 sighted near Gera was probably either Bill's or Kenneth Crawford's aircraft. No other US Fighters were in the area at that time.

32 Patterson was no stranger to war. He had been awarded the Distinguished Service Cross during World War I. He frequently toured the front lines during the Second World War while serving as an Undersecretary.

33 This scheme was instituted in August 1944.

34 This color scheme was discontinued at the end of August 1944.

35 Later, I discovered the USAAF Combat Chronology. This lists World War II missions by number and date, and is very valuable when researching specific dates and casualties. It is available on the Internet.

36 Pilsen aviation society.

37 Frank Birtciel of the 343rd flew with three mirrors on his canopy. These looked very much like the one I found. They were taken from British Spitfires by crew chiefs and mounted on the Mustangs. Subsequent searches failed to find these objects.

38 For a detailed description of these events, see "Lucky Forward; The History of Patton's 3rd US Army," by Col. Robert S. Allen.

39 Army Almanac Government Printing Office. 1950.

40 The control of internal security was carried out by the Ministerium fur Staatssicherheit, the Ministry for State Security, known by the acronym of STASI.

41 The author graduated from this institution in 1966.

42 Laminar flow refers to the movement of air across a wing. Laminar flow is orderly and smooth, while turbulent flow has eddies and whirlpools of air. Laminar as opposed to turbulent derives from improved wing design, improves lift, and generally makes for a faster aircraft.

43 See *Air & Space Magazine* online, *June/July 1999, Supplemental Info "The Meredith Effect."*

44 Of the more than 160,000 Merlin's built during the war, 60,000 or more were built by Packard Automotive. These were placed not only in P-51s but also in British bombers. Rolls-Royce employees increased from 7,000 before the war to more than 50,000 at war's end.

45 It was discovered during the writing of this book that a restored Focke-Wulf 190 was being readied for flight-testing.

46 Refers to the split-S, a maneuver in which the aircraft first inverts, then rolls downward in a half loop, heading in the opposite direction from the pursuer.

47 Indicated Air Speed.

48 A maneuvering formation named for the famous World War I ace, Raoul Lufbery. It is a circular formation of aircraft, primarily defensive in nature. The circular arrangement gives everyone a wingman.

49 These two were Lts Lewis and Crawford. Only Crawford was seen during the initial engagement south of Erfurt.

50 Jinking is a rapid evasive maneuver, usually up and down, some-times combined with rolls and turns. Its purpose is to keep the pursuer from maneuvering into a good firing position.

51 This aircraft was confirmed to have been a British Mosquito, not an Me-410.

52 This refers to the combat over Kovarska, at 1200 hours and minutes before the bomb run began.

Appendix II.
Military Aircraft Development 1937-1944

At the heart of American aircraft development was the Boeing-designed B-17. The strategy of battle had evolved, and airpower was being envisioned as a new approach.

Beginning in the early 1930s, air power advocacy gained support in the US Army. The Army Air Corps laid out the technical specifications for a new long-range bomber. The idea was for an air campaign that would defend shores of the United States against shipping and carry the fight against an enemy well within his borders. The airplane would have to fly on extended missions for ten hours or so, at moderately high altitudes, and carry large bomb loads.

As was the case with the P-51 fighter, the British, already at war, provided Boeing with the first orders. This was a useful introduction. British experience allowed Boeing to incorporate much needed improvements to the original design. By September of 1944, world events in the Pacific and in Germany soon began to indicate the desirability for full-scale production. The improved versions had greater armor, self-sealing fuel tanks, larger caliber machine guns, a tail gun position, and the ability to carry a 6,000-pound bomb load. With a range of 3,400 miles and a cruise speed of 182 miles per hour, the B-17G was the first really capable strategic bomber. Boeing shared production with Douglas and Lockheed, and a total of 12,371 B-17s were produced between the late 1930s and 1945. More than 8,600 of these were "G" models. Of the total production, nearly 5,000 were lost to accidents and combat action.

At the time of the Ruhland mission on September 11, 1944, Boeing had produced the B-17 from the initial "A" models to the "G" version in production since 1943. It was also not until 1943 that the USAAF realized that the long range of the B-17 was also its early weakness. When the bombers were used to the limits of their range, there were no allied fighters able to accompany them. Not until the advent of the P-51 with external tanks could bombers expect to have fighter support throughout their entire mission.

In early 1937, the US Army Air Corps, as it was called then, began to solicit potential providers for a new airplane. What they had in mind was not a fighter, but rather an interceptor. The idea was that threats to the US mainland could come from the sea or from long range land based strategic bombers. A requirement of this new airplane was to be the capability to climb quickly to high altitudes and attack successfully. Long range was not a high priority, since it was assumed that such intercept operations would be carried out over American territory. This limited range feature was to prove critical when the first P-38's deployed to England in the bomber escort role in 1943. Lockheed won the competition in June of 1937. One of the design team leaders was a man named Kelly Johnson. Johnson would later become the director of the Lockheed *"Skunk Works."* The Skunk Works operated largely in secret during the Cold War years and developed such aircraft as the U-2, the SR-71 Blackbird spy plane, and the F-117 Stealth Fighter in remarkably quick order. But Johnson's job on the P-38 was not carried out under those conditions in 1937. America was not at war, and the Army was not rushed to build or buy. The prototype was developed the next year, but a crash on a test flight ruined the chances of its becoming production ready. Instead, Johnson and his team had to start over, delaying the production by two years. The P-38 was improved in many respects and had many advantages over previous designs. During World War I, airplanes possessing machine guns had only two methods of employing them. One was to use an observer with a fuselage-mounted machine gun who fired independently of the pilot. On those planes with only the pilot aboard, sighting was a challenge. Engineers developed a mechanism whereby the gun actually fired through the propeller, using a system of cams linked to the propeller shaft that fired when the propeller blade was clear. This further limited the amount of armament the aircraft could carry. It was not too difficult to fire one gun through the propeller. Two guns required more precise calibration, and sometimes caused propeller damage or worse when the timing was improper. Later designs solved the problem by mounting the weapons on the wings and calibrating the guns, which fired at a slight inward angle, to converge on a point representing the center of mass of the enemy airplane. This was better than firing through the propeller, but if the convergence point was not calibrated properly, the effect could be a missed opportunity. If the convergence was set at an arbitrarily low range, the pursuing pilot had to take more time to maneuver closer in for the attack. It is reported that armorers who sought perfection in their work would view the combat camera films of their pilots in order to improve convergence. In combat in the air, time and accuracy are life itself. The P-38 had two engines mounted several feet outboard of the pilot. These engines were essentially the composition of two separate fuselages, each with a separate tail. The pilot sat in the third, or middle fuselage cockpit. The guns were placed in this section. Convergence was no longer a problem, since this arrangement aligned the guns with the fuselage and permitted the pilot to fire straight ahead. The center fuselage contained one 20-millimeter cannon and four .50 caliber machine guns with an effective range of 1,000 yards. The first large order for P-38s came in 1940, when the Army Air Corps committed to 600 units of the new interceptor.

The fledgling science of aerodynamics had expanded its boundaries dramatically during the decade of the 1930s. Despite the fact that people had flown for nearly forty years, high performance issues in aircraft are typically driven by the military. Dogfights and UFAs (unusual flight attitudes) are routinely a subject of military flight training and seldom so in the civilian ranks. These maneuvers place pilot and aircraft in stress and often danger. From 1939 through 1941, several new developments forced Johnson and his Lockheed team to rethink their science. The speeds the P-38 developed opened new problem areas in such issues as high-speed compressibility stalls, locked or unstable controls, and in some cases disintegration of the airplane itself. Johnson's team developed a new tail structure and dive brakes to offset the compressibility problem. Compressibility was a new challenge. Airplanes had never flown as fast as the P-38 before, and earlier aircraft could not enter dives and speeds needed to actually compress the air passing over the wing surfaces without crashing. When compressibility was reached, the airplane was difficult to control, buffeting and shaking while undergoing great stress. Another issue was the maneuverability of the aircraft while attempting to turn in tight patterns. Johnson's teams designed flap devices to allow the fast aircraft to make tighter turns. This feature was critical in the air-to-air encounters over the Pacific, where P-38s were already operational, and later in Europe. There is always a tradeoff in air combat. If you are fast enough to catch up to a slower opponent, you must then be able to reduce your turn radius to his as he sees you and begins his evasive moves. In level flight, being able to turn inside your opponent gives you the advantage. If you cannot, he may escape. Survival when pursued in level flight is the exception, and not the rule. The survivors and aces all know how to use the energy balance, seeking the advantage of altitude and practicing the violent evasive maneuvers that may save their lives. The USAAF Pilot Encounter Reports written the day of the Ruhland mission will give even an experienced reader of aviation subjects an eye opening lesson in combat maneuvers. The aircraft Bill flew when he arrived at the 55th was a P-38J. After many revisions, most of which came about because of American involvement in the Pacific war, the airplane had matured. At a weight of 21,600 pounds, it was surely the heaviest he had flown and was also the most powerful. It employed new turbo superchargers to allow engine efficiency at the high altitudes, where combat had never taken place. Early in the European Theater though, problems still confronted the mechanics and their pilots. Cabin heat was a problem, and sometimes the windshields frosted over on the inside during combat. Having two engines is fine, as long as both are running properly. Lose one in a fighter-to-fighter engagement, and you have a challenge keeping the aircraft in flight, much less fighting in it. There were problems with fuel mixtures, problems relating to the superchargers, and a lack of range for bomber escort missions. Two engines means two times the power, and two times the maintenance as well. Despite the problems encountered by pilots and mechanics, the Germans had a name for the fighter plane they respected. It was *"der Gabel Schwanz Teufel,"* the fork-tailed devil.

Most Americans, including some aviation enthusiasts, consider the P-51 Mustang fighter a purely American airplane. It is true that the Americans built it, but in the early years after its production it was used nearly exclusively by the British. British fliers had experienced a good deal of air combat since 1940 against the Germans, and they had extensive knowledge of aircraft flight characteristics. What they needed was more capacity for manufacturing war equipment. North American Manufacturing was solicited to manufacture more of the Curtiss P-40s for the British using their facilities in California. North American considered this arrangement, but there was little enthusiasm for manufacturing some other company's design. They countered with an offer to build a new fighter, incorporating much of the British experience against the Germans. North American had never built a fighter plane before, and the British imposed some strict deadlines on the time of delivery, demanding a 100-day deadline. North American actually delivered the airplane in 117 days, having had to wait for an engine for the new fighter. The prototype was called the North American 73, later the P-51. The first shipments of this American airplane went to the British, and the first success of a P-51 in an air-to-air encounter was the downing of a German Aircraft by a British pilot in 1942. It would be some time before the American Air Corps would adopt the P-51, since America was not yet engaged in the war in Europe. The USAAF was now fully committed to the P-38, and it would be the front line aircraft to be used in the Pacific once hostilities began. The P-38 enjoyed success in the Pacific, but the USAAF was evaluating the role the P-51 played in the European Theater of Operations (ETO). Realizing that the P-51 may have been more suitable for the fighter role because of its single engine and great maneuverability, the USAAF set aside two production units, numbers 5 and 10, for test use, designating them XP-51s. Later, when the Eighth Air Force committed to the P-51 fully and began to fly it from bases in England, some of the P-51s they acquired still had British insignia when they were turned over to the Americans.

The P-51 had clean aerodynamic lines, a laminar flow wing, wing-mounted converging fire machine guns, and a top speed of more than 400 miles per hour in level flight.[42] The fuselage was narrow, with a large air duct beneath the cockpit. The air duct was an interesting feature. The duct housed a radiator. As air rushed in, it cooled the engine lubricating oil, but also produced a drag, or decreased the speed. A British scientist, F.W.Meredith, determined that the proper design of the duct could deliver a significant improvement to the thrust of the airplane. This effect has been negated by jet airplanes, but was a real breakthrough for its time.[43] The British admired the aerodynamics and airframe of the design, and the build out of the airplane was completed with an Allison engine.

Within a few months of intense operations in England, the P-51 revealed its weaknesses. The Allison engine did not give the airframe a chance to excel. Underpowered for such a sleek design, the P-51 as first flown by the British squadrons was unable to fight well at altitudes much above 12,000 feet. It saw heavy use instead as a strafing, dive-bombing and reconnaissance platform, where its great speed was a clear advantage. Then the British provided the solution. The Rolls-Royce Merlin engine had been in use in RAF aircraft since 1937, including the famous British Spitfire and Hurricane. By some accounts, the Merlin had been installed in nearly 20 various aircraft types by the time that North American had built the NA-73 prototype. A British test pilot commented after a flight in the P-51 that what it needed was a Merlin.[44] That observation was put into practice and changed the tone of the air war. Fitted with the Merlin, the P-51 showed what the airframe could do with a properly matched engine. Almost immediately, the new marriage of machine and frame became a deadly opponent against the German fighters. At altitudes of 25,000 feet, it had a better fuel efficiency than the Allison had at lower altitudes. It had greater speed and climbing characteristics, and now could climb rapidly to 25,000 feet and fight there. A test model developed a speed in level flight of 490 miles per hour, faster by far than the prototype had flown, although the standard versions would not fly that fast. For much of the remaining war years, the Merlins used in the American version of the Mustang were built under contract by the Packard automobile company. There was one remaining improvement to be addressed. Even with the Merlin, range was still a problem. The bomber groups intended to use their ships to the maximum limits of range, bombing the manufacturing plants and oil refineries deep inside Germany. As production models, the first Mustangs just could not fly that far. Most bomber missions in the early years of the war were escorted only for the first and last few hundred miles because of this limitation. It was the development of the external drop tanks that held 100 gallons of fuel each that gave longer legs to the Mustangs, increasing their range to just over 2,000 miles. Typically, the P-51s would carry two of these, mounted on the wings. Pilots managed fuel by draining external tanks first, switching from one to the other to balance the load on the wings. While these contributed to drag and reduced speed somewhat, they could be dropped in a hurry if a fight erupted, and the two main fuel tanks in the fuselage provided plenty of fuel to return to base. Since these tanks were disposable, large numbers of them were required. In some photos of the 55th Fighter Group while based at Wormingford, stacks of these tanks can be seen in the background. And the airmen, ever resourceful, managed to turn the large crates used to ship the tanks into auxiliary huts to be used on their airfields.

Aviation historians sometimes argue over the effect of the P-51s. Some contend that the Luftwaffe was spent and strategically bankrupt before the P-51s came on the scene and that the effect of the P-51 was overstated. What cannot be argued is that by design and performance, the P-51 was a fighter vastly superior to anything else flying.

P-51s continued on active service for many years, and were flown by the US Air Force in Korea. Many Mustangs survived even past the 1950s when small countries with limited Air Force roles acquired them, and these could be found well into the 1960s. Of the original 15,586 built during the war years, approximately 290 or so have survived. Of those survivors, there are about 143 flying today, about 60 of those in the United States. Aeronautical engineers and pilots cite this as enduring evidence of the strength and reliability of the airframe. The Messerschmitt 109, one of the usual opponents of the P-51, was produced in greater numbers than any airplane of the war years, more than 30,000 being built, but now there are only 38 existing, only a few of which are being flown. Nor are there any flying survivors of the original 2,068 Focke-Wulf 190s built by the Germans.[45] The men who flew all of these airplanes were pioneers in aerial combat. Flying at speeds and altitudes never reached before, they set the standards for modern fighter pilots.

The two aircraft that escort pilots and the bomber crews most commonly faced were the Messerschmitt 109 and the Focke-Wulf 190. Many aviation experts will argue that the 109 was the first truly modern fighter plane. The Me 109 was designed in the early 1930s and flown in the Spanish Civil War, so that by the time that Germany faced British and American pilots in combat, its designer, Dr. Willy Messerschmitt, and his team had acquired significant experience with the airframe and power plant. The Me 109 was comparable in many respects to the P-51. With a top speed of 387 mph, it was only about 50 mph slower than the production Mustang. It was also lighter than the Mustang by almost 4,000 pounds. It could operate at an altitude of 38,000 feet, high enough to have the energy advantage as it waited for the bombers and their escorts. Its range was not competitive at 450 miles, but this was not a problem over Germany. The Daimler-Benz engine was comparable to the Merlin, and rated at 1475 horsepower. One area of advantage was its armament. While its two 13 mm machine guns were not as powerful as the Mustang's .50 calibers, it carried 20-millimeter cannons, fitted with explosive shells. On some variants, cannons were upgraded to 30 millimeter, and others also carried two removable 20 mm cannons under the wings. One burst from either of these formidable weapons could destroy something as large as a bomber, and against the P-51 one hit to the Merlin engine or its radiator assembly often brought the airplane down. A strike that penetrated the cockpit and struck the pilot directly would be fatal. For the reader unfamiliar with weapons specifications, a short primer is helpful. Caliber refers to fractions of inches. Thus, a .50 caliber machine gun delivers a bullet one-half inch in diameter. Millimeters are harder to comprehend unless you have familiarity with the metric scales. A 20-millimeter cannon delivers a projectile about three quarters of an inch in diameter, and just less than three inches long with a much higher velocity, greater range, and a much greater weight than the .50 caliber weapon. The 30-millimeter cannons found on some of the specially modified FW 190s fired a shell about one and one quarter inches in diameter and longer than the 20-millimeters. Again, there is a tradeoff. Heavier, more destructive weapons and their ammunition will weigh more, and take up more space. The pilot must still maneuver the aircraft in range, and make accurate shots to prevail in air combat. Weapons would not do the job for him if he could not fly with skill.

Near the end of the war, Willy Messerschmitt would build improved versions of his existing models and vastly improved new aircraft, including the first jet propelled fighter aircraft, the Me 262.

The FW 190 was somewhat closer in specifications to the P-51. Fully loaded, it would weigh just less than 11,000 pounds, only a few hundred pounds lighter than the Mustang under the same conditions. The top speed of the Focke-Wulf was 408 mph, close to the 420 or so of the production model Mustang. With a range of 500 miles, they were comparable to the Me 109s. The engines of the FW 190s were much more powerful than either the Mustang or the Me 109. They were 2,100 horsepower BMWs, and they utilized an injection of water and methanol to boost performance. Special variants of the FW 190s were developed for attacking the bomber formations. These *"Sturmjäger"* had armor plate and armored cockpit glass. In addition, 30-millimeter guns on each wing replaced the outboard 20-millimeter cannons. The addition of the special armor plate would increase the weight of the FW 190s upward to as much as 10,000 pounds, rendering them hard to maneuver. But the tactics developed by the Luftwaffe were to use the Focke-Wulf machines in a single-pass slashing attack to be accompanied by the more maneuverable Messerschmitt 109s. Light by comparison to the .50 calibers of the Mustang, two 13-millimeter machine guns completed the armament.

The Jadgeschwader 4 that rose in defense against the 55th Fighter Group on September 11, 1944 was one of only three Luftwaffe units equipped with the special variants of the FW 190. They also had the regular complement of production model Me 109s.

Appendix III.
Archival documents related to the 55th FG's combat mission on September 11, 1944 (examples)

PILOT'S PERSONAL ENCOUNTER REPORT

A. Combat
B. 11 September 1944
C. 38th Fighter Squadron, 55th Fighter Group
D. 1150
E. Near Erfurt
F. 5/10ths broken clouds at 5,000 feet
G. Me-109
H. Two (2) Me 109's destroyed

Lt. Francis M. Matney

I. *I was flying Hellcat Red 4 at about 22,000 feet in the vicinity of Erfurt when we got into a fight with 30 plus Me 109s. Breaking into the attack, I got on the tail of the Huns when I saw another one coming in on me. In attempting to reef it in, my plane snapped and went into a spin, and seeing the 109 still there, I let it spin to about 5,000 feet before pulling out. On recovery I observed another Me 109 below me and to the left. I turned and opened fire from about 30 degrees deflection and 200 yards range and immediately observed hits on the wings, canopy and engine. Closing to about 150 yards and still firing and hitting the 109, I saw coolant gushing from the engine. When the E/A went through the edge of a cloud, I followed him down and saw him split S into the ground and explode. Lt. Thorsen, who followed me down and chased the first E/A from my tail, saw him go in. I therefore claim the Me 109 destroyed.*

After the above combat I pulled up in a wide climbing turn and at 5000 feet spotted an Me 109 slightly below me and about a mile away flying paralleled to my course. I made my bounce and fired one short burst at 45 degrees and 1200 yards, but didn't see any strikes. As I was closing in behind him, he dove below the clouds — but I followed him and from dead astern fired a short burst, observing hits on his wing roots and fuselage. Then a P-51 from Acorn Squadron came between us and fired a short burst and got some hits on the tail of the E/A. But he was going too fast and overshot after that short burst. When the E/A started a tight turn to the left, I turned with him and let him have it with a 10 second burst from 30 degrees and 150 yards, registering hits on his wing, canopy and engine. The E/A then started into a shallow spiral.

*He tried to pull out right on the deck, but flipped over, crashed
and exploded. The Acorn '51 was above us and saw him go in, for he
wagged his wings and pulled up into the clouds.*

*As a result of this fight I claim one Me 109 destroyed for a total
of two Me 109s during the entire combat.*

FRANCIS M. MATNEY
2nd Lt. Air Corps

PILOT'S PERSONAL ENCOUNTER REPORT

A.   Combat
B.   11 September, 1944
C.   38th Fighter Squadron, 55th Fighter Group
D.   1150
E.   Southeast of Erfurt
F.   4 to 5 tenths clouds, 2500 to 4000 feet
G.   Me-109
H.   Destroyed

Lt. Arthur L. Thorsen

I.   *I was leading Hellcat Blue Flight at 24,000
feet in the vicinity of Erfurt on withdrawal support of B-17s when many
bandits were called in by Acorn Squadron of the same escort. We went
up front to join Acorn and saw our P-51s engaged with about 30 plus
Me 109s about 4,000 below us. We also observed a strong force of
enemy top cover, but when we decided they were not coming down
we joined the fight below. I immediately got on the tail of a blue-nosed
109, but was well out of range — 700 to 800 yards. I tried to close
but the E/A split-essed.[46] Attempting to follow him I somehow lost
my wingman and then my second element was forced to break as the
result of a head on enemy attack from some other E/A. Picking up the
chase, of my original 109 in a vertical dive, I opened up at 500 yards
almost dead astern, closing all the time. I didn't observe strikes, but the
E/A suddenly began to belch black smoke, then went out of control.
Because he began snapping to the right, it was impossible for me to
keep him in my sights. All this time we were still in a vertical dive-and
when I checked my air speed it registered 500 mph. The Me 109 pilot
tried to regain control but over-controlled and began snapping to the
left. By this time we were nearly out of altitude(the splits had started at*

22,000 feet). Suddenly the E/A popped its canopy, went into a cumulus cloud and I followed-starting my pull out in the cloud. When I burst out and leveled off I was scarcely 300 feet above the treetops. When my vision cleared I saw a terrific explosion on the ground and am positive that this was the E/A I had followed into the cloud. In my opinion the pilot had tried to bail out but failed in his attempt because there were no chutes in the area. As a result of the above combat I claim one Me 109 destroyed.

ARTHUR L. THORSEN
1st Lt. Air Corps

PILOT'S PERSONAL ENCOUNTER REPORT

Lt. Walter J. Konantz

On a bomber escort mission to Ruhland, Germany, I was flying Blue 2 in Acorn Squadron. South of Meiningen, we saw about 150 unidentified small dark ships flying in a swarm, like bees. At the time we were flying at 24,000 feet going east. The bogies crossed our path 90 degrees to our course quite a distance ahead of us and 5 to 6,000 feet above. This is the last time I saw them for about 3 or 4 minutes, when someone called, "109s," over the radio. Just then a single Me 109 dove across my path about 100 yards ahead in an attitude of 45 degrees.

Immediately I peeled off from my flight and followed the e/a. He evidently saw me, because he steepened his dive to 90 degrees. I followed him clear down in a wide-open near vertical dive. By the time I was giving full chase the e/a had increased his range to 600 yards. My I.A.S.[47] was 600 and I hit compressibility at 15,000 feet, resulting in violent buffeting and oscillation of my ship. I noticed the Me 109 in the same condition; he was bucking and skidding violently. At about 10,000 feet his right wing ripped off about 4 feet from the fuselage. He went straight in and exploded in a wooded area. The pilot did not get out. I did not fire at this ship nor did I take any pictures of the crash ...

WALTER J. KONANTZ
2nd Lt. Air Corps

PILOT'S PERSONAL ENCOUNTER REPORT

A.   Combat
B.   11 September 1944
C.   338th Fighter Squadron, 55th Fighter Group
D.   1148
E.   South of Meiningen, Germany
F.   2 to 3/10 cumulus clouds at 2000 feet
G.   Me-109s
H.   Three (3) Me 109s destroyed, 1 of those shared with unknown P-51 pilot of the 38th Squadron, one (1) Me 109 damaged

I.   *I was flying Acorn Red 3 as the squadron was proceeding in front of the escorted bombers. I called in bogies at 12 o'clock high to our position, which was then at 22,000 feet. Acorn leader made a 90-degree turn into the sun on our right. As the squadron entered the turn, another group of e/a, positioned to the left of the gaggle called by me, turned to pursue us and came in over our tail at about 6 o'clock. On the command to break, I turned about to engage an Me 109 coming on my flight leader's tail. As my flight leader broke to the left, the e/a split S'd and continued in a diving turn to the left. I followed and opened fire at about 500 yards, 30 degrees deflection, and observed strikes along the fuselage, and white smoke pouring from both sides of his engine. At 16,000 feet the e/a jettisoned its canopy and the pilot bailed. I did not see the chute open. I claim this e/a as destroyed. At this time I was alone. I took snap deflection shots at an Me 109 I caught in range, observing several strikes on his fuselage. He split S'd and went down to the deck. I did not follow, because there were too many e/a in the area. I claim this Me 109 as damaged. Following this, I tried to find a P-51 to join, and located one in a lufbery[48] with an Me 109 . The P-51 ran out of ammunition and the pilot told me over the R/T to finish the e/a off. I pulled up in a zoom and nosed down on the e/a, registering hits on his wing roots, fuselage, and canopy. It rolled over on its back, burning furiously, and crashed into the ground from 9,000 feet. I did not see the pilot get out. I claim this Me 109 destroyed (shared with an unknown pilot of the 38th squadron). As I turned away from this encounter, I came up on the tail of anther Me 109 at about 9,000 feet, and opened fire at 700 yards. The e/a skidded and slipped evasively, but I scored hits along the fuselage and wing roots. Pieces flew off the Me 109, and white smoke billowed out from under the wing. He fell off, and I saw him hit the ground. I did not follow, being at this time out of ammunition and alone. I did not see the pilot get out. I claim this Me 109 destroyed.*

WILLIAM J. INGRAM
1st Lt. Air Corps

STATEMENT

A careful check has been made with pilots of the 38th squadron to determine the identity of the pilot who was attacking the Me 109 and ran out of ammunition, asking Lt. Ingram to take over. Apparently, he was one of the two pilots of the squadron who failed to return.[49] No claim for this plane has been made by the 38th squadron.

WALKER H.GABBERT
Captain, Air Corps
Intelligence Officer

P-51D Mustang of Lt William J. Ingram

PILOT'S PERSONAL ENCOUNTER REPORT

A. Combat
B. 11 September 1944
C. 38th Fighter Squadron, 55th Fighter Group
D. 1150
E. Near Erfurt
F. 4 to 5/10th broken clouds
   - 2500 to 4000 feet
G. Me-109
H. One (1) Me 109 destroyed

Lt. Clifford C. Sherman

I. *I was flying Number three in Hellcat Red Flight in support of heavy bombers when 30 plus Me 109s were called in far ahead at 12 o'clock. We were at about 23,000 feet in the vicinity of Erfurt at the time. Our squadron leader took us to the area where Acorn Squadron of our Group was already engaged. Making certain first that an enemy formation up top wasn't going to attack, we joined in the scrap. I spotted an Me 109 at our level approximately 9 o'clock and called to my wingman to stick with me on my bounce, expecting more Me 109s to come in. As I made a left turn and closed in on the E/A from astern, I noticed that the enemy pilot was jinking his ship violently.[50] I fired from 150 yards to zero at 15 degrees deflection to dead astern without observing a strike. I was tempted to ram him, but thought better of it and skidded out to the right and flew formation with him. Then I swung out to the side and back in on his tail. By this time he was turning to the left. At 100 yards I opened fire with 20 degrees deflection. The concentration of fire around the wing roots and canopy was so intense that his cockpit literally disintegrated. I ceased firing as the E/A straightened out, fell off first on one wing then the other and then went down in an uncontrolled spin with the engine on fire and gasoline, smoke and white vapor streaming behind him. Lacking power and out of control, the E/A was obviously finished and the pilot killed, so I didn't follow it down to watch it crash but left to find some more victims. As a result of this combat I claim One (1) Me 109 destroyed.*

CLIFFORD C. SHERMAN
1st lt. Air Corps

PILOT'S PERSONAL ENCOUNTER REPORT

A. Combat

B. 11 September 1944

C. 38th Fighter Squadron, 55th Fighter Group

D. Approximately 1150

E. 5 miles east of Meiningen

F. 4 to 5 tenths broken clouds, 2500 to 4000 feet

G. Me-109

H. Destroyed

Lt. Tunis H. Holleman

I.   *I was flying number 4 in Hellcat White Flight on an escort mission at an altitude of 24,000 feet when Acorn Squadron made a bounce on 30 plus Me 109s at 21,000 feet just east of Meiningen. We then spotted a large force of E/A above, so our squadron leader committed us momentarily to top cover. But when the E/A led to attack, we followed Acorn into the fight, which had now progressed to a low altitude. I got split up from my element leader as I went into a tight diving turn with an Me 109 on my tail, but another P-51 drove the E/A off. As I pulled out of my dive at approximately 3,000 feet, I saw another Me 109 on my tail and immediately went into a diving turn. At 200 feet he tried to square the corner and get deflection, but I anticipated this move and did a reverse snap roll ending up in a right turn at about 20 feet. At the moment of recovery I glanced back and saw an explosion underneath and slightly behind me — obviously the Me 109. He apparently had tried to follow me in my maneuver — admittedly unorthodox — and did not make it. I therefore claim one Me 109 destroyed as a result of this combat.*

TUNIS H. HOLLEMAN
1st Lt. Air Corps

PILOT'S PERSONAL ENCOUNTER REPORT

A. Combat
B. 11 September 1944
C. 38th Fighter Squadron, 55th Fighter Group
D. 1150
E. Approximately 10 miles south of Erfurt
F. 4 to 5/10ths cumulus
   – 3,000 to 5,000 feet
G. Me-109
H. Three Me 109s destroyed

Lt. Earl R. Fryer

I. *I was leading the second element of Hellcat Yellow Flight at 23,000 feet in the vicinity of Erfurt when many bandits were called in at 12 o'clock high. Acorn, the other squadron of our group in the area, was attacked first and took the fight down toward the deck. Our squadron remained above to protect them from another gaggle of E/A who appeared above us when two Me 109s started an attack on us. I immediately turned into them and they broke off making a convenient turn that put my wingman and me on their tails. I fired a short burst at approximately 550 yards line astern, getting a few strikes; then opened up again and closed to about 200 yards at 15 degrees deflection and observed very many strikes on the Me 109s wing roots and fuselage. The E/A straightened out and I pulled off to the side to avoid over-shooting. As I was coming in for another pass, the pilot bailed out. I therefore claim this Me 109 destroyed.*

By this time the main 109 gaggle was in a big dogfight with Acorn and Hellcat and my wingman clobbered his E/A, so we set out for two more approximately 2000 feet below us. I immediately got in a turning engagement with one of them, firing from about 250 yards at from 20 to 5 degrees deflection and observing lots of strikes all over him. When he straightened out I again pulled off to the side to avoid over-shooting and this pilot also bailed out. As a result I claim this Me 109 destroyed.

Being by myself now, I climbed to about 15,000 feet off to the side of the main fight and after I got above it headed back into the melee. A Me 109 made a head-on pass at me and got a hit on my right wing. Upon seeing the strike on my ship, I didn't fire but pushed over and split-essed around. This 109 was a little slow in entering his original turn and in the turning encounter that followed — lasting about 3 minutes — I got on his tail and observed many strikes on his wings and fuselage. He then straightened out, and as I turned to clear my tail the pilot bailed out. I claim this Me 109 destroyed — making a total claim of three (3) Me 109s destroyed during the entire combat.

Additional remarks:
(1) all enemy pilots delayed opening their chutes
(2) I do not believe that I could have out-turned the 109s
at my over-taking speed had I not been wearing a G-suit.

EARL R. FRYER
1st Lt. Air Corps

55th FIGHTER GROUP MISSION SUMMARY REPORT

I. Rendezvous made with 3 boxes of B-17s of 3rd Division at 1040/24,000 feet in vicinity of Verviers. Tudor Squadron remained with bombers and Acorn and Hellcat Squadrons combed area ahead of bombers on their planned track. About 1145 Acorn leader sighted two large groups of contrails at 30,000 feet 12 o'clock to him in vicinity of Rudolstadt near Erfurt. The Group turned starboard to get in position to attack out of the sun, when two 109s somewhat over eager attacked out of the gaggle, were engaged and destroyed by Hellcat Yellow Flight. It is believed that these two E/A committed the large formation of 50 plus 109s to the attack sooner than was planned. The Group swung back engaging the 109s head on, and combats ensued from 26,000 feet to the deck with claims of 24-0-7. The E/A were aggressive and fought tenaciously, breaking into flights of twos and fours. White section of Hellcat Squadron remained above, bouncing E/A when it was definite that none were coming down from the enemy top cover group. Combat lasted about ten minutes, squadrons then reforming into flights and proceeding home because of lack of ammunition. One lone Me-410 was seen circling at 35,000 feet in this area during engagement [51]... Tudor Squadron went on with bombers, sighting 200 plus Me 109s and FW 190s flying in a large gaggle at about 30,000 feet in the vicinity of Meiningen. Tudor ... pursued ... unable to overtake them. On course out, 3 combat wings (18 a/c each) were sighted headed east in vicinity of Sonneburg, and the last two combat wings were under heavy attack. [52] ...Tudor chased E/A, destroying 3 in engagement from 25,000 feet down to 10,000 feet. On climbing back up about 100 chutes were seen in this area and only about 18 B-17s remained out of the 3 combat wings. ... Lt. Rosenoff was seen to explode in the air after being attacked by E/A in engagement at Sonneburg. Lts. Crawford and Lewis were last seen in area of first engagement.

ANALYSIS OF DEVIATIONS AND DIFFICULTIES

A. BOMBING

1. WEATHER PREVENTED THE PRIMARY AND SECONDARY TARGETS FROM BEING BOMBED VISUALLY.

2. GROUPS ATTEMPTED TO BOMB VISUALLY AFTER WEATHER REPORT FROM MAYPOLE A/C.

3. FULDA BEING CLEAR WAS BOMBED BY 8 GROUPS AS A LAST RESORT TARGET.

B. 92nd WING, LEADING THE DIVISION, TURNED LEFT IN VICINITY OF I.P. TO GO TO THE LAST RESORT TARGET, INSTEAD OF TURNING TO THE RIGHT TO GO TO THE PRIMARY.

1. 13th WING CONTINUED TO THE PRIMARY TARGET AND IN SO DOING BECAME SEPARATED FROM DIVISION COLUMN.

2. ACCORDING TO CONTROL POINT REPORTS THE INTERVAL BETWEEN 92ndA AND 13B WAS PROBABLY OVER 16 MILES. THE 13thA WING WAS LATE AT C.P.1 AND WAS UNABLE TO MAKE UP THIS TIME. TO ADD TO THIS CONFUSION, THERE WAS NO RADIO COMMUNICATION BETWEEN 92ndA AND 13A WINGS.

WHEN THE DIVISION LEADER MADE THE DECISION NOT TO BOMB THE PRIMARY, HE GAVE THIS INFORMATION OUT ON CHANNEL B BUT IT WAS NOT PICKED UP BY 13A. THE 13thB WING RECEIVED THIS INFORMATION FROM THE DIVISION LEADER AND TURNED SHORT OF THE I.P.

THE RESULT OF THE ABOVE DIFFICULTIES LEFT THE 13A WING SEPARATED FROM THE DIVISION COLUMN. IT WAS AT THIS POINT THAT THIS WING RECEIVED THE SEVERE FIGHTER ATTACK.

References

- Astor, Gerald *The Mighty Eighth-The Air War in Europe As Told By The Men Who Fought It* Dell Publishing, 1997
- Allen, Col. Robert S. *Lucky Forward: The History of Patton's 3rd US Army* Vanguard Press, New York, 1947
- Bekker, Cajus *The Luftwaffe War Diaries* Da Capo Press 1994
- Center for Air Force History *Wings at War: Air and Ground Teamwork on the Western Front* Washington, D.C.
- 55th Fighter Group Mission Summary, USAF Historical Research Agency, Maxwell AFB, Alabama
- Gray, John *The 55th Fighter Group Against the Luftwaffe*, Specialty Press, 1999
- Hot Springs National Park, Arkansas, *The Sentinel Record*, Sunday, August 6, 2000 *"Out of the Ashes: Researcher finds history in hometown"*
- Individual Deceased Personnel Files, US Army Total Personnel Command
- Littlefield, Col. Robert *Double Nickel, Double Trouble*, private correspondence
- Middlebrook, Martin *The Schweinfurt-Regensburg Mission* Cassell & Co.
- Mombeek, Eric *Sturmjäger* — History of the JG 4
- Missing Air Crew Reports, US Army Total Personnel Command, Alexandria, Virginia
- Patist, Paul private correspondence
- Russell, Edward T. *Leaping the Atlantic Wall: Army Air Forces Campaigns in Western Europe, 1942-1945* Air Force History and Museums Program
- 390th Bomb Group Museum, private correspondence
- 100th Bomb Group Mission Summary, Crew Reports, 11 September 1944, United States - National Archives and Records Administration, College Park, Maryland
- United States Air Force *Headquarters, Air Force Education and Training Command*
- US Army Memorial Affairs Activity, Europe, Archives
- United States Government Printing Office *The United States Strategic Bombing Survey - Summary Report (European War)*
- Yeager, General Charles and Leo Janos *Yeager* – An Autobiography Bantam Books, New York
- Zdiarsky, Jan *Black Monday over the Ore Mountains*, Museum of Air Battle over the Ore Mountains on September 11th, 1944, private correspondence, Kovarska, Czech Republic, 1994-2005

Internet Resources and URLs

American War Orphans Network — www.awon.org
Army movements on 7 April, 1945 — www.4point2.org/hist-93.htm
A Brief History of Flying at Wormingford — www.esgc.co.uk/history.htm
Bases of the 8th AF in East Anglia — www.455th.ukpc.net/tomfeise/8thusaaf
Historic Wings — www.historicwings.com
Little Friends - Eighth Air Force Fighter Groups — www.littlefriends.co.uk
Museum of air battle over the Ore Mountains — www.museum119.cz
Ohrdruf — www.scrapbookpages.com/EasternGermany/Ohrdruf/OhrdrufNord.html
Kovarska — www.kovarska.cz
USAAF Combat Chronology, September 1944 — members.aol.com/jlowry3402/sep44.html
12 o'clock high — www.xs4all.nl/~rhorta
The P-51 Merlin Engine — thierry.lie.free.fr/aero/p51/merlin.html
100th Bomb Group Web-birds — www.web-birds.com/8th/100/100.html
100th Bomb Group Foundation — www.100thbg.com
The 55th Fighter Group - Major General Edward Giller USAF — www.55srwa.org/55_giller.html

COME TO TOUCH BILL LEWIS' STORY

visit personally the musuem that is devoted to the air battle described in "Courtesies of the Heart," one of the greatest air battles of WWII fought in the skies over central Europe

MUSEUM OF AIR BATTLE OVER THE ORE MOUNTAINS ON SEPTEMBER 11, 1944

member of the 100th Bomb Group Foundation

The displays of the musuem are appraisals of both tactical and technical backgrounds of the air war that took place in 1944, history of the various units that took part in the battle, the continuance of the conflicts of September 11, 19944, the fortune of the shot-down airmen of both sides, and data on all the aircraft involved. The wreckage of the planes shot down in this battle, including wreckage of Bill Lewis's P-51, are supplemented with unique historical photos, documents and personal items of the shot-down airmen, uniforms, aerial equipment and accessories and memories of battle participants who survived.

Displays are schematically divided so they depict in detail particular phases of the battle and correlate to each individual crash. Displays are supplemented with several hundred exhibits. The museum commemorates some other conflicts over this region and over the Czech Repubic in general.

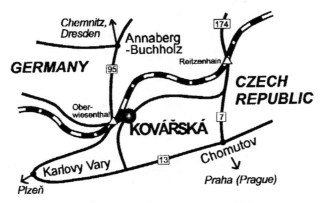

MUSEUM HOURS
SATURDAY 2PM - 6PM
Collective visits and visits at other times available on request.

Museum of Air Battle over the Ore Mountain
Albert E. Trommer Street 696
43186 Kovarska, Czech Republic

WWW.MUSEUM119.CZ

Credits

Photos

William M. Lewis, Jr. family (historical photos): 9, 10, 11, 19, 22, 23, 27, 46, 91, 102, 118, 135

Kenneth Breaux: 137, 146, 149, 226; archival: 14, 15, 16, 169

Archive of the Museum of air battle over the Ore Mountains (historical):
17, 43, 69, 70, 78, 86, 130, 192; via David Jewell: 29, 53, 104, 250, 255, 256, 257;
via USAMAA-E: 167(2), 210; via Russel Abbey: 251, 252, 254; via Adelbert Wolf family: 170(2)

Jan Zdiarsky: 114(2), 138, 140, 141, 147, 160, 166, 178, 179, 180, 181, 187(2), 189(2), 191(2),
194(2), 196(2), 198, 199(3), 200, 203(15), 204(14), 208(2), 219(2), 220, 221, 223, 224(2), 225

Petr Frank: 177, 188, 203   **Charlie Cole:** 220(1)   **US Army:** 215(2), 216(2)

Randy Finfrock: 217(1), 221, 232   **Col. James Tonge:** 210(2), 222   **B. Bond:** back cover

Reproduced documents

William M. Lewis, Jr. family: 11, 33, 94, 96, 98, 99, 109, 112, 217(3)

Archive of the Museum of air battle over the Ore Mountains: 202; via US National
Archives: 88, 143, 144; via USAMAA-E: 168

Maps, charts and emblems

Jan Zdiarsky: 25, 32, 42, 51, 55, 56, 60, 61, 66, 67. 68, 84, 183, 197, 207, 261

Courtesies of the Heart
by Kenneth Breaux

**Published in Canada
in 2005 by Trafford Publishing
ISBN 1-4120-1165-5**

**Front cover, graphics and book design
© Jan Zdiarsky, 2005**
Graficke studio Promeny,
Kovarska, Czech Republic
Additional production by Jen Cooper, USA.

**Trafford Publishing
Suite 6E, 2333 Government Street
Victoria, BC Canada
V8T 4P4**

toll-free at 1-866-638-6884

Library cataloguing
Breaux, Kenneth, 1943-
Courtesies of the Heart / Kenneth Breaux. — Victoria, B.C. : Trafford, c2005.
Includes bibliographical references and index.
ISBN 1-4120-1165-5
I. Title.

ISBN 141201165-5